MAGGIE JORDAN

Also by Emma Blair

WHERE NO MAN CRIES
NELLIE WILDCHILD
HESTER DARK
THIS SIDE OF HEAVEN
JESSIE GRAY
THE PRINCESS OF POOR STREET
STREET SONG
WHEN DREAMS COME TRUE
A MOST DETERMINED WOMAN
THE BLACKBIRD'S TALE
SCARLET RIBBONS
THE WATER MEADOWS
THE SWEETEST THING
THE DAFFODIL SEA
PASSIONATE TIMES

MAGGIE JORDAN

Emma Blair

BANTAM BOOKS
TORONTO · NEW YORK · LONDON · SYDNEY · AUCKLAND

MAGGIE JORDAN

All of the characters in this book are fictitious, and any
resemblance to actual persons, living or dead, is purely
coincidental

A BANTAM BOOK : 0 553 50502 5

Originally published in Great Britain by Bantam Press,
a division of Transworld Publishers Ltd

PRINTING HISTORY
Bantam Press edition published 1990
Bantam edition published 1991
Bantam edition reprinted 1991
Bantam edition reprinted 1995
Bantam edition reprinted 1996

The Cockburn speech which appears in this book is
extracted from *Reporter in Spain* © Patricia Cockburn, 1986.
Reproduced with kind permission of Lawrence and Wishart.

This book is set in 10/11pt Plantin
by Colset Private Limited, Singapore

Bantam Books are published by Transworld Publishers Ltd,
61–63 Uxbridge Road, Ealing, London W5 5SA,
in Australia by Transworld Publishers (Australia) Pty Ltd,
15–25 Helles Avenue, Moorebank, NSW 2170,
and in New Zealand by Transworld Publishers (NZ) Ltd,
3 William Pickering Drive, Albany, Auckland.

Printed and bound in Great Britain by
Cox & Wyman Ltd, Reading, Berkshire

PART ONE

The Sea Outside the Hill

'But all the middle of the valley was a place to rest in, to sit and think that troubles were not if we would not make them. To know the sea outside the hill, but never to behold it.'

Southey

CHAPTER ONE

Maggie Jordan entered Reception from the back door to find her best friend Susan staring out of the window. 'Are you all right?' she queried when she saw the expression on Susan's face.

'Come and have a dekko at this, will you. It's right queer,' Susan said without turning around.

'What is it?' Maggie asked, joining her at the window.

'Just *look* at that sky!'

A heavy bank of clouds, very dark and tinged with deep red and purple, was creeping across the sky, while at the same time a lower bank was moving rapidly in the opposite direction. The overall effect was weird and uncanny.

'I've never seen a sky like that in my life before,' Susan said softly, wonder in her voice.

Neither had she, Maggie thought, feeling she could have stood there all day gawping up at it. For some unknown reason prickles sprang up all over her shoulders and down the length of both arms. She ran a hand through her wavy auburn hair.

'At least it's stopped raining,' Maggie said. It had been bucketing down when she'd left home that morning.

'Aye, but not long since. And there's more to come, that's obvious,' Susan replied. She and Maggie worked at The Haven hotel where they'd been employed since leaving school three years previously.

Susan turned on Maggie. 'Are you away then?' It was Maggie's half-day.

'I am. And twenty minutes past my knocking off time. But lunch was pandemonium. I was fair run off my feet.' She'd been waitressing in the dining-room for breakfast and lunch. Her duties weren't merely confined to waitressing however;

like all the girls at The Haven she did whatever was required of her from changing bed linen to washing dishes.

'It's been a busy summer right enough,' Susan commented. It was already 12 August 1935.

'Which has pleased Mr Lawler,' Maggie smiled. Mr Lawler owned The Haven.

'You can say that again. He's been positively coining it since the season started.'

'Aye. Last season was good, but this one is even better.'

Maggie changed the subject. 'Now about tonight, are you still on for the pictures?'

'Darned tooting I am!' Susan enthused. 'I wouldn't miss Douglas Fairbanks Jnr for the world.' The film playing at the local cinema was *Chances*, a war-time romance also starring Anthony Bushell and Rose Hobart.

'I'm really looking forward to it too,' Maggie smiled.

'And we'll have fish and chips afterwards. Just like always.'

'Couldn't do without the fish and chips,' Maggie agreed. Her brown eyes suddenly twinkled. 'I wonder . . .?'

'Wonder what?'

'If those two English lads from Northallerton will turn up at the pics? They said they might.'

Susan giggled. 'I think you fancy that Tom. Can't say I blame you, he's very nice.'

'He's all right. Cyril's nice too.'

Susan giggled again. 'Cyril! What a name! But a lovely kind face and such broad shoulders.'

He certainly had those Maggie thought, broad as the proverbial barn door. Tom's were broad, but not a patch on Cyril's.

'We must make sure we get there before the start of the programme,' said Maggie, giving Susan a wink.

'You mean while the lights are still up?'

'Precisely,' Maggie nodded.

'So that if they're there they'll see us.'

'And hopefully *join* us.'

Susan giggled a third time. She was about to say something further when the telephone rang.

8

'I'll knock on your door at quarter to six,' Susan said as she hurried to answer it.

'I'll be ready.'

'Good afternoon, The Haven hotel,' Susan said into the telephone, waving to her as Maggie left Reception through a wooden flap which was part of the counter.

Outside the hotel Maggie turned up the collar of her mac. Straight home? she wondered, then decided she'd go down to the front and see if her dad was there. She'd have a natter with him if he were, something she often did on her half-days.

The air had a peculiar smell to it, she noted, as she made her way down the street towards the front and the spot where her dad tied up his boat. It was a metallic smell that you could somehow taste, which she found quite unpleasant.

'Hello Maggie, and how are you the day?'

The friendly voice belonged to Mrs Caskie who lived just along from Maggie and her family. 'Fine, Mrs Caskie. What about yourself?'

'I'm not too bad, thank you. Mustn't grumble. What an awful day, eh?'

'Awful,' Maggie agreed.

'And this August too.' Mrs Caskie shook her head. 'If it wasn't so warm it would be more like November or December.'

Maggie glanced up as lightning flickered across the sky, followed seconds later by a loud crack of thunder.

Leaving Mrs Caskie, Maggie waved across the road to Clarice McKechnie who was a year older than her and was engaged to a lad from Oban whom she was marrying early in the new year.

It started to rain again, a light drizzle that caused umbrellas to pop up all over the place.

When she reached the front, Maggie stared out to sea. The sea was a dull murky green, and angry. Waves broke on the shore and eventually expired in a froth and myriad of bubbles.

There wasn't a seagull to be seen Maggie suddenly realized. At this time of afternoon there were usually hundreds swooping and screeching overhead.

Charlie Jordan was sitting beside his boat enjoying a pipe while he repaired some tackle that had been damaged. A blackboard set on an easel at the rear of his boat proclaimed, Fishing Trips, Shark Fishing a Speciality.

'It's yourself, Maggie,' Charlie smiled as she came up to him. 'I wondered if you might come down and say hello.'

'How's business?'

He pointed a horny finger at the sea. 'Anyone taking a small open craft out on that needs his head examined. I wouldn't even chance it by myself, far less take holidaymakers with me.'

Further along the shoreline a wave crashed, followed by another, louder than the last.

Maggie exclaimed when spray lashed against her face.

'I'll walk you back if you like. I only hung on here thinking you might turn up,' Charlie said.

'What about the boat?'

'Tide's on the way out so she'll be all right for now. I'll come back and check the situation this evening.'

Maggie gazed at the twenty-foot-long boat that was her father's main source of livelihood. She was called *Lucky Lady* and had originally been bought by grandfather Alec, some forty years ago. During the season Charlie used the boat to take holiday-makers out on fishing and pleasure trips. Out of season, he fished by himself, selling his catch on the quayside to the fish agents and passers-by.

Mid-winter he carved figures in wood and whalebone, the latter called scrimshaw, which Mr Lambie, who owned Lambie's Shop & Gift Emporium, sold for him, taking a percentage profit from every item bought.

Charlie's scrimshaw was particularly beautiful, an art that had taken him years to perfect and of which he was extremely proud. He had the whalebone sent to him from the port of Leith from where several whalers operated.

'So what do you make of this weather?' Charlie asked.

Maggie shifted her attention from *Lucky Lady* to her dad. 'You tell me.'

Charlie secured the tarpaulin with a length of hairy string

from his pocket. 'It's going to get worse before it gets better. I'll bet on that.'

More lightning flickered overhead, followed this time by several cracks of thunder, each a tearing whiplash of sound.

'I'm sure you're right,' Maggie replied.

He snorted, and rubbed his nose with a finger. 'There's a funny smell been about for—'

'A sort of metallic smell?' she cut in. 'I noticed it when I left the hotel.'

He considered that, then nodded, 'Aye, metallic. That describes it exactly.'

'And you can taste it - at least I can.'

Charlie stood up. 'I can too. What we both need is a good strong cup of tea to wash it away. So let's go on home eh?'

'Anything you want me to carry?'

He shook his head, and started walking away from the boat, Maggie falling into step beside him.

'Is it the pictures tonight?' Charlie asked as they reached the road that ran along the top of the shore.

Maggie nodded. 'Susan and I are going. Douglas Fairbanks Jnr is in the big film so it should be good.'

Charlie thought of the kinema, the dear old kinema! and smiled to himself. It was years since he'd been there, but there had been a time when he'd gone every week, sometimes twice. He and April, Maggie's mum, had done a great deal of their courting in the back seats of the stalls.

There had been no sound in those days of course, twenty odd years ago now. Mrs Wedderburn had been the piano accompanist, a reed of a woman who wore wire-framed spectacles and reputedly drank like a fish.

His smile widened as many fond memories came flooding back. He must go to the kinema again soon, he and April. And perhaps, though he doubted she'd agree, they could sit once more in the back seats for old times' sake.

They stopped briefly at Smellie's tobacconist while Charlie bought a half ounce, then continued through the drizzle to the narrow cobbled street where their cottage was.

'I'm back!' Charlie yelled as he hung up his oilskin coat.

'Me too!' Maggie also called out.

Wee Charlie, aged seven and the youngest in the family, appeared out of the parlour where he'd been playing. He had an impish look about him, and the most beguiling manner, a combination which never failed to capture the hearts of all who came into contact with him.

'Hello horror,' said Charlie, clapping his hands and gesturing Wee Charlie to come to him, which Wee Charlie did at a run.

Charlie laughed as he gathered his only son into his arms. If there had been room in the hallway, he would have swung Wee Charlie round in a circle.

'Miss me horror?' Charlie demanded.

'Not in the least, Dad,' Wee Charlie replied, teasing him. He might be young but he still had a highly developed sense of humour.

Charlie feigned outrage, then hurt. 'What! Not at all?'

'Not at all. Though . . .' Wee Charlie trailed off.

'Though what?'

'If you were to give me a ha'penny I might tell you different.'

Charlie laughed, and gently cuffed him on the head. His son was a continual source of amusement and delight to him.

'Get away with you, you Philistine!'

'All right, make it a farthing then,' Wee Charlie instantly retorted.

'I'll make it a smack on your backside for cheek if you're not careful,' Charlie declared, joking as well.

Maggie went through to the kitchen where April was rolling pastry and Pet, her fourteen-year-old sister, paring and cutting up apples. The remaining member of the family was her big sister, Laura, who was married and living in Glasgow.

'Apple tart or pie?' Maggie queried. She loved both.

'Tart and some jam turnovers,' April replied.

'Yummy,' Maggie said as Charlie and Wee Charlie, arms twisted around one another, came into the room.

'I thought you'd be back early,' April said to Charlie.

'I only hung around as long as I did thinking Maggie

12

might come and see me, which she did,' Charlie replied.

'Have you heard the thunder?' said Pet to Maggie, and gave a mock shudder. She was terrified of thunder.

'Are the rivers up?' April asked Charlie. She was referring to the North and South Heys which flowed from their source at Ranlodden Moor towards the six-hundred-foot hills that towered over Heymouth.

'A bit, but not as much as they might be considering the rain we've had,' Charlie answered.

That was all right then, April thought, and got on again with her pastry rolling.

'I'm dying for a cup of tea,' Charlie announced.

'I'll make it,' Maggie told him, crossing to the range where the kettle was boiling, as it was more or less constantly throughout the day.

'Can I have some lemonade?' Wee Charlie asked hopefully.

'Yes,' replied Charlie.

'No,' said April simultaneously.

April looked at her husband. 'Don't you go spoiling him now. He had a glass earlier on.'

Charlie gave his son a wry smile. 'Sorry, wee fella, but if your mum says no then no it is.'

'Oh Mum!' Wee Charlie complained.

April glared at him. 'Don't you start now! Don't you start.'

'Come with me – I want to show you something,' Charlie said to Wee Charlie. He'd just remembered he had a couple of toffees in his oilskin coat pocket. April might have forbidden Wee Charlie to have any more lemonade, but she'd said nothing about sweets.

'Half fill this from the tap, will you,' requested April, passing Maggie a saucepan.

Maggie thought of Tom from Northallerton and hoped he would come to the pictures that night. He was in Heymouth for another eight days and . . . She exclaimed in surprise as water ran into the saucepan.

'What is it?' April asked, glancing around from what she was doing.

'This water's filthy. Just look at it!'

Wiping her hands on her pinny April came over to the sink. Sure enough, the water gushing from the tap was the colour of brown sauce.

'Well that's never happened before,' April mused.

Maggie emptied the pan. 'We certainly can't use that. So what are we going to do?'

'It will probably clear itself before long,' Pet commented from across the kitchen.

'It might. Then again it might not,' said April. 'If the system has broken down it could take days for it to be sorted out. What a nuisance!' she muttered darkly.

'I've an idea. To be on the safe side why don't we stand the zinc bath out the rear and let that fill up with rainwater?' Maggie suggested.

'That's a thought,' April nodded. Looking out of the window she saw that the drizzle had become heavy rain. The zinc bath would soon be filled.

Charlie came back into the kitchen and was told the news. He frowned as he stared at the brown water still gushing from the tap.

'I presume it is the system and not us in particular?' April queried.

'Has to be the system,' he confirmed, wondering how on earth this had come about.

'It was working a few minutes ago,' Pet stated.

'It's over an hour since we last used the tap,' April corrected her.

Pet's brow creased. 'Seems like just a few minutes ago.'

'It's been over an hour,' April repeated for Charlie. Then told him about Maggie's suggestion of putting the zinc bath out the rear.

'I'll do that right away,' he said.

Maggie turned off the tap as there was no point in letting it continue to run.

When Charlie returned, he instructed Pet, 'Run over the road and knock on the McDougalls' door. Ask them if they're having the same problem.' To April he explained, 'I believe

14

they're on different pipes to us so it's just possible their water might be unaffected.'

'Send Wee Charlie. I'm busy with these apples,' Pet answered, quite the little madam.

Charlie didn't reply, just gave his daughter a stare – which was enough. She hurriedly left the room.

A few minutes later Pet was back. 'Their water is just as bad. I told Mrs Mack about us putting the zinc bath outside and she said she'll do the same.'

'You never know the minute till the minute after,' murmured April, shaking her head.

'Who else for tea?' asked Maggie. April and Pet declared they'd have a cup.

'And a biscuit?' said Charlie.

'There's a bought tipsy cake in. You can have a slice of that,' April told him.

Charlie's face lit up. Tipsy cake was a great favourite of his. While they were drinking their tea and talking about the filthy tap water, there was a knock on the outside door.

'I'll get it!' Wee Charlie yelled through.

'Mr Lawler!' Maggie exclaimed, jumping to her feet when her boss appeared in the kitchen.

'I'm sorry to trouble you on your half-day Maggie, but I sorely need your help,' Lawler explained.

'Here, let me take that from you,' said Charlie, reaching for the bowler hat Lawler was holding.

'That's kind, Mr Jordan, but I can't stay,' replied Lawler, hanging onto his bowler.

'Surely you'll have a cup of tea with us?' April smiled. 'As you can see it's already made.'

Lawler shook his head. 'I'd love to but I'm afraid I just don't have the time. I must get straight back to the hotel.'

'So what can I do for you, Mr Lawler?' Maggie queried.

'As you know it's the twelfth, the start of the grouse season, and I ordered thirty brace from the Ranlodden Estate which are supposed to be collected about now. They're on tonight's menu.'

15

Maggie nodded. The grouse were to be a special feature on the menu.

'The plan was for Bryce to drive up and get them, but he's up to his eyes in trying to draw substantial amounts of water from our well. The normal supply of water has turned brown and unusable.' The Bryce he was referring to was the general handyman.

'Same here,' Maggie commiserated.

'I would have driven myself except we've had a party of Australians land on us looking for accommodation on the off-chance. We're able to put up most of them, while the remainder I've sent round to The Beach Hotel.'

Here Lawler pulled a face. He loathed turning business away. He went on. 'And as you know Mrs Lawler has gone to . . .'

'Are you asking me to collect the grouse for you?' Maggie interrupted with a smile.

'I'd be ever so appreciative if you could, lass. And as I'm putting you out on your half-day I'll make it up to you, there will be something extra by way of a thank you in your pay packet on Friday.'

Maggie had always wanted to drive and passed her test first time. She often drove errands for Lawler.

'I'll be happy to go for you, Mr Lawler. To be truthful I'd nothing special planned for this afternoon anyway.'

'Oh that's good of you, Maggie! Thank you very much. I do appreciate it,' he replied gratefully.

'Where's the van?'

'Outside. I brought it over for you,' Lawler said, groping in a pocket. He produced the van key on a ring, which he handed to Maggie. 'It's just been filled up with petrol so you've no worry there.'

'I'll leave right away,' Maggie promised.

'You're a darling!' he beamed.

Lawler rubbed his hands together. 'Right then, I'll away back to the hotel and see how those Australians are settling in.' To Charlie he said in a confidential tone, 'Strange people the Australians. Very brash and loud, though nice and

16

friendly with it. No class though, certainly none of that.'

Maggie smiled to herself. Lawler was renowned as a snob which was in total contrast to his wife. But then Mrs Lawler came from a 'good' background, while it was well known that Lawler was an entirely self-made man.

Maggie saw Lawler out, then returned to her tea, finishing it in a single swallow. 'I'd better scoot then,' she said.

'Listen, I've got nothing special planned for this afternoon either. Do you mind if I come with you?' Charlie asked unexpectedly.

'Not at all, Dad. I'd enjoy the company.'

'Good.' Then to April, 'I'll have a word with Parkinson the gamekeeper if there's anything you'd like. How about a couple of rabbits?'

'We haven't had rabbit for a while. They'd make a change. And how about a brace of grouse for ourselves? We could have them on Sunday as a treat.'

'I'll see what I can do,' Charlie nodded.

Maggie and Charlie went out into the hallway, where she put her mac back on and he his oilskin coat. 'I haven't been up top for some time,' he said.

'Can I come?' Wee Charlie asked, having appeared out of the parlour.

'If you like,' smiled Maggie.

'Och, I don't think I will then,' said Wee Charlie contrarily.

'You're a horror,' laughed Charlie, tickling his son under the chin.

'Will you play with me when you get back, Dad? I'm playing knights of the round table.'

'I'd love to,' Charlie agreed.

'Promise? Cross your heart and hope to die?'

'Cross my heart and hope to die,' Charlie stated solemnly.

'You can be in charge of the baddie knights and I'll be Sir Lancelot, the bravest and best knight of all.'

Charlie was chuckling as they left the cottage. 'What a boy!' he said. The game with Wee Charlie would be fun – they always were.

The van was old but a good and reliable runner. Once they were under way Charlie pulled out his pipe and lit up.

'It's like a winter's afternoon, not a summer's one,' commented Maggie, switching on her lights.

Charlie nodded. In all his years he'd never known an August day quite like it.

They drove into the High Street, then turned into Bridge Road, which crossed the North Hey.

'That river has risen quite a bit since earlier on,' murmured Charlie.

Maggie glanced sideways at the river, having been concentrating on the fairly heavy traffic. It was now well up, and flowing very fast indeed. The South Hey would be the same, as they both acted in tandem.

She sniffed. 'And that smell's got worse.'

It had indeed, Charlie thought. He wondered if it were connected in some way with the fouling of the water system.

Charlie spotted and waved to Don Gillies, a drinking partner of his who also arranged fishing and excursion trips during the season.

Don waved back and then gestured towards The Bell Inn where he was clearly heading. Charlie shook his head and mouthed the word 'Tonight!' Don gave the thumbs up.

'Are you sure you don't want to join him?' Maggie asked, having caught this little exchange. 'I can get your rabbits and the brace of grouse. Nor will I be offended, I assure you.'

Charlie gave her a thin smile. 'It's a matter of economics, lass. I would like to go with Don, but don't feel I can afford the pub twice in one day. I'll have my pint this evening.'

A few minutes later they were starting up Heymouth Brae, the road that connected Heymouth with the summit and world beyond.

The brae was extremely steep, bordered on either side by meadows and patchy woodland. In the old days it had taken six horses to haul a vehicle the two thousand yards from the bottom of the brae to its top.

Charlie watched as Heymouth and the sea dropped away beneath them. A holiday-maker had once described the ascent to him as 'like going up to Heaven'. It was an apt description.

They passed a house which seemed to hang perilously onto the hillside. The Thorns lived there, newcomers who'd only moved in the year before.

'When you get to the summit can you stop in the lay-by?' Charlie requested.

'If you want.'

He puffed on his pipe.

'Any particular reason?' she probed.

'It's a grand view. Is that particular enough?'

Maggie laughed. 'Aye, all right then.'

She was amused by his dry tone. Not for the first time she thought her father would have made a wonderful actor.

The van laboured its way up the final stretch of the brae, its engine protesting at the strain. They were now at the summit and Maggie pulled into the lay-by, positioning the van so that they overlooked Heymouth.

Maggie stared at people walking about far below, tiny creatures that could hardly be recognized.

There was The Haven, and to the right, the kinema where she'd be going later. She gazed at the stubby brick lighthouse, which was over two hundred years old, and had been built to guide the fishing boats home safely to harbour.

She shifted her attention to the main car park which was full. There were a lot of holiday-makers currently in Heymouth, as it was an extremely popular resort.

Someone had 'discovered' Heymouth years before, and the beauty of this little fishing village cast an irresistible spell on those who, undaunted by its remote situation and the lack of organized transport, began to stream in from all over Britain. In time, the ever-increasing number of visitors had opened up an entirely new source of income for the Heymouthians, and instead of having to depend on fishing as their primary source of income, they found the tourist trade was theirs for the developing.

'It's a view I never tire of looking at. I think it must be one of the most beautiful in the world,' Charlie sighed.

'Do you think you might be biased, Dad?' Maggie teased.

'Of course I'm biased! But I also believe it to be true. As far as I'm concerned what we're looking at could be Paradise itself.'

Paradise itself! 'Even in this gloom and with the rain pelting down?'

'Even in this gloom with the rain pelting down,' he confirmed defiantly.

Leaning across she kissed him on the cheek. 'You're lovely, Dad. A 100 per cent gold-plated smasher. I think comparing it to Paradise is a bit strong, but I know what you mean.'

'Does that mean you agree or disagree with me?'

She smiled. 'It means I know what you mean. Now we'd better get on if Mr Lawler is to get those grouse in time.' And with that she reversed the van, turned it round and drove back on to the road. Soon they turned down a side road which led to Drumbreck House where Sir Ewen McLay lived. He owned Ranlodden Estate, which consisted of all thirty-nine square miles of the moor.

They drove in silence, Charlie contentedly puffing on his pipe, the only sounds being the patter of rain on the van roof and the brushing of the windscreen wipers.

'Look!' said Charlie suddenly, pointing out of his window.

'What?'

'The sheep in the burn.'

Maggie stopped the van so she could see what he was talking about. The burn was swollen, the sheep in question bobbing up and down in the middle, apparently held there by something under the water.

'Is it alive or dead?' Maggie queried.

'Can't tell from this distance.'

'You want to go over there then?'

'If it is alive we might be able to help.' Charlie glanced at his daughter. 'I'd hate to think we passed on by if the beast is suffering.'

'Come on then,' she said and, opening her door, hopped out.

The moment they stepped on to the moor itself their feet sank almost to the ankle. Their feet made loud sucking noises as they tramped over to the burn.

The branch of a tree, embedded in the bottom of the burn,

20

was supporting the sheep which had become firmly wedged against it.

Maggie blinked and wiped the rain from her face. 'It's as dead as a dodo,' she said, referring to the sheep.

Charlie stared at the sheep, whose eyes were wide open while its mouth was pulled back to reveal two rows of large, yellowy teeth. A cold shudder ran through him. 'It's dead all right. Drowned probably.'

They stared at the dead sheep for a few seconds longer, then went back to the van. As she got in, Maggie glanced up at the sky. The heavy bank of clouds was still there, the areas of red and purple had expanded, their colours now violently intense. In the distance lightning flickered. For some reason it made Maggie think of silent music, each flicker a celestial note.

Between there and Drumbreck House they came across a number of swollen burns and encountered streams where no streams had existed before.

It was with relief that they reached Drumbreck House, parking among the outbuildings where they hoped to find Parkinson, the gamekeeper.

Inside the first, they came across Bob Merryfield, chief ghillie, sorting out part of the day's bag.

'Mr Parkinson is with Sir Ewen in the big house, but he'll be along in a few minutes,' Bob informed them after Maggie explained why she was there.

'Terrible day,' commented Charlie by way of making conversation.

'Terrible indeed,' Bob agreed. 'The "guns" had to call it off by mid-day.'

'The weather?' asked Maggie.

'Partly that, and the birds themselves. They just refused to be flushed.'

Maggie immediately thought of the lack of seagulls she'd noticed when she'd been down at the sea-front. She was about to mention it when Parkinson appeared. He was positively grim-faced.

'Good afternoon, Mr Parkinson. Mr Lawler has sent me

from The Haven to collect the thirty brace of grouse he ordered,' Maggie said with a smile.

Parkinson snorted. 'There will be no thirty brace for Lawler the day. I can let you have eight brace, and that's all.'

'Only eight!' Maggie exclaimed, disappointed.

Charlie saw his brace disappearing down the plug-hole.

'Eight brace and Lawler's lucky to get that. I've never known such a disastrous twelfth!' Parkinson replied.

'Sir Ewen won't have been pleased,' Charlie said. Sir Ewen was a fanatical sportsman.

'He was cross enough to spit. Nor were matters helped by the fact he has two very important business associates here whom he'd guaranteed an excellent day's shooting. They didn't get a single bird between them.'

'From the way Himself carried on you would think it was all our fault,' Bob Merryfield grumbled.

Parkinson frowned at the chief ghillie.

'Well, it's true!' persisted Merryfield.

Parkinson agreed, but considered it disloyal of Merryfield to say so in front of outsiders.

'Are you sure you can't do me more than eight brace?' Maggie suggested, trying to cajole Parkinson.

'I'm sorry. Normally there's no problem filling all the orders I get from the Heymouth hotels and others in the area, with dozens of braces over and above that to send to Edinburgh, Glasgow and London. But not this year. The bag has been far and away the smallest in my lifetime. And in fact, I overheard Sir Ewen say it's been the smallest for the past hundred years.'

'Then I'll settle for the eight brace and be thankful,' Maggie said, accepting defeat.

Parkinson reached into an inside pocket and brought out a leather bound silver flask. 'How about a dram all round, eh? I feel it's that sort of occasion where one is merited.'

'You can count me in,' said Merryfield, who made no bones about enjoying a drink.

Maggie held up a hand. 'Not me, thank you. But I'm sure my father will.'

Parkinson unscrewed the top of the flask and handed it to Charlie.

'Here's hoping you have better luck with the grouse tomorrow,' Charlie toasted.

'That's good stuff,' he acknowledged after he'd had a deep draught.

As Bob Merryfield was having his dram Charlie broached the subject of rabbits and Parkinson said he could have a pair, as a number had been shot the previous day. Charlie could have as many as he wished, but Charlie replied that a pair would be sufficient.

'I'll have to leave you now I'm afraid, I have matters to attend to,' Parkinson said to Charlie and Maggie. He then instructed Merryfield to see to their grouse and rabbits.

'Only halfway through the afternoon and it's like night!' Maggie commented to Charlie when they were once more outside. It was certainly a great deal darker than when they'd arrived.

Charlie loaded up the van, then climbed in.

'Mr Lawler will be upset that I'm only bringing him eight brace, but I did my best,' Maggie said as they pulled away. She then literally jumped in her seat as a huge peal of thunder crashed directly overhead.

Charlie grinned. 'That's set my ears ringing. You?'

'What?'

He raised his voice. 'That's set my ears ringing. Has it done the same to you?'

'Ding dong,' she replied, which made him laugh.

More thunder followed, while off in the far distance the small arrows of lightning, the silent celestial music, were still flickering.

It had been raining steadily, but suddenly the rain became torrential in its fierceness.

'Has to be a cloud-burst,' Charlie stated softly. 'You all right?'

'Why, do you want to drive?' That was a jibe, her father couldn't.

23

'What I meant was do you wish to pull in somewhere till this has eased a bit?'

She considered that. 'I don't think so. I'm fine.'

They drove on slowly because Maggie's visibility was limited. All the traffic on the road was also crawling along.

'Knowing our weather the sun will probably be cracking the skies tomorrow,' Charlie joked as they started down Heymouth Brae.

'No doubt. Trust it to be like this though on my half-day!'

The deluge still hadn't abated when Maggie drew up outside their cottage. 'You away in and I'll go on to the hotel by myself. There's no point in the two of us getting drenched,' she said.

He nodded. That made sense. 'I'll see your mum has a nice cup of tea waiting for you.'

'Thanks, Dad,' she smiled. 'I won't be long.'

Charlie got out of the van, took his rabbits from the rear and hurried indoors.

When Maggie reached The Haven she parked the van in its usual spot, collected the grouse and then went directly into the kitchens where she dumped the birds in front of Harry Harrison, the chef. After exchanging a few words with him, she went in search of Lawler.

She found him in Reception talking on the telephone. He was cradling the telephone and gave a long, heartfelt sigh. 'You got the grouse?'

'Only eight brace I'm afraid, Mr Lawler.'

His face clouded with irritation. 'But I ordered thirty brace! I told you Maggie, thirty brace.'

'I know what you ordered, Mr Lawler. There just wasn't thirty brace to be had!' She repeated to Lawler what Parkinson had told her.

'Blast!' Lawler exclaimed. He opened his mouth to say something else, but before he could, the lights went out.

'Jesus Christ, what next?' Lawler exploded.

'They'll probably come on again right away,' Maggie said. But they didn't.

Lawler groped his way to the wall switch which he flicked up and down, to no avail.

'Hello, what's happened?' a female voice called out.

'There seems to have been a power failure,' a male voice replied.

'Maggie?'

'I'm here, Mr Lawler.'

Lawler moved away from the wall and immediately stubbed his toe against a heavy cast-iron ornament that had been placed out of the way while the small oval table it normally stood on in the lobby was being repaired. He swore vehemently, causing Maggie to clamp a hand over her mouth to stop herself from laughing.

She crossed over to the wooden flap set in the counter where she bumped into Lawler.

'Sorry, Mr Lawler,' she apologized, thinking this whole thing was rapidly degenerating into a farce.

'Must find Bryce,' he muttered agitatedly.

'Henry!'

Maggie recognized Mrs Lawler's voice.

'Over here, my dear.'

'What on earth has happened, Henry?'

'I don't know yet dear, but I'm about to try and find out,' Lawler replied.

'It's a power failure,' the same male voice as before repeated.

'Is it just the hotel?' a new female voice asked.

'No,' said the man, 'Look outside. The entire street's blacked out.'

'He's right,' said another man who was standing by a window.

'We're going to have to get organized, Henry,' Mrs Lawler said.

Alarm bells rang in Maggie's brain. Time to get out of there before she was roped in to help, she thought, and sneaked out of the main doors into the deluge that was still cascading down.

'Well, isn't this a to-do!' Pet laughed as Maggie entered the kitchen. The kitchen was filled with the soft cosy glow of

25

candlelight, as there were two lit candles on the mantelpiece and another on the table.

'All of Heymouth is out,' Maggie stated.

'I thought that was probable from the looks of things,' Charlie said, and shook his head.

'I think it's fun!' Wee Charlie beamed.

'You would,' muttered April from the sink where she was peeling potatoes. At least they could cook, as the stove was gas.

Maggie found a towel and began rubbing her hair. 'Are these all the candles we've got?' she asked her father.

'No, I have a full packet if we need them.'

Thank goodness for that, Maggie thought. It would be awful to sit around in pitch black.

'I wonder how long this will last?' Pet queried.

'No telling,' Charlie said, drawing on his pipe. 'It could be one hour or ten. It all depends what the problem is.'

'This rain possibly. It's still chucking it down,' Maggie said.

'I can hear it,' Charlie nodded at her.

Promptly at quarter to six there was a knock on the outside door. Wee Charlie let Susan in.

'I came over as I said I would,' Susan smiled at Maggie.

'But the pictures won't be on if there isn't any electricity!' Maggie replied.

'My dad said the kinema might have its own generator. Would you know about that, Mr Jordan?'

Charlie shook his head. 'I've no idea, Susan. But they could. It's worth your trying anyway. It would be a shame to miss the programme if it were actually on.'

'That's what I thought,' Susan said.

'Well, you'll have to give me a few minutes to get myself ready. I hadn't bothered, thinking we wouldn't be going,' Maggie told Susan.

'Hurry up then. I don't want to miss the start of the big picture.'

Charlie pulled out his fob-watch and glanced at the time. 'I'd better away and check *Lucky Lady*.'

'Then it's a pint, I suppose?' April said drily.

'I did intend to have a couple. You don't mind, do you?'

'Glad to be rid of you for a while,' she retorted. 'When you're at home you just get under my feet.'

Maggie grinned at this exchange. She didn't know of a more loving couple than her mum and dad. They idolized one another.

'If that's the case I'll stay out longer than I'd planned, and do you a favour!' Charlie teased.

Their eyes met, and a look passed between them.

'Ach, away with you, you big pudding!' April said gruffly. She knew what was going to happen later when they were in bed together. It was something to look forward to while the hours ticked by. She might have four children, but still thoroughly enjoyed that sort of thing. She was only thirty-six after all!

It took Maggie ten minutes to get herself sorted out, then she and Susan were off, heading towards the kinema.

'It's like fairyland,' Susan commented referring to the candle light and the light from the storm lanterns that illuminated the various windows they passed.

Maggie agreed. 'Just think, this is what Heymouth must have been like before electricity was discovered,' she said.

'Wait a minute,' said Susan, and stopped. She sniffed, then sniffed again.

'That stink's gone,' she declared.

Maggie realized that Susan meant the metallic smell. It had gone. All she could smell now was the clean salty tang of the sea.

'And the rain's stopped at last,' Maggie stated. The earlier deluge had eventually given way to more normal rain, and now finally that too had passed.

'I'm surprised Mr Lawler let you away at the end of your shift,' Maggie said.

'The Haven has been in a right uproar since the power failure, I can tell you. When it was time I didn't tell Mr Lawler that I was going, I just left. I'm sure he would have asked me to stay on if I had.'

'A shrewd move on your part,' Maggie nodded.

'Oh, I'm not daft! I know that Lawler through and through. Mind you he's been worse than he usually is today. First the water, then the electricity. By the time I left he was quite demented.'

Eventually they arrived at the kinema, only to find it dark and locked. There clearly wasn't going to be any Douglas Fairbanks Jnr that night.

'Damn!' muttered Susan.

'No generator after all,' Maggie said with a resigned smile.

'So it appears.'

'Well, as my dad said, it was worth the try.'

They turned on their heels and started back the way they'd come.

'So, what do you fancy doing now?' Susan queried.

'I don't know. You?'

'I'm easy. Open to suggestions.'

They were both thinking about it when they were hailed from across the street.

'Hello there! How are you?'

They stopped as two figures hurried over – Tom and Cyril, the lads from Northallerton.

'Imagine bumping into you pair,' Cyril said.

'We've just come from the kinema. It's shut,' Susan informed him.

'Well, what do you expect when there's a power cut!' Tom jibed.

'Don't be so clever,' Maggie admonished him. 'The kinema might just have had its own generator.'

'We never thought of that,' Cyril admitted.

'Just shows you who's got the brains then,' Susan said as a good-natured put-down.

'Brains is it! I'll let you know I've got stacks of brains,' Tom retorted.

'Aye, right where you sit,' Maggie replied quick as a flash, which earned a laugh from Susan.

'I'll ignore that,' Tom told her, pretending to be piqued.

They stood for a few moments in shy silence, staring from one to another.

'How about a drink in place of the pictures?' Cyril suggested at last.

'Maggie?' Susan queried, trying not to look too eager.

'A drink would be very nice.'

'That's agreed then,' said Tom, moving beside Maggie, staking his claim.

Cyril moved to stand next to Susan. 'Where would you recommend?'

'The Lobster Pot's nearby,' Susan replied.

'Sounds great,' murmured Tom.

'Let's go then,' said Cyril, taking Susan by the arm. Tom immediately did the same with Maggie.

Both the girls were under age for drinking, but knew they'd be served without any trouble. Jack Smith and his wife Maisie were pets who'd known them all their lives.

The Lobster Pot had loads of candles stuck in bottles, littered about the pub. As they went inside, Jack Smith was roaring with laughter, having just been told an extremely rude story by one of the regulars.

They chose a table in a corner. As the girls were sitting down Tom asked them what they'd like to drink. Maggie said she'd have a half of shandy, Susan ordered the same.

Susan giggled when the two lads were up at the bar. 'We've fallen on our feet tonight, eh?'

Maggie nodded.

'It was obviously fate we met up. It must have been in the stars.'

'Tosh!' Maggie smiled.

'In the stars I'm telling you.' Susan shivered. 'Just look at that Cyril's shoulders! I could positively eat them.'

'Boiled or fried?' Maggie joked, tongue in cheek.

'You know what I mean!'

Tom glanced over at Maggie and winked.

'Ooooohhhhh!' murmured Susan quietly.

'Ssshhh!' Maggie scolded her.

Maisie Smith bustled into view, saw the girls and waved. They both waved back.

'Isn't this candlelight romantic,' Susan said.

It was, Maggie thought. She'd never known the Lobster Pot to have so much atmosphere. 'All we need now is a gypsy violinist,' she said, which made Susan giggle again.

Tom and Cyril returned with the drinks.

'Now, tell us all about yourselves. We know very little,' Susan prompted, eyes wide and beguiling.

What a *femme fatale*! Maggie laughed inwardly. That sort of thing wasn't her style at all, but Susan was a past master at it.

From there on, they all relaxed and conversation flowed freely.

When last orders were called and they had to leave the pub, they went round to the fish and chip shop to see if it was open, but like the kinema, it too was closed.

'I'll walk you home,' Tom whispered in Maggie's ear.

She smiled at him. She'd been hoping he'd offer. She'd taken a shine to Tom Rudge whom she now knew to be an apprentice fitter, as was Cyril, his mate.

'I'll see you later,' Tom said to Cyril.

'And I'll see you tomorrow at work,' Susan said to Maggie.

They exchanged a few further words of parting, then Maggie and Tom walked away, heading towards her house, while Cyril and Susan headed for Susan's.

'Smashing night tonight,' Tom said.

'I enjoyed it too.'

'It was great that we bumped into you.'

'Yes.'

He took her hand and squeezed it. 'I like Heymouth. I'm glad we came here.'

'I'm glad you came too.'

He laughed softly, and drew her closer to him.

Many of the candles and storm lanterns that had been lit when Maggie left the house were now out so it was a dark journey home, the pair of them stumbling more than once. There weren't even any stars to help them.

Finally they arrived at Maggie's cottage and stopped outside the front door.

'Thank you for the drinks and everything,' she said.

'Thank *you*.'

He was suddenly awkward, shy again. 'I was wondering . . . How about tomorrow evening? We could go and see that picture we missed tonight.'

'You mean just you and I, or with Cyril and Susan?'

'I'd prefer just you and I.'

So would she, she thought. 'All right then. The pictures tomorrow night.'

He edged even closer to her. 'I'll look forward to that.'

'So will I.'

'There's no chance of seeing you through the day is there?'

'I'm afraid not, Tom. I'm completely tied up at the hotel.'

'Pity.'

He was going to kiss her she thought. Normally she would never have allowed such a thing on her own doorstep, but with the street lights out and only a few candles glimmering, no-one would see.

Well come on! she urged him mentally when he hesitated. Come on!

'Maggie, I . . .'

Then his lips were on hers and she could taste his sweetness. He pulled her tight against him, squashing her against his chest. It was sheer heaven.

She stiffened as a hand crept up her side, knowing its intended destination. It was time to go inside.

Reluctantly she pushed him from her. 'I really must go, Tom.'

'But, Maggie . . .'

'I must,' she insisted.

His face fell. He would happily have stood there kissing her till the next morning.

She placed a finger across his lips. 'Outside the kinema at six.'

'I'll be there.'

'Till then,' she breathed.

'Till then.'

She twisted the door-knob, knowing the door would be unlocked, and went in. She stood for a few moments catching her breath, then continued through to the kitchen.

Charlie glanced at her and smiled. 'The pictures were open after all, eh?'

'No, they weren't.' She told her parents how she and Susan had bumped into the two lads from Northallerton and that they'd all gone together to the Lobster Pot for a drink.

'I see,' said April, laying aside the sock she'd just finished darning.

'They're nice lads, Mum. You'd approve.'

April wasn't worried on that score. She knew Maggie was very sensible and that she wouldn't take up with any riff-raff, nor would she do anything she shouldn't.

'Anyway, I'd better get off to bed. I've got work in the morning,' Maggie said.

'We won't be long behind you, lass,' Charlie stated.

Maggie kissed her mother on the cheek. 'Goodnight then.'

'It's obvious you enjoyed yourself. Your eyes are sparkling.'

'Are they?'

'Like diamonds.'

Laughing, Maggie kissed her mother a second time, and then kissed her dad.

'Now don't disturb Pet,' Charlie warned.

'I won't Dad. I promise.' He said that to her every night she went up behind Pet, and every night she promised she wouldn't.

'See you in the morning then.'

She left them and went up the stairs which led to the bedroom she shared with Pet.

As she was undressing it began to rain again, and soon it was bucketing down. Poor Tom she thought. He must be caught in it as he couldn't possibly have had time to get back to where he was staying yet.

Lightning flashed, an enormous zigzag of it ripping across the sky, followed by a deep rumble of thunder.

She fell asleep with a smile on her face, and dreamt of Tom.

Maggie woke up imagining it to be morning, only to discover it was still dark. Now what had wakened her she lazily wondered? It was most unlike her to wake before it was time to get up.

The rain was still battering down she noted, and from the sound of it even heavier than when she'd got into bed. She was about to close her eyes again when she heard a far-off roaring.

She sat up and frowned. What in the world could it be? She whimpered as the noise filled her ears. It was now unbelievably loud.

Throwing back the covers she was about to get out of bed, when the far wall suddenly exploded inwards and a broiling mass of water burst into the room.

One moment the cottage was intact, with five people safely inside. Seconds later it had disintegrated.

And the Jordan family with it.

CHAPTER TWO

Maggie was being sucked into a pit of water that seemed to go down forever. This is it, she thought. I am about to die. Strangely she felt quite calm about it, which amazed her.

Perhaps it was all a dream. She was still tucked up in bed and this was simply some horrible nightmare. However, the pain in her chest confirmed that this was no nightmare, but grim reality.

Her head broke the surface and she gratefully gulped in air. Water swirled her round till she started doggy-paddling, exercising some control over her movements.

Her previous calm gave away to terror that escalated until it threatened to overwhelm her.

'Mum! Dad!' she called. But there was no response.

She banged into something solid which she immediately grabbed hold of, imagining it was part of a house. She couldn't decipher it in the pitch black.

Someone screamed, a high shrill piercing noise that caused her to break out in goose pimples. She was freezing cold, she realized. But then what else could she have expected as she was only clad in a thin night-gown. The cold began to seep into her.

'Help me someone! Help me!' a young female voice wailed only feet away.

Maggie lunged out an arm and hauled the girl towards her.

The girl started clawing at Maggie.

'Careful, you'll pull us both back under!' Maggie warned.

'I'm drowning! I'm drowning!' the young girl yelled hysterically. Maggie now recognized the voice of Faith Caskie who lived across the street.

She felt the front of her night-gown rip in Faith's clutch. 'Get hold of this wall or whatever it is,' Maggie instructed.

A searching, frantic hand savagely grasped Maggie's hip, and she yelped as sharp nails pierced her skin.

Somewhere close by there was an almighty splash, followed almost immediately by a large wave washing over them. The wave had a great deal of undertow.

Faith cried out as she was carried off.

There was absolutely nothing Maggie could do. Faith was gone. There was a brief flash of white that could have been Faith, then nothing.

A large piece of wood hit the building Maggie was desperately clutching. From the feel of it she thought it could be a telegraph pole.

Letting go of the masonry she dived under water and swam beneath the pole, emerging on its far side. The first time she attempted to climb onto the pole she failed, but succeeded the second.

With her left foot she pushed herself and the pole away from the building. The pole moved off with her straddling it, slowly to begin with, then faster as it was caught in a current.

Her fear was almost choking her, making it difficult to breathe. She drew in a number of shallow breaths. Driving rain pounded into her hunched back and shoulders. Suddenly, a light appeared at a window and a terrified face peered out. 'Jesus Christ and all the Angels!' a male voice exclaimed.

A dog barked, and continued barking. Maggie was listening to it when something nudged her leg. Her groping hand made out the outlines of a fully-clothed man, who was floating face downwards.

The sea! she suddenly thought. She and the pole must be being drawn towards the sea. She must get off. But where? And onto what?

Hundreds of yards away a fire suddenly broke out, a bizarre sight in the midst of all this water. From the shape of the building Maggie thought it might be Ralston's Fruitshop, but couldn't be sure.

Nearby, she heard a male and female talking together. 'Hello!' she called.

'Who's that?'

'Maggie Jordan. Who's that?'

'Rory and Harriet McPherson. Where are you, Maggie?'

'Sitting on what I think is a telegraph pole. Where are you?' The McPhersons lived close to The Haven.

'Over here.'

'I can hear you, but can't see a thing other than that fire.'

'It looks to us like Ralston's Fruitshop,' Harriet said.

'That's what I thought.'

A series of lightning flashes crackled overhead, briefly illuminating the scene. Dreadful destruction and carnage was everywhere, reminding Maggie of pictures she'd seen of the Great War. She also spied the McPhersons to her left standing on the roof of what she presumed to be their house. Using her hands she began paddling in that direction.

'Come on, Maggie!' Rory urged, also having spotted her.

More lightning flashed overhead, followed by loud thunder.

Maggie sobbed with exertion as her hands dug repeatedly into the water. But it was to no avail – she was no nearer the McPhersons than when she'd started.

'I can't make it!' she shouted.

'Swim to us then!' Rory suggested.

She was tempted by that suggestion but remembered what had happened to Faith. At least she was relatively safe astride the telegraph pole.

She began to cry, thinking that if Wee Charlie was out in this he couldn't swim. Pet could, but Wee Charlie . . . Get a grip! she admonished herself, dashing her tears away.

A building collapsed. She heard it give way and then plunge into the water.

'Rory? Harriet?' she called out.

There was no reply.

'Oh my God!' she whispered. 'Rory? Harriet? Are you still there?'

Again there was no reply.

She swallowed hard, thankful she hadn't made it to their house.

Then she heard a mysterious gurgling noise. She was

36

wondering what caused it when all of a sudden there was an enormous explosion. For a moment she thought it must be gas, but there was no smell. Gradually the bubbling and gurgling faded as she drifted away.

Suddenly, the pole thumped so hard into an unseen object it almost dislodged Maggie. She hung on tightly as the pole veered violently round. Under water what felt like gravel brushed against her legs and feet. Then without warning a green flare exploded, which had to have been shot off by one of the fishermen. In the light Maggie found herself staring directly at Bryce, the live-in general handyman at The Haven. He was framed in a window less than a yard away.

Bryce threw up the sash window, leaned out, hooked Maggie under her arms, and dragged her inside.

'Is this your house?' she gasped.

'No, The Haven. You're in the hotel, lassie.'

She swept her sodden hair back from her face thinking she must look a proper sight. Then she remembered her night-gown was torn down the front where Faith Caskie had ripped it.

'Everyone is upstairs. I've been on the mooch trying to see what I could find,' Bryce explained.

'In this dark!'

He clicked on a torch and a weak beam shone forth. 'I've been using this, but conserving the batteries as much as possible as they're very low. I'm hoping to lay my hands on some new batteries down here.'

Bryce now realized that Maggie was covering herself. 'Sorry lass,' he apologized, swinging the beam away from her.

Maggie gave a hollow laugh. 'Ridiculous to be modest in the midst of all this!'

'Aye,' he agreed. Then said, 'Wait a minute.'

Going to a built-in wardrobe he opened it and flicked through the many articles of clothing hanging there.

'Try these,' he said returning with a dress and coat which he handed to her.

'Which room are we in?' Maggie questioned, now knowing that they were in one of the guest bedrooms.

37

'Number twenty-three.'

'So we're on the second floor.'

'Aye, that's right.'

Twenty-three was *en suite* she remembered, which hope fully meant towels. She'd dry herself and change in the bathroom.

'Fine. I'll wait for you out in the corridor,' Bryce replied when he told him of her plan. 'And you'd better take the torch with you.'

She appreciated that.

Maggie went into the bathroom where, to her delight, she found a large, unused towel. She hurriedly rubbed herself dry, and then put on the dress Bryce had taken from the wardrobe. Unfortunately it was a size too big, but that didn't matter. It covered her and was warm.

In the corridor she gave Bryce back his torch and he then led the way. A little further on he stopped before a cupboard door.

'This is what I was looking for,' he said, and opened it.

It was a cupboard used by the cleaners that contained a number of other odds and ends. Bryce exclaimed when he found the box of batteries he'd come in search of.

'I was sure these were in there,' he said.

They stood in the darkness as he replaced the fading batteries.

Maggie had a sudden thought. 'Bryce?'

'Yes?'

'If you knew the batteries were in this cupboard what were you mooching in the bedroom for?'

Bryce paused, and she could sense a sudden change in the atmosphere.

'Why?' he queried harshly.

'Just wondering that's all.'

There was a short hiatus, then he said unconvincingly, 'I was checking all the rooms for food. We don't have any upstairs.'

He's lying, she thought. Whatever the reason he was in that room it wasn't for food. And then she guessed. He'd been stealing! There must be jewellery, cash and all manner of valuables lying around the hotel.

'And cigarettes,' he added lamely. 'I'm positively gasping.'

Pity he hadn't said that to begin with. No, he'd been stealing. But it was none of her business, especially not now.

The beam from the new batteries was strong and bright. 'I'll guide you upstairs so you can be with the others,' Bryce said.

Maggie was about to reply when she suddenly became aware that her feet were wet again. 'Shine your torch onto the floor,' she instructed.

There was about an inch of water covering the floor that she was certain hadn't been there when they'd stopped at the cupboard. A little wave rippled over her feet, then another.

'It's rising and rising fast,' Bryce muttered.

'Is Mr Lawler upstairs? I mean he isn't . . .?'

'He's upstairs, and safe. So is Mrs Lawler. There were folk on the ground floor who didn't make it though.' Bryce shook his head in disbelief. 'The whole thing happened so fast.'

'But *what*? What happened?'

'Flooding off the moor. I can't think of any other explanation.'

'We've never had flooding in the past as catastrophic as this though,' Maggie protested.

'That's true enough. But you know the old saying, there's always a first time for everything.'

When they reached the nearest stairs the water was over Maggie's ankles and still rising.

'Maggie!' Lawler exclaimed when he saw her. 'I didn't know you were in the hotel.'

With Lawler were his wife, members of staff and dozens of guests. Candles had been lit which cast weird flickering shadows on the walls.

'I wasn't,' Maggie replied, and went on to tell them her tale.

Lawler gave a heartfelt sigh when she finally finished. 'Both your parents and your brother and sister?'

It was as if a fist had punched her very hard in the stomach. She felt a lump in her throat. 'I don't know, Mr Lawler, I really don't. They could be safe somewhere, just as I am here. At least that's what I'm hoping, praying for.'

'The water's rising down below,' Bryce said to Lawler.

At which point there was a massive crash which shook the entire building.

'My God, what's that!' Mrs Lawler exclaimed, her hand going to her mouth.

A second crash rapidly followed, and then a third. Plaster dust floated down from the ceiling making some people choke and one little girl shriek that it had got into her eyes.

'Let's have a look,' said Lawler, marching to a window and opening it. 'Your torch Bryce,' he requested.

As Lawler shone the torch outside Maggie listened to the protesting groan of timbers and prayed the hotel wasn't going to suddenly collapse as the McPhersons' house had done.

'Can't see a thing,' Lawler stated agitatedly.

'Shall I have a look, sir?' Bryce offered.

'I tell you there's nothing to be seen!' Lawler snapped.

'Yes, sir. Very good, sir,' Bryce replied obsequiously.

'Oh, damn it!' muttered Lawler, running a hand through his hair. 'Yes, of course have a look. Why not!'

'Mummy! Mummy!' a toddler started to cry.

'There, there, poppet,' a female voice soothed.

There was another crash which shook the building. Then the building began to rock on its foundations.

'Holy Mary, Mother of God!' a broad female Irish voice exclaimed.

'Well, I can't see anything either,' Bryce declared. He was about to close the window when something made him pause.

Maggie's heart leapt. It was the same roaring she'd heard just before she and the cottage were swept away.

'Water!' she whispered. 'More water.'

Mrs Lawler took her husband by the hand and held it tight. Then they were both knocked from their feet, as were many others, by the sudden impact.

Maggie found herself clutching a young man. 'Sorry,' she apologized.

He gave her a strained smile as she extricated herself. 'A bit frightening, eh?'

'A bit,' she agreed.

'There's nothing we can do but hang on here and wait for morning,' Lawler said to his wife, helping her onto her feet.

'I suppose not. But I wish there was. It's a long time till then,' a distraught Mrs Lawler answered.

Maggie noticed the young man she'd been thrown against had a watch. 'What time is is exactly?' she asked.

He glanced at his watch, bringing it close to his face because of the poor light. 'Eighteen minutes past three.'

Hours till dawn, she thought. It seemed a lifetime since she'd gone to bed the night before. As for being out with Susan, Tom and Cyril, that seemed like an eternity ago.

How were they? she wondered. Were they all still alive? Or were they dead as so many others clearly were.

'Cigarette?' the young man with the watch offered.

'I don't smoke, thank you.'

He lit up. 'I wish I could have a drink. Do you think there might be any available?'

'I've no idea.'

'I could certainly use one.'

The hotel began to rock again on its foundations. Maybe it had never stopped, Maggie wasn't at all sure. Everything was so confused.

'Excuse me,' the young man said to her. He turned away, gagged and vomited.

Mrs Docherty, a member of the hotel staff, came to his assistance. After exchanging a few words with him, she led him off into a corner.

A blue funk, Maggie thought. That was what that young man was in, a blue funk. Not that she blamed him, she had every sympathy with him.

'Cold!' someone complained. 'I'm absolutely freezing.'

Lawler looked at the person who'd spoken, then bit his lip.

'Mr Lawler?'

'Yes, Maggie?'

'Would you like me to organize a small party to go downstairs and get what bed-coverings we can?'

'Splendid idea, Maggie.'

She knew she'd be happier with a specific task to take her

mind off things rather than just sitting about waiting for whatever might happen next, even if it was only the passing of time.
She wouldn't take Bryce though, recalling what had happened
earlier. In the end Maggie dragooned four Australian chaps,
and a Cockney girl who'd volunteered as soon as she'd heard
help was needed.

'I'm Ethel from Aldgate, London. Pleased to meet you,' the
Cockney girl said to one of the men as they went downstairs
with Maggie. She led the way holding a candle stuck on a
saucer.

'And I'm Casey from Brisbane, Queensland. We're all from
Queensland,' the Australian replied.

'Too right sport,' another said.

Ethel giggled. Suddenly this had become fun.

The top floor of the hotel, where they left Lawler and company, was mainly used as a loft. It contained various bits of
junk that had been stored there over the years, but nothing was
even remotely useful in the present crisis. The floor below
that was the staff quarters, the rooms small, but with bed-
clothes in them.

Maggie had every bed on that level stripped and the bed-
clothes taken upstairs. She and two of the Aussies then proceeded to the next floor where guest bedrooms were to be
found. Again beds were stripped and the bedclothes carried
upstairs.

Food and drinking water, Maggie thought. If only they
could find either, preferably both. But so far they'd drawn a
blank in that direction.

She and Ethel were halfway down the next flight of stairs
when they were suddenly joined by Bryce.

'I thought I'd come along and lend a hand,' he smiled at
Maggie.

She wasn't pleased by that, but could hardly tell him to go
away.

'This is my room and I'm going to get changed!' Ethel
announced excitedly, and vanished inside.

Bryce opened another bedroom door, and went in. Maggie
quickly followed him.

'This is what we need,' Bryce said, picking up a carafe of water from the top of a chest of drawers.

'Good,' approved Maggie.

'And there's a bar of milk chocolate.'

'Stick that in your pocket.'

Bryce opened a drawer, laughed, and drew out a skimpy pair of silk knickers. 'I wonder who these belong to?'

Maggie felt her face flaming. 'Put them back,' she instructed in a cool, disapproving voice.

He did, smirking as he closed the drawer again.

In another room they had a stroke of luck when they came across a large paper bag of fruit, a couple of packets of biscuits, a tin of shortbread, a jar of butterscotch and an unopened bottle of Johnnie Walker whisky.

Maggie asked two of the Australians to take these items, along with the carafe of water and chocolate bar, back upstairs.

'How are we off for bed-clothes now?' Maggie asked Ethel who'd just returned from the top level.

'We can still use more.'

'Right. We'll go down to the next floor.'

Maggie had just stepped onto that floor when there was a sudden miaow! Blackie the hotel cat shot directly across her path.

She stopped and sucked in a breath.

'Bad luck!' commented Ethel. Then, 'Oh I am terribly sorry, perhaps I shouldn't have said that?'

'It's all right, I'm not very superstitious,' Maggie said.

On that floor they found a variety of soft drinks, and took some bottles of lemonade, soda water and Irn Bru, and also half a bottle of Gordon's gin. They also found more fruit, and lots of dry bed-clothes.

'I think that'll do us now. Our little foray has been a success,' Maggie announced.

'Back we go then,' Bryce said.

'Everyone else can. I want to check downstairs to see just how far the water has now risen,' Maggie said.

Bryce frowned at her. 'If anyone does that it should be me. You're only a lassie, after all.'

43

She thought again of the incident in room twenty-three. 'No, I'll go, Mr Bryce. I may be only a lassie but I can assure you I'm quite capable.'

'I never doubted that for a moment,' he replied in an extremely charming, yet at the same time insolent, tone.

Maggie decided she didn't like Bryce. He wanted to be alone down here so he could steal. Well, not if she could help it.

'I'm going,' she declared.

'It's my place to do so,' he countered.

'*I'm* going,' she repeated with determination.

'Then we'll go together, and that's that.'

She glared at the handyman. Better he came with her than go off on his own to do his dirty work. 'All right then,' she conceded.

There was a splintering sound of wood snapping. 'What's that?' she queried.

'Heaven alone knows.'

Ethel and the Australians had no sooner left Maggie and Bryce than the building began rocking again. Maggie couldn't help but think she was in the middle of a death trap.

'Wait a minute,' said Bryce. He produced a packet of cigarettes, and lit up.

'I thought you didn't have any?' Maggie queried.

He gave her a straight, no-nonsense look. 'I borrowed this packet from one of the guests.'

She believed that as much as she believed the moon was made of green cheese. 'Let's get on then,' she said.

The next floor down was split level. They were standing on the lower section, with a fire door leading onto a split-level landing. This was closed with its bar lock on.

Maggie pushed on the bar lock but couldn't shift it. 'Damn!' she muttered in exasperation. The door wasn't usually difficult to open.

'Here, let me,' offered Bryce.

He tried, and couldn't open it either. 'That's odd,' he frowned, and tried again. This time he failed as well.

'There's another door this way, we'll try that,' said Bryce.

They were moving away from the fire door when there was a loud report, like a large cannon going off. Seconds later they were engulfed in a seething torrent of water that appeared as though by magic.

The water rose incredibly quickly till it was touching the ceiling. Maggie found herself submerged, and completely disorientated. She swam in what she hoped was the direction of the stairs, only to come up against a wall. She pulled herself along it thinking she might reach the stairs. She jerked in surprise, bubbles streaming from her mouth, when a hand clamped onto her shoulder.

A beam of light flashed in front of her, the distorted face of Bryce behind the beam. He let her go and beckoned her to follow him.

He propelled himself away, reached the bottom of the stairs and hauled himself up them.

Maggie gasped, then greedily gulped in air when her head broke through the surface.

'I thought I'd lost you there,' Bryce said, sitting on one of the stair treads.

'That's the second time tonight I've nearly drowned.'

'Aye well, there you are. Your number just isn't up. That's what we used to say during the war. If your number was up there was absolutely nothing you could do about it. If it wasn't you could walk through a hail of machine-gun fire and come out the other end without even a scratch.'

'You were in the war, Mr Bryce?' She hadn't appreciated that before. He'd always struck her as too young.

'I was lassie. The last year of it. Fought in France.'

He groped in a pocket and pulled out a now useless packet of cigarettes. 'Buggeration!' he swore, and tossed the packet onto the lapping water.

'Thank goodness for that torch,' said Maggie, rising to her feet.

'Fortunately for us it's waterproof. I'd never have got out of that without it. Or found you again either.'

She swivelled on him. 'Are you telling me you got out and then went back in again after me?'

'I could hardly let you drown, could I! What do you take me for?'

A thief perhaps, but also a lot more than that. 'I don't know if you saved my life earlier, but you certainly did now. Thank you very much, Mr Bryce,' she stated solemnly.

'You're welcome. I'm sure you'd have done the same if you'd been in my shoes.'

Would she? She hoped she would have done.

'I see you lost your coat,' Bryce said, shining the torch at her.

So she had, she now realized.

'Let's get back upstairs,' she said.

En route Maggie hunted through several bedrooms until she found suitable dry clothes, while Bryce stopped off at his bedroom on the staff floor and also changed.

'Good work you two,' Lawler greeted them.

Maggie glanced about her. People were sitting huddled in groups, many of them thoroughly dejected and miserable. Ethel and the four Australians were the exceptions. They appeared in buoyant spirits, and seemed to be telling each other jokes.

'The water's risen two floors from where Bryce pulled me in off the telegraph pole,' Maggie reported.

Lawler paled to hear that. 'Which floor has it now reached then?'

'The split level one. And still rising.'

'Dear God!' Lawler whispered. Then, desperation in his tone, 'Surely we're safe this high up?'

Maggie remembered how the building had been rocking on its foundations. If the hotel doesn't collapse under us, she told herself, but refrained from saying so out loud. Who knew what would happen between then and the morning? Each minute, each second, had to be played as it came.

Then she had another thought. What if the outside world was unaware of what was happening at Heymouth? That was possible if the telephones were down. She'd been counting on rescue services arriving with the dawn, but maybe they wouldn't be coming after all.

Lawler glanced over to his wife, who was sitting wrapped in an eiderdown. 'It's all so unbelievable,' he choked.

Maggie couldn't have agreed more.

'I think the rain might just have slackened,' Bryce said.

Maggie stared out of the nearest window, but all she could see was Stygian darkness. Her shoulders sagged, she felt completely drained.

Tiredness crept over her, making her eyelids droop. Sleep. She had to get some sleep. She was utterly worn out.

Curling up beneath the window she sank into gorgeous oblivion.

She awoke stiff and sore, puzzled as to why that should be. Then it all came flooding back. She sat bolt upright, aches and pains quite forgotten.

Bryce, Lawler, Ethel, one of the Australians and a few others were standing at the windows gazing out.

'Christalbloodymighty!' the Australian breathed.

Maggie rose to her feet, and looked out of her window. The scene that greeted her eyes was even worse than she'd expected. It was horrific in the extreme.

'The water's gone,' someone said.

So it had, Maggie realized. That meant they could leave the hotel by themselves. Turning, she rushed to the stairs and started down to the ground floor.

The hotel below the line where the water had finally peaked was a complete mess. The air was heavy with the stink of damp and foulness. Slime and sludge covered the floors, everywhere wallpaper hung in tatters, while in places ceilings had come down.

With relief Maggie finally left the hotel, realizing that it now was a most unsafe place to be.

Outside the hotel's front doors were a pair of bent and twisted motor cars, one on top of the other. The mangled remains of a bicycle were sticking out of the windscreen of the lower car.

All sorts of debris was scattered in profusion. A multitude of household effects, iron bars, timbers, glass, bricks, a chimney stack, seemed to have been shaken by some giant hand and strewn any which way.

Maggie came upon a pile of massive boulders, which had been swept down off the hills. When they were moving they must have demolished everything in their path.

'Maggie Jordan?'

It was Mrs MacDonald who owned the post office. She was wearing a coat over her night-dress.

'Yes, Mrs MacDonald?'

'Have you seen my Graeme?' She was referring to Mr MacDonald.

'I haven't I'm afraid.'

'He's around here somewhere. I just know he is.'

Maggie glanced about, but saw no sign of Graeme MacDonald.

'I just know he is,' Mrs MacDonald repeated and then beat one hand ineffectually against the other.

'Was he with you this morning?' Maggie queried, beginning to realize the truth.

'No. I missed him some time during the night. But he's around here somewhere. I just know it.'

Mrs MacDonald went wandering off. 'Graeme? Graeme? Where are you darling? It's Janey calling. Your Janey.'

When the demented Mrs MacDonald had disappeared, Maggie put a hand to her forehead and gently rubbed it. She then became aware that she was shaking all over.

A little further on a surprisingly clean rag doll caught her eye, which she recognized. Eileen Riddrie had proudly shown it to her the previous week, as she had been given it that very day for her birthday.

She next came upon the mud-covered carcass of a sheep, and another of a Friesian cow. The cow was bloated and a swarm of flies were already buzzing round it. Both animals, with many others, had come from the higher parts of the rivers.

The small Achray Hotel had vanished; all that remained was a foot of brickwork where its base had been. It reminded Maggie of a tooth broken off just above the gum.

The Pixie Tearooms were still intact. But she was wrong. The front and one side remained, the rear and other side had been swept away along with half the roof.

The North Hey itself was still well over its banks, and flowing like an express train. When Maggie glanced out to the mouth of the river she was amazed. The mouth of the river seemed ten times its normal width, while about half a mile out to sea hundreds of trees stood upright, supported by their enormous roots, just as they had been carried down in the flood. As far as the eye could see, the water was a dirty mud colour.

Then Maggie came across her first human body. She thought it was hideous, and turned quickly away. Although horrified, she couldn't resist having another peek to see if she recognized who it was. The face was unfamiliar. A holiday-maker she decided.

She moved on, and into a quagmire of silt which she had to wade through, making obscene sucking noises every time she took a step.

She spotted other figures moving about, and from some place close by she heard agonized sobbing.

The stone bridge across the North Hey was no more. She later discovered that eighteen bridges had been destroyed.

She became gradually aware of an awful stench. It smelt not only of mud and rotting materials, but also the unmistakable odour of human waste.

She paused to stare at a wooden gate swinging crazily on its hinges. The cottage the gate belonged to had disappeared, but perversely its gate had been left behind. Further along she came upon an upturned Welsh dresser with a hand protruding out from underneath it. The hand was caked in mud, the fingers hooked into a claw.

More boulders now barred her passage, and mixed with these, were trees and telegraph poles.

She worked her way round the obstruction, clambering over general debris as she went. And then, the worst moment so far, she stumbled across Clarice McKechnie.

Clarice would never now marry her lad from Oban, or

49

anyone else. Clarice was dead, her clogged-up mouth oozing dribbles of mud.

Maggie put a thumb in her own mouth, and bit it so hard she drew blood. Why only yesterday she'd waved across the street to Clarice. And now . . . She swallowed back bile and continued.

Where their street had been was a wasteland. Not one solitary cottage had survived. The entire area was so altered it took her several minutes to establish where their cottage had been.

She stood on what she judged to have been the centre of their cottage and, fearfully biting her lip, gazed about her. 'Oh Mum! Oh Dad!' she whispered. Pictures of her parents, memories, flashed through her mind bringing hot scalding tears to her eyes. And with April and Charlie, Pet and Wee Charlie.

She mustn't give up hope she told herself. There was no certainty they were dead. They might have had a miraculous escape. But somehow, she didn't believe that. Deep within her she knew they were dead. All four of them, most of her family, wiped out.

A screech made her look up. A seagull flew overhead, followed by another. They'd returned knowing danger was past.

Slowly she sank onto her knees, and tumbled forwards. She was crying profusely now, tears dripping onto that awful mud. She moved her right hand, and made contact with something which slid into her hand as though wanting to be there.

She held the object up, but it was impossible to make it out as it was coated in mud.

She scraped the mud away and revealed a piece of scrimshaw. It was her dad's favourite piece that he'd always refused to sell and which had had pride of place on top of the mantelpiece in the parlour.

Emotion stronger than any she'd ever previously experienced welled up within her, and overwhelmed her.

And for a while time stood still.

'Hello?'

Maggie dimly became aware that she was being spoken to.

50

'Hello? Are you all right?'

She gradually brought herself back from wherever she'd been. Her eyes were puffy and still full of tears.

'I'm fine, thank you,' she eventually mumbled.

'Would you like a cigarette?'

'I don't smoke.'

She could make out the man now. He was a member of the Salvation Army, the dear old Sally Ann.

'This was my home,' she said, gesturing vaguely about her. 'This!'

'You lived here with your husband?' he queried, squatting beside her.

'No, my mother and father, sister and brother. The water came, and now they're all gone.'

'There are many survivors Miss . . .?'

'Jordan. Maggie Jordan.'

'There are many survivors Miss Jordan. The homeless are being asked to gather at the Commemorative Hall. Shall I take you there?'

He was about sixty years old, she thought, with a kind face that expressed a lot of spirituality. Her father had always had a great deal of time for the Sally Ann. The salt of the earth, he'd called them.

She tried to move, but found her legs had somehow stuck. 'Can you give me a hand?' she asked, which he did.

'I'll walk you to the Commemorative Hall if you like?'

She shook her head. 'There's no need to trouble yourself, but thank you all the same. I'll find my own way. There will be others who need you more than me.'

'Are you sure?'

'Absolutely.'

She was about to move off when she had a sudden thought. Turning back she said. 'Tell me, I'm curious. Having seen all this do you still believe in God?'

His features contorted, then relaxed. 'God works in mysterious ways His wonders to perform. Yes I do, in answer to your question. Just because we don't always understand *why* doesn't mean there isn't a reason behind what He does. Yes, I still believe in Him, and love Him,' the Salvation Army man replied in a soft, gentle voice.

Maggie couldn't think of a suitable reply to that.

Maggie had developed a raging thirst and wondered if she could get a drink at the Commemorative Hall. She wasn't in the least bit hungry though. To have eaten at a time like this would have seemed all wrong.

'Maggie!'

She stopped as Don Gillies came hurrying over. He looked positively ghastly.

'How are Charlie and April?' he demanded.

She wondered if she looked as bad as he did. What did it matter anyway? Would anything ever matter again?

'Our house got washed away. The entire street did.'

Already a small man, Don appeared to shrink even further. 'But you're alive?'

'I'm alive,' she nodded. 'Though how is beyond me. I should be dead like the rest of them.'

He stared grimly at her. 'Have you seen their bodies?'

'No.'

'Then you can't be certain lass.'

'I suppose not,' she replied, humouring him. 'What about your family?'

'We were very lucky. Our first floor got flooded, but it never rose higher than that.'

'You *were* lucky,' she acknowledged.

He opened his mouth to say something, clearly changed his mind and said instead, 'The lighthouse has gone you know.'

'No, I didn't.'

He made a sweeping gesture with the side of his hand. 'Completely gone. Two hundred years it's stood there. And now, in a single night, gone!'

'Along with half of Heymouth. If not more than half,' she added heavily.

A large camouflaged painted truck caught their attention. 'The Army! Thank the Lord for that,' Don Gillies said.

A second truck appeared behind the first, and a third behind that.

'They've come quickly,' Don said.

'I thought it might take some while for the outside world to learn of what had happened here as I presumed the telephone lines were down. But apparently not,' Maggie said.

'Perhaps someone got through on a short-wave transmitter?'

Maggie had forgotten about them, but there were several – or had been several – in Heymouth, including one in the lighthouse. The keeper on duty at the time might have got a message out before the lighthouse went.

Don spotted someone and swore. 'My sister Morag! I was on my way to see her.' He waved frantically, and his sister did the same.

'Will you excuse me, Maggie,' he said, wetness in his eyes that hadn't been there a moment ago.

'Of course, Mr Gillies.'

He flew into Morag's arms and the pair of them hugged one another.

Maggie met and talked to others she knew before finally arriving at the Commemorative Hall. Going inside she found people milling aimlessly around, others sitting staring vacantly into space.

The Reverend Barr was sitting behind a table, flanked on either side by Mrs D'Arcy and Mrs Henry, both pillars of the church. Maggie joined the short queue in front of him.

She had shuffled forward several places when two soldiers entered carrying a metal milk churn.

'Fresh water!' one of the soldiers cried out. Instantly he and his companion were mobbed.

Stay in the queue or join those at the churn? Two more soldiers entered with another churn of water. That settled it, they wouldn't run out of water right away so she'd remain where she was.

'Hello, Maggie,' the Reverend Barr said when she reached him.

'Hello, Reverend. Ladies.'

'We're making a list of the homeless. That will also help eliminate—'

'I understand,' she cut in.

He wrote her name in the school jotter open in front of him. 'And the exact address was again?'

She gave it to him.

'We've been told your entire street has gone,' he sighed.

'That's correct.'

'What about the rest of your family?'

She stared at him, then replied, 'My surviving was a miracle. They might also have survived, but that's highly unlikely.'

'You mustn't be so negative, Maggie,' Mrs Henry admonished. Maggie glanced at the well-meaning woman. She could easily have slapped her for that remark, which was silly really, but nonetheless that was how she felt.

'Have your family all lived through last night?' she queried instead.

'Yes. But then we're very protected where we are.'

Maggie focused on the Reverend Barr again. 'Is there anything else, minister?'

'I'm correct in believing you don't have any other relatives in Heymouth?'

She nodded.

'Temporary beds will be made up here tonight. We're also hoping to place others with those whose houses have remained intact.'

'I understand. Thank you.'

'The Army will be laying on food later. Though how much later I've no idea.'

Maggie wanted to say that the way she felt she doubted she'd ever want to eat again, but didn't.

'Thank you, Maggie,' the Reverend Barr said, dismissing her. She left him and joined those at the milk churns.

Outside again she glanced up at the sky which was a pale shade of blue. She recalled what her father had said about 'knowing our weather the sun will probably be cracking the skies tomorrow'. That brought fresh tears to her eyes. It was hardly likely the sun would be cracking the skies, but it looked as if it would soon be out.

'Oh Dad!' she whispered to herself yet again, feeling sick.

She went down to the front, or what had been the front, and stared out to sea. How many bodies were out there she wondered.

How bizarre those trees looked! Sticking straight up out of the sea as if they'd grown there. She knew that was one of many memories which would stay with her for the rest of her life.

Susan! she suddenly thought. What had become of Susan? She would go and try to find out.

Susan's house was still standing, its front door wide open. 'Anyone home?' she called out, sticking her head inside the door.

Mrs Lennox, Susan's mum, appeared from the rear of the house. 'Maggie! Come away in girl! I'm afraid you haven't caught us at our best. As you can . . .' She broke off having taken in Maggie's expression and general demeanour. 'How bad was it with you?'

Mrs Lennox's face drained to a pasty white as Maggie told her. 'Oh lassie!' she whispered, aghast, when she'd finished her tale.

Maggie took several deep breaths. 'I don't know if it's actually fully penetrated yet. I think it has, but I'm not sure.'

Mrs Lennox threw an arm around Maggie and drew her into the kitchen. A few seconds later Susan came bursting in as she had been upstairs when she'd heard Maggie's voice.

With a shriek of delight she threw herself at Maggie, enveloping her in the warmest of embraces. 'I was just about to come round and see you. Wasn't I, Mum?'

'Yes,' Mrs Lennox said softly.

Susan looked from her mum to Maggie, and back again. 'What is it? What's happened?'

'Maggie's lost her family. Mother, father, sister and brother. She's convinced they're dead.'

'Oh!'

'I'm certain of it,' Maggie added.

'I don't know what to say,' Susan whispered.

Maggie nodded. 'If I was in your shoes I wouldn't know what to say either. But I know what's in your heart.'

Susan kissed her friend on the cheek, then embraced her again. All three women were crying.

'Where's Mr Lennox?' Maggie asked when Susan had released her.

'Gone to do the round of our relatives. I only hope . . .' She trailed off, and bit her lip.

'I've got the impression some parts of Heymouth were more badly hit than others. So in many cases it's a matter of where you live.'

'What about The Haven? Any news of that?' Susan enquired.

Susan's eyes grew wide as Maggie told her about her ride on the telegraph pole, ending up at The Haven where she'd been rescued by Bryce.

'Well I never!' Susan exclaimed.

'I'd make us a cup of tea if I had some clean water,' Mrs Lennox said. She'd lit the range earlier intending to cook later. She had enough tins in the larder to see them through a few days at least.

'There's clean water at the Commemorative Hall. And the Army are bound to be establishing other water points. If you've got something I can put the water in I'll go and see if I can get some for you,' Maggie offered.

'We'll both go,' Susan declared.

Mrs Lennox found them a pail and a large enamel container.

They set off at once, everyone looking forward enormously to the proposed cup of tea.

The area immediately round Susan's house had suffered relatively little damage, but they soon left that behind to enter roads that were devastated.

Susan gaped at a fishing boat with a motor car embedded in its side, in what had been someone's front parlour. They both jumped when, with a loud crash, a two-storey house suddenly caved in on itself.

'It's dangerous out here,' Susan said, swallowing hard.

'Not as dangerous as it was last night, I can assure you.'

'And the smell!' Susan wrinkled her nose. 'It's a lot worse here than where we are.'

'The sewers are probably smashed to smithereens. They're going to have to do something fast about that if they don't want an epidemic on their hands.'

'Oohhh!' exclaimed Susan, fist flying to her mouth. The object of her alarm and disgust was a drowned collie dog.

'There are plenty of dead animals about,' Maggie said. And humans too, she thought grimly.

A little further on they came across a parked Army vehicle around which a number of people were clustered listening to the vehicle's wireless. Maggie and Susan joined the listeners, which included a lance-corporal and sergeant, the vehicle's drivers. The radio was tuned to a report on Heymouth.

'Flash flooding of the utmost severity . . . feared that many lives have been lost . . . great damage to property . . . Secretary of State for Scotland on his way to make a personal visit . . . Prime Minister Baldwin keeping in hourly touch with events . . . telephone calls enquiring about friends and relatives jamming all local switchboards . . . medical and other assistance on its way . . . the Army already there (this raised a cheer from the lance-corporal) . . . specialized equipment being mobilized, equipment necessary for the enormous clear up that will have to take place . . .'

They both listened to the end of the report, then continued. 'We're certainly national news,' Susan commented.

'We are that,' Maggie agreed.

'And you said that Mr and Mrs Lawler are safe?'

'They were when I left them this morning.'

They paused to watch as a stretcher was carried past, the person obviously a corpse as a blanket was covering its face.

Susan shivered. 'I wonder if we knew them?'

'It might be anybody,' Maggie mused. A sudden icy coldness ran through her. It could indeed be anybody, including her mum, dad or sister Pet. It wasn't Wee Charlie though, the body was far too big.

They followed the stretcher until they arrived at a large tent which had a hastily painted sign slung across its front. The sign bore the chilling legend Temporary Mortuary.

'I missed this when I came to your house,' Maggie said quietly.

'Do you want to go in and see if any of your family are there?'

Maggie thought, then shook her head. 'Not yet. Maybe later on.'

A woman in the uniform of the Women's Voluntary Service, approached them. 'Are you girls lost?'

'Hardly!' Maggie snapped back. 'We were both born and brought up in Heymouth.'

The woman's expression softened. 'Sorry. I'm only trying to help. There are locals wandering around in a state of shock you know. Some of them don't know which way is up.'

Maggie realized she'd been in the wrong. 'It's me who should be sorry. It just seemed such a stupid question that's all. But now I understand why you asked it.'

The woman glanced at their pail and enamel container. 'Are you after water?'

Susan nodded.

'The Army were dishing out some at the Commemorative Hall earlier,' Maggie said.

'No need to go that far. There's a stand-pipe that's been erected two streets over that way,' she said, pointing. 'It should save your legs a bit.'

Maggie smiled her gratitude. 'Thank you very much. And again I'm sorry I was short with you.'

'Think nothing of it.' And with that the woman bustled off.

'Right,' said Susan. 'Let's find this stand-pipe.'

Before they reached the stand-pipe they came upon Tom and Cyril. Subdued greetings were made all round.

'We're returning to Northallerton on the first transport available,' Cyril said.

'The sooner the better,' Tom added.

'That's completely understandable,' Maggie smiled.

When they'd been in The Lobster Pot, and afterwards, there had been a tremendous rapport between them. But now, their budding relationship had been reduced to one set of strangers discussing events with another.

'Our place was badly flooded. We've lost all our clothes and gear,' Cyril complained.

'Cost a mint to replace,' said Tom, sticking his hands in his pockets.

'An absolute mint,' Cyril agreed, gazing off into space.

'Maggie lost her family,' Susan stated levelly, suddenly angry with these two.

Tom blinked. 'You mean . . .?'

'Our entire street was washed away, and my family with it. It was a chance in a million that I came through it all alive.'

'Jesus Christ!' swore Tom, trying to remember Maggie's street. But all he could conjure up was darkness and the vague shape of houses.

'That's tough,' said Cyril.

Tough! Maggie raged inwardly. What sort of word was that to use. And delivered with such aggression. They didn't care, she suddenly realized. All the pair of them were concerned about was getting back to Northallerton.

'Goodbye, have a good trip,' she said, forcing her voice to remain steady.

'Try and keep your peckers up!' Tom said in an attempt to be cheerful.

Susan grabbed Maggie's arm and marched her friend away. 'What a couple of prats,' she said.

'It doesn't matter. We hardly knew them.' Maggie thought back to what the WVS woman had said about locals being in a state of shock. Was she? She wouldn't have been at all surprised if she were. She was certainly far from her normal state of mind. At times she was very subjective, at others quite detached as if floating outside her body.

And another thing, her hearing had gone peculiar. Right now she was hearing as though from a long way off, the sounds somehow muffled. A little earlier when they'd listened to the

Army vehicle's wireless her hearing had been so acute that every syllable spoken sounded as if it were being shouted directly into her ear.

They found the stand-pipe, and joined the queue. The water was supplied from an eight-wheeled tanker that had arrived in Heymouth only an hour before.

They filled their pail and container, and started the return journey. *En route* they met a number of people they knew, hearing their stories and telling their own. They also witnessed various nauseating sights including a cart piled high with dead animals. These, they gleaned, were being taken off to be burnt.

Mr Lennox was there when they arrived back. 'Maggie, I'm so awfully sorry to hear your news,' he said, taking her hands in his and squeezing them.

'Thank you,' she whispered.

'You'll of course stay here for as long as you like. I won't hear otherwise.'

She thanked him for that as well.

'The wife has already made up a spare bed in Susan's room. You can use that as long as necessary. Till you get yourself sorted out like.'

'What will you do?' Susan asked. It was something she'd been wondering about.

Maggie shook her head. 'I've no idea. To tell you the truth I haven't thought that far ahead.'

'Plenty of time for that,' said Mrs Lennox from the range where she was putting the kettle on. She glanced down at the linoleum in despair. It was quite ruined thanks to the filthy water that had covered it during the flood.

'What about your relatives?' Maggie asked Mr Lennox.

'Old Auntie Mary, she's seventy-six you know, had a heart attack and Uncle George broke a leg getting her upstairs away from the flood water. Now they're both being looked after, and our only casualties I'm happy to say.'

'Our family got off light altogether,' Mrs Lennox said.

'Aye, indeed,' Mr Lennox agreed.

His wife's face clouded. 'Do you know the McLeans in

Fisherman's Wynd? McLean won the big money prize in the draw last Christmas.'

'I know them,' Maggie nodded.

'Their son Hector was a hero. Apparently he saved a child from certain death, at the expense of his own.'

'His father saw him swept away,' Mrs Lennox said heavily.

'A hero,' her husband repeated, and shook his head. 'From accounts there were quite a few last night. Or early this morning as it actually was.'

'They say adversity always brings out the best in folk,' Susan stated.

Maggie immediately thought of Bryce returning to the flooded corridor to save her. It was certainly true in his respect.

The kettle was soon singing, and the tea made. Mrs Lennox placed some sliced corned beef on the table along with some griddle scones she'd had in the larder wrapped in a cloth. 'No bread I'm afraid,' she apologized. 'I normally get that first thing in the morning, which I didn't today. So you'll have to make do with scones.'

Susan went up to the table. 'Maggie?'

Maggie shook her head. 'Not for me.'

'Are you sure, lass?' Mrs Lennox queried.

'Yes, thank you. The tea's enough.'

Maggie held the cup clasped in her hands, letting its warmth seep into them. The heat rose from her hands into her tired, battered body. Closing her eyes she felt the warmth spreading throughout her body, relaxing her.

'Maggie?'

She started as Mr Lennox removed the cup from her grasp.

'Would you like to lie down, lass? You were just about to nod off there.'

She was tired, she thought. She'd only had those few hours at The Haven. 'Please, I could do with some sleep.'

'Susan will take you up,' Mrs Lennox said.

Maggie yawned. Yes, sleep was what she needed. To recoup her strength and escape all this . . . this horror for a while.

Upstairs Susan looked out a night-gown into which Maggie

61

shrugged. She would have given anything for a bath, but that was impossible.

'I'll leave out some of my clothes to replace those,' Susan said, gesturing towards the clothes Maggie had acquired at The Haven.

'Thank you, Susan.'

She climbed into bed. She would go to the mortuary when she woke up, she told herself. And then there was her sister Laura, but she'd think of her later.

She smiled when Susan kissed her on the cheek. 'I think I must have aged a dozen years today,' she said.

Susan didn't reply, but stroked her friend's dirty and matted hair.

Within seconds Maggie was sleeping soundly.

She heard the roaring approaching and knew what to expect. She had to warn the rest of the family! She tried to get out of bed, but couldn't. Every time she was about to put a foot on the floor she suddenly found herself tucked up under the bedclothes again.

Shout a warning, she thought. But nothing emerged, not even a croak. Dad! Mum! Watch out! Run for your lives! she silently cried. Pet! Wee Charlie!

The roaring was stupendous now. She clapped her hands over her ears waiting for the water that was almost upon them, aware of the damage it was going to cause.

Her mother appeared, a horrified expression on her face. Wee Charlie was with her, clutched to her bosom. 'We're all going to die!' April said, and shook all over.

Wee Charlie started to cry, enormous tears running down his cheeks. 'I don't want to die! I don't want to die!' Then, looking directly at her, 'Save me, Maggie! Please save me!'

Now Pet was there, and her dad behind Pet. 'Who would ever have thought it would end like this?' Charlie said calmly.

'But not for you!' Pet stated, pointing an accusing finger at her. 'Not you!'

All of a sudden the far wall exploded inwards and a broiling mass of water burst into the room.

Maggie felt herself being sucked into a pit of water that seemed to go down forever.

'I can't swim!' Wee Charlie shrieked in fear. 'I can't swim!'

She tried to call out to him, but again no words came. She thrashed her arms, attempting to swim towards him. But every stroke took her further and further away.

'I can't swim!' Wee Charlie shrieked a last time, and promptly vanished from view.

'Goodbye, Maggie!' said April, waving. 'Goodbye!'

She watched her mother shatter into a million pieces. From nowhere a swarm of fish appeared who promptly gobbled up the pieces.

Her father was choking for breath, clutching his throat as he fought for air. His face got redder till finally, like a squeezed pimple, it suddenly burst sending his head's gory contents flying in all directions.

She was sobbing as the remains of her dad simply drifted away.

She twisted round and saw Pet up to her shoulders in ooze, sinking fast. Pet writhed, which only succeeded in making her sink even quicker.

Pet's shoulders disappeared, then her neck was swallowed up. Pet screamed, a horrendous scream which was abruptly cut off as her mouth vanished.

Maggie's gaze was locked onto her younger sister's agonized eyes, then the eyes too had gone.

'No!' She'd found her voice at last. 'Nooo!!'

She sat bolt upright in bed. She was covered in cold sweat, her chest heaving.

A nightmare! she realized. She'd been having a nightmare. But how excruciatingly real it had seemed.

The door opened and Mrs Lennox rushed in. 'Are you all right, Maggie?'

'Just a nightmare, Mrs Lennox. It's over now.'

Mrs Lennox sat on the bed beside Maggie. 'You're bound to have a few of those. It would only be natural after what you've been through.'

Maggie wiped the sweat from her forehead. 'My

imagination ran wild there for a bit. It wasn't very pleasant.'

She didn't know how it happened, but she found herself in Mrs Lennox's arms, who comforted her as though she were a child.

'Was it your family you were dreaming about?' Mrs Lennox shrewdly asked.

Maggie nodded.

'I'm sure they felt no pain. It would have been all over very quickly.' She paused, then added softly, 'If they are dead, that is. That hasn't been proved yet.'

Maggie didn't argue with Mrs Lennox. But she knew the truth.

'If you get dressed and come down I'll give you another nice cup of tea,' Mrs Lennox proposed.

'Sounds grand.'

'And a bite. You must want one now.'

'No, I couldn't. I'm not in the least hungry.'

Mrs Lennox held Maggie at arms' length. 'You have to eat, girl, you'll make yourself ill if you don't. I can understand your not feeling hungry, but you must force yourself. And I tell you this, that's the advice your own mother would give you. So, for her sake you'll make an effort, eh?'

Maggie couldn't help but be won over by this appeal on her mother's behalf. It was precisely the advice April would have given her.

'A little something then,' she smiled.

Mrs Lennox matched Maggie's smile. 'I'll see if I can find you a treat.'

When Mrs Lennox had gone Maggie got out of bed and dressed in the clothes Susan had left out for her.

As she ate her treat she announced she would pay the mortuary a visit directly she'd finished her tea.

'I'll come with you. We need some more water,' Susan said.

'And I'll have to think about contacting my sister Laura in Glasgow,' Maggie went on. 'Though I don't know how I'll do that as she doesn't have a telephone.'

Mr Lennox paused. He was ripping up the ruined linoleum. 'Speak to the police. They're bound to be able to help.'

Maggie thought that was a good idea.

'And see if you can find out when the water and electricity are going to be back on?' Mrs Lennox asked.

'That could take days if not weeks,' her husband told her.

When Maggie and Susan left the house they were carrying the same pail and enamel container that they'd used earlier. As they walked along the street they heard the strident clang of a fire engine. A little further on they caught sight of a rising column of smoke.

'Wait a minute,' Susan said shortly. She went over to a man sitting on a front doorstep.

'Mr Darling?'

Mr Darling looked up at Susan. His eyes were red-rimmed with black bags underneath. He stared uncomprehendingly at her.

'It's Susan Lennox. You know my dad.'

Recognition dawned. 'Oh aye, of course. How are you, Susan?'

'Fine. And yourself?'

'I lost my Gladys. She was at the rear of the house here when it was hit by something or other and knocked down. I identified her at the mortuary not an hour since.' Gladys had been his wife. And it had only been the rear of the house that had been knocked down.

'I'm so sorry,' Susan said softly.

'She was a good woman and wife,' Mr Darling went on. 'I'm going to miss her sorely.'

'We're on our way to the mortuary ourselves,' Susan explained.

'Your mum or dad?'

'No, Maggie's here. Most of her family are missing.'

'You have my every sympathy. I know exactly what you must be going through,' Mr Darling commiserated with Maggie.

She looked into his eyes and saw terrible pain and inconsolable grief. She nodded her thanks and reciprocal sympathy, and then moved on. Susan caught up with her after a few words with Mr Darling. The encounter with

65

him had left Maggie with an enormous lump in her throat.

'Look!' Maggie said. She was pointing at a massive crane inching its way down Heymouth Brae. Behind the crane was a bulldozer, tiny by comparison.

When they arrived at the temporary mortuary they halted outside. 'Do you want me to come in with you?' Susan queried.

Maggie thought about it. 'Yes, I would.'

'Right then.'

Susan couldn't think of anything she'd like to do less, but she would support Maggie. After all she was her friend and she was in no doubt that had the positions been reversed Maggie would have done the same.

Maggie took a deep breath, and made for the tent entrance.

'Can I help you?' asked a man belonging to the Army Medical Corps.

Maggie explained the situation.

'I see.' The man then asked her some gentle questions.

'Please come this way,' he beckoned.

There were lines of double-banked trestle tables with bodies lying on top. Each body was covered by a blanket.

The first body they passed had a piece of paper pinned to its blanket, Smith, Maisie. The Lobster Pot, if still in existence, had lost its landlady.

They stopped by a body as yet unidentified. 'From your description this could be your mother,' said the man from the Army Medical Corps.

Maggie braced herself as he reached for the top of the blanket, which he then drew down to reveal a corpse's face. The breath hissed from her when she saw it wasn't April.

'No?' the man asked.

Maggie shook her head. 'No,' she confirmed.

'Any idea who she is?'

The woman was roughly her mother's age, the face rounder and fatter with hair on the upper lip which her mother didn't have. The face was streaked with mud and had a gash on the left cheek.

'I've never seen her before in my life. Susan?'

'Me neither?'

'Must have been a holiday-maker,' Maggie suggested.

The man replaced the blanket, and then moved on to another corpse.

Finally the ordeal was over and they could escape the tent. Maggie had drawn a blank, none of the bodies were of those she was looking for. But there were still a great many bodies to come in, the Army Medical Corps man had grimly told her.

They returned to the stand-pipe where they'd got water from earlier, to find the tanker gone. They decided to try the Commemorative Hall.

There they found a tanker and stand-pipe, also a stall where bread was being doled out. After filling the containers they queued up and were given two large plain loaves.

'Have you been into the hall to let them have your particulars?' queried the WVS woman running the stall.

'I've reported to the minister if that's what you mean,' Maggie replied.

The woman nodded. 'And what about you?' she asked Susan.

'No, I'm afraid not.'

'Then you'd better. The powers that be have decided that various lists have to be drawn up, including one of all those who survived. They apparently need them for all manner of reasons.'

'That makes sense,' Maggie commented, and Susan agreed.

On leaving the stall they plunged into the hall which was bedlam, and far fuller than it had been that morning. The minister was still there, but now Mrs D'Arcy, Mrs Henry and a Mr Ker had tables of their own.

While Maggie was waiting for Susan, Mr Crosland, one of the town councillors, appeared out of the mêlée to pin a sheet of paper onto a wall. Curious, she went over to see what the paper said. It was a list of all bodies that had been positively identified to date.

It made sad reading, with five entire families from her street numbered among the dead. The Caskies, including Faith, were one of the five.

A band of children were careering about, playing tig. How

resilient children could be Maggie thought. The children all looked as if they didn't have a care in the world, that this was just another ordinary day, and what was taking place within the hall some sort of social occasion.

Her reverie was broken by the sound of a loudhailer coming from the street. She went out to listen and discovered it was a policeman in a car. There were other police present, and after the announcement she spoke to one of them about her sister Laura.

'We're home!' shouted Susan, and went through to the kitchen leaving Maggie to close the front door.

Susan placed the pail of water on the table. 'We're being evacuated, starting tomorrow,' she declared.

'Evacuated?' Mrs Lennox queried with a frown.

'Those in authority are worried about the spread of disease, plus the sheer danger of remaining in Heymouth. Everyone is to be evacuated until it's safe to return.'

'Well, I'm not going,' Mr Lennox stated defiantly.

'You won't have any choice, Dad. You're not being asked to go, you're being told.'

'Where to though?' Mrs Lennox demanded.

'There's a camp being put together right now on the moor at the top of the brae,' Maggie explained.

'What sort of camp?'

'Tents and caravans the police said. Facilities will be provided, lavatories and bathing, that sort of thing.'

'What about eating?' Mrs Lennox queried, eyeing the loaves Maggie had laid beside the water containers.

'There are to be mobile canteens,' Susan said.

Mr Lennox grumbled and glowered. Stay in a tent or caravan! The idea was appalling. They might be ideal for daft holiday-makers, but certainly not for him. He liked the comfort of his own bed.

'Those who still have homes have to take no more than a suitcase each. Those of us who lost everything will be given clothes and other necessities,' Maggie informed the older Lennoxes.

'What about the house while we're out of it?' Mrs Lennox asked anxiously.

'It'll be safe, you don't have to worry about that,' Susan assured her.

Maggie sat at the table, thinking that she didn't know about the proposed camp but couldn't wait to get at the promised bathing facilities. She didn't care whether it was a bath or a shower just as long as there was lots of hot water and soap.

'We stopped by The Haven and saw the Lawlers,' Susan said.

'How are they?'

'Beside themselves,' Maggie answered. 'The hotel has been condemned and is to be pulled down within the next couple of days.'

'Surely it's insured though?' Mr Lennox chipped in.

'Mrs Lawler did mention that it was, so at least they've got some safeguards,' Susan replied.

'It's still a terrible blow to them,' Maggie said. 'They loved that hotel, it was their pride and joy.'

Mr Lennox gave a thin smile. 'At least hotels can be rebuilt, dead people can't be brought back to life.'

Maggie dropped her head.

'I'm sorry lass, I wasn't thinking,' he said quickly. 'How eh . . .?' He glanced at Susan, who shook her head.

'I'll go back to the mortuary again tomorrow,' Maggie stated heavily.

'And what about once we're in this camp?' Mrs Lennox demanded.

'I'll be able to come and go to the mortuary. Those with a reason will be allowed access to Heymouth. The police were quite definite about that.'

Mrs Lennox crossed over and picked up one of the loaves. 'You managed to find some bread I see.'

They chatted for a while longer, then Mrs Lennox and Susan set about packing, getting ready for the next day's evacuation.

Mr Lawler never mentioned again that he'd refuse to go, aware now that was a stance he'd have to back down from when the time came.

69

Besides, he knew in his heart of hearts evacuating Heymouth was the right thing to do. But he was still going to miss his own bed!

They were having dinner the following day when there was a loud knocking on the front door.

'I'll get it!' said Susan, jumping to her feet.

She opened the door to reveal an Army officer, who promptly saluted her. He then consulted a notebook.

'Is this the Lennox household?'

'It is.'

'Therefore you must be . . .' He peered at his book. 'Miss Susan Lennox?'

'I am.' He was quite dishy she thought.

He cleared his throat. 'Have you heard about the intended evacuation?'

'Yes. Would you like to come inside?'

He smiled. 'Sorry, I've a lot to do.'

'We've just made a pot of tea.'

'Sorry, Miss Lennox. I really can't.'

Pity, she thought.

He went on. 'I have to inform you that this street will be evacuated this afternoon between nineteen and twenty hundred hours. That's seven and eight p.m. Transport will be provided, and each person is limited to . . .'

'One suitcase each,' she interjected playfully.

'That's correct, miss. One suitcase each.'

'Will you be with the transport, colonel?'

'*Captain*,' he blushed. 'I'm only a captain. And yes, I will be. I shall be in command of the convoy.'

'We'll be ready in time,' she promised.

'Please. It will make matters so much easier all round if everyone is.'

Very, very dishy, she thought.

He saluted her again. 'Till later, Miss Lennox.'

'Till later.'

He moved away, and she shut the door. She went through to tell the others about the arrangement.

Susan had no sooner sat down than there was another knocking at the door.

'I'll get it!' she said, jumping up, thinking it was the captain again. But it wasn't. It was Maggie's older sister, Laura McNair.

'Laura!' Maggie exclaimed when she saw her sister framed in the kitchen doorway.

'The police told me you were here. I hurried over as quickly as I could.'

Maggie rushed over to her sister, and they fell into one another's arms. Laura began to cry and, despite herself, Maggie did the same.

Mrs Lennox crossed to a cupboard and took out another cup and saucer for Laura.

'So just what do you know?' Maggie demanded when the emotional embrace was over.

'The wireless and newspapers have been full of the flood. I tried to ring the emergency telephone lines all day yesterday from a public phone box, but could never get through. Then last night the police called to tell me that Mum, Dad, Pet and Wee Charlie were missing, but that you were safe. Have they been found yet?'

Mrs Lennox filled Laura's cup and placed it on the table. She then signed to her husband and Susan to leave the room. It was best that Maggie and Laura were left alone for a while.

When the Lennoxes were gone Maggie asked, 'Have you been home or talked to anyone else since arriving in Heymouth?'

Laura shook her head. 'The police directed me straight here, and apart from them I haven't spoken to anyone.'

'Then you'd better sit down and I'll tell you all about it right from the beginning.'

Laura was rigid with shock when Maggie finally finished her story. 'You're certain they're dead?' she queried in a strange, hollow voice.

'I can't be that until their bodies are found. But within myself I am.'

'I thought . . . I don't know what I thought! I knew lots of

71

people had died, but couldn't bring myself to . . .' She stared up at Maggie, eyes glistening with tears. 'I kept telling myself it would·be all right. That when I got here they wouldn't be missing anymore. That they'd be among the lucky ones. I just couldn't conceive that . . . that . . .' She broke off to bite her lip.

'Drink some of this tea,' Maggie urged, handing it to Laura.

Laura took several sips. Her face was screwed up with grief.

'Is John looking after Margaret and Rose?' John was Laura's husband, Margaret and Rose their two-year-old twins.

'He offered. But he's so useless with them, typical man! I thought it best I leave them with a neighbour. She'll keep them till I get back.'

A few silent seconds ticked by, then Laura said, awe in her voice, 'The whole street washed away?'

'All of it. Every last house. I'll take you there later and you can see it.'

Maggie glanced at the table. She didn't want any more to eat herself, and it wasn't fair that the Lennoxes were kept from what remained of their dinner.

'Would you like to come to the mortuary with me? I intended heading there after I'd finished eating.'

Laura nodded. 'I suppose so.' She wasn't at all enthusiastic.

'Right then.'

Laura groped in her coat pocket for a scrap of hanky, and used it to dab at her eyes. When the Lennoxes returned, their faces were filled with sympathy and concern.

'Are you all right?' Mrs Lennox asked gently.

'Yes, thanks. I'll manage.'

What a business! Mrs Lennox thought. What an awful business.

Outside in the street Maggie linked arms with Laura. They held each other close, deriving comfort from one another, being sisters in a time of crisis.

'I saw the pictures in the newspapers, but they didn't give the overall extent of the damage,' Laura said as they walked along. 'I was expecting it to be bad, but nothing prepared me for this!'

They paused to stare at a cistern hanging on the wall next to a wash basin, the rest of the house having disappeared.

'The place is full of sights like that,' Maggie commented.

A little further on they had to skirt an area where a gang of workmen were shovelling rubble onto a lorry.

Work was in progress everywhere, cellars were being cleared and pumped free of foul water, men salvaging goods and destroying perishable stores, windows being boarded up, and, the most urgent job of all, lashings of disinfectant being applied in all manner of places.

When they arrived at the temporary mortuary they halted outside. As one, they each took a deep breath.

'You know I've never seen a dead body before,' Laura murmured.

Well, she was going to now, Maggie thought. 'Come on, let's get this over with,' Maggie replied, and pulled Laura into the tent.

It was the same Army Medical Corps man as the day before, except now he looked positively haggard.

'Miss Jordan, wasn't it?' he said, recognizing Maggie.

'Yes. And this is my sister from Glasgow. We'll go round together if you don't mind?'

'Not in the least. If you could just give me those descriptions again to refresh my memory?'

As Maggie described her family, she gazed about her. There were more trestle tables and more corpses than before.

'If you'll come this way please,' the man said when Maggie had finished.

McPherson, Rory Finlay Gordon stated a piece of paper which caught Maggie's eye. The same Rory she'd been talking to just before he and his wife Harriet died. If she had managed to join them as they'd urged her to do, she would also be lying there.

They stopped at a body which hadn't been identified. 'Ready?' the man asked.

Maggie glanced at Laura, then nodded. When he drew down the top of the blanket Laura gave a cry, staggering where she stood.

'That's our mother,' Maggie said in a choked voice. She was holding Laura up, because if she'd let Laura go she would have slumped to the ground.

'There's whisky if you'd like a drop?' the man proposed.

We could both certainly use something, Maggie thought. 'Please,' she replied.

The man hurried off.

Maggie stared at her mother through a haze of tears. How much older April looked in death, and somehow so much smaller.

'Thank you,' Maggie said when he returned with two thimble glasses of whisky. She accepted hers, and Laura did the same. Laura threw the fiery liquid down her throat, and grimaced.

'Do you know where she was found, and under what circumstances?' Maggie asked.

'I'm sorry. I don't.'

Maggie sipped her whisky, which helped steady her.

'I have more bodies for you to see,' the man murmured.

'Just a minute,' Laura, partially recovered, went to April and placed a hand on her mother. She swallowed hard as tears ran down her cheeks.

Maggie finished her whisky and laid the glass aside. 'Let's move on,' she said.

Laura rejoined Maggie, and they linked arms again.

They viewed two bodies of young girls, neither of whom was Pet. Then they were asked to look at a young boy. It was Wee Charlie.

When Maggie and Laura emerged from the mortuary tent they were both severely shaken, but Maggie less so than Laura.

'I don't think I could have done that on my own,' Laura confessed.

'Oh, you would have done if you'd had to.'

'No,' insisted Laura, shaking her head.

Maggie glanced at Laura, realizing for the first time in her life that she was stronger than her sister. It was quite a revelation. In the past, probably because she was four years older,

74

Laura had always seemed the more dominant figure. But now, the boot was on the other foot.

'Do you want to go and sit down some place?' Maggie asked.

'No, I'd prefer to keep walking.'

'We could go to where the cottage was then.'

'You were right about them being dead,' Laura said after a while.

'I just knew it somehow. No doubt they'll find Dad and Pet before long. If they are to be found, that is.'

Laura frowned. 'How do you mean?'

'Folk must have been swept out to sea. Some of those will never be seen again.'

Laura gripped Maggie even more tightly.

Maggie went on. 'You know how it was always said that Wee Charlie was the spit of me? Looking at him I saw myself stretched out in his place. It was an eerie feeling.'

They didn't speak again until they neared the Commemorative Hall where they came across a mobile canteen manned by the Sally Ann. It was doing brisk trade.

'Fancy a cup of tea?' Maggie suggested.

'That would go down a treat.'

They queued up, and eventually got two cups of strong steaming hot tea.

'How's John?' Maggie asked.

'Fit as a flea. Gets irritated by the children, mind, but I suppose that's natural in a man. He adores them really and is certainly very proud of them.'

Maggie thought of John McNair whom Laura had met in Glasgow when she'd gone to work there, when she'd decided she wanted to leave home and broaden her horizons. She liked John; he had a sunny disposition and was always fun to be with.

'He has every right to be proud of them, they're bonny children.'

'Aye,' agreed Laura, a smile brightening her face. It was the first smile Maggie had seen since Laura's arrival in Heymouth.

When they'd finished their tea, they returned their

cups to the mobile canteen and continued on their way.

'God Almighty!' whispered Laura when they arrived at where the Jordan's street had been. 'No wonder you were convinced everyone else was dead.' Then, in a lower tone as she gazed about her, 'No wonder!'

'Faith Caskie also survived the initial impact, but drowned shortly afterwards. I would have died too if it hadn't been for that telegraph pole.'

Laura stooped and picked up a gym shoe half buried in the mud. D McKay was written inside. David McKay had lived three cottages up and had been friends with their Pet.

They both started when an explosion went off. 'From over that way I think,' said Laura, pointing.

'Someone's blasting. Army engineers probably.'

'Unless it's gas?'

Maggie considered that. 'I don't think so. It sounded too controlled.'

They remained there for over twenty minutes, occasionally exchanging comments, but mainly gazing about in silence, each deep in thought and memory.

Finally Maggie said, 'Shall we get back to Susan's?'

Laura sighed. 'I suppose so. If we stay here I know I'll only become more maudlin.'

Maggie felt exactly the same. They linked arms again, and retraced their steps.

'I hate to go,' Laura said to Maggie.

'It's best you don't leave the twins for too long. And anyway, you can't stay, what with the evacuation and all!'

The two of them were at the bottom of Heymouth Brae where official transport was ferrying people up and down, and to and from the railway station. The station buildings had been damaged in the flood, but the railway itself, after some minor repair, remained functional.

'Now you've got the number of our newsagent. You can leave a message there for me anytime,' Laura went on.

'I'll let you know if and when they find Pet and Dad.'

'I'll be back to see the bodies if they do.'

76

'Time to leave!' the Army driver called out.

Maggie and Laura warmly embraced. Then Laura was on board the single-decker coach, its door clicking closed.

Maggie waved, till it was pointless waving any more. Turning, she hurried away to Susan's where the Lennoxes, and the rest of their street, was waiting to be evacuated.

An hour later she followed Laura up Heymouth Brae.

The metal ball swung in a ponderous arc to go crashing into the front of The Haven. A large section of the building immediately collapsed inwards.

Maggie glanced over at the Lawlers who were about a dozen feet from her. They'd come from the camp to witness the demise of their hotel.

That wasn't the reason she'd come to Heymouth. She'd paid the mortuary another visit, and this time was able to identify Pet's body. Her father's body was still missing.

Another chunk of wall collapsed, sending up a billowing cloud of dust. Before long all that would remain of The Haven would be yet another pile of rubble.

Maggie turned away. She didn't want to see any more.

All she wanted was to be alone.

She found herself wandering, thinking about Pet. The worst thing about Pet's body was that it had been badly crushed below the waist. She consoled herself with the thought that Pet would have been dead before it happened.

Her aimless meandering eventually brought her to the top of Heymouth, directly underneath the towering cliffs. She stared up at them, bitterness and pain welling within her.

'I can't imagine it either,' a male voice said.

She turned to gaze at the man who'd approached silently and stood a little behind her on her left. 'I beg your pardon?'

He gestured at the cliffs. 'I said I can't imagine it either. The force of the water must have been incredible.'

'It was,' she stated simply.

Something she didn't recognize flashed in his eyes. 'You're one of the survivors?'

A ghoul! She suddenly thought. How horrible! She swept away.

He caught up with her, placing a restraining hand on her shoulder. 'I'm terribly sorry. Was it something I said?'

An American ghoul to boot, she now realized, as she registered his accent.

'Please take your hand off me,' she snapped.

He did so promptly. 'Look! I am sorry. I didn't mean to upset you. Honest I didn't!'

Tall and slim with a strong, handsome face, he didn't look like a ghoul. How old? Mid-twenties she decided. With exceptional warm, light green eyes. It was these that made her carry on the conversation.

'What are you doing here?' she asked.

He removed his brown felt hat. 'Allow me to introduce myself. I'm Howard Taft on special assignment for *The New York Times*.'

'A journalist!'

'Yeah, all the way from the States to cover the Heymouth tragedy. I flew in yesterday, travelled up last night and this morning came straight to the scene.'

'Scene?' she questioned.

'Scene of the tragedy,' he explained.

She gave a soft laugh. 'What a funny way to express yourself. The *scene*! Sort of shorthand.'

'Exactly,' he smiled.

'And you've come all the way from America to write about Heymouth?'

'I surely have. What happened here has touched heart-strings all over the world.'

That took her aback. 'I knew we were headlines throughout Britain, but hadn't realized we were worldwide.'

'Your story is of enormous interest to the American people. Hell! Quite a number of Americans have been here you know, and many of them wrote to us after we printed what came across the wire services. It's because of that interest, and those letters, that I've been sent to do a special report.'

She blushed. 'I eh . . . I must apologize. I thought you were some sort of ghoul come to . . . come to do what ghouls do.'

'Holy Harry, do I look like one of those!' he replied, genuinely shocked.

'Not in the least now that I've had a chance to study you,' she reassured him. 'It was just that you seemed so interested in my being one of the survivors that I got quite the wrong initial impression.'

Relief flooded his face. 'I'm glad to hear that. You had me worried there for a moment, I can tell you.' He laughed. 'A ghoul! Jeesus!'

'Now it's my turn to say sorry.'

He gave her a mock bow. 'Apology accepted, Miss . . .?'

'Jordan. Maggie Jordan.'

'And you live in Heymouth?'

Her expression became grim. 'I did, with my family.'

'Did?' He was gently probing.

'I've just come from identifying my sister in the temporary mortuary. Several days ago I identified my mother and little brother in the same place. They haven't found my father yet.'

'He's dead too?'

'Has to be. I'd have known long before now if he wasn't.'

Taft took out a packet of Camel cigarettes. Maggie shook her head when he offered her one.

'Would you care to sit down?' he asked.

'Where?'

He glanced about. 'There are some rocks over there. We could sit on those.'

The rocks referred to were boulders that had come down off the moor in the flood. When Maggie had perched herself on one she said, 'Does this mean I'm being interviewed?'

'Do you mind?'

She thought about that. 'No, not really.'

'The job I do can be somewhat intrusive at times. I guess this is one of those times.'

She appreciated that. For someone who worked in what she believed to be such a hard-nosed profession he retained a sensitive streak. She approved, and liked him for it.

'I'm told that nine inches of rain fell during the twenty-four hours prior to the flood, and that five of those inches were in one single hour,' he said.

'I haven't heard those figures.'

'Yeah, nine inches in twenty-four hours apparently. More than you'd normally get here in three months.'

'There was certainly a lot of rain. Most of that day it simply bucketed down.'

'Bucketed down?' he repeated, smiling thinly. 'English expression, eh?'

'I don't know about England but we do use it here in *Scotland*.'

The thin smile turned into a grin. 'Do I get the impression I just made a boo-boo?'

'We Scots are a very independent race, and totally different to our English neighbours. Their background is Teutonic, ours Celtic, of the Gael. Two entirely different fish.'

'I take your point,' he nodded. He paused, then went on mischievously. 'Of course it could be that when I said "English expression" I meant expression in the English language. Which is what we're talking, right?'

'An Englishman might not agree with that,' she countered.

'But basically it's true,' he persisted.

'*Basically*,' she agreed, and they laughed.

'Laughing suits you,' he said. 'I just hope you don't think it's disrespectful of me saying so in the circumstances.'

She shook her head. 'It's good for me to laugh. It makes me feel better.'

'How old are you?' Howard Taft asked suddenly.

'Seventeen. And you?'

The swiftness with which she'd put the same question surprised him. Quick-witted and intelligent he thought. There was none of the country bumpkin about this young miss. 'Twenty-four.'

'*The New York Times* must think highly of you to send you abroad at your age,' she stated disarmingly.

He shrugged. 'I guess they do.'

That pleased her for some unknown reason.

'Maggie, is it OK if I call you that?'

She nodded.

'And you'll call me Howard.'

'All right, Howard.'

'Or Howie if you prefer?'

'No, Howard. Howie is too juvenile. Or . . .' Careful! she warned herself. She didn't want to insult him.

'Or what?' he prompted.

'Nothing, *Howard.*'

Howard reached inside his brown leather jacket and pulled out a notepad and pencil. 'I'd like to take notes. Would you mind?'

'Go ahead.'

He opened his pad and stared at it, obviously thinking. The atmosphere between them changed and became serious.

'Precisely what do you know so far?' Maggie asked.

He glanced up at her. 'Statistics, such as the nine inches of rain. I'll give you another, it's reckoned that ninety million tons of water, I'll repeat that, ninety *million* tons of water, sufficient to supply the needs of this immediate area for over a hundred years, cascaded down off the moor that morning. The water converged on Heymouth, having dropped hundreds of feet in its half-mile race to the sea, at a velocity of over twenty miles per hour. Water that had started ten miles away at the far end of the moor and then fallen fifteen hundred feet overall. The wall of water that finally hit Heymouth is believed to have been over forty feet high. You know what happened next.'

'A wall of water over forty feet high,' she repeated, recalling the roaring which had made her ears ache, and had grown unbelievably loud just before the wall hit her home.

'Statistics are all very well and good, but what I want is the human angle. To hear from those directly involved. That's why I've come over from the States,' Howard said.

'I understand,' she replied softly.

'So, when were you first aware you were in danger? Let's start there.'

Maggie began to speak, recounting what had happened during that early morning of the flood. The only thing

81

she omitted was her suspicion of Bryce the handyman.

After a while Howard stopped scribbling, and just listened.

The funeral took place on 19 August, six days after the flood.

The weather was bright and sunny, as the procession slowly wound its way to the cemetery nestling beneath the cliffs, within sound of the sea.

Maggie, dressed in black, walked between Laura and John McNair. The twins had been left behind in Glasgow.

The procession was one of sombre colours, khaki and air force blue predominating. All who had gone to help the stricken townsfolk mixed with those who had lived through the disaster, and were present to mourn and pay a last tribute to their relatives, friends and neighbours, whose coffins, borne by men of the Fire Service, they now followed.

As she walked Maggie thought of her father whose body had been one of the last recovered. A diver had found it out at sea trapped beneath the underground storage container from a petrol station, the container having been ripped right out of the ground.

Laura sobbed, and dropped her head. A hand holding a scrap of hanky pressed on her veil where her mouth was.

John glanced at his wife. He should have placed himself in the middle between Laura and Maggie he thought. As if reading his mind Maggie tugged him across in front of her so that he could comfort his wife. His arm supportively slipped round Laura.

Inside the cemetery, Maggie couldn't imagine a more peaceful setting. When the whole procession finally had arrived, and everyone was in place, the Moderator of the Church of Scotland began the service.

Many fine words were spoken, and sentiments expressed. In the middle of Reverend Barr's address a woman Maggie didn't recognize completely broke down and had to be led away. Mr Baldwin, the Prime Minister, who was there, also gave a speech.

At the conclusion of the service the deep silence was broken by the mournful and pathetic notes of 'Land of the Leal' and

'Flowers of the Forest', by a lone piper of the Argyle and Sutherland Highlanders.

'Aye,' said John when at last it was all over, and the final notes had faded away.

People began to talk among themselves, others to drift off.

Laura had composed herself now. 'It went well I thought,' she said, lifting back her veil.

Maggie agreed with her.

There was a brief pause, and then John prompted his wife. 'Laura.'

Laura grasped Maggie by the arm. 'There's nothing left for you here. The house and your job have gone. Come and live in Glasgow with us. John and I have talked it through, and if you'd like to come we'd love having you living with us.'

It was true, Maggie thought. There wasn't anything left in Heymouth for her. Why not make a completely fresh start someplace else? The idea appealed.

'Are you sure I wouldn't be in the way?' she said hesitantly.

'We wouldn't have suggested it if we'd thought you would,' comforted John.

Maggie put a hand in her coat pocket, and with the tips of her fingers touched the piece of scrimshaw she'd found in the mud where their house had once stood.

A new start was exactly what she needed she told herself. She'd be daft to turn down this opportunity. 'When would you want me to move in?' she asked.

'Today, come back with us. There's no time like the present,' Laura replied.

So soon! But there again, why not? 'I'll have to get my things from the camp, and say goodbye to the Lennoxes and a few others.'

Early that evening when John and Laura boarded the train to take them home to Glasgow, Maggie was with them.

CHAPTER THREE

The moment the alarm clock went off Maggie was up and out of the cavity bed she slept in. She had a big day ahead.

She switched off the alarm clock, then lit the fire that had been laid the night before.

As the fire was crackling into life she headed for the small lavatory in the hall. When she was finished there she hurried back to the kitchen where she washed herself at the sink. That done she got dressed.

She was in the middle of making the porridge when Laura, a thick dressing-gown covering her night-clothes, put in an appearance.

'Sleep well?' Laura smiled.

'Tossed and turned a bit.'

Laura's smile widened in sympathy. 'A little nervousness is only to be expected when you're starting a new job.'

Maggie's new job was at Templeton's carpet factory in Tullis Street. She'd tried to get another position in hotel work, but nothing suitable had been available. Then she'd contacted Templeton's, at John's suggestion, and struck lucky. She was to be employed as a cop winder, whatever that meant. Training would be given, she'd been assured.

'Let's have a look at you then,' said Laura.

Maggie stopped what she was doing to face Laura. Her dress was one she'd bought specifically for work in the factory.

'You'll do,' Laura nodded.

'Let's hope they think that.'

Laura laughed. 'I'm sure they will.'

Maggie *was* nervous. Life was terribly hectic in the city, she thought, all hustle and bustle. Quite the opposite to the calm peacefulness that had existed in Heymouth prior to the flood.

It was a month now since she'd left Heymouth, and she'd

read in the newspapers that a great deal had been accomplished there. People had moved back into their own homes though the camp was still in existence.

Maggie got on with making the breakfast. It was part of the morning routine she'd adopted, a routine that had her up and dressed before John came through. Having to rise first for the privacy that afforded was one of the penalties of living in a two-roomed house where the kitchen also doubled as a bedroom. Her cavity bed was built into the wall, like some ancient Roman grave.

Laura took a large plain loaf from the bread bin, and began slicing it. When she'd cut sufficient slices she buttered them.

'I bought some chocolate biscuits as a treat,' Laura said.

'For breakfast?'

'No, you ninny, for your dinner piece. Don't expect them every day mind, we don't run to such luxury in this house.'

Maggie was touched by the gesture. Typical Laura! 'Thank you,' she said.

'Don't mention it. Now what about your piece, I'm giving John tomatoes and lemon curd. That suit you, too?'

'Not in the same piece I hope?' Maggie joked. A piece was a sandwich, or collectively sandwiches in this case.

Laura pulled a face. 'Just think what that would taste like, yuch!'

'What would taste like yuch?' John asked, coming into the room. He was wearing trousers but his chest was bare. His braces hung down the outside of either leg.

'Tomatoes and lemon curd in the same piece,' Laura explained.

'Oh, I don't know, could be quite nice.'

'He's teasing,' Laura said to Maggie. 'Ignore the bugger.'

John yawned, and scratched his stomach. While he was doing this Maggie took a pan of boiling water from the cooker and laid it by the side of the sink. This was John's shaving water. They could get hot water, but only after the fire had been going for a while and the back boiler had heated up.

'Today's the day then, eh?' John grinned at Maggie.

'It is.'

'Don't worry. This time next week it'll be as though you'd been there all your life. It's always the same.'

Maggie stared at John's bare back, his creamy white skin punctuated by large freckles both fascinated and repelled her. He poured his boiling water into the enamel basin, then started to strop his razor on the leather strap that hung by the side of the sink.

'You're looking a bit tired,' Maggie commented to Laura as she gave the porridge another stir. It was ready now, waiting for John to sit at the table.

'Rose woke me up several times during the night,' Laura explained.

'Teeth?'

'No, upset tummy. I'm surprised you didn't hear her. Particularly as you were restless yourself.'

Maggie shook her head. 'Never heard a thing.'

'Well, I damned well did,' John grumbled, dragging his razor down one cheek.

Laura glanced at John, and Maggie sensed friction between husband and wife. But it quickly vanished as they got on with the morning's proceedings.

'Good porridge that. The sort that sticks to a man's ribs,' John said, pushing his bowl away from him. He glanced at the wag-at-the-wall clock. 'We'd better be getting a move on. I'll walk you to the tram stop, Maggie. It's on my way.'

That was kind of him, she thought.

Several minutes later, each clutching their dinner piece wrapped in waxed paper, they kissed Laura goodbye and went off downstairs.

'Good luck!' Laura called after Maggie.

Outside the closemouth they crossed the street, and walked down the hill to the nearest tramstop. From here, they had a marvellous view over Dennistoun and beyond.

There was a keen nip in the air, winter only just round the corner Maggie thought. She hoped it was going to be reasonably warm in Templeton's.

They stopped when they reached the tramstop. 'You'll be all right now? You know where you're going?'

'Of course I do. Don't worry about me, I'll be fine,' Maggie smiled in reply.

'Right then, see you the night.'

Maggie was turning away from John when, in a sudden darting movement, he kissed her on the cheek which made her start because it was so unexpected.

'Ta-ra then!' he cried to her as he hurried off.

Wasn't that nice of him, she thought. John was proving to be a good friend as well as brother-in-law.

When her tram clanked to a halt in front of her Maggie climbed aboard and went upstairs. She adored the upstairs in Glasgow trams, the only drawback being that it was where the smokers went. Sometimes, particularly at night, the fug could be so thick you could hardly see from one end of the tram to the other.

The tram schoogled away again, and Maggie gazed eagerly out at the passing scene.

How dirty Glasgow was, Maggie thought, and yet, despite that, it had tremendous charm. Like the Glaswegians themselves, hard and uncompromising on one side, charming and friendly on the other.

When she reached her stop Maggie got off and paused to stare out over Glasgow Green, spotting the People's Palace in the distance. She'd heard about the People's Palace, a museum concerned with Glasgow and its past, and promised herself she'd pay it a visit in the near future.

As she walked up Tullis Street, Templeton's came into view, and she headed for the entrance that would take her to the offices where she'd been told to report. Her heart was hammering as she went up the narrow, cheerless stairs she'd last climbed before her interview.

The girl she spoke to was as nice as pie. She was told she'd soon be attended to, and instructed to take a chair.

'Miss Jordan?'

A thin, middle-aged man addressed her, sporting a walrus moustache. His expression was severe and disapproving as if he'd just been sucking on a slice of lemon.

Maggie quickly rose to her feet. 'Yes, I'm Miss Jordan.'

'I'm Mr Kerly, your supervisor. If you'll follow me I'll take you down and introduce you to your department.'

He walked so fast she almost had to run to keep up. They went through a series of corridors until they reached the factory floor. It spread before Maggie, and she'd never heard such a din. No doubt she'd soon get used to it she told herself as she followed Kerly down a metal spiral staircase.

There must have been hundreds of men and women at work there, but they all looked happy enough which cheered her. It would be awful to work in a place where everyone was miserable.

Something hissed – steam escaping, from the sound of it. But she couldn't see what or where.

They left that area behind and entered a partitioned, quieter section. Here there were long benches with various lengths of carpet on top of them.

A man was on his knee next to a woman, and for one wild insane moment Maggie thought he was proposing. Then she realized he was examining a small rectangle of carpet.

'Everything as it should be, Singleton?' Kerly asked.

'Yes, sir. Everything's quite in order.'

Kerly harumphed, and moved off again, walking just as fast as before.

The walls were lined with wooden pigeon holes. Many of them contained pieces of carpet and what appeared to be spindles of thread. A number of the people smiled at her as she went by – she liked that.

They plunged from that area into another. She heard that steam sound again. She glimpsed a man busy at a cylinder, and again there was a hiss! verifying that the cylinder was the source of the noise.

They stopped alongside a bench at which a fat, cross-eyed girl was working.

'Miss McGinley, this is Miss Jordan. I want you to explain the factory to her, and then teach her your job. Report to me when you consider she is proficient enough to manage on her own,' Kerly said.

'Yes, Mr Kerly.'

Maggie had thought there might be a sign of deference in the fat girl's voice when she replied to the somewhat intimidating supervisor, but there wasn't. The girl stared boldly at Kerly awaiting further instructions.

'Right then,' said Kerly, giving the fat girl a curt nod. He addressed Maggie, 'Miss McGinley will show you the ropes and answer any general questions you might have. Before I leave you, is there anything you want to ask me personally?'

Maggie couldn't think of a thing. 'No, Mr Kerly.'

He harumphed again, then strode quickly away.

'Don't be put off by his manner, he's a sweetie really,' the fat girl said to Maggie sticking out her hand. 'I'm Natasha.'

'And I'm Maggie.'

They shook hands. 'Unusual name, Natasha, I've never heard it before,' Maggie commented.

'It's Russian. My da's a great admirer of Marx and Lenin. I've got two other sisters and they're called Polena and Anya.'

Maggie had never heard of those names either.

'Have you ever worked in a carpet factory before?' Natasha asked.

Maggie shook her head. 'I've been working in a hotel since I left school – up until the flood that was. I've recently moved here from Heymouth.'

Natasha's cross-eyes opened wide. 'Heymouth! You were in that terrible flood?'

There was a sudden tightness in Maggie's chest. 'Yes, I lost my mother, father, sister and little brother.'

'Oh, I am sorry,' Natasha muttered, not knowing what else to say.

'Well it's over and done with. I've just got to carry on as best I can.'

'Is that your dinner piece?' queried Natasha, pointing at the waxed paper parcel Maggie was holding.

'Yes.'

'Put it in here. This is where I keep mine.' Natasha opened a cupboard built into the bench and Maggie popped it in.

'So, who are you staying with in Glasgow then?' Natasha asked.

Maggie explained that she lived with her sister and brother-in-law, and how all this was a new start for her.

'You've certainly landed on your feet getting a job at Templeton's. Everyone loves it here.' She lowered her voice. 'Hard graft, mind, but at least they're decent to you, aye, and fair too which goes a long way.'

'Everyone seems happy enough. I noticed that right off.'

'Believe me, they are. Now back to business. You'll be taking over my job as cop winder, and when you do I'll be promoted to the looms, just as you'll be in time.'

A female squealed, and then came up to them rubbing her backside. 'That sod McAvoy got me again. Talk about wandering hands!'

Natasha laughed. 'You should be so lucky. With a face like mine I never get my bum pinched or felt! So don't complain!'

Maggie's heart instantly went out to the fat, cross-eyed girl. She really was ugly.

'Agnes, this is Maggie Jordan who's starting today and will be doing my job in future. Maggie, this is Agnes Mitchell who works in the sample room.'

'Please to meet you, Maggie,' said Agnes, extending a hand.

'And to meet you,' Maggie replied as they shook hands.

Agnes looked Maggie admiringly up and down. 'I'll warn you now, the wandering hands will be after you. Just don't take offence that's all, it's all meant in good part.'

'Right, we'd better get rid of your coat before I show you round,' Natasha said to Maggie.

'See you about,' Agnes smiled at Maggie, and continued on her way.

'I could tell you tales about that one which would make your hair curl,' Natasha whispered to Maggie in a conspiratorial tone, and winked.

'What sort of tales?' Maggie was intrigued.

'Tales about married men, some of them not all that far away from here either.'

'Oh, really?'

'*Really*,' Natasha confirmed. 'You wouldn't believe some of the things that go on in here. Absolutely in . . . credible!'

Maggie laughed. The way Natasha had said incredible was hysterical to hear. Long and drawn out, it positively oozed insinuation.

She had a right character here, Maggie thought.

'Come on then, let's hang up your coat and go from there,' Natasha proposed.

They spoke to several people *en route* to the cloakroom, all of whom Natasha introduced Maggie to, explaining who the person was and what they did. Without exception all were friendly.

The cloakroom was a sparse wood-panelled room with a legion of metal pegs screwed into the walls. It reminded Maggie of the cloakroom at her primary school.

'First things first,' Natasha declared as they emerged from the cloakroom. 'We make chenille carpet here, which is different from other carpets. Do you know what chenille means?'

Maggie shook her head.

'It's French for caterpillar. So there you are.'

'Caterpillar!' Maggie found that delightful.

'What makes chenille different from other carpets is that it's the product of two distinct processes, the *formation* of the chenille fur, and the *weaving* of that fur, which is the weft, into a carpet.'

'Weft,' Maggie repeated.

'As opposed to the warp. But we'll come to that.' Natasha went on to describe the difference between chenille and other carpets. She paused mid-flow, and smiled. 'Don't look so worried, it's not that difficult. I picked it up in no time, and I'm a dummy.'

Maggie doubted that. Natasha was far too articulate to be stupid.

Natasha continued, explaining the weaving process in precise detail. 'Do you follow that?'

Maggie nodded.

'Repeat it to me then.'

Maggie did, to be corrected on several minor points she'd got slightly wrong.

'Good,' said Natasha, beaming approval.

'So what is a cop, and a cop winder?'

'A cop is what a single woollen thread is wound onto, which in turn fits inside the shuttles for the weft looms. Cops can also be wound with skeins of fur, which are chopped up and steam treated, forming strips of cloth from the first process. We use these in the setting looms. Understand?'

Maggie nodded again.

'When making weft cloth, before starting to weave the weaver needs a supply of cops of all the colours required in the carpet. The weaver works from a paper design which shows the full size, the pattern repeats, in the colours that are to be used. The design is cut up horizontally into strips two squares wide, and the weaver works this paper strip, inserting and changing the shuttles which carry yarns of the various colours.'

Natasha laughed at Maggie's bewildered expression. 'We'll go and watch what I've just explained on machine, which should make it easier for you to understand. At least that's the way it is with me, if I can see something in operation I can understand it far more quickly than when someone tries to describe it.'

They'd only taken a few steps when a man gave an appreciative wolf whistle. 'Who's your friend then, Natasha?'

'She's new here, Eddy Boyd, and far too good for the likes of you!'

'What do you say, darling?'

Maggie blushed, aware that quite a few men were looking at her now. Or leering at her, to be more precise, but in a good-humoured way.

'Ignore him,' said Natasha, taking Maggie by the arm and pulling her on.

'What's your name, hen?' Eddy Boyd shouted after Maggie. Then, when he got no reply, he said to his pals, 'I'll just call her "gorgeous".' That earned him a laugh.

'Cathy Henderson better not hear him on like that,' Natasha said.

'Who's Cathy Henderson?'

'Only his fiancéee!'

Again Maggie had to laugh at Natasha's exaggerated pronunciation.

Some while later they stopped at a large setting loom, manned by five men 'beating up', as Natasha explained, the chenille fur.

The young man at the far end of the loom glanced at Maggie, and for an instant their eyes locked. Then, blushing, he addressed himself once more to what he was doing.

Nice, Maggie thought.

'Now this is important,' Natasha went on.

Maggie quickly brought her attention back to the cross-eyed girl and forgot all about the young man.

Maggie arrived home to find John already there, but then his firm was closer to Dennistoun than Templeton's.

'So, how did it go?' Laura asked eagerly, wiping her hands on a towel.

'My head's buzzing. There's so much to learn!'

'As bad as that!' John said, teasing her.

'Worse. I don't know whether I'm coming or going. Do you know what chenille means?'

She looked at Laura, who shook her head, then at John who did likewise.

'Caterpillar,' she stated. 'It's French for caterpillar.'

'Never!' exclaimed Laura.

'It is apparently.' She stared at her sister, positively glowing with excitement.

'What's the talent like?' Laura asked, eyes twinkling.

'Can't say I noticed.'

'Fibber!'

John sat back in his chair and made a pyramid with his hands in front of his face. His lips were twisted into a peculiar lop-sided smile.

'Come on, what's it like?' Laura cajoled.

'Lots of men, a great many of them single, I believe.'

'Any possible clicks?'

'How should I know, Laura! I've only been there five minutes,' Maggie protested.

'Shouldn't be surprised if there were. What do you say, John?'

The lop-sided smile didn't leave his face. 'There's bound to be. But what about the work itself, Maggie? Tell us about that.'

'Well, I've learned what a weft and a warp are. And what a cop winder does.'

'We'll hear about it over tea. I've made a special one for you because this was your first day at work,' Laura said.

'Oh, Laura! That's lovely of you.'

'It is an occasion after all.'

Maggie glanced over at where Margaret and Rose were playing. 'How about the twins?'

'They've been fed so we don't have to worry about them. John, you sit in and Maggie will help me dish up.'

John slowly rose and sat at the table where he was soon joined by the two women. Throughout the meal Maggie, continually prompted by Laura, talked about Templeton's, describing who she'd met, what she'd learned and what conditions there were like. Laura and John listened attentively.

'This Natasha sounds quite a case,' Laura commented when Maggie had finally finished.

'She is that. But great fun.'

'And cross-eyed,' said John, crossing his own.

Maggie giggled at the sight of him, he looked utterly ridiculous. 'You shouldn't judge a book by its covers. Natasha is an extremely nice person,' she scolded.

'Oh, I'm sure!' he replied in such a way it made Maggie giggle again.

'That was a fabulous tea, Laura, thank you very much,' Maggie said when the meal was over.

'Don't mention it. I'm just pleased today went well for you.'

'It certainly did.'

John rose, and stretched. 'I think a walk down to the pub for a pint is in order. That all right, Laura?'

'Of course,' his wife answered, starting to pick up the dirty dishes.

John paused in the kitchen doorway. 'I'll tell you what, Maggie, to further celebrate your first day, why don't you come with me and I'll buy you a drink?'

She wasn't tempted in the least, as she was far too tired. All she wanted was to sit down and maybe read a book. 'If you don't mind I'd rather stay in. But listen, why don't you take Laura? I'm sure she'd like a wee turn out and it's no problem for me to look after the twins.'

John's face creased into what was almost a scowl.

'I'd like that. It's ages since we've been out for a drink together,' Laura enthused.

'Then on you go. Get your coat. I'll see to those dishes.'

The black look vanished. 'Then Laura and I it is. And I only hope you're bringing some money with you.'

'You're paying!' Laura replied, wagging a finger at him. 'You would have paid for Maggie, wouldn't you!'

John didn't reply.

When they'd gone Maggie gathered up the rest of the dishes and piled them in the sink. She was going to enjoy working at Templeton's, she told herself. She was going to enjoy it a lot.

Maggie arrived at Charing Cross to find Natasha already waiting for her. The two of them were bound for Templeton's Christmas dance which was being held in the St Andrew's Halls.

'God, it's cold enough to freeze the proverbials off a brass monkey!' Natasha greeted Maggie, clapping her gloved hands together.

Maggie winced as an icy blast swirled up the bottom of her dress and coat. 'It's bitter, right enough,' she agreed.

'Don't let anyone ever tell you that fat folk don't feel the cold just as much as you skinny ones. I can assure you we do!'

They fell into step, heading for the pub where they'd arranged to meet some of the other girls prior to going on to the dance.

'What are the Templeton dances like?' Maggie asked.

'Oh, a good laugh, if nothing else. And in my case it's always nothing else.'

'Perhaps your luck will change tonight and Prince Charming will be there to whisk you off your feet,' Maggie said.

Natasha knew her friend was only being kind and that there was no dig behind the remark. 'Aye sure! And maybe he'll be a millionaire as well!' she replied sarcastically.

'Stranger things have happened.'

'To you maybe, but not me.' She sighed. 'I'm destined to die an old maid, so I am. I know that as certain as I know no-one will ask me onto the floor tonight.'

Poor Natasha, Maggie thought. If only she could have waved a magic wand to turn the fat girl into a raving beauty.

They arrived at the State Bar in Holland Street, and hurried in.

'That's better,' said Maggie as the heat enveloped her. As they went down into the cellar bar they were given a loud hello! by Mary Mauchline, one of their party.

Pleasantries were exchanged then Natasha said to Maggie, 'I'll get them in. What would you like?'

'I don't know. What are you having?'

'My favourite, gin and orange. Very p*ooo*sh!' She pronounced the o as in po.

'The same for me then.'

'I'll make them doubles, we need them after that weather out there.'

Maggie sat with the others and Natasha made for the bar where Muriel, an orange-haired dragon somewhere in her seventies, held sway as chief barmaid.

'We're telling dirty jokes,' Mary Mauchline announced to Maggie. 'Do you know any?'

Maggie shook her head. 'Sorry.' She did actually, but was far too shy to tell them, even in all-female company. That sort of thing embarrassed her dreadfully. But then she was different from the vast majority of girls at Templeton's, being of a more refined, though certainly not prissy, nature.

'Have you heard the one about the three-legged sailor?' piped Bunty Abercrombie.

'*Three* legs, oh aye!' smirked Moira Law, giving them a coy wink. 'Big lad was he?'

They all guffawed at that, with the exception of Maggie who nevertheless found it funny. The punchline actually brought tears to her eyes and caused Isa Peebles to laugh so hard she almost fell off her stool.

'Here, get that down you,' Natasha said to Maggie, handing her a drink. 'So what's the hilarity?' This remark was addressed to the table in general.

Mary Mauchline explained again that they were telling dirty jokes.

'Is that a fact! Well, have you heard the one about . . .?'

Maggie smiled to herself. Trust Natasha! Her joke proved to be the dirtiest yet.

'Well, look what the cat's dragged in,' Moira Law said a little later, gesturing to the bottom of the stairs.

Maggie recognized a group of chaps from Templeton's. Some she knew to speak to, others she didn't know at all.

Mary waggled an almost empty glass at them. 'We're open to offers?'

'Away and rattle your can!' Andy Ramsay replied.

'Charming!' said Mary sarcastically, and plonked her glass on the table.

Maggie found herself staring directly into the eyes of the young man she'd noticed at a setting loom on her first day. He smiled tentatively, and she smiled in return.

He smiled at her again later when she was up at the bar ordering a second round for her and Natasha, as he and his friends were standing further along the bar. She, naturally enough, smiled back.

Maggie had never been to the St Andrew's Halls, and was looking forward to it. The exterior was grand and imposing, though black from the ravages and continual onslaught of grime, smoke and soot, like so many buildings in the centre of Glasgow.

Inside was something of a disappointment. She'd expected it to be more sumptuous than it was. Faded was the word that sprang to mind – everything had a rather tired quality about it.

A man in uniform directed them to the hall booked by Templeton's. Before they went in, they left their coats in a cloakroom nearby and changed into their dancing shoes.

Maggie, Natasha and the rest of the girls went into the hall together and immediately Moira was asked to dance.

The band, dressed in evening wear and sitting on a raised dais, were at the far end of the hall. They were playing a schottische.

'There's Kerly with his wife,' hissed Natasha, nudging Maggie in the ribs, and then discreetly pointing with a finger.

Mrs Kerly wasn't at all what Maggie would have expected. For a start she was a lot younger than her husband, and extremely attractive.

'Are you sure that's her and not his daughter?' Maggie said in disbelief.

'Of course I'm sure!' Natasha smiled wickedly. 'He must have hidden talents, eh?'

Sandy Roughead, a maintenance engineer, came striding in their direction. 'One of us is up,' Mary Mauchline said in a low voice.

It was Maggie he was after. 'Delighted,' she replied, and followed him onto the floor. As she went into his arms, she saw Natasha give her the thumbs up.

'Quite a do, eh!' Sandy said.

'Quite a do,' she agreed.

'All the nobs are here. Every last one.'

'I've seen a few already.'

And with that Sandy ran out of conversation. At the end of the dance Maggie thanked him and beat a hasty retreat back to Natasha.

'If I hadn't known he was wearing shoes I'd have sworn he had clogs on,' Maggie said.

Natasha sniggered. 'Don't be cruel!'

'I'm not. Just stating a fact.'

'Who's for the punch bowl?' Bunty Abercrombie asked.

They all were, so they went over *en masse*. As they queued Natasha said to Maggie. 'It's chilly in here but no doubt it'll soon warm up.'

Maggie was about to reply when she spotted the young man from the pub heading towards her.

'Miss Jordan, would you care to dance?'

The speaker was Mr Fairley, one of the nobs Sandy Roughead had mentioned. Maggie didn't know exactly what his position was, but he was high up on the management side.

'Why, thank you,' Maggie replied, and hooked an arm around the one extended to her. She saw the young man hesitate, then veer away.

'And how are you settling in at Templeton's?' Fairley asked politely as they took the floor.

'Very well, thank you.'

An hour later it was steaming hot inside the hall and sweat was running down Maggie's back and front. She'd been on the floor for nearly every dance, and was having a whale of a time.

'Have a sip of that,' said Natasha when Maggie joined her yet again. She handed her a glass that had originally contained punch.

Maggie studied the amber liquid in the glass, then sniffed it. 'Whisky?' she asked.

'A lot of the lads are carrying half-bottles. I scrounged that off Tom McAskill who owes me a favour.'

Maggie gave the glass back to Natasha. 'Not for me, thanks. You have it all yourself.'

'Don't you like whisky?' Natasha queried.

'To be truthful, I'm not much of a drinker. Those gins were more than enough for me.'

Natasha swallowed the whisky, and smiled. 'Rare!'

Maggie glanced over at the punch bowl thinking she wouldn't mind some. The punch was non-alcoholic; there was no alcohol available, other than what was secretly brought in.

'Excuse me.'

Maggie turned round to find herself staring into the eyes

she'd stared into in the pub. It was the young man.

'Would you like to dance?'

There was something about his voice that moved her, made her go weak at the knees. A man's voice had never had such an effect on her before.

'Please,' she replied, her own voice quavering slightly.

'I'm not very good, I'm afraid,' he said when they were on the floor waiting for the band to strike up.

'Neither am I.'

'Oh, but you are! I saw you earlier with Mr Fairley and thought you were terrific.'

'Why, thank you,' she smiled.

'My name's Nevil, by the way. Nevil Sanderson.'

'I'm Maggie Jordan.'

'I know. I've seen you around. You're a cop winder.'

'And you operate a setting loom. But not one of those I service.'

'Hello Nevil. All right!'

The chap who'd called out was the one in the pub who'd told Mary Mauchline to go and rattle her can, the same Mary Mauchline he now held in his arms.

'All right, Andy!' Nevil answered. To Maggie he explained, 'That's Andy Ramsay. He and I live in the same street. We went to school together and now both work at Templeton's.'

'Your best pal?'

Nevil gave a soft laugh. 'You could say that. We're as thick as thieves, the pair of us.'

She looked over again at Andy Ramsay. A handsome fellow, but not nearly as handsome as Nevil. She found herself blushing.

'What is it?' he asked.

'Nothing.'

'But you've gone all red.'

'The heat,' she lied, and prayed for the band to start playing, which it promptly did, this time a waltz.

She could feel and sense the strength in him, not merely physical. She liked it.

'I warned you, two left feet, I'm afraid,' Nevil murmured.

'You're doing fine. Stop worrying about it and just relax.'

He tried.

All too soon as far as Maggie was concerned the waltz was over and they were clapping the band. She continued clapping as long as she could, hoping he'd asked her to stay. She was on the point of thanking him and leaving the floor when he asked.

'Why not?' she smiled. And then immediately wondered if she should have given a more positive reply.

'How long have you been at Templeton's?'

'Since leaving school at fourteen, which was six years ago. How, eh . . .' He broke off apologetically. 'It's rude to ask a lady her age, isn't it?'

A lady! That was lovely. 'I'm seventeen.'

He nodded. 'That was what I guessed.'

He looked older than twenty, she thought. But didn't say so. Perhaps that was because he was very dark round the chin and lower cheeks. His eyebrows were thick and bushy.

The next dance was another waltz, which pleased them both as a waltz was more intimate than some of the other dances. It also gave them more of an opportunity to chat.

A number of dances later when the two of them were quite relaxed and thoroughly enjoying themselves, Nevil said, 'Why don't we take a breather? And you can meet the lads I'm with.'

'Fine.'

She thought he might take her hand as they left the floor, but he didn't.

'Andy, say hello to Maggie Jordan. Maggie, Andy Ramsay.'

'I was beginning to think you pair were dancing for the duration,' Andy joked as he shook hands with Maggie.

'I'm dying for some punch. My throat's like sandpaper,' Maggie said.

'I could use some too,' said Mary Mauchline who was standing beside Andy.

'How about a dram instead?' Andy offered, patting the inside pocket of his jacket.

'A dram *in* the punch,' suggested Mary coyly.

'Just the punch for me,' Maggie stated.

'Right then,' said Nevil. 'Who's doing the honours?' He glanced about the assembled company.

'I'll go,' volunteered a fair-haired chap. 'I'm parched myself.'

'Thank you, Bob. Maggie, this is Bob Kinloch. He doesn't work for Templeton's but a firm producing sheet metal. That right, Bob?'

Bob nodded. 'So it's two fruit punches for the girls, and one for myself?'

Nevil seemed to be the leader among this lot, Maggie thought, which bore out the strength she'd felt and sensed in him. Natural charisma was what he had, she realized. He stood out from the pack.

She was then introduced to the other chaps from work she didn't know already, and to the girls a few of them were with. She only knew one of these girls, who operated a weft loom she serviced.

Bob was soon back with her punch for which she thanked him gratefully. When she'd drunk that, Nevil proposed they danced again, and she agreed. Now she knew beyond any doubt that they were going to spend the rest of the evening together.

'Whheeccchhhh!' shouted a female voice as the band robustly played the Gay Gordons, announced as the last dance.

'She's having a good time,' Nevil laughed.

'Whheeecchh!' another female voice yelled.

'She's not the only one,' Maggie replied.

And then, with a final drum roll, it was all over.

Maggie's heart was suddenly thumping as they slowly left the floor. Would he or wouldn't he?

'Where's Natasha?' she wondered aloud, just for something to say.

She spotted Andy and Mary Mauchline heading for the door together. Come on! she thought, glancing sideways at Nevil. Come on!

'Where do you live?' he asked.

'Dennistoun.' She named the street.

'That's not all that far from me.'

'Oh?' She tried not to sound excited.

'Would you like me to walk you home?'

She acted surprised, as if the idea had never crossed her mind. 'Walk me home? You mean in case the bogeyman gets me?' she teased.

He smiled. 'Maybe I'm the bogeyman.'

Maybe you are, she thought. But if he were she was all in favour of bogeymen.

'That would be nice,' she replied, her tone earnest.

His brows twitched. Then he put a hand on her elbow to guide her to the door.

It had started to snow, huge flakes swirling in the cold evening. Visibility had been reduced to no more than a few yards.

'Steep hill this,' Nevil commented as they trudged upwards.

'It's certainly easier to go down than come up.'

He laughed. 'Aren't all hills? Except for the electric brae, that is.'

'Electric brae?'

'I read about it somewhere, the *Sunday Post*, I think. Apparently when you imagine you're going up you're actually coming down, and vice versa. Therefore, you can get on a bicycle and freewheel *uphill*! It's all some sort of optical illusion.'

'Fancy that,' she mused.

'It's in Scotland, but I can't recall where.' He shivered, his coat being a thin one. 'I'm going to look like a snowman when I get in.'

'You already do,' Maggie told him. His black hair was now white, as were his shoulders and the front of his coat. She looked much the same herself.

Silence fell between them for a few steps, then he said, his tone slightly different, 'I've heard on the grapevine that you came to Glasgow from Heymouth, and that you were involved in the disaster there last August.'

'Yes,' she answered softly, a sadness falling over her.

'I presume you don't like talking about it?'

'I don't mind.' She gave him a weak smile. 'What do you want to know?'

'Nothing in particular. I just wanted to say it must have been awful.'

'It was. I lost my father, mother, sister and wee brother, you know.'

'Aye. That's what I heard. I'm sorry.'

Four months, she thought. That was all it was, four months. And yet it felt like four years. Timewise, the period of the flood and directly afterwards had become completely distorted in her mind.

'I read about it in the newspapers, a terrible tragedy,' Nevil sympathized.

She nodded in agreement. 'But tell me about you and your family.'

'Nothing much to tell really. My da works in a foundry; I have a brother who's an apprentice electrician, and then there's my ma. That's about it.'

'What's your brother called?'

'Jimmy. He's not a bad sort, for a brother if you know what I mean.'

She smiled knowingly. Hadn't she felt precisely the same about her sister Pet?

'Here we are,' she said when they arrived at her close. She moved just inside the close, but he remained outside.

'It was kind of you to walk me home,' she smiled.

'As I said, it's not that far out my way.'

'Still kind of you.'

She could see his face quite clearly, as it was lit by the gas street lamp just a few feet behind him. The close mouth itself was shadowy, lit by the gas mantle further back along the close.

'It was a good night,' he said.

'Very good.'

'A lot better than last year's dance.'

Get on with it, come and kiss me, she thought. 'I wouldn't know about that.'

'No.'

Something had come between them. A barrier had risen where no barrier had been before. Come on! she mentally

104

urged, stop hanging back. She was damned if she was going to make the first move.

He shuffled his feet in the snow creating patterns on the pavement. 'Right then, I'll see you at work.'

She smiled again, but this smile was strained. 'I suppose so.'

'Thanks for the dances.'

'And thanks again for walking me home.'

He gave her a curt wave. 'Bye!' And with that he started off, crossing the road and going back down the hill.

She stared after him in disbelief, filled with disappointment and a growing anger. She'd been certain he'd take her into the darkness and privacy of the back close. And she'd been blind positive he'd ask her out. But he'd done neither!

She silently swore and for good measure swore again. Then she stamped up the stairs.

To hell with you, Nevil Sanderson! she thought as she inserted her key into the keyhole. Your arse in parsley!

She laughed at that expression which she hadn't heard in years. Your arse in parsley! How utterly ridiculous.

'You look as though you've enjoyed yourself,' Laura said when she went into the kitchen. Laura was ironing at the kitchen table, John sitting at the other end of the table with a bottle and glass in front of him. His glazed eyes and silly expression told her he was half-cut.

'I did, thank you very much,' she replied, going to the fire to warm herself.

Laura stopped what she was doing. 'Here, catch this!' she instructed, throwing Maggie a towel which she deftly caught.

Maggie wiped her face, and then ran the towel over her hair.

'Snowing, is it?' John asked, lips drawn back in a sarcastic sneer.

'No, it's a gorgeous summer's evening, what do you think?' she jibed in return.

He waved a finger at her. 'Now don't you be cheeky with your elders, young woman.'

She'd been wrong, she realized. He wasn't half-cut, but

105

completely so. She'd never seen John drunk before, and didn't particularly like it.

'John!' Laura scolded in a disapproving tone.

'Only a joke!' he protested.

Maggie pulled a chair up close to the fire. She was frozen through.

'Did you meet anyone nice?' Laura queried, dying to know.

John poured himself another drink without taking his eyes off Maggie.

'There were lots of nice people there,' Maggie prevaricated.

'You know what I mean!'

Maggie picked up the poker and jabbed the fire with it, rearranging the coals so that even more heat was thrown out.

'Well?' Laura insisted.

'There was a chap there I danced with a great deal. He's one of our weavers.'

'Did he walk you home?'

Maggie glanced at Laura, then John who was studying her intently. 'He did actually,' she confessed.

John had a mouthful of whisky, and another. 'The back close was it, eh?' he leered.

Maggie didn't answer that.

'No doubt it was. Slap and tickle. Or did you not bother with the slap because you were enjoying the tickling so much?'

'John!' Laura exclaimed.

'Oh, don't you act so shocked. You were hardly the innocent when you were in the back close with me. My God, you weren't!' he retorted and laughed nastily.

Laura had gone white. 'John?' she pleaded.

John winked at Maggie. 'She was a right goer, I can tell you. Some nights I could hardly keep up.'

Maggie would have left at that point, but as her bed was in the kitchen she couldn't get into it until after he'd left the room. She stared back at him. This was a new side to John, and a very unpleasant one.

'Not another word. You're drunk,' Laura said tight-lipped.

'As a lord! Oh aye, you can bet on that. As an effing lord!'

'I'm sorry, Maggie. He wasn't like this before you came in.'

'But I was, woman, you just never noticed.' He turned his attention again to Maggie. 'How about a drink?'

She shook her head.

'Aw go on, just a wee one?'

'No, thank you, John. I really don't want a drink.'

John grunted, and topped up his glass once more. 'So what's he like, this Don Juan you went into the back close with? Did he get his hand up your skirt?'

'That *is* enough!' Laura said, banging down the iron.

John laughed. 'I haven't seen you so passionate in a long time. And I mean a long time!'

Laura glared at her husband. She was now seething.

John addressed Maggie again. 'She used to be passionate, you know. But then I just told you that. In our courting days she was red hot. She fair sizzled!'

He paused, then said very softly, 'You remind me of her, Maggie. Only you're far more attractive than she ever was.'

Maggie could have slapped him for being so cruel. What an absolute pig he was this evening. And she wished he wouldn't stare at her – it made her feel unclean.

Laura placed her iron by the sink to cool off. 'Bedtime for us, John,' she stated firmly.

'It's early yet. And I want to hear more about the kissing and canoodling.' He smiled lecherously at Maggie.

'We didn't go into the back close if you must know.'

He raised an eyebrow. 'Oh?'

'And in case you don't believe me I wouldn't still have been covered in snow when I came in if I had.'

'That's true enough,' he acknowledged.

'Now, can we change the conversation please?'

Laura crossed to the doorway. There was a glisten of tears in her eyes. She felt humiliated. 'John?'

'Aw I . . .'

'John!' she snapped.

For several moments it seemed as if he might refuse to go with her, then he decided that he would. He threw what remained in his glass down his throat, and lurched to his feet.

'Goodnight Maggie,' he slurred, swaying on the spot.

'Goodnight John.'

'Don't be upset now.' He glanced sideways at Laura. 'There was no harm meant.'

'No offence taken,' she lied.

He belched, scratched his stomach, and then stumbled from the room.

'I am sorry, Maggie,' Laura apologized.

'Just the drink talking. He'll have forgotten all about it in the morning,' Maggie smiled in reply.

'I can't think what suddenly got into him. He's not usually . . . well like that. He can normally hold his drink.'

Maggie went to Laura and kissed her sister tenderly on the cheek. 'Away with you now. Nothing further needs to be said.'

'Marriage!' Laura sighed. 'It's not all you imagine when you're single. Remember that.'

'I will,' Maggie said, smiling again.

Laura wiped tears from her eyes. 'Goodnight then.'

'Goodnight.'

Maggie closed the door behind Laura, and leant against it. What an evening! It had begun so well. Then suddenly, right out of the blue, it had gone straight down the drain.

She'd thought Nevil fancied her, but perhaps he didn't! That would certainly explain why he hadn't taken her into the back close, or asked her out.

There again, he might just be shy? No, he wasn't that – tentative possibly, but not shy.

So what had gone wrong? She was damned if she knew. One thing she did know however was that she wasn't running after him. If he was at all interested it was up to him to make the first move.

She frowned as her thoughts shifted to John. How awful he'd been to Laura, how unforgivable. You just didn't say those sort of things, or divulge such secrets, about your wife. Poor Laura must be mortified.

She suddenly giggled. So Laura had fair sizzled, as John

108

had put it, in her courting days. She couldn't imagine it, Laura had never seemed the sizzling type. But then did you ever really see your own sister objectively? She doubted it.

That night she dreamt again about the flood, and this time Nevil was one of those who drowned.

Maggie was sitting reading a magazine when Laura came into the kitchen having just got the twins off to sleep. John was out at the dog racing with a couple of his pals.

'They take it out of you those two,' Laura said, falling into a chair.

'They're certainly hard work.'

'But worth every moment of it, don't you think?'

'They're gorgeous,' Maggie smiled.

Laura leaned forward, clasping her hands in her lap. 'I've been wanting to speak to you about that business the other night.'

'I told you, there's no need to say anything else on the matter,' Maggie replied.

'But I want to. Simply to explain a bit, I suppose.'

Laura stared down at her clasped hands. 'Things haven't been quite the same between John and I since I had the twins. It was a difficult birth if you remember.'

'I was never given the details, but Mum did remark that you hadn't had an easy time.'

Laura held out one of her hands. 'Look at that, skinny as anything. Same goes for the rest of me. Thin as a rake.'

'You appear to eat properly?'

'I do. But my weight's still down. It's the continual tiredness, you see. The twins are a constant drain on me. Morning, noon and night, demand, demand, demand! And then there's John . . .' She broke off to bite her lip.

'What about John?' Maggie prompted.

'He just can't seem to understand that it's different now. That I don't always feel up to . . . the way I used to. I'm not unreasonable, mind! And it's not as if I've gone off it within myself. It's simply the tiredness that makes me so unresponsive on many occasions.'

Maggie considered that. 'Have you spoken to the doctor?'

'He put me on an iron tonic which bucked me a little. He told me that the way I felt was quite normal for someone in my situation.'

'You said difficult birth?' Maggie probed. 'Does that mean you've had after-effects? I mean physical ones.'

'It's very tender where it wasn't before.'

'You mean painful?'

'It can be,' Laura admitted.

Maggie took a deep breath. 'It seems to me that John is the one who's being unreasonable.'

'He doesn't think so. God knows what he really does think, but he certainly doesn't think that. I've explained the situation to him again and again, but he refuses to accept it.'

Maggie had a sudden thought. 'Is my being here making matters even worse for you? If so I could go into digs.'

'No, no, on the contrary! It's easier with you about. You're a big help.'

'Are you sure about that?'

'Positive. You take a considerable load off my shoulders.'

Maggie was relieved to hear it. She would have been appalled to think she'd added to her sister's problems.

'Anyway!' exclaimed Laura, coming to her feet, 'I suppose I've said what I wanted to. How about a nice cup of tea?'

'Only if you let me make it.'

'I'm already up.'

'Then sit down again. This cup of tea is being made by *me*. And that's an order.'

Laughing, Laura did as she was told.

Maggie and Natasha were having their dinnertime piece, and a right old gossip, when Natasha suddenly whispered, 'I think you're about to have a visitor.'

Maggie glanced up, and there was Nevil Sanderson bearing down on her. It was now the second week in January and she hadn't spoken to him since the night of the Christmas dance.

'I'll take a powder,' said Natasha and, picking up what remained of her piece, rose and strolled away.

110

'Hello, how are you?' Nevil smiled at Maggie.

'Fine. And yourself?'

'In a way glad all the festivities are over. They become too much of a good thing after a while.'

'I know what you mean,' she agreed.

'Do you mind if I join you?' He indicated Natasha's stool.

'Help yourself.'

'What's in your piece?' he asked after he'd sat down.

'Dates. What did you have in yours?'

'Some sort of mayonnaise spread that tasted like chopped up cardboard with bits in it. I'd have much preferred dates.'

She was about to offer him one of her sandwiches, then decided not to. 'So to what do I owe this honour?' she asked instead.

'I was wondering if you'd like to go out with me?'

She felt a flush rise up her neck. Don't appear too eager! she warned herself. 'Oh?'

'To the pictures, I thought. Or we can go some place else if you want?'

He'd caught her completely off-guard. When she hadn't heard from him she'd presumed he wasn't keen.

'Why?' she queried.

He blinked. 'Why what?'

'Why has it taken you so long?'

'You mean to ask you out?'

She nodded.

'Well, I was going to that night of the dance and then I thought it was a bad time with it being Christmas and the New Year coming right afterwards. Folk are always so tied up round about then.'

It was a reasonable explanation, except his voice lacked conviction. He was lying, or covering up something. Another female?

'I see,' she smiled, and watched him relax. 'But is that all?'

Instantly he was on his guard. 'I don't understand.'

'Is there more to why you didn't ask me out that night?'

'Why should there be more?'

She was right, she told herself. He'd gone all defensive. 'I just think there might be.'

'Oh well, if you don't want to go out with me!'

'I didn't say that, Nevil. I didn't say that at all.'

He frowned at her. 'You're intelligent, aren't you? But then that's part of it.'

'Part of what?' she probed.

He glanced around, ensuring they weren't being overheard. 'You're different to the other lassies. Brighter for a start, and you speak nicer.'

She was delighted. 'Are you telling me I put you off?'

He squirmed and looked uncomfortable. 'You didn't put me off exactly. I liked you tremendously. It's just . . . Well, if you want the truth, I wasn't certain we would hit it off together on a regular basis.'

'In other words you thought I might be better than you?' she said softly.

'I know you're only a cop winder, but you're not from round here. And you have . . . a certain way with you!'

'I'll take that as a compliment.'

'It's certainly meant as one. You're class, Maggie. That was the first thing that struck me when I asked you to dance. You're class through and through.'

She couldn't have been more touched. Nor was he trying to butter her up, he meant every word he said. 'The nicest thing is that you consider me intelligent. I appreciate that most of all,' she replied.

He stared full into her face, and she stared back.

'What's your answer then?' he asked in a slightly husky voice.

'I'd love to go to the pictures with you.'

They agreed a time and place to meet.

Maggie gazed anxiously up at the sky as she and Nevil emerged from the Sauchiehall Street picture house that he'd taken her to. It had been lashing down when they'd gone in.

'Thank God, it's stopped raining,' Maggie said as they stepped onto the pavement. Judging from the smell of the air

112

and the large pools of water on the street it had only recently finished.

Nevil grunted.

'I thought the big film was marvellous,' Maggie enthused. She was referring to *The Glass Key* starring Edward Arnold, George Raft and Claire Dodd.

'Hmmh!'

She rounded on Nevil. 'Didn't you like it then?'

'It was all right,' he replied vaguely.

'I thought it a lot more than that!'

'It was the News that caught my interest.'

'The Movietone News?'

He turned to her, eyes positively glowing. 'The bit about the forthcoming election in Spain. It would be a disaster for Spain and the rest of Europe if the Fascists came to power.'

'I must say I didn't pay much attention to that,' Maggie confessed.

He linked arms with her. 'The Fascists at the moment are gaining ground throughout Europe while democracy and Socialism are in disarray. That's why it's so important that Spain chooses the right, by which I mean Republican, government to lead it.'

'You're interested in politics then?'

He burst out laughing. 'Of course I am! I'm a Glaswegian, aren't I? We're brought up to live and breathe politics.'

She decided to tease him a little. 'What if I told you that I was a Conservative?'

He stopped in his tracks, his expression a combination of horror and contempt. 'You're not, are you?'

She didn't reply.

'Jesus bloody Christ! I never dreamt . . .' He let go of her arm.

'That serious, eh?'

'It's more than serious, it's . . . shattering!' His voice pleaded, 'You're not really, are you, Maggie? Tell me you're only pulling my leg!'

'Does this mean you won't take me out again?'

'I can't go out with a Tory!' he virtually wailed.

113

He was so beside himself she had to laugh. 'Don't worry, I'm Labour. I *was* only pulling your leg.'

His face collapsed with relief, and then he took her arm again. 'You gave me the fright of my life there. Nevil Sanderson going out with a female Tory, ye Gods and little fishes!'

She would have liked to have kissed him then, but couldn't because they were in the street. She drew close to him instead.

'Can we have some fish and chips before we go home? I'll pay,' she said.

'You'll do nothing of the sort. When you're with me, I'll pay.'

'I can afford it, Nevil. I'm a working girl, don't forget.'

'It's got nothing to do with whether you're working or not. It's a matter of principle.'

The fish and chips he did buy were simply scrumptious.

This time there was no hanging back on his part. When they arrived at her close he took her inside, along past the stairs to where it was dark and they couldn't be seen by the rest of the close.

'Maggie!' he whispered as his eager lips sought hers.

Nothing had ever felt quite so right as finding herself in Nevil's arms and being kissed by him. They belonged to each other.

When she finally left him to go upstairs her heart was over-flowing, and she was beaming from ear to ear.

Nevil caught up with Maggie as she was leaving Templeton's. 'What are you doing tomorrow night?' he asked, falling into step beside her.

'Nothing special. Why?'

'I've just heard that Harry Pollitt is addressing a meeting in Parkhead and I wondered if you'd fancy coming with me?'

'Who's Harry Pollitt?' she questioned.

'General Secretary of the Communist Party of Great Britain. Do you honestly mean you've never heard of Harry Pollitt?' Nevil's expression was one of complete amazement.

'Never,' she confirmed.

'Why, the man's an institution!'

'He might be. But I've still never heard of him.'

Nevil shook his head in disbelief. 'Incredible!'

'Is he a good speaker?'

'Tremendous. He can really fire the blood. So will you come with me?'

'You know I will.'

He smiled at that.

Arm-in-arm they continued on their way.

Harry Pollitt was a fine speaker, Maggie thought. And yes, Nevil was right, he did fire the blood. He'd certainly succeeded in firing hers.

She glanced sideways at Nevil who was sitting entranced. He might have been listening to Moses when he came down from the mountain.

She brought her attention back to Pollitt, who was sitting beside Willie Gallacher, a Communist MP and one of Glasgow's most famous and well-loved sons. Pollitt thundered on about Italy's invasion of Abyssinia which he and his party roundly condemned.

'What did you think of that then?' Nevil demanded as they left the meeting.

'It was all right.'

'Only all right!' he exclaimed, scandalized. 'It was utterly brilliant.'

He took his politics so seriously, she thought, smiling to herself. But there again, as she knew he would have argued, politics were a serious matter.

'I thought your Harry Pollitt spoke extremely well,' she relented. 'He had me on the edge of my seat a couple of times.'

'Aye, gripping stuff. And Gallacher was good too. The only Communist in Parliament, you know. I have heard, though I can't say whether or not it's true, that Winston Churchill is an admirer of his.'

'Churchill?'

'Apparently so. Funny that, eh?'

A nearby clock tower chimed the hour. It was still early.

'How about a drink before we catch the tram home?' Nevil suggested.

'Are the pubs round here safe?' Maggie asked. She'd learned that many Glasgow pubs were far from desirable.

'Oh aye! Safe as houses. Anyway, they'd never bother a couple.'

A couple! It thrilled her that he'd called them that. They weren't just Maggie and Nevil any more, but a *couple*.

To her it was indicative of how he'd come to view their relationship.

The bell rang announcing dinnertime. Maggie laid down the job in hand and wiped her forehead. She had a slight headache from the noise of the factory which, for some reason, seemed worse than usual.

She was opening the cupboard containing her piece when she saw Nevil hurrying over.

'Have you heard the news?' he demanded eagerly.

She immediately presumed it was something to do with Templeton's, but she was wrong. 'No. What?'

'The Spanish have elected the Popular Front to government. Isn't that fabulous?'

'It certainly is.'

'The news broke on the wireless just a short while ago. Hopefully all the details will be in this evening's newspapers.'

'One in the eye for Hitler and that lot, eh?'

'It'll sicken him, right enough. He's probably jumping up and down with fury. Him and the entire Nazi party.'

'Good news,' said Maggie, nodding. She was extremely pleased.

'Couldn't be better,' Nevil agreed. He was so excited he seemed to vibrate with it.

Maggie opened up the cupboard and took out her piece and the thermos flask she now brought to work with her. 'How about a cup of coffee?'

'I couldn't eat or drink at the moment. Besides, there are a few other people I want to tell about this. But I wanted you to be the first I told.'

116

She put her lips together and blew him the tiniest of kisses. 'Thank you.'

He was about to move when he remembered something. 'My ma has suggested I ask you home to tea. She and the old fella are dying to meet you.'

She was also keen to meet them. 'When do you have in mind?'

'What about this Saturday? Then we could go on to a dance in our local Labour Hall? Andy Ramsay is going with Mary Mauchline, so they'll be there.'

'Tea and dance it is then,' she agreed.

She watched Nevil walk away, thinking how much, in such a short while, he'd come to mean to her.

And she believed it was the same with him.

Maggie woke up to hear the sound of voices, one of which was raised in anger, John's, she now realized. He and Laura were arguing.

Maggie glanced at her alarm clock, but couldn't make out the time. She still felt dreadfully tired so couldn't have been asleep all that long.

'No!' Laura said quite distinctly.

That told Maggie what her sister and brother-in-law were arguing about. Laura was denying him.

Laying her head on the pillow she closed her eyes and tried to get back to sleep.

What was that? It could have been a slap. Had Laura hit John? Or . . . Maggie sat up in bed. Had John hit Laura?

In their bedroom something crashed to the floor, which immediately woke one of the twins who began to howl.

Recriminations followed. Although Maggie couldn't make out the exact words, she knew they were from both sides.

And then the other twin started crying.

Should she go through, knock on their door and offer to help? Don't be stupid, she berated herself. That was the last thing she should do, for a number of reasons.

She curled up again and closed her eyes. The next thing she knew her alarm was ringing and it was time to get up.

117

The atmosphere was strained during breakfast. But it altered when John took her down the hill to her tramstop. He couldn't have been more chatty and pleasant.

The street Nevil lived in wasn't nearly as nice as the McNairs'. The tenement was very old, the stairs concave from constant use. She noticed outside lavatories on the first landing – thank goodness she didn't have to put up with that. The idea of a shared lavatory appalled her.

Nevil opened his door, smiled at her and ushered her in. The smell of wax polish hit her as she walked through the hall. The linoleum beneath her feet shone and sparkled.

'We're here!' Nevil called out loudly.

The Sandersons were gathered in the kitchen, Mr Sanderson and Jimmy standing as though at attention. They were just as nervous as she, Maggie realized.

'Ma, Da, this is Maggie Jordan.'

Mrs Sanderson was a slender woman with pepper-and-salt hair pulled back into an old-fashioned bun. Her face beamed welcome.

'How are you, Maggie? Nevil has told us so much about you,' Mrs Sanderson said as she shook her hand.

Maggie wasn't quite sure how to reply to that. 'I've been looking forward to meeting you too,' she answered, which was true.

'And this is Father.'

Mr Sanderson stepped forward to shake Maggie's hand. His own was hard and calloused, the hand of a manual worker. 'Nevil said you were pretty, but he didn't do you justice.'

Maggie blushed. 'Thank you very much. That's kind of you.'

'Not kind, lassie, just the truth.'

'And this is my brother, Jimmy.'

Jimmy was about her own age, maybe a little younger. He was as fair as Nevil was dark.

'The apprentice electrician,' Maggie grinned as she shook Jimmy's hand.

'I'd have preferred to be a jockey. But as you can see I'm far too big and heavy for that,' he replied.

'You like horses then?'

'I love them. And the countryside. Some day I'll live in the countryside, I've promised myself that.'

'Then I hope you manage it.'

'Have a seat, Maggie,' Mrs Sanderson said, pointing to an armchair by the fire whose back was covered with an anti-macassar. The anti-macassar was boiled as white as newly fallen snow.

Maggie sat down, and Mr Sanderson cleared his throat. 'I thought a wee something might be in order before tea. Would you like some sherry, Maggie?'

Maggie could tell from the expression on Mr Sanderson's face that much thought had gone into this. She really would have preferred a cup of tea, but couldn't refuse when they'd gone to so much trouble.

'Some sherry would be lovely, thank you,' she replied.

'And you, Grace?'

'Please,' his wife answered.

As Mr Sanderson was pouring the drinks Maggie had time to quickly glance about her. The range, similar to that they'd had in Heymouth, was black-leaded, the brass parts gleaming. There was yellow distemper on the walls, and the ceiling was a mushroom colour. All the wood in the room had recently been polished, and the ornaments and various knick-knacks dusted. Was this all for her benefit? No, Maggie thought. Mrs Sanderson was an excellent housewife.

'Thank you,' she said when Mr Sanderson handed her a glass of sherry. A whisky glass, she noticed, and immediately chided herself for being unkind. She had had the benefit of having worked in an hotel after all.

'I hope that's to your liking,' Mr Sanderson said to her.

'I'm sure it will be.'

He hovered, waiting for her to taste it. Surprisingly, the sherry was an excellent one and had certainly cost a shilling or two. He'd probably asked for the best sherry available, she rightly guessed.

'Very nice indeed,' she acknowledged, which clearly delighted him.

'Something smells good,' Maggie commented as Mr Sanderson poured out whisky for himself, Nevil and Jimmy.

'Steak-and-kidney pudding, a speciality of mine,' Mrs Sanderson replied. Then, with a sudden frown, 'I hope you like steak-and-kidney pudding?'

'I love it. My own mother . . .' She trailed off, and sipped her sherry hurriedly.

'Nevil told us about your family. A terrible, terrible thing,' Mrs Sanderson said softly.

'Yes.' Maggie paused, then went on, 'As I was saying, my own mother used to make steak-and-kidney pudding. It was a great favourite of ours too, particularly mine.'

'And mine,' piped up Jimmy.

'Everything's a favourite of yours, gannet. The way you eat no wonder you're far too large to be a jockey,' Nevil jibed.

'It was my heavy bones that did for me, as you well know!' Jimmy retorted hotly.

Maggie smiled to herself. It could easily have been her and Pet having a go at one another.

Silence settled on the little group.

'I understand you went with Nevil to hear Harry Pollitt,' Mr Sanderson said to Maggie after a while.

'That's right.'

'Marvellous, isn't he!'

'He certainly spoke well. He fires the blood.'

'So does this stuff,' muttered Nevil, knocking back his whisky.

Jimmy laughed. 'Too true!'

Mr Sanderson glared at his sons, then turned back to Maggie. 'Tell me then, lass, what stance do you take on rearmament?'

Mrs Sanderson groaned. 'Not politics, please, Hector! This is supposed to be a *social* occasion.'

'There's nothing wrong with talking politics during a social occasion. Is there, Maggie?'

'I'm not taking sides!' she smiled.

'Does talking politics bore you then, lass?'

'Far from it.' As long as that's not the only topic of conversation, she might have added, but didn't.

'There!' exclaimed Mr Sanderson triumphantly to his wife.

'Well, it bores me,' Mrs Sanderson retorted.

Her husband ignored that. 'So what *is* your stance on rearmament?' he asked Maggie again. 'I'm against it myself. It will lead to nothing but trouble, you mark my words.'

'And I'm for it,' Nevil stated.

'Attlee's against it,' Mr Sanderson said to his son.

'Attlee might be, but Bevin and Dalton are for it,' Nevil countered.

'The unions are against it,' Mr Sanderson said.

'Oh no, they're not. The unions are divided on the subject. So don't tell fibs.'

Mr Sanderson harumphed.

'Maggie?' Nevil prompted.

She didn't reply at once, but then said, 'There are pros and cons to both sides of the argument. But I do believe, which is maybe an unfeminine view, that history shows that the weak always lose. They are always dominated by the strong. I'd say, whenever possible, you should always try to be in a position of strength.'

'Aha!' exclaimed Nevil. 'Good for you, Maggie.'

'You might adopt a different view when you become a mother,' Mrs Sanderson chipped in quietly.

Maggie knew what the older woman was driving at. 'I might, but I doubt it, Mrs Sanderson. If only we humans were less ambitious, and more tolerant of one another, then there wouldn't be a need for arms at all, and every mother's child would be safe. At least from war, that is. But unfortunately people are what they are, and because of that I agree with rearmament as a safety measure.'

'Give a man a weapon and he'll use it,' Mr Sanderson argued.

'But will he if the person facing him has the same weapon? He would certainly think twice where he wouldn't have done before,' Maggie replied.

'The bullies must be stood up to,' Nevil said. 'That's something you learn early on. Give a bully an inch and he'll end up walking all over you.'

'At least you'd still be alive,' Mrs Sanderson said.

Nevil smiled. 'Would you? Perhaps and perhaps not, depending on the circumstances. But I for one am never going to let anyone walk over me.'

'Me neither!' Jimmy declared.

Mr Sanderson shook his head. 'Rearmament is a mistake, I tell you. Look what happened the last time Europe armed, millions dead on both sides. And for what? Nothing in the end, nothing at all. It was all debit and no credit.'

'You can blame Kaiser Bill for the Great War. The man was a lunatic,' Nevil said.

'And now there's this Herr Hitler. Folk laugh at him and his funny wee moustache,' Mrs Sanderson said, 'but I don't find him funny at all. Quite the contrary, he scares the living daylights out of me.'

'Aye, another lunatic,' Jimmy agreed.

'God save us from another war,' Mrs Sanderson murmured, a glance taking in her two sons.

'Amen,' Maggie whispered.

The steak-and-kidney pudding turned out to be absolutely delicious, even nicer than her mother used to make.

She asked for, and was given, the recipe before going home.

Maggie and Nevil walked hand-in-hand through a pine wood. It was a Sunday afternoon and they were out for a stroll in the park.

She smiled at him, and he smiled back. 'It's a gorgeous day,' she said.

'Not nearly as gorgeous as you.'

'Flatterer!'

'I'm told that flattery will get me everywhere.'

'Not with me it won't.'

'Are you quite sure about that?'

'No,' she laughed, thoroughly enjoying herself.

With a startled squawk a rook flew from one tree to another where it perched complaining loudly.

122

'It's very lucky to see a solitary rook on a Sunday,' Nevil said.

'Is it? I didn't know that.'

'Neither did I till now. I just made it up.'

'Fool!' She kissed him on the cheek.

'How about more of the same?'

This time he kissed her on the lips.

'Hmmh!' she murmured when it was over. She was gloriously content. She didn't need a mirror to know her face was glowing with happiness.

They wandered down a small incline where they stopped on a bridge and stared down into the browny green water.

Maggie suddenly shuddered, and twisted away, her happy expression replaced by one of painful memories.

Nevil drew her towards him. 'What is it?' he whispered.

'The water. It just . . . for a moment there . . .' She broke off and bit her lip.

'Heymouth?'

'Yes,' she mumbled in a tiny voice.

He put both arms round her and held her tight to his chest. He could feel her thudding heart.

'Oh Maggie!' he whispered, and tenderly kissed her neck.

She looked up at him and they kissed on the lips, this time not frivolously, but full of heat and passion.

'You know I've fallen for you, don't you?' he murmured finally.

Those were words she'd so desperately wanted to hear. 'Have you?'

'Head over heels.'

'In love?'

'In love,' he confirmed.

'I feel the same about you.'

'In love?'

'In love,' she stated.

They were about to kiss each other again when they both heard another Sunday afternoon walker approaching.

Laughing, hand-in-hand, they continued on their way.

*

'That's them off,' declared Maggie, coming back into the kitchen. She and Nevil were looking after Margaret and Rose as John and Laura had gone out to the theatre for the evening.

Nevil glanced at his watch. It was a quarter past eight.

'I'll make a cup of tea,' Maggie said.

As she was filling the kettle, Nevil crept up behind her, and slid his hands round to cup her breasts. She caught her breath, then closed her eyes as he gently rubbed and caressed. He pressed against her, and she could feel him hard against her.

'Do you know this is the first time you and I have been alone together,' he whispered.

'What about the back close?'

'I mean in a house.'

She'd known perfectly well what he meant. She put the kettle down and turned to face him. She desperately wanted to touch him.

'This room has one serious drawback,' he said.

'Which is?'

'It doesn't have a couch. Only chairs and . . .' He paused before adding, 'a bed.'

'Are you suggesting we go and lie on that?'

He nodded.

'I'd crease my clothes.'

'Then take them off. I'll do the same.'

The twins were fast asleep, and it would be hours before John and Laura returned. They would be quite safe, she told herself.

'Well?' he prompted.

'I'm a virgin, Nevil. I want you to know that.'

'Then that's two of us.'

That pleased her enormously. Previously she hadn't been able to work out whether he was or not.

'We'll have to be careful,' she said. 'I don't want to get pregnant.'

'Don't worry. I have the necessary with me.'

'Prepared, were you?' she teased.

'I've been hoping you'd agree for some time. Do you think less of me for that?'

She could hear a quiver in his voice. He was nervous, but then so was she.

'Tell me again.' she asked.

'That I love you?'

She nodded.

'I love you.'

Her lips curved into a small smile. How marvellous it was to hear him say that. She could have stood there all day listening to him repeat it over and over again.

She crossed to the fireplace, and put some more coal on the fire. Standing up she began undressing. When she was completely naked she turned to stare at him. She'd never seen anyone so transfixed, but then he'd never seen a naked woman before.

'You can put your clothes on the other chair,' she said, and went over to the cavity bed.

She threw back the covers, and climbed in. Luckily she'd changed the sheets several days before and they were good Egyptian cotton sheets, a pair of Laura's best. She watched him undress just as he'd watched her.

His body was a fine one. Young, hard and well muscled. His buttocks were clenched as he moved towards her.

She wriggled over to make room for him. How strange, yet exciting, it was to have him there with her, she thought.

After a while their nervousness vanished and was replaced by the glory and wonder of each other.

'All right?' he asked.

They were both lying on their backs staring at the top of the cavity.

'Yes.'

'Was it . . . I mean . . .'

She twisted slightly, and kissed his upper arm. 'Of course, silly. It was beautiful.'

'For me too, Maggie.'

She didn't feel any different. She'd always imagined she would somehow, but she didn't.

'Maggie?'

125

'Hmmh?'

'Wouldn't it be fabulous if we could do this every night?'

'Fabulous,' she agreed.

'We could, you know.'

She pulled herself up onto an elbow to gaze at him. He looked totally vulnerable, and for once far younger than his years. 'How?'

'You know as well as I do.'

She went very still, and literally stopped breathing. She waited for him to go on.

'Will you marry me?'

'Is that a proposal?'

'That's what it sounded like to me.'

Her eyes welled up with tears of joy. 'Then I accept.'

They began talking about the future, and later made love once more.

The second time was even better than the first.

'That's them now,' said Maggie hearing scuffling at the front door. A final glance at the cavity bed reassured her that it looked just as it should. No-one could tell she and Nevil had been in it. She flicked back a stray lock of hair as Laura and John breezed into the kitchen.

'You two appear to have had a good time,' Maggie said with a smile.

'Terrific! Absolutely terrific,' Laura enthused. 'Wasn't it a great night out, John?'

'A great night. I can't remember the last time I enjoyed myself as much. Or laughed so hard. They had a comic on the bill who had me in stitches.'

'How were the twins?' Laura asked.

'Not a peep out of them since shortly after eight. They couldn't have been better.'

'Good,' said Laura, nodding. 'I'll go and have a look at them. I want to go through there anyway.' And with that Laura hurried from the room.

John entertained Maggie and Nevil with tales of the show until Laura returned, and then Maggie said, 'I have some news. Or I should say, Nevil and I have some news.'

Laura guessed immediately what it was, and put a hand to her mouth.

'What is it?' John asked.

'Nevil and I have decided to get married.'

Laura gave a delighted squeal and flew at her sister. 'Oh congratulations! I know you're both going to be happy together. You're just made for one another.'

Laura kissed Maggie on the cheek, and hugged her. Then she did the same to Nevil.

John was standing rooted to the spot, his expression stony.

'Well, John, aren't you going to say something?' Laura urged.

He took a deep breath, and managed to smile. 'Congratulations. All the very best.' He may have been smiling, but his tone didn't match the smile. It had a brittle edge to it.

Laura began to pump Maggie for details. When was it going to be? Would it be in church or at a registry office? Where would the reception take place? She'd be matron of honour, of course!

John produced the remains of a bottle of whisky and they all had a dram to celebrate.

CHAPTER FOUR

It was the morning teabreak at Templeton's and Natasha had
come over to chat with Maggie as usual.

'I think the King should marry Mrs Simpson, don't you?'
Natasha said. 'I mean, he seems absolutely besawaaaaated by
her!'

Maggie always laughed at Natasha's exaggerated pronunciation. 'He certainly gives that impression,' she agreed.

Natasha leaned closer. 'Mind you, I don't think she's that
attractive. In my opinion she's quite plain.'

'Now don't be bitchy!' Maggie chided.

'I'm being nothing of the sort. Take away all those fancy
glad rags and jewels and what are you left with? Something
very ordinary. Why, many of the lassies here knock spots off
her. Myself excluded, of course. I couldn't knock spots off
anyone.' Natasha gave a soulful sigh. 'Not anyone.'

Maggie smiled in sympathy, then glanced down at the
diamond ring she was wearing. 'I'll tell you this, if the King
does marry Mrs Simpson he'll give her a bigger engagement
ring than I've got.' She waggled the ring in front of her. 'Still,
I'm not complaining. It does me.'

'*Any* engagement ring would do me,' Natasha lamented,
which made Maggie laugh again.

The solitary diamond on her ring was very small, Maggie
reflected, but she had no-one but herself to blame for that.
Nevil had been willing to buy a more expensive ring but she'd
talked him out of it, arguing that it was better they saved the
money and put it into their house fund. It was a thrifty suggestion on her part, and a practical one. However, she
thought wistfully, a bigger diamond would have been nice.

Mr Kerly, who'd been talking to one of the other girls at a
bench a short distance away, now came over to where Maggie

and Natasha were sitting. They both immediately rose, Natasha desperately chewing in order to swallow the sausage roll that was in her mouth.

'Well, Miss Jordan, how are you today?'

'Fine, Mr Kerly. No complaints.'

'Nine months you've been with us now, and settled in very nicely. We're all extremely pleased with you.'

'Thank you, sir.'

'In fact we're so impressed, we're going to promote you earlier than we normally do.'

Maggie's face lit up. This was completely unexpected.

'So how do you feel about taking over a weft loom? Think you can cope?'

'Yes, please. And I'm sure I can,' she replied eagerly.

'Good. There will be a new lassie starting next Monday whom you'll train for your present job. When you consider her competent you'll move up. Miss McGinley can train you if you like, as the pair of you seem to get on together.'

'I'll train her well,' Natasha promised.

'Right then. I'll bring the new girl to you on Monday,' Kerly said to Maggie. He treated them to one of his rare smiles, then moved on.

Maggie clapped her hands in glee. 'This means more money in my pay packet! I can't wait to tell Nevil.'

'You've got time before the end of the teabreak. If you hurry, that is.'

Maggie hurried. Nevil was just as thrilled as she was, and said they'd discuss it at dinner time. He said that as it was sunny they should take their pieces and have a wee picnic on Glasgow Green.

'More beer, son?' Mr Sanderson asked Nevil. It was a Saturday night and Maggie and Nevil were spending it with the Sandersons in order to save money. They were both saving as hard as they could for the wedding and the house they'd have to furnish.

Nevil nodded. 'Aye, please, Da.'

Maggie gathered up the cards – they were playing rummy – and started shuffling. She was dealing when Jimmy arrived home, who had been out for the past couple of hours.

'Have you had the wireless on?' Jimmy asked.

Mr Sanderson shook his head. 'No. Why?'

'A group of generals in Spain, led by someone called Franco, have revolted against the Government. Apparently fighting has taken place.'

Nevil was appalled. 'Franco,' he repeated. 'That one's a right bas . . .' He didn't complete the word as he remembered his mother was in the room, but they all knew which word he'd been about to say.

'You know of him?' Maggie asked.

'I read an article on him somewhile back. He was first noticed when he put down a miners' rising with, I think the expression was, "considerable brutality".'

'A hard man then,' mused Mr Sanderson.

'Hard and utterly ruthless. The sort who crushes anything or anyone who gets in his way.'

'So do you think he'll succeed in toppling the Government?' Maggie asked.

'I suppose it depends on how many troops he's got backing him.' To Jimmy, 'Was there any mention of numbers?'

'None. The whole thing only started earlier today so what report there was was sparse and somewhat muddled. It didn't even give the names of the other generals involved.'

'Is Franco a Fascist?' Mrs Sanderson queried.

Nevil pulled a face. 'Is the Pope Catholic?'

That earned a laugh all round. 'He's a Fascist and no mistake,' Nevil said. 'And if he could overthrow the Popular Front then Spain would become a Fascist state just like Germany and Italy.'

'But they lost the election,' Maggie mused.

'It seems Franco and his bully boys have decided not to abide by the election results,' Nevil replied. 'Like all Fascists they're only prepared to accept democracy when it's going their way. Vote against them and they have a nasty habit of smashing the ballot box.'

'Will Britain do anything to help the Spanish government?' Mrs Sanderson asked.

Her husband shook his head. 'I shouldn't imagine so. It's really got nothing to do with us after all.'

'That's where you're wrong, it's got everything to do with us!' Nevil stated hotly. 'If it's Spain today, who is it tomorrow? Just remember this, the Fascists view Britain as an enemy. An enemy they would one day like to convert to their own cause.'

'Britain will never turn Fascist!' Maggie exclaimed.

'Sir Oswald Mosley doesn't agree with you,' Nevil countered.

'Mosley is a brilliant orator, but surely that's all?' Mrs Sanderson said.

'He has his followers, those Blackshirts, whose ranks are growing all the time, according to the newspapers,' Nevil replied.

'But they still only number a tiny percentage of the population,' Mr Sanderson said. 'I can't see them ever coming to power. At least . . .' he added ominously, 'not by legal and democratic means.'

'A Fascist Britain.' Nevil murmured. 'The very thought makes me go cold all over.'

'It doesn't bear thinking about,' Jimmy agreed.

Nevil punched a fist into his other palm. 'The Government in Spain must beat off this rebellion. It must!'

They had no heart for rummy after that, so abandoned the game. Jimmy's bombshell had ruined the evening for them all, even Mrs Sanderson.

Labour against Fascism! the placard proclaimed, while another said Spain Today – The Truth!

The large co-operative hall was packed to bursting, with many standing at the back and round the sides. Maggie and Nevil had been fortunate and were sitting near the front where they had an excellent view and would hear every syllable.

Willie Gallacher introduced the speaker who was sitting behind him on the right.

'And so, ladies and gentlemen, Mr Claud Cockburn will

now relate to you in his own inimitable way some of his recent experiences in Spain, beginning with, I believe, events of 18 July, a date destined to go down in Spanish history. Mr Claud Cockburn!'

Cockburn stood to rapturous applause. His face behind the glasses was sensitive, and very intelligent. When he spoke the power and thrust of his descriptive narrative held his audience spellbound.

'Looking back, it would appear obvious that the situation of the men and women who rushed out that morning to defend themselves and their towns against the army attack was quite hopeless.

'It did not occur however to the sleepy and mostly unarmed men who rushed the Montaña barracks in Madrid against all the rifles and machine guns of the biggest garrison in Spain, that by all the laws of war they could never take those barracks.

'They took them, and when they got inside they saw a line of twenty or thirty officers with big automatic pistols, lined up behind a parapet, green and shaking not with fear only, but with astonishment, at the huge heroism of the people who had thrown themselves against the machine-gun emplacements and the riflemen, and broken their way in against odds which were intended to be, and ought to have been, overwhelming.

'The half-dozen men who held the inside of the telephone building at Barcelona, the three who held the radio station against a whole troop of Fascist officers, that white-haired Communist woman, Caridad Mercadet, who led a little band of men and women with rifles, sporting guns and two airguns against the Army Command building at the bottom of the Rambla, did not, it seems, grasp that such things are impossible.

'The officers who planned the betrayal of Spain thought, and admitted afterwards that they had thought, the thing impossible. They thought they would have a walk-over. They had, and they admitted it, no remote notion of the heights of courage and tenacity of which the people, once united in

132

defence of democracy and the most elementary rights of humanity, is capable. It was only days later, when defeat at the hands of the people stared them in the face, that they realized treachery must go further and deeper, and opening the gates of their country wider still to the enemy, called for new reinforcements from Germany, Italy and the Moors, just as French grandees had tried to betray France to foreign enemies against the French people more than a hundred years before.

'I came out that Sunday morning into Hospital Street and saw tense-faced boys and girls, clutching miserable old weapons, including a number of broken airguns taken from a sporting gun shop, advancing slowly but unwaveringly up the pavements against a towering red-brick church with sandbagged loopholes in its walls from which a machine-gun and a score or more of modern army rifles cracked and spat continuously.

'A boy fell over suddenly on the pavement and rolled into the roadway. A girl bent hurriedly over him. He whispered something. She took the Republican emblem from her arm and gave it to him and he kissed it and so died. The advance went on.

'It did not occur to me then that the boy who died under a priest's rifle fire in Hospital Street would shortly be accused in the British reactionary press of "an outrageous attack on a Church" and reminded that to use violence against priests is a barbarous act, forfeiting the respect and support of respectable people.

'We thought that when the Church takes up arms against the people, the people has the right to defend itself even against priests.

'You only had to twiddle radio knobs to hear something of what was happening in the places where the people had failed in their defence. You tuned into Seville, and heard drunken General Queipo de Llano hiccuping out his endless ugly polemic against civilization, progress and democracy. In Seville, the democrats got no arms, and in the poorest quarter of the city they held out for four days fighting street-to-street, house-to-house, room-to-room, with knives and boiling oil.

'The women heated the oil, and under the volleys of rifle fire brought it in jugs and saucepans and slop-pails to the men lodged on window ledges and the angles of roofs, when they poured it down on the advancing soldiery.

'They died fighting, and the others – who had not died in that first struggle for the city – were massacred and many of them burned alive later, when the generals met at Cadiz to plan a northern drive with the Moors and agreed that the wiping out of the working population of Andalusia was a military necessity "to keep the country quiet".

'Turn the knobs again and hear what the generals have to say to you. Here is Franco, there is Mola, and there Cabanellas, all roaring into the microphones in a nightmare chorus of things to come, filling the air of tortured Europe with the menace of the warlords, the horror of great darkness, spitting fire and slaughter and slavery, the brasshats and the inquisitors and the enemies of the people, marching on . . .'

Finally, after weaving his web of words for almost half an hour, Claud Cockburn paused, took a deep breath, and then concluded. 'That, ladies and gentlemen, is the Spain I have just left, and which I intend returning to shortly. Thank you.'

Cockburn returned to his seat in profound silence. Maggie realized there were tears in her eyes, and when she glanced about her she saw that it was the same with many people, both male and female.

Jack Morrison, a well-known trade-union leader, who'd been sitting on the other side of Willie Gallacher, rose to his feet.

'Ladies and gentlemen, we will now take a collection for those trade unionists currently fighting so gallantly on the streets of Spain. The money raised from this meeting and other meetings that Mr Cockburn speaks at will be used to buy arms, food and clothing. Please give generously, thank you.'

When it was Maggie and Nevil's turn to contribute they

gave every last farthing they had on them, as did many in the hall.

Maggie and John hurried down the hill to her tramstop. They were a little later than usual, as it was one of those mornings where nothing had gone right or according to plan.

Maggie didn't see the deep crack in the pavement, which caused her to stagger and stumble. Immediately John grabbed hold of her, steadying her against his body.

'Are you all right?' he said anxiously.

'Fine, thank you.' She tried to move away, but it was impossible. She literally had to wrench herself out of his grasp.

She glanced into his eyes, and quickly looked away, not liking what she saw there. Side by side they continued on their way.

For too long she'd tried to ignore the fact that John fancied her, pretending it was all a figment of her imagination. But eventually she'd had to admit it to herself.

There were times when she could feel the desire oozing out of him. Frequently he made her feel uncomfortable and these days she contrived never to be alone with him other than in a public place.

She told herself again that she could live with the situation until the spring when she and Nevil married and moved into their own house. She could only hope and pray that until then John kept his passion at bay, and didn't attempt to do anything about it.

Was Laura aware of John's feelings towards her? She had to be, Maggie thought, as Laura was nobody's fool. But so far Laura hadn't mentioned it. She guessed that Laura was waiting for the spring and her departure from the house just as much as she was.

Nor had she mentioned it to Nevil. She wasn't sure what Nevil would have done if she had. He might even have insisted on a confrontation with John which was the last thing she wanted.

How wearisome! she thought. She'd always liked John

up until recently, but now he gave her the creeps.

Nor was she to blame. She'd never given John any indication that she was sexually attracted to him. Heaven forbid, the man was her sister's husband! Even if she had fancied John, which she most certainly did not, out of loyalty to Laura she'd never have admitted it.

'Goodbye, see you later,' she said when they got to her tramstop, and turned away so that he couldn't try to kiss her.

However, he managed to brush against her as he moved away.

John felt wretched as he strode along, still smelling Maggie's distinctive odour. It was a smell that had come to mean so much, unlike any other he'd known.

How he wanted her! Not simply for sex, but to be with all the time. Night after night he dreamt about her and then when he reached out there was Laura. And Laura usually said no. But when she didn't reject him, he imagined that he was making love to Maggie. If only he could wave a magic wand and turn Laura into Maggie! God, he was so miserable. Talk about Tantalus! So near and yet so far.

'Maggie,' he whispered, taking comfort in saying her name.

He'd always thought she was attractive. But it wasn't until she'd started living with them that he'd realized just how attractive she was. And that gorgeous exotic smell of hers, how it aroused him! It was a strange scent, like a mixture of herbs and pungent spices. You would have thought that Laura would have smelled slightly similar, but she didn't. Laura smelled ordinary.

As for Nevil Sanderson, he could quite happily have stuck a knife in him and twisted it. Just as he would have given anything to have turned Laura into Maggie so he would also have given anything to be turned into Nevil, Maggie's fiancé and future husband.

Were they sleeping together? He hated to think about that, it made him far too upset.

He couldn't believe they were. Maggie must be saving

herself. And yet, there was something about the two of them when they were together, a shared intimacy, as if . . .

He was beginning to hate Laura, he realized. He'd loved her once, but not any longer. He'd look at her, then at Maggie and it was as if he'd been hit in the stomach.

Maggie. Beautiful, gorgeous-smelling Maggie, but quite out of reach.

He groaned in anguish.

'I went round to Bob Kinloch's house last night to suggest a quick pint,' Andy Ramsay said to Nevil as he hung up his jacket. He and Nevil were in the men's cloakroom, about to start work.

'Oh aye?'

'Only he wasn't there. He left yesterday afternoon for Spain.'

Nevil turned to stare at Andy in astonishment. 'Left for Spain?'

'Apparently it was a sudden decision. He's gone off to fight the Nationalists.' The Nationalists and Fascists were one and the same.

This was a turn up for the book. Bob had always seemed rather a meek and mild type, Nevil thought, not the sort to go rushing off suddenly to fight in a foreign war.

'His mother was in a terrible state,' Andy continued. 'She tried her best to talk him out of it but he wouldn't listen. His mind was made up and that was that, he told her.'

'He's not the only one either by all accounts,' Nevil mused. 'I have heard of others doing the same thing. All off to fight on the Republican side.'

'There was a bit in last night's *Evening Citizen* that said a group of Nottinghamshire miners are en route to enlist. And it is expected that more from the same area will join them.'

They began to leave the cloakroom, streaming through with the others. Charlie Menzies, a close friend of Nevil's, caught his arm.

'Have you heard about Bob Kinloch?' Charlie demanded.

'Just a few minutes ago from Andy.'

'Good for him, eh?'

'Good for him,' Nevil agreed.

137

'I wouldn't mind doing the same myself. If nothing else it would be a change from grafting in dear old Templeton's.'

Nevil smiled. 'I don't think you should go just for a change of scenery. They're using real bombs and bullets over there, don't forget!'

A dreamy look came into Charlie's eyes. 'It can't be all fighting, there must be socializing too. Lots of vino and senoritas. I wonder how you say "I love you darling" in Spanish?'

Trust Charlie, Nevil thought. Women and drink were never far from his mind.

'I can speak the French lingo, you know,' Charlie went on. '*Voulez-vous coucher avec moi ce soir?*'

'Dirty bugger!' grinned Andy Ramsay.

'There are lots of European volunteers fighting for the Republicans as well, I'm told,' Charlie said. 'And even some Yanks.'

'But there are Germans and Eyeties on the Nationalist side,' Nevil replied.

'The newspapers insist that's not true,' Charlie commented.

'Claud Cockburn, who writes for the *Daily Worker* and has recently been there, confirms it. According to him the Germans and Italians have supplied Franco and his mob with the very latest aeroplanes and pilots to fly them – not to mention the bombs.'

'Baldwin says that's nonsense. He says the Germans and Italians are following the same policy of strict non-intervention,' Norman Currie, another pal, chipped in.

'Baldwin's half a Fascist himself!' declared Tom Currie, Norman's brother, which produced a laugh all round.

'Baldwin might be following a policy of strict non-intervention, but according to Cockburn the Germans and Italians most certainly are not. They're liars to pretend they are,' Nevil said.

The conversation would have continued but they'd run out of time. Their looms were waiting.

*

138

Maggie was smiling broadly as she and Nevil left the factor's office. He'd just promised them a house early in the new year. They'd agreed to take the house sight unseen as they knew the street, and the factor had assured them the house was in excellent repair.

'So that's agreed, we've got what we were after,' Maggie said.

Nevil could see how pleased she was and he was delighted himself.

'I knew we'd land something nice if we kept badgering him,' Maggie said. They'd been visiting the factor's office every Saturday without fail.

'Well, you were right.'

'Maybe we should have asked to see the inside first? No! It was best to grab it while we could.'

Nevil nodded. 'It was the correct thing to do. Getting houses isn't easy in Glasgow nowadays. And Green's a fair factor, he won't cheat us. If he swears it's in excellent repair, then you can guarantee it will be.'

'I've got so many ideas for it!' Maggie declared, her voice bubbling with enthusiasm.

'Let's just hope we do well with the wedding presents,' Nevil muttered.

'You know we will. With the amount of friends and relatives you've got, and not forgetting Templeton's, we won't go short.' She thought of Susan Lennox with whom she kept in regular contact. Susan and her parents were sending a present, though so far hadn't said what it would be. In a roundabout way they had enquired about bedding, so she presumed it would be something along those lines.

'How about celebrating with tea and cakes?' she suggested. There was a lovely tearoom just along from the factor's office.

Nevil pulled a face. 'How about a drink instead? It is Saturday after all.'

'Tea and cakes,' she insisted. 'It's far too early for pubs.'

'Well, if there's an eclair on the plate it's mine,' he joked, having a fairly sweet tooth.

'That's a deal. As long as I can have the eccles cake.'

'It's a deal,' he smiled, echoing her. He would rather have had an eclair any day.

Outside the tearoom stood a newspaper vendor. 'Fresh fighting in Huesca and Zaragoza!' he proclaimed. 'Fresh fighting in Huesca and Zaragoza!'

Nevil bought a newspaper from him. Zaragoza was where Bob Kinloch was.

'A letter for you, son,' said Mrs Sanderson, laying the letter beside Nevil's plate. He was in the middle of breakfast.

Nevil picked up the letter and studied the fancy multicoloured stamp stuck to the envelope.

Opening it up he glanced at the signature on the last page. As he'd guessed, it was Bob's.

He began to read.

Maggie was aware that John was watching her. He appeared to be engrossed in a book, but she was certain that this was a pretence.

What were his thoughts? She hated to think. Recently, she'd felt exhausted. It was hard work at Templeton's, and when she came home there was always someone about, John being suggestive or the twins underfoot.

If only she had her own room as she'd had in Heymouth, but there was no such luxury here. She craved solitude, longed to be on her own. The only privacy she got here was when she went and locked herself in the lavatory, and even that she couldn't do for too long.

She glanced over to where Laura was mending some clothes, and as she did was certain she caught the flicker of John's eyes returning to the page he was supposedly reading.

'Auntie Maggie, will you play with us? Please?' Margaret begged.

'We want to play nurses. You can be matron,' Rose added.

God! This was the last thing she needed. She felt like screaming.

Calm down, Maggie told herself. The days and weeks

might be dragging, but the wedding and the proposed move were drawing near.

She forced a smile. 'Nurses eh? Do we have any patients?'

'Teddy has a sore tummy,' Margaret explained, waving Teddy at Maggie.

'And Golly is expecting a baby,' Rose said.

'But I thought Golly was a boy? Boys can't have babies,' Maggie replied.

'Oh!' Rose stared at Golly, then back at Maggie. 'He's also got a sore tummy same as Teddy.'

'You don't mind, do you?' Laura asked, looking up from her mending.

'Not at all. Delighted,' Maggie lied, getting out of her chair.

She would have adored to go to bed early, but knew that was impossible. John and Laura were great ones for staying up late, even when there was work the next day.

'Let's play over here, shall we?' she suggested, indicating a part of the kitchen that was difficult for John to see properly from where he was sitting.

A few minutes later John changed chairs.

As Maggie was playing with Margaret and Rose Mrs Sanderson was gazing anxiously at Nevil. 'Are you all right, son?' she asked eventually.

He blinked, sighed quietly, and then focused on his mother. 'Perfectly. Why?'

'There was such a strange, pained, expression on your face. I thought maybe you had bad wind. That can be excruciating.'

He laughed. 'No wind, Ma. I was just thinking.'

'It looked as if it was painful.'

'Maybe in a way it was,' he replied vaguely, and somewhat mysteriously.

He rose. 'I'm going out for a walk. Won't be long.'

'Aye. Suit yourself.'

He'd had some queer moods of late, Mrs Sanderson reflected. She hoped nothing was wrong between him and

Maggie. She was such a nice lass, and just right for him. Still, if something were wrong better it happened now than after they were wed.

There again, perhaps he was merely getting cold feet. That was understandable, and common enough. After all, marriage was a big step.

She smiled, remembering her own courting days.

Maggie woke up suddenly, fear clutching her insides. She half sat up, then with a gasp fell back onto her pillow. This had happened before, she reminded herself. It wasn't the morning of the flood, that was past history.

She wiped cold sweat from her brow, and breathed in deeply. How marvellous it was going to be when Nevil would be in bed with her every night. He'd be there to cuddle up to, a reassuring, loving presence that would . . .

Her thoughts froze as a floorboard creaked, and then creaked again. A shadow moved in the darkness, but there was no moon or starlight in the room thanks to the heavy window curtains.

'Who's there?' she whispered.

There was no answer.

'Who's there?' she demanded again, this time more loudly.

'Ssshhh! It's only me,' replied John's voice.

The fear returned. 'What are you doing in here?'

'I've got an awful thirst and wanted some more water. I've already drunk the glass I have by my bed so I've come through for a refill.'

This was a new departure, John had never returned to the kitchen once she'd gone to bed. 'Does Laura know you've come back through?'

'She's asleep.'

Maggie pulled the bedclothes right up to her chin. 'You'd better get the water then,' she said.

He filled his glass at the sink then padded back across the kitchen.

'Maggie?'

She'd known damn well he wasn't going to leave, that there was an ulterior motive. 'What?'

He came closer. 'I'd like to talk to you.'

'No!'

He came closer still. 'I think we should talk. Only for a little while, it won't take long.'

She shrank back in the bed. 'You've got your water, now goodnight, John,' she said as firmly as she could.

Another floorboard creaked. Funny, she thought, they never seemed to creak during the day.

Bending down he sat on the edge of her bed. The moment she felt his weight on the bed she quickly wriggled up against the wall. 'Lay one finger on me and I'll scream the place down,' she threatened. This was the first time ever she'd acknowledged that he fancied her.

'There's no need for that. I only want to talk,' he replied soothingly. But he had more in mind. How he longed to crawl in beside her and make love to her. Every last bit of him ached with desire.

He placed his glass on the floor and reached into the cavity. 'Maggie, can you feel my hand?'

'I'm giving you to the count of five and then I'll scream. So help me God. Then you'll have to sort this out with Laura.'

'Be reasonable, I only want to . . .'

'One!'

'Maggie, I . . .'

'Two!'

'You don't understand!'

'I understand only too well. Three!'

'Oh, for fuck's sake!' he swore angrily, losing his temper.

'Four and . . .'

'All right! I'm going.' He slid from the bed and straightened up.

'Goodnight, John.'

'Are you sleeping with him?'

'Who?' she prevaricated, knowing full well who he meant.

'Nevil of course! Who else?'

'That is none of your business.'

143

'I must know. I have to.'

Her brother-in-law was stark raving mad, she thought. 'I said it's none of your business!'

'You are then!'

'No, I'm not,' she lied.

'Yes, you are, I can tell.'

'John, get out of here. Now!'

'If only I could . . .'

'Now!'

'Maggie, I . . .'

'Five!' She opened her mouth, fully intending to scream as hard as she could.

But before she could, she heard him rush to the door which closed with a click behind him.

She collapsed. That had been simply horrendous. Not surprisingly, she realized she was shaking.

If only the kitchen door had a lock and key. Nor could she suggest to Laura that they have a lock put in. Laura would surely know why, and the last thing she wanted was to cause her sister any more humiliation or pain.

It took her ages to go back to sleep, and when she finally did it was fitful.

In the morning John refused to meet her eye.

'We're doing well, eh?' a slightly flushed Maggie said to Nevil, as she gazed about. She was in charge of the white elephant stall belonging to the jumble sale being held for the Spanish Republican Cause.

'Yes,' he agreed.

'So much stuff has been donated. Folk have been terribly generous. Why, I've taken pounds here all by myself, which is incredible, considering this isn't the wealthiest of communities.'

'Folk have been generous,' Nevil acknowledged softly.

Maggie spotted one of the girls from Templeton's and waved. 'What a turn out! Couldn't have been better,' she enthused.

'And yet . . .'

'And yet what?' she prompted.

144

'They need much more help than they're getting.' He paused, then said, 'They're losing, you know. The Nats are advancing again.'

She fully understood his concern, and shared it. 'We're doing all we can for them, Nevil.'

One eyebrow rose quizzically. 'Are we?'

She was about to reply when another customer came up and asked her the price of a pair of matching saucers, bearing the image of Queen Victoria.

Looking thoughtful, Nevil moved away. He'd promised to relieve Andy Ramsay at the second-hand book stall. He, Andy and several other lads from work had agreed to take turns at the stall.

'Bob Kinloch's been killed.'

The words, whispered to Nevil at his loom, were like a bucket of ice-cold water being thrown over him. He glanced sideways at Betty Yellowtrees, their cop winder. 'What?'

'Bob Kinloch's been killed. That's the message I was asked to give you by Charlie Menzies.'

'What's up?' asked Tom Currie who was working on Nevil's right.

'Bob Kinloch's been killed.'

'Christ!' Tom swiftly passed the message on to Bobby Farquharson.

'Are there any details?' Nevil asked Betty.

'Charlie says your friend died a hero.'

'Died a hero!' echoed Tom who was listening. 'Died a hero apparently,' he handed on to Bobby Farquharson.

'Kerly and Singleton!' Nevil hissed to Betty, having suddenly caught sight of these men walking towards them.

Betty immediately scooped up some empty cops and strode purposefully away.

Nevil continued 'beating up', but was doing it automatically, his mind miles from the job.

Bob dead! Killed in action, from the sound of it. He couldn't wait for teabreak to find out more.

*

'I heard it from Gavin Millar the engineer who works in the basement,' Charlie Menzies explained. 'I went to the lavatory and Gavin was in the next stall to me.'

'How did he find out Bob's been killed?' Nevil demanded.

Nearly two dozen of them were gathered round Charlie's loom. Although Bob hadn't worked at Templeton's he was well known to many who did.

'It seems he lives up the same close as the Kinlochs. Well, early this morning an ambulance had to be called for Mrs Kinloch who'd collapsed and had to be taken off to the hospital. They'd received a letter from Bob's commanding officer, an Irishman would you believe, in the first post informing them of Bob's death and giving them the details.'

'What about his father?' Andy Ramsay asked.

'He's in a state of shock, but that's only to be expected. He went to the hospital with Mrs Kinloch.'

'And what are the details?' Norman Currie demanded, as anxious as the rest of them to know.

'Part of his group had been captured by the Fascists who proceeded to torture them for amusement. The remainder of Bob's group could hear the screams of their fellow men but, because they were hopelessly outnumbered, were unable to do anything. Bob apparently decided otherwise. Holding a Lewis gun at his hip, single-handedly he attacked the Fascists, setting such an extraordinary example that those whom he'd left behind were inspired to follow. Miraculously the superior force fled and many of those who'd been tortured were saved. Bob survived his mad attack, but was severely wounded. He died several days later.'

Silence settled over the band as Charlie finished his tale. It was finally broken by the quiet muttering of Maurice Cairns, who was a Catholic, saying a prayer.

'Single-handed with a Lewis gun at his hip!' said Norman Currie, his voice filled with awe.

'And him normally such a quiet, sane chap,' commented Tom, Norman's brother.

'He was a good lad, none better,' said Andy Ramsay, and agreement ran round the group.

Maurice Cairns, whose brow had been furrowed in thought, now announced, 'I've been considering it for a while, and somehow this settles it for me. I'm going over there as well.'

'What about your job, Mo?' Tom Currie demanded.

'To hell with the job. This is far more important – at least to me it is. Anyone else feel the same? Will anyone else come with me?'

Nevil found all eyes focused on him. It was as if everyone present was suddenly holding his breath.

'Maggie!'

She turned to find Nevil running after her. She'd looked for him at the end of the day, but hadn't seen him, so she'd decided to go on with Natasha and Ida Hope. She and Nevil didn't always leave together.

'I have to talk to you,' he stated on joining her.

'A wee lovers' chat is it?' joked Natasha in broad tones, nudging Ida in the ribs.

'Has to be!' Ida agreed. 'Don't you think they make a lovely pair together, Natasha?'

'Oh luvvvvelly!'

Maggie laughed. Natasha was a born comedienne.

'Quit the hilarity,' Nevil said in a no-nonsense tone.

'I don't think he's amused,' Ida said to Natasha.

'I don't think so either. Are you not amused then, son?'

Nevil grasped Maggie by the arm. 'We'll see you girls later. Goodbye now!' And with that he pulled Maggie across the road.

'There was no need to be rude. They were only teasing,' Maggie admonished.

'I'm sorry. But I'm just not in the mood for that sort of thing.'

'Obviously.'

She studied him for several seconds, then said, 'Is there something wrong, Nevil?'

'Whether it's wrong or not depends on your point of view. I'll explain it in Conti's Café. We'll stop there for a coffee.'

147

Maggie frowned. 'But that will make me late for tea which Laura will have prepared.'

'It'll just have to wait, I'm afraid.'

They walked on in silence, then she said, 'I've heard about Bob Kinloch. His parents must be devastated.'

'His ma collapsed and was taken to hospital. His da, in a state of shock, went with her.'

'Poor woman,' Maggie commiserated, shaking her head.

Nevil shot her a sideways glance. He felt curiously elated, and rotten at the same time. It was a strange mixture of emotions.

At Conti's Café he sat her at a corner table and ordered some coffee.

'Now what's this all about?' she asked.

When he didn't reply immediately, she smiled and said, 'Not having second thoughts about getting married, are we?'

'Maggie, I love you. You know that, don't you?' he said heavily.

'Of course I do! I wouldn't be marrying you if you didn't.'

He took a deep breath. 'There's no easy way to do this. Myself and a number of the lads from work are going to Spain to fight for the Republicans.'

Her smile faded, while her stomach felt as though it had just dropped through the floor. 'I see,' she murmured.

'I have to, Maggie. I feel so strongly about the whole thing. Fascism stands for everything I hate in this world and I must do my bit to oppose it. If I don't go, I know I'll regret it for the rest of my life.'

She fought to keep the tears out of her eyes. 'And what about us?'

'We'll get married the minute I get back. I promise.'

If you get back, she thought. Bob Kinloch had gone and he wasn't coming back. He was dead and buried. The same Bob who'd got her a glass of punch at the Christmas dance.

'I suppose I should have seen this coming. All the signals have been there,' she said.

'Maggie, I must stand up and be counted.'

Reaching out she took his hand and squeezed it. Her whole

world, all her dreams, had just collapsed around her. 'Who's going with you?' she whispered.

'About fifteen of us. We agreed to keep it quiet for the rest of the working day. I insisted on that because I wanted to tell you myself. We'll tell Templeton's tomorrow.'

'What do you intend giving them, a fortnight's notice?'

'Yes. But we will work longer than that, if they wish, until our passports come through. We're not sure how long it will take, none of us have ever applied for a passport before.'

She thought of Kerly and the other supervisors. 'Templeton's are going to have a fit! Fifteen trained setting loom weavers leaving at the same time. They'll never replace that number in a fortnight, or whatever.'

'We appreciate that, but feel if we are going to go then we should leave as soon as possible.'

She spooned a little sugar into her coffee, and stirred it. 'What about our house?' she asked softly.

'We're going to have to tell Green we won't be needing it for now. Unless you want to rent it on your own until I get back?'

She shook her head. 'I don't earn enough for that.'

This time he reached out and took her hand. 'I feel I'm letting you down dreadfully . . .'

'You are!' she interjected, and instantly regretted saying it. She was going to cry, she thought. She couldn't suppress the tears much longer.

'I'm sorry – truly I am,' he whispered.

'But only a little.'

'I'm sorry I'm hurting you. But I honestly believe that the Republican cause is bigger than you and I. What if the Nats do win in Spain, and the tide sweeps on to Britain and Mosley somehow comes to power? Would you want your children, our children, brought up in a Fascist state? I know I certainly wouldn't. Now's the time to stop this evil before it spreads further. Or at least to—' He broke off, realizing what he'd been about to say.

'Or at least to die trying as Bob Kinloch has done?' she finished for him.

149

'Leaving you is the hardest thing I've ever done in my life. I want you to know that.'

She believed him, she could see it in his face.

'And letting you go without falling on my knees and pleading for you to change your mind and stay is going to be the hardest thing in mine. Even after all I've been through.'

He hung his head. 'I have to go, Maggie.'

She managed a weak smile. 'I know that, Nevil. And as I have just said I won't try and stop you – though your going will break my heart.'

'You're a woman in a million, Maggie. That's why I love you.'

She hadn't touched her coffee, but didn't want it any more. The only thing she wanted was to get outside.

'Let's go,' she said, rising.

He didn't argue, but followed her to the door. Outside he put his hand in hers, and they walked along side-by-side, tears trickling down Maggie's face.

John and Laura were just finishing their tea when Maggie arrived home. She felt completely numb and utterly drained.

'You're late. What happened?' said Laura as Maggie wandered into the kitchen.

'Great fish that!' exclaimed John, pushing his plate away.

'Yours is in the oven,' a now frowning Laura informed Maggie.

'I know it's a waste but I couldn't eat a thing,' Maggie stuttered in a cracked voice.

Laura rose and went to her sister, her expression one of concern. 'What is it? What's wrong?'

She didn't really want to talk about it, but realized it was unavoidable. 'It's Nevil, he and some of his mates at Templeton's have decided to go off and fight in Spain,' she said.

John's eyes opened wide with delight, then swiftly contracted again as he disguised his reaction to Maggie's news.

'Oh Maggie!' Laura whispered.

'They're going just as soon as their passports come through, however long that will be.'

'I don't suppose he'll change his mind before then?'

Maggie shook her head. 'Not a hope! Nor will I try and change it – I've promised him that.'

'Come and sit down,' instructed Laura, and led her to a fireside chair.

'I have a half-bottle in. Would you like a dram?' John asked.

Maggie shook her head.

'You look like you could use one,' he went on.

'No, thank you. I think I'd be sick if I had a drink.'

Margaret and Rose came bursting into the kitchen having been playing in the other room.

'Auntie Maggie! Auntie Maggie!' they cried in unison, running towards her.

Laura warded them off. 'Not now, girls. Auntie Maggie isn't feeling very well.'

Margaret pouted. 'Has she got a sore tummy?'

'Something like that. I want the pair of you just to go back into the other room and leave her alone.'

'But we want to be in here!' Rose protested.

'It's fine,' said Maggie, staring into the empty fireplace, seeing Nevil there.

And while she stared into the empty fireplace John stared at her.

With a gasp Nevil collapsed on top of Maggie. 'Oh that was wonderful! The best ever,' he said.

They were in Maggie's cavity bed, the twins were asleep and John and Laura out at a party. They were bound to be there for several hours yet.

'You're too heavy for me,' she whispered.

With an apology he pushed himself off and onto his side so that he was lying facing her. 'You're sweating like billy-o,' he said, running a finger along her damp skin.

'Thank you very much. How romantic of you!'

'I didn't mean it like that!'

'I know.' She paused, then grinned. 'As a matter of fact you're sweating like billy-o yourself.'

Leaning over he kissed the nipple nearest to him, then gently licked it with the tip of his tongue.

Maggie closed her eyes. 'Hmmh!' she murmured.

'Like a big ice-cream with raspberry on top.'

'You're determined to be romantic tonight, aren't you!'

'Well, it is like a big ice-cream with raspberry on top. And I *love* ice-cream.'

She laughed softly. 'Idiot!'

'Ice-cream and . . .' He lowered his voice, 'honey.'

'Don't be disgusting!' she retorted, realizing what he meant.

'It's not disgusting!'

'Yes it is!'

'Not!'

'Is!'

She squealed as his hand delved between her legs to find her. 'Not!'

'Don't do that!'

'What? This?'

'That!'

'Don't you like it?'

'You know I do.'

'Then why should I stop?'

'Because . . .'

'Because what?'

Her mood changed as quickly as if a switch had been thrown. One moment it was frivolous, the next all raw emotion. She threw her arms round him, crushing him against her body.

'I just can't bear the thought of you leaving me,' she whispered in a distraught tone.

He removed his hand from where it had been and placed it on her naked thigh, which he then began to slowly caress. This could be the last time they ever made love together, he thought, which was precisely what she was thinking. It was unlikely that they would find another opportunity before he left.

'Oh Nevil!' It was now that she came closest to breaking her

152

promise and begging him to change his mind and stay. It was only with supreme willpower that she stopped herself and kept her promise.

Their mood for the rest of the evening remained sombre, but extremely loving and tender.

She'd thought long and hard about what to give him as a going-away present, and had decided on a good pair of gloves. The weather could be bitter in Spain during late autumn and winter, she'd found out, so a pair of gloves would be both practical and useful.

Daly's was her favourite department store in Glasgow and one she adored browsing through even when she didn't intend buying anything. However that day she went straight to the glove counter.

'Can I help you?' the assistant, a woman in her fifties called Mrs Grierson, enquired.

'I'm looking for a pair of men's gloves.'

'Size?'

'I'm afraid I don't know. But I'm sure I'll be able to pick out a pair that fits.'

'Wool? Leather?'

'Whichever is the warmest,' Maggie said.

'You appreciate there is quite a difference in price?'

'The price doesn't matter. Just as long as they're warm.'

'Then I'd recommend fleecy-lined kid.'

'Fine,' Maggie nodded. 'Would you mind showing me a selection of those.'

Less than a week to go, Maggie thought. How the time had flown. The days had just zipped past. But then wasn't that always the way! When you wanted time to go slowly it went quickly, and when you wanted it to go quickly it did the reverse.

Less than a week! Five and a half days to be precise. Five and a half days and then . . . She fought against the anxiety which suddenly rose within her.

'Now what about these,' smiled Mrs Grierson, placing half a dozen pairs of gloves in front of Maggie.

Maggie picked up a pair and slipped on the right one. 'This would be the size, I think.'

'Can I just . . .?'

Maggie gave the gloves to Mrs Grierson who peered in one of them to establish the size. 'Right!' She whisked the other gloves away and returned with another selection, this new lot all the same size.

Maggie picked up a light grey pair that had caught her eye. They were gorgeously soft, not like leather at all.

'Those are three pounds two and six, I'm afraid,' stated Mrs Grierson.

'As I said, the price is irrelevant. They're for my fiancé. He's going off to fight in Spain.'

Mrs Grierson's smile disappeared, then returned, but now seemed strained. 'I see,' she muttered.

'I want to give him some gloves because it can get bitterly cold there, so I'm told.'

Mrs Grierson nodded.

Maggie examined the light grey pair of gloves, noting the neat stitching and how well made they were overall. These would do, she wouldn't find a better pair.

As Maggie was examining the gloves Mrs Grierson's mind had flown back twenty years to recall her beloved George who'd died in the Battle of Albert as part of Haig's Third Army. She remembered the fear and anxiety she'd felt just before George had gone away. No doubt this young lassie was going through precisely that experience right now. Her heart went out to her.

'I'll take these please,' Maggie said.

Mrs Grierson wrapped the gloves, wishing she could give them to her, but that was impossible.

'And if they don't fit bring them back and we'll be happy to change them.'

'Thank you,' said Maggie, accepting the parcel Mrs Grierson handed her.

Before relinquishing the parcel Mrs Grierson said in a voice ringing with sincerity, 'All the very best of luck to your fiancé. I hope everything goes well for him.'

Maggie could see this was more than politeness or good service. 'Thank you again,' she said quietly in reply.

Mrs Grierson watched Maggie walk away, the strains of Tipperary running through her head.

It had been a happy day up until that point, but now it was quite spoiled.

Maggie heard the arguing from the half-flight landing down, Mrs Sanderson's voice fraught with anxiety. She chewed her lip as she climbed the remaining stairs to Nevil's door.

Mrs Sanderson's voice was reminiscent of an animal in pain. Then Maggie heard the bass of her husband, his soothing, placatory tones trying to calm her hysteria.

Should she knock or go away and come back again? Maggie wondered. If she did go away it might be just as bad when she returned and Nevil was expecting her. She knocked.

Mrs Sanderson answered her. Her cheeks were tear-stained, her colour a whitey-green. She looked dreadful, a woman at the end of her tether.

'I'm trying one last time to talk some sense into him. You come away through and see what you can do,' Mrs Sanderson said, grasping Maggie's arm and almost dragging her inside.

She'd told Mrs Sanderson repeatedly that she wouldn't interfere. Nevil must do what he wanted. Nor did she break her promise now though Mrs Sanderson continually tried to provoke her.

The worst moment was when Mr Sanderson suddenly broke down and started to weep.

Muttering he couldn't stand any more of this Nevil bundled Maggie out of the house, and together they fled down the stairs.

'God almighty!' was Nevil's only comment as they marched swiftly along the street. Maggie had occasionally to break into a run in order to keep up.

The alarm clock was ticking away remorselessly. Maggie lay gloomily listening to it.

The day of Nevil's departure for Spain had arrived. If she'd slept the night before she wasn't aware of it. It seemed to her she'd lain there all night listening to that clock ticking the hours away.

She wouldn't be going to the station. Nevil and the others had decided they didn't want a tearful farewell, so they'd be leaving without anyone there to wave them off.

She and Nevil had said their goodbyes in the back close where she'd clung to him, and they had sworn undying love.

The actual moment of parting had been so horrible Maggie thought she might pass out from the intensity of the pain. She'd wanted to run after him and kiss him yet again. But she'd restrained herself.

Instead she'd forced herself upstairs and into bed, where she'd curled up consumed with the grief of their parting.

God, please keep him safe, she'd whispered a thousand times throughout the night. And alternatively, please bring him back to me whole and sound.

Like a knell of doom the alarm finally went off. Another working day had begun, but a working day with a difference. Today there would be no Nevil. And no Nevil for an indefinite length of time to come, if indeed there would ever be a Nevil again.

From where she stood at her weft loom she had a clear view of a large wall clock. It was five to ten, Nevil's train was scheduled to depart on the hour.

Her hands were shaking so badly she could hardly operate the loom, and she was constantly making mistakes which she was having to correct.

He'd be on the train by now, she thought. What would their mood be? Were they laughing and joking, or sombre? Knowing that lot probably laughing and joking as if they were off on holiday rather than to some place where they could be maimed or killed.

Was Nevil thinking about her? She was certain he must be . . .

She yelped in pain as she nicked her hand. Luckily the skin hadn't been broken.

Three minutes to go now!

She took a deep breath, and tried to steady her hands. But they wouldn't stop shaking. It was as if they had a life of their own.

'Miss Jordan?'

When he got no reply Kerly spoke again, 'Miss Jordan?'

She heard him then and turned to face him. She was unaware that her eyes were glistening.

Kerly looked at the cloth she was weaving, then back at her. While he was doing this she'd hidden her hands behind her, but he'd noted earlier they were shaking.

'The lads leave this morning, I understand,' Kerly said mildly.

She nodded.

'What time?'

'Ten.'

They both glanced at the wall clock. One minute to go.

She tried to move her eyes away from the clock, but couldn't. They were glued to it. She watched the big hand tremble then, swift as a darting snake, click onto the hour.

Ten o'clock! In her mind she could visualize the guard blowing his whistle and waving his flag, the train shuddering and . . .

'Miss Jordan?'

She swallowed, and swallowed again.

'Maggie,' Kerly said in a soft yet commanding voice. It was the first time he'd ever called her that.

The train would be moving out the station now, gathering speed as it . . .

'Maggie!'

She wrenched her attention away from the mesmerizing clock, and onto the supervisor. 'Sorry, Mr Kerly,' she whispered.

'You're no use to me the way you are, girl. Take a half-hour's break and pull yourself together. No, make that an hour.'

That was kind of him, she thought. He was an absolute gem. 'Can I leave the factory?' she asked.

'If you like.'

'Thank you, Mr Kerly.' If they hadn't been where they were she would have pecked him on the forehead.

As he moved away her gaze strayed back to the clock. Five past ten now. The train would be over the Clyde and . . .

Abruptly, she left her loom and the clock. She stared at the floor as she walked, her heart thumping inside her.

In the lavatory she bumped into Mary Mauchline.

'Jesus! You look . . .' Mary trailed off, having just remembered what day it was. 'Sorry,' she mumbled.

'That's all right.'

'Is there anything I can do to help? How about a ciggy?'

'I don't smoke.'

'Oh, neither you do!'

Maggie suddenly felt faint. She steadied herself against a cubicle wall.

'I should go, but do you want me to stay with you?'

Maggie shook her head. 'I'd actually prefer to be on my own if you don't mind.'

Staring at Maggie, Mary was glad her romance with Andy Ramsay had only been a brief affair. Christ, men could be so bloody selfish! Hell mend the lot of them.

When Mary had gone Maggie stumbled over to a sink where she dipped her hanky in cold water, and then pressed it to her face and neck. It made her feel a little better. As she left the factory she picked up her coat and walked into Tullis Street.

It wasn't cold, but she was. She pulled her collar up around her ears and began walking aimlessly away from Templeton's.

She considered going on to Glasgow Green, and decided against it. It brought back too many memories.

The church was a small one, and out of the way. Maggie noted with surprise that its doors were open, unusual for Glasgow. She went inside.

She almost sighed with relief at the calmness that greeted her. Peace, quiet and a feeling of holiness was just what she needed. She sat in a pew near the front.

She'd lost faith in God after the flood, but that had only been temporary. She was still confused as to why God acted as he did, but she just had to believe there was some reason for it all.

Closing her eyes she began to pray and gradually a sense of peace crept over her.

Laura rushed into the kitchen with the morning mail. 'The one you've been waiting for!' she announced excitedly, thrusting a letter into Maggie's eager hands.

Maggie stared at the envelope. Nevil had been gone for two and a half weeks now, and she'd been desperate for news. This was her first letter.

'Excuse me,' she said, and went to sit by the fire. There she opened the letter and started to read.

The journey had been a fairly uneventful one, the only real drama was that Charlie Menzies had been terribly sick on the boat going over. Once they reached Spain they'd travelled to Madrid where they'd soon joined up.

They were currently in the middle of training which they were enjoying. It was a far less disciplined business than it would have been in the British army. They were finding Spanish food, on the whole, utterly revolting.

The Francisco Rodriguez Street Barracks where they were stationed was large, ugly, draughty and at one time had been the church and monastery school of the Salesians. (Who were the Salesians? Maggie wondered. She'd have to look them up.)

Madrid was bombed daily by Fascist planes, one of which had been shot out of the sky the previous day.

He was well, feeling as fit as a fiddle. And guess what? He'd met up with Claud Cockburn who was back in Spain.

Cockburn had been delighted to meet him and the others and had chatted with them for some considerable time. Cockburn was in Madrid en route for Catalonia where fierce fighting was currently taking place . . .

'Well?' Laura demanded anxiously when Maggie had finished the letter.

'They're all fine and obviously having quite an adventure,' Maggie replied.

She related some of the letter's contents to her sister and brother-in-law, then began reading it all over again.

She read it a dozen times and more during the course of the day.

Maggie was making her way back to her loom, having just spent the teabreak with Natasha, Moira Law and Bunty Abercrombie, when she was hailed by Mr Fairley from management.

'So how's Sanderson doing?' he demanded on reaching her side.

'Very well, thank you.'

'Has he seen any fighting yet?'

'He's been involved in a number of actions. All the lads have, and luckily they've been kept together.'

A look of irritation crossed Fairley's face. 'It was damned inconvenient the way they went off like that. They could have been more thoughtful.'

A sharp retort was on the edge of her tongue which she bit back. 'I suppose it must have seemed like that from the management point of view,' she answered instead.

'We certainly weren't pleased when we learned what they intended. Far from it!'

'They gave you fair notice, Mr Fairley. You've no complaints.'

'But fifteen of them at once! You can imagine what that did to production.'

And profits, she thought.

'At least they're all safe and well,' he said, which redeemed him a little in Maggie's eyes. She still suspected, however, that he cared more about Templeton's than he did about the lads who'd gone to fight.

Typical boss, she thought. She couldn't see him going off to fight for democracy. She could only envisage him fighting for his position, and another step up the ladder.

Nevil was in a different class altogether. Nevil might only

be a weaver and Mr Fairley high up in management but as far as she was concerned Nevil was the better man and human being, by a long chalk.

That evening when she got home, Maggie felt the atmosphere as soon as she walked into the kitchen. John was huddled behind his newspaper, and Laura busy at the stove. Neither glanced at her as they normally did. They've been fighting again, she guessed, wrongly.

'Any mail?' she asked. It was the first thing she asked every evening as she walked in.

'On the mantelpiece,' Laura answered, still without looking at her.

'Where are the girls?'

'Over at Jean Moon's for tea.' Jean lived several closes along and had a little girl the same age as Margaret and Rose.

Maggie went to the mantelpiece where the letter stood propped against the wall. Picking it up, she glanced at it.

It wasn't Nevil's handwriting! The letter was from Spain, but it wasn't Nevil's handwriting on the front! The writing was completely different.

That explained the tension and why the twins were at Jean Moon's. Laura had engineered it.

'Do you want us to leave the room?' Laura asked quietly.

'No,' Maggie answered in a voice she barely recognized.

She made a right hash of tearing open the envelope, ripping it almost in half. Inside were three sheets of paper. She had to force herself to look at whose signature was on the last page. It was Andy Ramsay's.

'Dear Maggie', the letter began.

'Oh!' she exclaimed at one point as she read, staggering on the spot. Then, 'Thank God!'

When she'd finished the letter she dropped the hand holding it and heaved a sigh of relief.

'He's been wounded, but not too seriously,' she said.

Laura slumped with relief. 'Wounded where?'

'In the shoulder. The bullet lodged there and had to be removed. Andy Ramsay says the operation was completely successful and Nevil is now on the road to recovery.'

John was staring at Maggie over the top of his newspaper. 'Is he coming home?'

'No. Andy mentions nothing about that.'

John grunted, secretly pleased.

'We thought . . . feared . . . well, you can imagine!' Laura said.

'Andy has asked me to go and tell the Sandersons personally. Nevil has asked me to do it.'

Directly after her tea she left for the Sandersons and luckily all three of them were in.

When Jimmy said he'd like to go and fight in Spain his mother slapped him so hard she knocked him to the floor.

'Right, we're away then!' Laura declared. It was a Saturday afternoon and she was taking the twins into town to buy them some new clothes. John was off to watch Rangers play Hibs.

'Have a good time then, all of you!' Maggie replied.

'She always has a good time when she's spending money,' John grumbled, which made Laura laugh. It was true – she adored shopping.

When the McNairs were gone Maggie closed her eyes, and sighed. Sheer bliss! She'd have the house to herself for the next couple of hours at least.

She put some more coal on to the fire, for it was a chilly day, and then decided to wash her hair and have a wash.

Once a week, she went to the local public baths. She and Laura often went together while John looked after Margaret and Rose. She never failed to enjoy her wash at the baths, there was always lashings of piping hot water.

She and Laura were due to go to the baths again on Monday night, so a top wash would suffice till then. Humming a tune she'd heard earlier on the wireless, she stripped to the waist.

She filled the enamel basin in the sink, and washed her top first. Then she slopped out that water, and refilling the basin, started to wash her hair. She was on her second rinse when she happened to glance into John's shaving mirror standing against the window, and there he was staring back at her, the strangest of expressions on his face.

With a gasp she grabbed for the towel, desperately trying to cover herself up.

Turning, she demanded, 'What are you doing here? I never heard you come back.'

'I forgot my wallet,' he replied in a tight, strained voice.

She was horribly aware that she was naked from the waist up. 'How long have you been standing there?'

He smiled thinly. 'Long enough to get a good look. You're bigger and fuller than I imagined.'

She swallowed. 'Please go, John. I was only washing myself because I thought you were out.'

'It wasn't contrived on my part. I didn't mean to leave my wallet behind. Honest!'

'I believe you. Now please go!'

His gaze dropped to where her breasts bulged beneath the towel. 'You're beautiful, Maggie. An absolute knock out.'

Panic rose inside her. 'Will you please go!'

Instead he did the opposite, and walked very slowly towards her.

'John, please!' She flattened herself against the sink.

He stopped in front of her, his expression now pleading. 'You must know how I feel about you, Maggie.'

'Stop it!' she commanded. 'Don't be stupid.'

'Being in the same house as you is driving me out of my mind. There are times when I feel I'm literally going crazy.'

'Stop being so ridiculous. You're my brother-in-law. You're married to my sister.'

'I don't care for Laura any more. You're the only one I want, who I want to spend the rest of my life with.'

She would have dashed for the door, but knew she'd never get round him. 'I don't feel anything for you that way, John, nor have I ever given you the slightest indication that I do. I love Nevil.'

'Nevil!' John spat. 'Your precious Nevil loves you so much he's deserted you to go off and fight in some daft foreign war.'

'It's important to him. It's—' She stopped in mid-sentence as John's hand reached for her. 'No!'

His hand rested on her bare shoulder and, gently, tenderly,

caressed it. 'God, how I want you,' he whispered.

She brushed his hand off. 'Leave me alone.'

His hand returned. 'I've touched you a thousand times like this in my dreams.'

She tried to brush his hand away again, but he dug his fingers into her, preventing her from doing so.

'You're hurting me!' she hissed.

'That's the last thing I want to do, Maggie.' John's hand twisted to clasp her neck.

She resisted as he tried to pull her to him. His eyes, glittering with desire, were fastened on to hers.

His other hand came up to grasp the top of her towel which she was hanging on to for dear life. She was frightened, filled with repugnance for him, and bloody angry.

'Maggie!' he groaned and, despite her efforts, pulled the towel away exposing her breasts.

She let go of the towel and covered her breasts with her hands. She attempted to dodge him, knowing it was useless but trying anyway. He stopped her. His arms went round her and he squashed her to him, his mouth falling greedily on hers. She writhed in his grip, refusing to open her mouth to his probing tongue. She brought her knee up forcefully but, realizing her intention, he swivelled his crotch out of the way so that her knee merely thumped into his leg.

The delicious smell of her was making his head reel, a smell he could quite happily have drowned in. This was the closest he'd ever been to it.

He left her mouth to kiss her cheek, again and again, and then her neck.

She hit him on the shoulder as hard as she could, but he was so carried away he never even felt the blow. His mouth darted down to fasten on to a breast.

He groaned with pleasure. Then he had her breast in his hand, squeezing it as he kissed her nipple.

He was past reason, she thought, grabbing his hair and desperately pulling at it. She tore away a chunk which caused blood to spurt out.

He groaned again as he buried his face between her breasts.

Then he dropped one of his hands to catch hold of the bottom of her skirt.

The same hand was wriggling inside her knickers when she suddenly spotted the milk jug on the far side of the sink. She stretched, but couldn't quite reach it. Then he shifted position as he fumbled with his flies.

He was pulling himself out of his trousers when she brought the heavy stone jug down on his head with a resounding thud.

He wasn't knocked out, but totally stunned. He exhaled loudly as he fell sideways to land on his knees.

Maggie seized her opportunity, scuttling past him to snatch up the sweater she'd taken off earlier. Throwing it on in the hall, she whipped her coat from the peg where it was hanging. Out the front door she flew and clattered down the stairs.

At the close-mouth, panting for breath, she paused to slip on her coat and cover her soaking hair with a scarf that had been in her coat pocket.

She decided where she would go as she walked smartly up the street.

'Tried to rape you!' Natasha exclaimed, her cross eyes popping.

Maggie nodded. 'It was horrible.'

'Jesus Christ!'

Maggie then told Natasha about John's obsession with her, and how it had been going on for months. It was the first time she'd ever confided in anyone.

'And he actually came to your bed one night?'

'Pretending he wanted some water from the kitchen tap. The tension has been building up for ages. I thought it would naturally defuse when Nevil and I married and moved into our own house, but now Nevil has gone to Spain and the house has fallen through.'

'So what are you going to do?' Natasha queried.

'One thing I'm not doing is going back there. I couldn't after what has happened.'

Natasha glanced about the room she shared with her sisters. 'You can stay here for a short while if you like. I'm sure Ma and Da won't mind, not when I explain the circumstances to them. But it can only be for a short while, I'm afraid, as you can see how cramped we are.'

A short while with Natasha and family, then what? Digs, she supposed. Digs with full board. She didn't know of any, but surely if she . . .

The idea came to her in a blinding flash. It was so obvious, she thought, smiling. There and then she made up her mind that's what she'd do. She had enough money after all, what with the savings she'd put by for the wedding, so money wasn't a problem.

'Spain!' Natasha squealed when Maggie told her.

'Spain,' Maggie confirmed. 'Just as soon as I can get a passport.'

They both were silent for a few moments, then Maggie said, 'In the meantime I have to get my clothes and belongings from my sister's.'

'Do you want me to come with you?'

'That would be a help, Natasha. I doubt I'll have to tell Laura why I'm leaving. She'll guess.'

Natasha had a sudden thought. 'I just hope you didn't kill that brother-in-law of yours.'

Maggie smiled. 'I'm sure I've given him a headache, but I certainly didn't kill him.'

'Served him right if you had,' Natasha muttered, thinking she wouldn't put up any resistance if anyone ever tried to rape her. Resist would be the last thing she'd do.

Maggie was right, Laura did guess. Maggie didn't give any explanation for moving out, she didn't have to, and for most of the time she and Natasha were there John hid in the lavatory.

She never mentioned Spain, or what her plans were. When she came to say goodbye she had the distinct feeling that Laura was relieved to see her go, which was wholly understandable.

PART TWO

On the Arid Square

*'On that arid square, that fragment nipped off
   from hot
Africa, soldered so crudely by inventive Europe;
On that tableland scored by rivers . . .'*

W. H. Auden

CHAPTER FIVE

Noisy, Maggie thought. That was her first impression of the Spanish. Noise that was usually accompanied with violent gesticulations, hands and arms flapping like an out-of-control windmill.

She yawned, desperately tired. It was nearly forty-eight hours since she'd disembarked at the port of Corunna where she'd caught a train for Madrid. The subsequent journey was proving interminable.

Her trip from Southampton had been fairly nasty, the weather bad and the sea foul. She hadn't actually been sick, but had been delighted to leave the ship for dry land. Her companion, Evelyn Loup from London, had vomited, not just once but a number of times. Evelyn's face had been a pale shade of green throughout the crossing, and had taken almost a full day to resume a more normal colour.

She'd been lucky to fall in with Evelyn, as she spoke fluent Spanish, and was on a mission similar to her own. Evelyn's husband Harry was a militiaman fighting on the front around Siguenza. Harry had joined the Republicans a fortnight before Nevil.

The train shuddered to yet another stop. 'What now?' Maggie muttered.

Evelyn peered out of the filthy window she was sitting beside. 'Someone with a flock of sheep,' she reported.

'You mean they're blocking the track?'

'No, they seem to be coming on board.'

A few seconds later, accompanied by much laughter, a sheep scampered down the corridor.

Maggie had to smile. Spanish trains, at least during the war, were quite incredible. She had no doubt now that the sheep would be allowed to mingle with the passengers. Who would have believed it! But it was true.

Not that the oncoming sheep would be the only animals on board. A number of passengers travelled with live chickens, some trussed, others in cages, while one had a large sack that continually looped and writhed all over the floor. It contained several dozen rabbits, they'd been told.

More sheep followed the first. Then one appeared which stopped directly outside their carriage door and relieved itself.

'Charming!' Maggie commented.

A deep male voice in a carriage further back began to sing a revolutionary song. It raised a cheer, after which others joined in.

A man in their carriage produced a goat-skin wine bottle and squirted a long stream of red wine into his mouth. A friend of his facing him requested some and, instead of passing the goat-skin over, the man simply took aim and squirted a jet into his friend's open mouth across the distance separating them.

Maggie marvelled at this trick, the first time she'd ever seen it done. The man caught her staring at him and, smiling, rapped out a question.

'He'd like to know if you'd care for some wine?' Evelyn translated.

Maggie was parched, and hungry. They had brought provisions onto the train with them, but they had now run out, the journey proving far longer than anticipated.

'Please,' she replied. 'But tell him I'll have the bottle over here if he doesn't mind.'

The man asked another question when Evelyn returned the bottle to him. She nodded, and instantly the man dived into his pack to produce a long reddish-coloured sausage. He gave this to Evelyn with a sizeable chunk of coarse bread and two onions.

'*Gracias*,' said Maggie which won her a beam of approval. Her fellow travellers already appreciated that she didn't speak Spanish.

With a jolt the train moved off once more. It started slowly, and gradually gathered speed.

170

'How long till Madrid, do you think?' Maggie asked as she ate the bread and sausage.

'God alone knows.'

'What do you think of the sausage?' Evelyn asked.

Maggie considered that before replying. 'I would describe it as similar to chewing pulped paper, only in this case greasy pulped paper.' She kept a straight face as she said this, not wanting to upset the Spaniard who'd given it to them and who was watching them closely.

Evelyn's eyes twinkled. 'That's it to a T. But at least it's filling. What about the onions?'

The last thing Maggie wanted to do was munch on a raw onion. 'Save them for later?' she answered.

Evelyn understood perfectly. 'Save them for later,' she agreed.

A drunken militiaman paused in the corridor to glance into their carriage. He delivered a small speech and jabbed his carbine in the air. Then he lurched on his way.

'He said, "Long live the glorious revolution!"' Evelyn translated to Maggie before Maggie could ask.

Evelyn bent down to rummage in the bag she had under her seat, an action that saved her life. Glass tinkled, and suddenly there was a hole in the window in line with where her head had been. Then the entire pane of glass shattered inwards.

Everyone looked at everyone else, none of them yet realizing what had caused the glass to shatter. Then simultaneously they all heard the crackle of automatic gunfire sounding just like a string of firecrackers going off.

Another bullet shot into the carriage, this one lodging in a strip of wood, causing splinters to fly. The man who'd given Maggie and Evelyn the wine cursed as one of the splinters sliced open his cheek.

Evelyn was staring at the broken window in disbelief, as it slowly dawned on her how close a call she'd just had.

'I believe we're under attack,' Maggie croaked to Evelyn.

Pandemonium now reigned in the train. Windows were being thrown open, others smashed as the Republican militiamen aboard returned fire.

Maggie grabbed Evelyn and pulled her down on to the floor, which she calculated was the safest place. It dawned on her that the train had slowed right down. Why had the driver done that? Had the engine been taken over by their attackers?

A grinning black face suddenly appeared in what remained of Evelyn's window. A woman at the other end of the carriage screamed in terror when she saw it.

The black face, teeth shining like polished ivory, roared with laughter. Then a rifle barrel slid through the window.

The friend of the man with the goat-skin wine bottle leapt at the rifle barrel, grabbed it and pointed it harmlessly into the seat. In the ensuing struggle the rifle was fired filling the carriage with the reek of cordite.

Another male passenger joined in the fray. Brandishing a fearsome knife he slashed repeatedly at the black rebel who, with a cry of pain, fell away. Goat-skin wine bottle's friend was left panting and holding on to the rifle which he'd succeeded in wrenching from the rebel.

The passenger with the knife stuck his head out of the broken window. Bringing it back into the carriage he spoke swiftly in Spanish.

'Moorish cavalry, he says there are hundreds of them,' a wide-eyed Evelyn translated.

Maggie had read about the Moorish levies who fought for Franco. They were reputedly the most feared of all his troops.

'Pray to God they don't take this train,' Evelyn whispered.

Maggie stared at her companion. 'You mean they'd massacre us?'

'It's what they'd do to you and me before that I'm thinking about.'

Maggie realized what Evelyn meant, and went cold all over. A solitary rape by John McNair would be nothing compared to that.

Voices throughout the train were shouting and yelling. Then someone shrieked hysterically, the most awful, blood-curdling sound.

The man with the captured rifle kneeled at the broken window and began shooting, continuing to do so until the automatic weapon ran out of bullets.

Maggie and Evelyn clung to one another, Evelyn literally shaking with fright.

The train stopped. And almost instantly started up again. There was a screeching of tortured metal, then the train leapt forward so quickly it might have been a greyhound coming out of a trap.

They could clearly hear the engine working flat out. The reassuring chugs came closer and closer together until, the train now going so fast, they were indistinguishable from one another.

Their attackers had been left behind, the crisis was over. Maggie sighed with relief and dropped her head onto Evelyn's shoulder, Evelyn doing the same with her.

The woman at the far end of the carriage, who was in her mid to late fifties, began to weep. Her huge pendulous bosoms heaved up and down.

The firing had stopped, but pandemonium still reigned throughout the train.

They discovered they'd suffered one casualty in their carriage. The man with the goat-skin wine bottle had been hit by a second splinter, this one piercing his left temple and brain. They all agreed he couldn't have felt a thing.

Evelyn gently nudged Maggie in the ribs. 'Madrid – we're here,' she said.

At last! Maggie thought, coming awake. Glancing out of the broken window she saw a sign which read Chamartin, the name of the city's main railway station.

The train came to a halt in a great hiss of steam, and straight away passengers began clambering off. The dead man had long since been removed to somewhere at the rear of the train. The man's friend who'd captured the Moor's rifle had gone with the corpse.

Maggie was sore and stiff, hardly surprising after such a long and cramped journey. Long and cramped it might have

173

been, but hardly tedious, she thought grimly. Would she have a tale to tell Nevil when she saw him!

She pulled her suitcase down off the overhead rack and dumped it where she'd been sitting. She and Evelyn then said their goodbyes to the others in the carriage.

With Evelyn leading, they struggled on to the platform.

'I have to find a bathroom before I do anything else,' Maggie stated.

'We'll both find one,' Evelyn said as they made their way down the platform towards the main concourse.

Later they enquired about taxis and were directed to a rank where a solitary one stood waiting. Evelyn insisted Maggie had it and that she'd take the next.

It was now time for them to say their goodbyes, a sad moment for both as they'd become firm friends in a very short while.

Evelyn's plan was to book into a hotel for the night, then continue her journey the following day. Maggie's was to go straight to the hospital where Nevil was, and from there see what happened.

They shook hands, then embraced. 'Good luck,' Evelyn whispered.

'And to you.'

'Perhaps we'll bump into one another again?'

'Perhaps,' Maggie said, knowing that would be unlikely. Still, it was a nice sentiment.

They embraced again, then Evelyn bundled Maggie into the taxi and gave the driver the name of the hospital. She waved as the taxi bore her away.

Maggie waved back till Evelyn was out of sight, after which she sank into the taxi's deep leather upholstery.

She gazed out at her first sight of Madrid, drinking everything in. How utterly different it was from Glasgow, she thought. And how different the people looked.

Many of the Madrilenos were in blue overalls while others were dressed in very plain vaguely military-style outfits. There were militia everywhere, some of whom she noted with surprise were women.

174

And then there were the posters and graffiti, much of the latter being bewildering sets of initials. POUM was one set, FAI another. The most popular appeared to be UGT, with CNT running a close second. She wondered what they stood for? Something to do with politics, she guessed correctly.

There were masses of flags flying. Red flags, red and black flags, and one monster red flag flying from atop a high building that had the hammer and sickle on it.

She gawped when she passed a church that had been gutted by fire and whose walls were daubed with red paint. She didn't have to read Spanish to know the daubings were anti-Church.

When they arrived at the hospital, she paid the driver using a few pesetas she'd brought from Glasgow. She picked up her suitcase and made for the front entrance, glancing up at a large banner fixed above it which read *Resistir y Fortificar es Vencer*. This was the popular Communist slogan, Hold Out and Fortify, and You Will Win! There were thousands of these banners in and around Madrid. By far the great favourite was *Viva La Libertad!* Long Live Liberty!

Inside the hospital people were toing and froing, some laughing and joking, others hurrying silently about their business. The atmosphere was completely different from that of a British hospital. Spotting a man behind what appeared to be a reception desk, she went over to him.

'*Buenos dias señor*,' she smiled.

The man stiffened, then slowly looked up from the newspaper he was reading. His brows were knitted, his expression thunderous.

'Señor?' he said in disgust. '*Señor!*' He wagged a finger at her. '*Camarada! Salud Camarada!*'

She realized she'd somehow made an error. '*Salud camarada!*' she repeated, apologetically.

His brow cleared, and he rattled off something in Spanish which she of course didn't understand.

'I'm terribly sorry,' she said, and hastily consulted her dictionary.

'*Ah, Inglès!*'

'*No, Escocés.*'

'*Escocés!*'

'That's right, Scottish.'

'Scottish,' he repeated with a smile.

He smelled, she thought. Even with the broad desk separating them she could still smell him and it was atrocious.

'I don't speak Spanish, I'm afraid. Do you speak English?'

'Hello, baby,' he replied.

'Oh, you do!'

'Sure. Hello, baby. Tom Mix. Cucumber sandwiches. Ovaltine and tea. You pretty as film star. Metro Goldwyn Mayer. Four gallons, please.'

She stared at him quizzically. What sort of answer was that! 'Do you speak English?' she ventured again.

He held up a hand and brought his thumb and index finger to a point where they were about an inch apart. 'Leettle!' he said.

Well, at least that was something. 'I'm looking for a Mr Nevil Sanderson who's a patient here?'

The Spaniard regarded her blankly.

'A Señor . . .' She swiftly corrected herself. 'A Camarada Nevil Sanderson.'

The Spaniard shook his head.

'You mean he's not here any more?'

'Camarada Zanson?'

'Sanderson,' she repeated.

He thought about that. '*Escocés también?*'

She consulted her dictionary again. 'Yes,' she nodded. 'He's also Scottish.'

The Spaniard made a twirly motion with his hand, and gestured her to follow him. He came out from behind his desk and strutted off – there was no other word to describe it. Lugging her suitcase she hurried to keep up.

He led her a merry dance through a haze of corridors, until they eventually arrived in a small waiting-room. He pointed to a wooden bench, indicating that she should sit down. When she'd sat he strode away.

Minutes passed. Five became ten. She was beginning to

176

think he'd forgotten about her, or simply abandoned her, when he returned with a nurse.

He was speaking volubly to the nurse as he re-entered the waiting-room. His tone was stern, full of his own importance.

'*Si, si,*' the nurse said.

He then turned his attention to Maggie. 'Hello, baby, you pretty as film star.' Grabbing her hand he lifted it to his mouth and kissed it.

She tried not to gag. He did stink horribly.

The Spaniard strutted from the room, leaving her with the nurse who, in turn, crooked a finger at Maggie, indicating that she should follow her.

The ward was long, narrow and lined with beds on either side. One of the patients was groaning, another making a wheezing sound as he fought for breath. The floor, she noticed, could have done with a good clean.

The nurse stopped by a bed and pointed. Eagerly Maggie gazed at the bed's occupant, expecting it to be Nevil. It wasn't. The patient was Stuart Borland, a member of the party who'd left Templeton's. His complexion looked positively ghastly.

Stuart stared at Maggie in disbelief. 'I must be dreaming!' he exclaimed in a weak voice.

'No, you're not dreaming, Stuart. It really is me.'

'Well, I'll be . . .' He broke off to cough. 'Hospital cough,' he explained when he'd finished. 'Everyone gets it.'

'Have you been wounded?' she asked softly.

He gave her a wry smile. 'You could say that. I've lost my right foot. Blown clean off just above the ankle.'

'I am sorry.'

'So it's back to dear old Glasgow for me as soon as I'm fit to travel. Which is more than Kevin McGee will ever do, poor sod. He got killed the same day I got this.'

She hadn't really known Kevin McGee, and as far as she could remember had only once spent some time with him. He'd always struck her as a pleasant enough lad though. 'Any other casualties?' she enquired.

He shook his head. 'As far as I know that's it.'

Stuart had aged, she thought. He looked a dozen years older than when he'd left Templeton's.

She glanced round, hoping to speak to the nurse, but she had gone.

'I suppose you're here to see Nevil?' Stuart said.

'Yes. I couldn't make myself understood very well, I'm afraid. My Spanish is limited to my dictionary and the chap I talked to only spoke a few odd English phrases.'

'One of the hospital attendants?'

'Well, he certainly wasn't a doctor. At least I hope he wasn't, smelling as he did.'

Stuart nodded. 'He would have been a hospital attendant. All bastards! Within minutes of my arrival they'd stolen my money, my watch and my lighter. I tell you, they'd steal the hair off your head if they thought they could make a profit from it.'

'Do you need any money?'

His face lit up. 'A few pesetas wouldn't go amiss. Perhaps I can buy some fags, though they're getting much harder to come by. Franco holds the Canaries, you see, where all the Spanish tobacco is grown, so the only stocks left on our side are those that existed before the war.'

'I can do better than that. I can give you some cigarettes. I brought some with me, thinking the lads would enjoy a British brand. I didn't realize there was a shortage or I would have brought even more.'

His face lit up when he heard that. 'British fags! By God, that's wonderful! I'd murder for one of those.'

She laughed as she laid her suitcase flat beside his bed and took out two packets.

'Senior Service, my favourite,' he beamed, clutching them to him as though they were the crown jewels.

'Now what about Nevil? Where will I find him?'

'Wait a minute.' Stuart eagerly opened a packet, took out a cigarette and lit it from a book of matches he produced from under his pillow. He inhaled, closed his eyes in ecstasy, then blew the smoke slowly out.

'Oh, that is marvellous!' he exclaimed, and immediately had another drag.

'Nevil?' she prompted.

'Left the hospital, discharged himself some days ago.'

Her heart sank. 'You mean he's returned to his unit?'

'He's still not well enough for that. He's been ordered to have a period of convalescence before rejoining the 5th. He's staying at the Hotel Colon which has been commandeered by the 5th for use by their militia.'

Maggie knew the 5th he was referring to to be the 5th Regiment, Nevil had mentioned it in his letters.

Her spirits soared. Out of hospital and convalescing! It couldn't be better. 'Where is this Hotel Colon?' she asked.

'Do you have a map of Madrid?'

'Yes, I brought one with me.'

'Let's see it then.'

She spread it in front of Stuart.

'It's right . . .' He broke off as a coughing fit took hold of him. He fumbled under his pillow to find a handkerchief which he held over his mouth.

'Christ!' he muttered when the fit had finally subsided.

'You shouldn't smoke,' she chided.

'The coughing has nothing to do with cigarettes. As I said to you, all the patients get it. It kills off more than their rotten doctors do, and that's saying something.'

'Their doctors aren't good then?'

'Let me put it this way. I'd rather have a Scottish butcher operate on me than a Spanish doctor. I don't think any of them in here know what the word hygiene means. They're positively medieval.'

'Bad as that?'

'If anything I'm being kind to them.' He shrugged. 'Still, it's our own fault.'

She didn't follow that. 'What do you mean?'

'The good doctors were the successful, rich ones and as a result, almost without exception, Fascists. Those that didn't escape behind Fascist lines were either shot or hung. The Anarchists did for most of them.'

179

'The Anarchists are Republicans then?'

Stuart gave her a brief round-up of the political bias of all the different political factions, at the end of which Maggie realized she had a lot to learn. The situation wasn't nearly as simple as she'd initially imagined.

Mid-flow, Stuart suddenly gave a gasp.

'What is it?' she demanded.

His face grimaced. 'My right leg, I get terrible shooting pains in it from time to time. I'm told they'll disappear as my stump heals, and I can only hope that's right.'

He took a deep breath. 'Anyway, enough of me and politics. You'll want to find Nevil.'

He scrutinized the map. 'See here, Fuencarral Street. That's where the Hotel Colon is.'

'And where are we now?'

He pointed out the hospital.

'It isn't far then.'

'A few minutes' walk, that's all.'

'Will I be able to get a taxi there?'

'There aren't too many of those about now. You might be lucky, though.'

She thought of her suitcase and hoped she would be. 'I'll get started then,' she smiled.

He reached out and lightly touched her arm. 'Thank you for the cigarettes, Maggie. I really appreciate them.'

'Nevil and I will be back to visit you. I promise you that.'

'I dream of Glasgow, you know. Every time I fall asleep I dream of Glasgow and the folks there. I can't wait to get home, though how I'm going to earn my living when I get there is another matter. I'll certainly never operate a setting loom again, not with only one foot.'

'At least you're still alive,' she commiserated.

'Aye, that's right enough.'

'Now, how do I get out of here?'

Leaving the ward she retraced her steps through the hospital and from there headed in the direction of Fuencarral Street, and Nevil.

She stopped when she heard the sound of an aeroplane.

Louder and louder it grew till at last the plane roared overhead. A bomber, she thought. Three smaller chaser planes followed, their guns crackling when they caught up with it.

There was an explosion, immediately followed by others. In the distance Maggie saw a pall of smoke rise heavenwards. Then a second bomber appeared, and this time she actually witnessed the bombs being dropped.

It might not have been far but she was exhausted when she reached Fuencarral Street, her suitcase now seeming to weigh a ton. Luck hadn't been with her regarding a taxi.

She stumbled into the hotel, an unimposing building, to say the least, and went over to reception where she stood catching her breath.

'Hello?' she called out when no-one appeared to help her.

Two militiamen emerged from a side passage, each with a carbine slung over his shoulder. Both sported long moustaches that drooped to the chin.

'*Salud!*' the younger of them hailed.

'*Salud camarada!*' she replied.

They came across, the older one eyeing her clothes suspiciously. She'd already had a few odd glances on her way to the Hotel Colon. When they halted beside her the older one asked her something in Spanish.

'*Escocés,*' she explained, pointing to herself. '*Camarada.*'

Both nodded.

'I'm looking for *Camarada* Nevil Sanderson. *Entender?*'

'Ah!' smiled the younger militiaman. '*El Cabo!*'

She shook her head. 'No, Sanderson, Nevil Sanderson.'

'*Mujer?*' the older man asked.

She consulted her dictionary. He was enquiring if she was Nevil's wife. '*No, novia. Fiancée.*'

'*Ah si, si!*' the older man said.

'Can you tell me which room he's in?'

They frowned, neither understanding.

'Which room?' She had another quick flick through her dictionary. '*La habitación de Camarada Sanderson?*'

The younger one stated a number which she couldn't

interpret. The older one solved that problem by taking out a pencil and writing '46' on the palm of her hand.

That was clear enough. Nevil was in room forty-six. '*Gracias*,' she smiled.

She picked up her suitcase and headed for the stairs. As she thought, forty-six was on the fourth floor. She tapped the door, ready to say surprise! when he opened it.

When there was no answer she tapped again, this time more loudly. Still no answer, which meant he was out.

'Damn!' she swore. She supposed she could wait downstairs, but on impulse she tried the handle. It turned, and the door swung open.

The room was dark, the curtains drawn, and there was a heavy, pungent smell in the air.

She left the door open until she found the lightswitch. Light from an unshaded bulb flooded the room, and the first thing she saw Nevil in bed. Even at that distance she could see the globules of sweat dotting his forehead.

She flew back to the door, closed it, then rushed to him. His eyes were closed, his breathing shallow. His forehead when she felt it was afire.

'Nevil? Nevil, can you hear me?'

His mouth opened, then closed again.

'Nevil, it's Maggie.'

She pulled back the bed-clothes and intense heat wafted out. He was wearing a shirt and underpants, both of which were sodden.

His eyelids twitched, then fluttered open. 'Maggie?' he croacked.

'Yes, it's me, Maggie. What's wrong?'

He moved his mouth and it made dry, sticky noises. 'Water. Couldn't get out of bed. No energy. Water.'

She glanced about her, wondering where to find some water.

'Bathroom,' he said. 'Bottled water there.'

There was another door leading off the room, which proved to be the bathroom. There were a number of bottles standing in a cardboard box underneath the sink. She rinsed out a

182

tumbler which she filled and held to Nevil's lips, lifting his head slightly with her other hand.

He drank greedily. 'More,' he gasped when the tumbler was empty. She refilled the tumbler and he drank that too. She carefully laid his head back on the pillow.

What was she to do? Get a doctor, but how and from where? She couldn't help but remember what Stuart had said about the Spanish doctors left in Republican territory.

'What's wrong, Nevil?' she asked again.

'Wound,' he breathed. 'Become infected. Awful pain. How . . . how did you get here?'

'That's a long story I'll tell you later. Right now I have to do something about this.'

Alarm flashed on to his face. 'Not the hospital. Not there. Purposely left there. Most who go in don't come out.'

'Stuart Borland told me. I went to the hospital looking for you and saw Stuart instead. He gave me this address.'

'Pain,' he whispered. 'Awful pain.'

Don't panic! she instructed herself. That was the last thing she needed to do. She had a problem she'd have to solve as best she could. Start with the wound, she thought.

She explained to him what she was doing, then opened his shirt and exposed the bandage underneath.

'How long since you've had your dressing changed?' she asked.

'Don't know. What day is it?'

'Thursday.'

'Thursday? I seem to have lost a day or two.' He paused for breath, and thought. 'Monday. I changed it Monday.'

'Right then.'

She undid the two small brass safety pins securing the bandage, then said, 'I'm going to have to sit you up. Will you manage that?'

'I'll be fine.'

She gently brought him upright and used his pillows to prop him up. His hair was plastered to his head, his entire body slick with sweat, and she noticed he'd lost a lot of weight.

'I did try to get out of bed, but it was no use,' he mumbled.

'And no-one's been to see you?'

'The lads aren't about just now. They're out fighting in the Guadarrama.'

He whimpered when she removed his shirt from his wounded shoulder. She tossed the shirt aside, and started on the bandage.

'Oh Maggie, it's so good to see you,' Nevil said.

'And it's good to see you.' She kissed him on the cheek, which was sunken and thick with bristles.

He whimpered again when she gingerly pulled off the dressing, which had become stuck in places to Nevil's skin. The wound was highly inflamed, with pus seeping at the edges.

'Hold on, everything's whizzing round,' he said.

'Are you going to faint?'

'I don't know. Hold on.'

A few moments later he declared, 'I'm fine now. Still dizzy, but all right.'

'I'm amazed they let you out of hospital when your wound wasn't fully healed,' she said.

'I discharged myself. That place is a death hole.'

'Stuart said the doctors aren't very good.'

'They're useless. And so are the nurses. Nice girls, mind, but totally useless. They know how to take a temperature and tie a bandage. And that's it. Their training is non-existent.'

She stared at the wound. 'I'm going to have to clean this, Nevil.'

'Go ahead.'

'Can I leave you for a minute in this position while I get a few things together?'

'If I fall over you'll just have to pull me up again.'

She smiled at him. 'I do love you, you know.'

'And I love you, Maggie.'

She kissed his other cheek, then gave him a quick peck on the mouth.

She searched for some antiseptic in the bathroom, but couldn't find any. Then she had a brain wave – the whisky, of course! Besides the cigarettes she'd also brought a bottle of whisky. Alcohol was a perfect antiseptic.

184

The next thing she needed were some clean rags. The towel in the bathroom was dirty, so that was ruled out. One of her own towels would have to do, she decided. Selecting the oldest, she tore it into long strips.

'This is bound to hurt, I'm afraid,' she said, sitting beside Nevil.

'Then give me a slug of that whisky before you do anything.'

She poured a small measure into the tumbler, and held it to his lips. He gulped it down eagerly.

'Another of the same, Maggie,' he requested.

She hesitated.

'Oh come on!'

She gave him a small tot, and told him that was definitely his lot. Then she set about cleaning the wound with the whisky.

He clenched his teeth in agony. It felt as though acid rather than spirit was being used. Blobs of sweat steadily dripped from his forehead.

Maggie was as swift as she could be, but thorough. 'Now a fresh dressing and bandage,' she announced. 'Do you have any or will I have to improvise?'

'Under the bed,' he hissed.

She found a wooden box containing a number of his personal things plus several packets of dressings and four brand-new bandages.

'Brought those from the hospital. Managed to bribe one of the assistants,' he explained.

'Was bribing necessary?'

'Supplies are short. If I'd only asked they wouldn't have given.'

Maggie struggled with all the dressings but managed to bandage the wound without too much trouble.

'How's that?' she asked finally.

'Fine. Can I lie down again now?'

She moved his pillows, plumping each up, then eased him back into a prone position. The next step was to wash him all over.

'Do you get hot water in the bathroom?' she enquired.

'Sometimes. Why?'

'I want to give you a bed bath.'

'Oh lovely!' he replied, tongue in cheek.

As luck would have it, there was lashings of hot water and the bed bath was executed with a certain degree of hilarity, both of them delighted to be together again. Once Nevil was washed from top to toe, Maggie combed his hair. At last he was beginning to look slightly more himself. But Maggie had not finished yet.

'What about clean bed-linen?' she asked.

'There's a cupboard outside in the corridor. You should find some there.'

'Despite being commandeered by the 5th the hotel still has maids then?' she queried.

'Not maids! Comrade helpers. Maids in that context is a bourgeois expression, and like all bourgeois expressions it has been renounced and discarded by the Republic and all true democrats.'

His eyes were blazing with the twin fires of inner belief and conviction. Steel had strengthened his voice.

'I see,' Maggie answered. 'I've already learned that I must say *salud camarada* and not *buenos dias señor*.'

He softened fractionally. 'You must, otherwise people might think you were a Fascist and lynch you.'

'Well, I certainly don't want that to happen,' she replied, smiling. But he didn't smile back.

He continued in the same serious vein. 'The Spanish are a fine race, Maggie, but extremely excitable. They can very easily make mistakes because of that. They're always contrite afterwards, but by then it's too late. That's something we have all learned the hard way.'

'And something I'll remember.'

She left him to go out into the corridor, where she soon found the cupboard he'd mentioned. Inside were numerous articles, including several piles of sheets and pillowcases from which she extracted what she wanted. She also helped herself to a couple of toilet rolls from a large stack, believing they would come in useful.

Returning to Nevil's room she stripped his bed.

'How do you feel now?' she asked, when that task was over.

'Almost human again.'

His infected wound worried her, just cleaning it wasn't going to be enough. But it was all she could do for the present.

She yawned. God, she was tired! But doubted she'd sleep if she tried. Her mind was racing with thoughts about Nevil and how she'd found him.

She decided she needed a bath and told Nevil she was going to have one.

As she undressed she realized that she was longing to clean her teeth, so went through to pick up her toilet bag.

'I'd forgotten just how gorgeous and sexy you are,' Nevil said from the bed where he lay watching her.

'Thank you, kind sir!'

'Give me a kiss, Maggie.'

She kissed him, melting inside as she felt his lips on hers.

Afterwards he said, 'When I got shot I was convinced I would never see you again. Waiting for death I only thought of you. You filled my entire mind.'

'But you didn't die. You lived. And now we're together again.'

He ran a finger down her cheek. 'Hurry and have your bath. I want to learn how you came to be in Madrid.'

'And I want to hear about how you got shot.'

As she walked away he felt a large lump in his throat. Everything was going to be all right now that Maggie was here. There could be no doubt about that. He'd known he would miss her, but the actuality had been far worse than he'd ever imagined.

Maggie sighed as she slid into the tub. What a marvellous luxury to have your own bathroom, she thought as she relaxed. Already the aches and pains of her journey were disappearing, draining out of her to be replaced by warmth and contentment. When she'd finished, she then washed her hair at the sink, only happy when at last it was squeaky clean. Walking back into the bedroom she found Nevil fast asleep.

It was good that he was sleeping, she thought. The more sleep he had the better. Wasn't sleep supposed to be the best medicine after all! She felt his forehead and was delighted that it had cooled down considerably.

Maggie wandered across the room and drew the curtains back slightly. From her room she could see a courtyard with a street leading off it. A voluptuous, dark-haired woman, dressed in the same sort of blue overalls that she'd noticed earlier, was walking through the courtyard. She was clearly agitated about something, which made her think of Nevil's warning about how excitable the Spanish were.

Turning back into the room, she lovingly stroked Nevil's cheek and then settled down with a book.

'*Ya lo veo!*' Nevil cried out. '*Ya lo veo!*'

Instantly Maggie was out of her chair and kneeling at his bedside. His forehead was burning.

'Aaaahhhh!' he exclaimed, exhaling violently. His eyes snapped open to bulge like ping-pong balls.

'It's all right, darling. You're safe. This is Maggie.'

His gaze swivelled on to her. 'Maggie? I thought . . . I thought I only dreamed you were here. Is it real then?'

'Yes, it's real.'

'Really real?'

'Really real,' she laughed.

He took a deep breath, then another. His eyes had settled down.

'When you're out there fact and fantasy can merge so that you can't always tell one from the other,' he explained quietly.

'You mean when you're out fighting?'

'Yes.'

She could understand that. War, and the conditions of war, must have strange effects on the mind. 'I think I should change your dressing again. Your temperature's climbed up,' she said.

'My shoulder isn't as painful as it was. But it's still bloody painful.'

'Come on then.' She lifted him into a sitting position, and supported him there with his pillows as she'd done previously.

'Where were you fighting when you were shot?' she asked.

'As you know, Andy wrote and told me you'd been wounded but failed to give me any of the details.'

'The Sierra de Guadarrama. It's a range of mountains to the north of Madrid.'

She had a sudden thought. 'Won't be a minute,' she said, and hurried out into the corridor. The coast was clear, so she ran to the cupboard containing the bed-linen and stole another sheet.

Closing the door behind her she bolted it. 'As I'm obviously going to have to dress that wound of yours quite a number of times I need a fair amount of rags or cloths. This sheet will provide the necessary.'

'They'll never know it's missing,' Nevil said. 'The comrade helpers are very lackadaisical. Or I'll put that another way, efficiency isn't exactly one of their strong points.'

'Good,' she said, ripping a strip off the sheet.

'What were you doing when I was asleep?' he asked.

'Reading. Thinking.'

'Thinking about us?'

'Of course. But tell me about this Sierra de . . . What was it again?'

'Guadarrama. It was high up there that I was shot.' His tone changed to become soft and deadly. 'But we got the bastards. Killed every single last one of them. I swore we would. And we did.'

His tone had sent a chill up her spine. 'You make it sound like a personal vendetta.'

'It was, for all of us involved. You see, the Fascists had killed a group of our men, and then taken their heads.'

Maggie paused, aghast. 'What do you mean, took their heads?'

'Precisely that. They cut off the heads of those they'd killed, our comrades, and took the heads with them.'

'But why would they do such a horrible thing?'

'Out of sheer badness. Or perhaps they thought it would affect our morale. Who knows? For whatever reason, they did it.'

She sat beside him and undid the two small brass safety pins.

189

She couldn't imagine such an atrocity being committed in this day and age. Why, it was positively barbaric! Her hands trembled as she unravelled his bandage.

Nevil was staring straight ahead, back in the Sierra de Guadarrama. He went on. 'We were in sight of the high peak by Somosierra when we caught up with them. The ensuing fight was long and drawn out. But eventually we killed them, every single last one. Afterwards the heads were returned to where our comrades had been buried, and buried alongside. And I was taken to the Military Hospital.'

She continued unwinding the bandage until it fell away from his arm. This dressing had also stuck in places.

More pus had seeped from the wound, but not nearly as much as had been there before. She wiped it away, then washed his wound again with whisky.

She was rebandaging his arm when he said, 'Now tell me about you. How is it you've suddenly turned up out of the blue?'

Until that moment she hadn't known whether or not she'd include John McNair in her explanation. She decided she would.

Nevil swore viciously.

'After that the obvious thing to do seemed to be to come to you. And don't ask me what I'm going to do now that I'm here. I haven't the foggiest. I thought that would just sort itself out.'

'I'm glad you have come, Maggie. So glad I could burst.'

'I very nearly never got here either.'

He listened intently as she recounted how her train had been attacked by Moorish cavalry, and how one man and a sheep had been killed in their carriage. There had been other casualties, she knew, but was not sure how many.

'And how far away from Madrid were you at that point?' he queried when she'd finished her tale.

'Difficult to say really. The train stopped and started so much, and went at so many different speeds, from a slow crawl to a flying sprint, that it became impossible, at least for me, to judge distances in the end. But my feeling was we were relatively close.'

190

Concern settled on his face. 'Moors!' he spat. 'The scum of the earth.'

'The one who appeared at our carriage window was certainly frightening.'

'You were right to be frightened. You have no idea what they can do.'

She had at least some idea, she thought.

He reached across and laid a hand on her thigh. 'But you got through safe and sound, for which I'll be eternally grateful.'

His hand made her tingle inside as she remembered other times it had rested on her thigh. She felt a warm flush rise in her lower neck.

'What are we going to do about food? I'm starving,' she said quickly.

'Ah! What time is it?'

She glanced at her wristwatch. 'Seven twenty.'

'Then food isn't a problem. All you need to do is go down to the canteen just after eight, load a tray and bring it back up here.'

'There's a canteen in the hotel?'

'Indeed there is, at the rear. The civilian populace of Madrid might be on short rations because of the war, but not the militia. And certainly not the 5th.'

'But will they allow me to take food? I'm not in the 5th after all.'

'But I am, and you're with me. If questioned say you're with *El Cabo Sanderson*, and that'll be your password.'

'What does *El Cabo* mean?' she queried. 'The two militiamen downstairs called you that.'

'It's nothing exotic. It simply means corporal.'

She laughed. 'It does sound far more exotic than that! So you're a corporal.'

'In charge of the lads from Templeton's. We're a platoon and I'm the Corporal in Charge.'

'I should have guessed they'd put you in a position of command. You're a natural leader.'

His expression became sober again. 'That's what Bob Kinloch said.' He hesitated, then went on. 'I never told you,

191

but Bob wrote to me. A letter I received not long before he was killed. He said I was exactly the sort of man who was desperately needed in Spain, and urged me to come over and join the Republican cause. He said . . . he said I could do great things here.'

'Is that why you agreed to come with the others?' she queried, fixing him with a stare.

He shook his head. 'No, I would have come anyway. You know how strongly I feel about the matter. But I have to admit his letter was on my mind when I decided. I felt a decision had somehow already been made on my behalf.'

'You mean it was predestined that you came here?'

'Something like that,' he acknowledged quietly, rasping a hand over his bristles.

'As soon as we've eaten I'll give you a shave if you'd like,' she offered.

'Done! But getting back to eating, you're going to have to change before you go to the canteen.'

'I've already had some peculiar stares in that respect,' she told him.

'You would have done. You're dressed as a typical bourgeois, which is quite wrong.'

'We don't want anyone getting excited about me?' she joked.

'Precisely.' And this time he did smile. 'I think you should wear my uniform. That way you might not even be noticed.'

'Your uniform will never fit!' she protested.

'Listen, half the uniforms you see don't fit. It's not the Brigade of Guards we've got here.'

'So where is it then?'

He pointed at a free-standing wooden wardrobe. 'As my uniform isn't lying about I must have hung it in there before collapsing into bed.'

She recognized it straightaway as it was similar to those worn by the militiamen she'd encountered below.

She took the clothes from the wardrobe and laid them over a chair. She suddenly sniggered.

'What is it?' he queried.

'Can you just imagine me walking down Sauchiehall Street dressed up in this lot?'

He had to admit, the idea was somewhat mind-boggling. Pound to a penny she'd have stopped Sauchiehall Street dead in its tracks.

'How do I look?' she asked when she'd donned the uniform and boots.

'The truth?'

'Absolutely!'

He was about to make a smart reply, then changed his mind. 'I love you, Maggie. More than all the world,' he said instead.

She went to him, and kissed him on the mouth. A tender kiss that spoke volumes.

She frowned when the kiss was over. 'Are you all right?'

'I'm just so exhausted and weak, that's all. Can I have some more water?'

She filled the tumbler, which he emptied. She refilled it and placed it within easy reach for him.

'This infection hit me with the force of a sledgehammer, and about as quickly,' he said. 'I was well on the road to recovery, and then suddenly it all went to pieces. My worst fear is being taken back to the hospital. That would be the end of me, I just know it. Promise you won't take me back there, or let anyone else?'

'I promise,' she stated quietly.

He relaxed, seeing she meant it. That was one problem he didn't have to worry about any more.

For a while, at his instigation, she spoke about Glasgow, and Templeton's, though she didn't elaborate any further on the John McNair business. Then it was past eight o'clock, and time for her to go to the canteen.

'Anything you'd like in particular?' she asked.

'Whatever's going, I'm not fussy. Though a little red wine would be nice. If you have to ask for that, as sometimes happens, *vino tinto* is red, *vino blanco* is white, and a *chato* is a glass of red wine.'

'I see you're familiar with the local booze,' she commented drily.

'I prefer the wine to the water, I tell you. I counted myself lucky getting hold of that bottled water in the bathroom. The stuff out the tap tastes appalling. And you daren't even begin to think what nasties might be in it.'

In which case she'd drink wine as well, she decided. The best idea was to conserve all the bottled water they had.

'Remember,' he said. '*El Cabo Sanderson* is your password if you need one.'

'I won't forget.'

She was nervous as she made her way back down the hotel stairs. Just outside the canteen, which she found easily enough, she came upon a group of militiamen and women milling around. The din was terrific, everyone seemed to be talking at once. Still she joined a loosely bunched queue, and shuffled forward.

'Easy as pie,' she announced to Nevil when she returned to his room carrying a well-laden tray.

'No problems then?'

'Not a one.' She laid the tray on the bed beside him, then went back to shut the door.

Nevil murmured in appreciation.

'I don't know what it is, stew of some sort,' she said, sitting on the bed.

'It's called *cocido castellano*, and it is a stew containing beef, ham and potatoes. It's dished up regularly.'

'Are you hungry?'

'Yes. Even more so now I've got this in front of me.'

It was an encouraging sign that he had an appetite.

She lifted the full carafe of red wine that was on the tray and poured out two glasses. They were thick and amber coloured, their outsides dimpled below the rims.

'What shall we toast?' she asked as she handed him his wine.

'To us?'

'To *us*,' she agreed, and they both drank, after which they began tucking into their food.

'That was simply divine!' she pronounced when she'd finally finished. 'I think I've eaten enough for three.'

'The comrade cooks are very good. I've never had any complaints in that direction.'

'A little bit spicy perhaps, but then that's foreign cooking for you,' she prevaricated.

It suddenly dawned on her what he'd just said. 'Have you stayed here before then?'

'Several times. But never for long. Myself and the other lads know the Colon well.'

Maggie felt full, satisfied and very relaxed. If she lay down now, she knew she'd go straight to sleep.

She removed the tray. 'How's your shoulder?' she asked.

'Well, it hasn't fallen off yet despite your ministrations.'

She laughed. It was good that he'd regained something of his old sense of humour. 'Now what about that shave?'

'If you can still be bothered?'

'I'll enjoy it,' she said, getting off the bed. She went through to the bathroom, turned on the hot water tap, but the water ran cold.

'It'll have to be tomorrow then,' he said when she told him.

She stretched. 'So where shall I sleep, the floor or the bed?'

'The bed!' he replied instantly. Fortunately the bed was a very large single which made it more of a three-quarter size.

'I'm just worried that I might hurt you, or make it more difficult for you?'

'As long as I can lie flat, I'll be all right,' he assured her.

He lay watching, drinking her in as she changed into a brand new night-gown she'd bought before leaving Glasgow.

'Switch the light off,' he instructed when she was ready.

She did, then padded round the bed to his unwounded side. She got in and immediately put her arms round him, snuggling up close. After a few seconds she began slowly to caress his chest.

'Nice?' she queried.

'Very.'

He was sweating again, but nothing like he'd been before she'd washed him. His temperature was also up a little.

'I can't do anything, I'm afraid, Maggie. I simply couldn't manage it.'

195

'I never expected you to. It's enough just to be with you like this. To have you beside me, and in my arms.'

'This is the first time we'll ever have spent the entire night together, do you realize that?'

'You're right. I'd forgotten.'

'You and I were made for one another, Maggie. We were written in the stars.'

What a beautifully romantic thing to say, she thought. Written in the stars! Were they his own words or had he read them somewhere? No matter. He'd used, and meant them, and that was enough for her.

'Do you know what I've been thinking about recently?' he murmured.

'What?'

'That house we were going to rent. I don't know why I should think about that.'

'Guilty conscience?' she teased gently.

'Maybe. There again, maybe not.'

'Perhaps that's the house that you're hoping to go back to?'

He considered that. 'You know, you could be right. A subconscious longing.'

'I've thought about the house occasionally,' she confessed. But didn't elaborate to say that every time she'd done so it had almost broken her heart. She'd had such plans for it.

'Have you any regrets about coming to Spain?' she asked.

'None at all.' He paused, then went on. 'Of course I regretted leaving you behind, you know that. But that was something I had to come to terms with. I've no new, or overall regrets. I did the right thing, I'm utterly convinced of that.'

'I thought Stuart Borland looked a lot older when I saw him.'

'A lot of the lads do. You'll be surprised when you see them. War most definitely has an ageing effect on those involved.'

'You haven't aged too much, nothing like Stuart has. You have lost weight, though. Or is that just something that's happened since your wound became infected?'

'No, I lost it before then. Where we were diarrhoea was

endemic. That takes it out of you dreadfully. Especially when it's never-ending, but goes on forever.'

'You don't have it any more, though?'

'No,' he confirmed. 'That's one thing the hospital did cure. Though I'm sure more by luck than anything else.'

She kissed him on the shoulder. 'I'm going to sleep now. Good-night.'

'Good-night, Maggie. You know what?'

'What?'

'This is sheer heaven.'

She was smiling when she fell asleep.

Bang!

Seconds later the first explosion was followed by another, this one closer and therefore louder.

Maggie shot out of bed, and rushed over to the window. She pulled the curtains slightly apart and peered out.

'Artillery,' Nevil said matter-of-factly. 'They're shelling the city.'

In the distance she saw a flash of orange flame, followed by another explosion.

'Has this happened before?' she asked.

'No,' came Nevil's tight voice out of the darkness. 'It can only mean the Fascists are a lot closer to the city than they were.'

A siren rent the air, a harsh discordant sound that jangled the nerves and set the teeth on edge. She could hear frenetic shouting. Someone was panicking, she thought.

A shell whistled directly overhead. They both listened to the whistle fade, then abruptly end in an explosion, followed by the clatter of falling masonry.

'Should we do anything?' she asked, beginning to feel the cold.

'Like what? Hide in the basement? That's exactly what the bastards want.'

She could hear more and more voices. The city seemed to be in an uproar.

Nevil swore a stream of obscenities in which he called

Franco, the other rebel leaders and Fascists in general all the names under the sun.

'Don't get yourself too upset. Don't forget you're not well,' Maggie counselled.

'To hell with me not being well, that's unimportant! What is important is what's happening out there. Out there and in other parts of Spain! The damn Fascists have been winning and are continuing to win. And we can't stop them! We have the men and the will, by Christ do we have the will, but what we don't have are the necessary arms. Why, oh why, can't that idiot Baldwin realize it's against Britain's interests for Spain to fall to the Fascists!

'Just a little help, that's all it would take, and Franco would be beaten. But do you think we get that help? No, not a bit of it!'

Maggie got back into bed. She was chittering as Nevil raged on in a full-blown rage.

'As for the great British Press, they're so biased it's unbelievable. They print story after story telling lies about us. They say we've committed outrageous actions against churches, priests and nuns. They accuse us of being barbarians who've burnt down museums and destroying the treasures. They say . . .' He broke off to choke with anger, completely overcome with outrage and other emotions.

'Would you like a dram?' she asked, thinking that might calm him down slightly. Outside artillery shells were still exploding in all parts of the city.

She sensed rather than saw him nod.

She slipped out of bed again and went over to the light-switch. She threw the switch, but nothing happened.

'The electricity is off,' she said.

'There's nothing unusual about that, happens all the time. There's a candle on a saucer at the bottom of the wardrobe.'

Relying on the candlelight, she soon found the bottle of whisky. She rinsed out one of the glasses and poured out a reasonable measure.

Handing it to him, she put the candle on one side and scuttled quickly back to bed.

His eyes were marble hard with fury, and were staring

fixedly. She'd never seen them like that before and they frightened her a little. They were the eyes of a fanatic, she thought.

Nevil sipped his drink, glancing up at the window when it rattled from the closest explosion yet.

'I saw a burnt-out church when I was en route to the hospital,' Maggie said.

He focused his attention on her, and she found herself shrinking from those eyes. 'Some churches have been burned, that's true. But only churches belonging to clergy who were actively helping the Fascists. The Church is on their side, don't forget. That isn't supposition on our part, but hard fact. Priests and nuns have been witnessed loading weapons for the Fascist soldiers and sympathizers.'

'And what happened to them?'

'The same that happens to anyone caught assisting the enemy.'

'So there is some truth in the British newspaper reports?'

He regarded her frostily. 'The British Press is biased throughout, the only exception being the *Daily Worker* which all along, thanks to our friend Claud Cockburn, has given a fair and impartial view of what is happening today in Spain.'

'Nuns and priests have therefore been killed?'

'Not *en masse* as the British Press would have its readers believe. The vast majority that we took prisoner are alive and well, I swear to you that's true.'

More sirens shrieked, and a klaxon ululated its warning. Competing with these sounds was the clanging of a fire engine.

'What about the other accusation you mentioned, the museums?' she continued.

Nevil barked out a laugh. 'That's the biggest joke of all. Rather than destroy the museums and picture galleries the Cultural Commission was set up to provide them with many treasures that have been discovered mouldering in the depths of churches, private houses and, the most obscene of all in my opinion, locked in the strong rooms of the Bank of Spain, deposited there as a guarantee for the debts of some grandee.

'With the addition of these new pictures and other articles, new to the public that is, the picture galleries and museums have flourished. At the Museo del Prado a great exhibition was launched consisting entirely of works that have been discovered by the Commission. Day after day comrades have flocked to see them. When I'm better I'll take you there if you like.'

She looked over at the window, beyond which shells were still exploding. 'I'd love to go. If your Museo del Prado is still there after tonight.'

They both listened in silence as another shell whistled directly overhead.

Maggie woke up feeling terrible. The previous night's shelling had gone on for hours, and neither she nor Nevil had been able to go back to sleep.

Somebody was thumping at the door, she dully realized. Then the door handle jiggled.

'Get out of bed, you lazy sod!' a familiar voice cried. 'And why is the door locked, have you got a female *camarada* in there?'

'*Si!*' Maggie called back. She turned to Nevil, who'd also been rudely awakened. 'I only hope . . .'

'I've never touched another woman since leaving you. I swear!' he blurted out, tripping over some of the words in his haste to plead innocence.

'I hope *not*. You can pick up awful diseases,' she glowered.

He swallowed. 'You'd better open the door for Andy,' he said, changing the subject.

She put on her dressing-gown, and went to open the door. An astonished Andy Ramsay gaped at her.

'Well, are you coming in or are you going to stand there for the rest of the morning?' she said drily.

'Maggie!'

'Ten out of ten for observation.'

'But . . . but how?'

'Boat and train. I arrived in Madrid yesterday afternoon.'

His face broke into a broad smile. 'It's fabulous to see you, Maggie. You're a sight for sore eyes!'

He kissed her lightly on the cheek, then brushed past into the room. 'How are you doing, Nevil?' he asked, tossing a bundle he'd brought with him on to a chair.

It was Maggie who answered, explaining about Nevil's wound becoming infected and how she'd found him.

Andy crossed to sit beside Nevil, and then hurriedly changed his mind. 'I've got lice,' he explained.

'What's happening? We were shelled last night, which can only mean the Nats must be closer?' Nevil queried anxiously.

'They're closer all right. They've made huge advances all along what was the old front. We did everything in our power to hold them, but couldn't. We retired in as orderly a manner as possible, and have now taken up new positions not far outside the city. We've stopped them, but only for the time being. A number of the 5th, including our platoon, has been ordered into the city to throw up barricades and dig trenches. When they're completed the rest of our forces will fall back behind them. At least that's the plan.'

'Sounds pretty desperate,' Nevil said quietly.

'It is.'

'And how about the lads?'

'We lost Davey Law. He was gut-shot and took hours to die, screaming in agony because we didn't have any morphine. It was horrible.'

Nevil sighed. 'Davey will be sorely missed. He was a bonny fighter.'

'Rumour has it, and it's only rumour, mind you, that the Nats are going to use gas.'

'Gas!' Maggie exclaimed. 'You mean on Madrid?'

'That's what's they say. They'll do it too if they have gas available. Nothing is beneath these bastards.'

Andy spied the whisky bottle, and his eyes lit up. 'Can I have a belter?' he asked, indicating the bottle.

'You can have a couple, but no more. At least not until I can find an alternative antiseptic. I'm using it to clean Nevil's wound.'

Andy drank straight from the bottle. He took a large swig, burped, then had another. 'Oh, that's better!' he breathed.

Maggie went to her suitcase. 'How about some cigarettes? I brought some with me.'

'You're an angel, Maggie. A decent cigarette is virtually

impossible to come by nowadays. The last lot I managed to buy were absolutely disgusting. I dread to think what was in them, but it certainly wasn't tobacco.' He gratefully grabbed the two packets Maggie threw to him.

While he was opening a packet Maggie went to Nevil and felt his forehead. 'How's the shoulder?' she asked.

'Painful.'

'More or less than when we went to bed?'

He thought about that. 'A little more, I'd say.'

'I'll change the dressing in a minute.' She turned to Andy. 'I'm going to need some more dressings. In fact what I need are dressings, antiseptic, medicine and bandages. Can you help me at all?'

'What about Felicia?' Nevil suggested.

'Who's Felicia?' Maggie asked.

Nevil grinned. 'Andy's friend. Isn't she, Andy?'

Andy had gone a bright pink. 'She is my friend, and proud I am that she is.'

'A *girl*friend?' Maggie smiled.

The pink changed to red. 'Felicia's too good for me. She's got class, that woman. Let's just say we enjoy one another's company.'

'A sculptress who's studied at the Slade,' Nevil informed Maggie.

'A sculptress!'

'An amazing person,' Andy said, awe in his voice. 'Would you believe she went by herself to a remote part of Transylvania where she slept in the open and exchanged wood carvings for food.'

'She sounds quite a woman,' Maggie acknowledged, restraining herself from making an obvious crack about Dracula.

'Oh, she is! She is! You'll like her when you meet her. Everyone likes Felicia,' Andy enthused.

You certainly do, Maggie thought. 'So can Felicia get these things for me?'

'She knows an awful lot of people, I'm sure she'll be able to do something. I'll speak to her just as soon as I can,' Andy replied.

'Where are the lads staying?' Nevil queried.

'We haven't been billeted yet. We only arrived this morning, about three quarters of an hour ago. We heard last night's shelling from where we were camped.'

'How much damage has been done?' Maggie asked.

'Not nearly as much as I expected. But if they keep that intensity of shelling up there soon will be. And fatalities.'

'I wonder how many were killed last night.' Nevil mused.

'Anyway,' Andy continued, 'I left the lads at the barracks where they'll eat and get cleaned up. For myself, when I learned you were here I thought I'd come and see you and use your facilities. If that's all right?'

'Feel free.'

'I must say I never expected to find you like this. I was actually hoping you would be fit enough to rejoin us. We miss you, you know.'

Nevil gave a weak smile. 'That's nice to hear. And I can assure you I would rejoin you if I could. But yesterday I was so bad I couldn't even make that door under my own steam.'

'He won't be doing any more fighting for a while, you can tell your superiors that,' Maggie stated with determination.

'Speaking of superiors,' Andy said. 'I'm *El Cabo* now. I got promoted as soon as they heard what had happened to you.'

'Oh! So the platoon has two corporals now?'

Andy shook his head. 'Wrong!'

'You mean I've lost my stripes?'

'I mean you're now a *Teniente*. Congratulations, Lieutenant!'

'Lieutenant!' Nevil beamed. 'That's terrific. Isn't it, Maggie?'

She couldn't help but think of Davey Law and Kevin McGee, whose faces she could visualize quite clearly in her mind. 'Yes, I suppose so.'

Andy turned to Maggie. 'From what I've heard your train must have been one of the last to get into Madrid, if not the last. All railway links with the outside were severed yesterday. You're lucky to have made it.'

'I nearly didn't,' Maggie said, and told Andy the tale of her train being attacked by Moorish cavalry.

'But why have you come to Spain?' he asked when she'd finished. 'Just to see lover boy here?'

The truth or not? she wondered. And decided there was no need for Andy to know about John McNair. 'I got lonely without him,' she murmured. That was still the truth if not the whole truth. 'And just as well I did come when I did. He needs personal attention.'

Andy scratched himself. 'I'll have that bath now if I may. I can't tell you how much I've been looking forward to it.'

'There's a razor in there if you want to give yourself a shave,' Nevil stated quietly.

'I'll do that for you if you like. I've already promised Nevil one,' Maggie offered.

Andy smiled, as did Nevil. 'It wasn't just my face Nevil had in mind. He was thinking of the lice.'

Maggie flamed with embarrassment as the penny dropped. 'I see! Well I'm certainly not shaving you there. You'll have to do that for yourself.'

'Aww!' Andy joked. 'Just when I thought I was in for a treat.'

'I'll give you treat. Get on with you!'

Laughing, Andy picked up his bundle. 'Clean togs,' he explained, and headed for the bathroom.

'I hope the water's hot,' Nevil said.

'It is!' Andy yelled back, a few seconds later.

'Right,' said Maggie, 'I'd better get dressed. My clothes or your uniform?'

'Make it my uniform till we can find you something more suitable.'

Maggie dressed quickly, and then tended to Nevil's wound. Afterwards she drew back the curtains, the room instantly filling with hard October sunlight.

She gazed out. Everything looked so quiet and peaceful. It was hard to believe the city had been shelled the night before, or that fighting was taking place even now just outside its perimeters.

'Shall I get breakfast or wait for Andy to come with me?' she asked over her shoulder.

'Wait for Andy. He'll explain what the situation is and you'll be safe after that.'

Through in the bathroom Andy started to sing, a lullaby that brought back memories for Maggie. Her mother used to sing it to her when she was small.

She opened the window to let in some fresh air and then sat on the bed beside Nevil, talking to him until Andy re-emerged.

'I feel a new man, and that's the truth!' Andy declared.

'Manage all right with the shaving?' Maggie teased.

'Difficult to begin with, but easier as you got on. And no, I didn't nick myself. I was extremely careful.'

'I'll bet!' she smiled.

'I've rinsed out the bath and flushed bits and pieces down the toilet. I've also wrapped up my old clothes which need chucking out. The damn things are crawling.'

Maggie pulled a face.

'Inevitable out there,' Nevil said to her. 'Everyone gets lice. It can't be helped.' Changing the subject, he continued, 'Now how about you two going and getting some breakfast?'

That transpired to be chunks of coarse bread, sardines and red wine.

Andy explained the situation to the comrade in charge of the canteen, saying that *Camarada* Maggie would be looking after *Camarada* Sanderson until *Camarada* Sanderson was better. The comrade in charge said *Camarada* Maggie was welcome to use the canteen as long as she liked; a *camarada* was a *camarada* after all.

The sardines were delicious, quite unlike any other Maggie had ever tasted.

After breakfast Andy left them to return to the barracks for the platoon, but before he left he repeated that he'd contact Felicia just as soon as he was able.

It has been a lazy, lovely day as far as Maggie was concerned. She'd only left the room twice after Andy had gone, the first time to get lunch, the second for the evening meal.

205

She'd had another bath, and managed to wash Nevil's hair using a large container she'd discovered at the bottom of the cupboard in the corridor. Now it was evening and they were lying in bed talking softly to one another.

'Listen!' said Nevil suddenly. 'Can you hear it?'

'What?'

'Gunfire. In the distance.'

She listened, and there was something. But she couldn't say it was gunfire.

'It's definitely that,' Nevil told her, grim-faced. 'The direction of the wind must have changed which is why we can hear it now but couldn't before.'

She took his hand and squeezed it.

'What is it?' he asked.

'I don't know.'

'Scared?'

'A little. But as much for you as for me.'

'Are you sorry you came?'

'No, not at all!' She raised his hand to her lips and kissed it.

'That's nice.'

'Hmmh!' She kissed the hand again, then gently licked it.

'And that's nicer.'

She placed the hand on a breast.

'That's nicest yet!' he grinned. 'If . . .'

'If what?'

'If somewhat uncomfortable.'

He took his hand away, twisted himself round a bit, and put it back again.

'How's that?' she said.

'Worse than it was.' He dropped his hand to her thigh and caressed there.

'Better?'

'Much. Less strain,' he agreed.

She closed her eyes. How marvellous it was to be lying beside Nevil with his hand where it was. Love welled inside her, and desire.

'I wish . . .' he began, and trailed off.

'Wish what?' she prompted.

'Wish I didn't feel so exhausted. I'm utterly buggered, Maggie, and that's the truth.'

'That's only natural. It's going to take quite some time for you to recover.'

He sighed. 'I keep thinking of Andy and the others, wondering how they're getting on. I wish I could be with them.'

'Oh, thank you very much! I would have thought you'd rather be with me.'

'You know what I mean.'

'Do I?'

'I love you, Maggie, but what's happening all around us is so much bigger than you and I. So very much bigger. Lying here like this galls me in the extreme, I feel so useless!'

'You got shot, now you're recovering. That's a fact you're just going to have to live with for a while,' she told him.

'I appreciate that mentally. But I still desperately wish it was otherwise.'

'Even with me here to keep you company?'

His seriousness evaporated, and he smiled. 'If I have to be stuck in bed then this is the best possible way for it to be. With you, and with you looking after me.'

She matched his smile. Turning her face towards him, she kissed him, her tongue gliding passionately into his mouth. They were still kissing when there was a tap on the door.

'Nevil, it's Felicia!' a female voice said.

Maggie immediately shot out of bed, and reached for her dressing-gown. 'Coming!' she called out.

Unbolting the door, she opened it. Bright, highly intelligent eyes that sparkled beneath a mane of wild hair greeted her.

'You must be Maggie. I'm Felicia Browne,' the female said.

'I'm delighted to meet you,' Maggie replied, shaking hands with Felicia. It was a firm, positive grip.

'I've brought some goodies,' Felicia said, heaving up the canvas bag she was carrying.

'Come in!'

Felicia went straight to Nevil and pecked him on the cheek. 'An infection in your wound, Andy said.'

'It was lucky for me that Maggie decided to put in an

appearance. I don't know what would have happened to me if she hadn't.'

Felicia placed the canvas bag on the bed and opened it. 'Anti-septic, dressings, bandages and . . .' She pulled out a largish bottle of pills, 'Medicine to help clear up that infection.'

'What sort of pills?' Maggie questioned, moving to the other side of the bed.

'Sulphonamide, whatever that is. But the good doctor I got them from said they should do the trick.'

'He can start on those right away. I'll get a glass of water,' Maggie said.

Felicia opened the bottle, shook two pills into the palm of her hand, and gave these to Nevil. 'You're to take two three times a day,' she instructed.

'And I'll make sure he does,' Maggie said, handing Nevil a tumbler of water.

She glanced at Felicia to whom she'd taken an instant liking. 'I never realized you were in the militia,' she smiled at Felicia. 'Neither Andy or Nevil mentioned the fact.'

'She was one of the first women to join up,' Nevil stated, having swallowed his pills.

'I was over here on holiday when the Fascists rebelled against the government. When I learned the militia were accepting women I felt it my duty as a committed Communist, and active party member, to volunteer my service.'

'And do you actually fight?' Maggie queried.

'That's a bone of contention, I'm afraid. So far I haven't been allowed to. But with the Fascists at the gates of Madrid I'm certain that will soon change. They're going to need every able-bodied person they can get to man the barricades and fill the trenches.'

'Wait till she gets going. I'm sure she'll be a holy terror,' Nevil joked.

'A woman can do anything a man can, it's only hidebound tradition, and the male ego, that stop us being given the chance,' Felicia declared hotly.

'Couldn't agree more,' Maggie smiled.

'In fact there are many things a woman can do far better than a man, things that up until now have been considered strictly the male prerogative.'

Nevil held up his good hand in submission. 'I'm not getting into an argument with you, Felicia. You're far too clever and articulate for me.'

'And *right*,' she stated emphatically.

Nevil laughed. But it was with Felicia, not against her.

'I'm relieved you were able to get some dressings,' Maggie said to Felicia. 'The one he's got underneath that bandage was our last.'

Felicia reached into the canvas bag and extracted a huge bottle of clear liquid. 'The antiseptic,' she said, giving it to Maggie.

'I've been using whisky up until now.'

Felicia's eyebrows shot up. 'What a waste!'

'Would you like a drop?'

'Yes, please. And nothing with it.'

'Me too,' Nevil declared with enthusiasm.

Felicia tipped the remainder of what was in the canvas bag on to the bed. 'I have to take the bag away with me,' she explained.

Maggie eyed the mound as she poured out the whiskies. There were dressings galore, and many packets of bandages. 'That's terrific. Just what we needed. Were they hard to come by?'

'Not exactly easy. But after a bit of arm twisting a doctor acquaintance of mine did produce the goods.'

Maggie gave Felicia her drink, then Nevil his. She wasn't bothering herself.

'Bottoms up!' Felicia toasted.

'She's got a far bigger dram than me,' Nevil complained.

'You're ill. Felicia isn't,' Maggie retorted.

'Not fair!' Nevil pouted, and disposed of his in one swallow.

'Andy mentioned you had English cigarettes?' Felicia said to Maggie after she'd had a sip of her drink.

'Would you like some?'

'Not for me, but the doctor who gave me these supplies. It's not necessary, but would be a nice gesture. And also

209

stand in our favour if we wanted more in the future.'

That made sense to Maggie. 'How many packets?' she queried.

'Two would be fine. And oh! Almost forgot.' She opened a side zipper pocket in the canvas bag to produce a squashed pair of blue overalls. 'Andy also said you needed these.'

Maggie handed Felicia a couple of packets of Senior Service, then accepted the overalls. She shook them out in front of her.

'Not too small, I hope?' Felicia said anxiously, gazing at them.

'On the big side if anything,' Maggie answered, holding them against herself.

'It's best if they are. It means you can wear as much as you want underneath.'

'I can't thank you enough, for everything,' Maggie said.

'That's what friends are for. What comradeship is all about. As Dumas put it, one for all and all for one, eh?'

Maggie was about to reply when there was the sound of a far-off explosion.

'It's started again,' Nevil stated quietly.

'And earlier this time,' Maggie added.

There was a second explosion, and a third, followed by a series in rapid succession as the Fascist artillery got into its stride.

'Perhaps you'd better stay here the night?' Maggie suggested to Felicia.

The sculptress gave her a wry smile. 'I belong to the school that believes if a bullet or bomb has your name on it then it'll find you wherever you are. And conversely, if it doesn't you can walk into a hail of bullets with bombs falling all around and come out the other side completely unscathed. So I won't, thank you very much.'

'A remarkable woman, and in some ways a contradictory one,' Maggie commented after Felicia had gone.

'Andy worships her.'

Maggie could understand why.

At which point the lights went out as the electricity was cut off again.

CHAPTER SIX

'A prison wardress! Me!' Maggie exclaimed, aghast.

'Not exactly that, you won't be in a proper prison,' Felicia explained. 'The prisoners you'd be looking after are in a convent. And half of them are children.'

Maggie didn't know what to make of this proposal. It had completely surprised her.

'We need to release the militiawoman who's doing the job at present so she can fight in defence of the city,' Felicia went on. It was something she herself, as she'd predicted, was now doing. She'd been hastily trained in the use of the machine-gun and now did spells of duty manning a machine-gun post in the eastern part of Madrid.

'I see,' said Maggie, biting her lip. 'But what about Nevil?'

'I don't need you about all the time, as I have done. Now that I'm up and walking there's no reason why I can't go to the canteen under my own steam,' he replied. It was a week since Maggie's arrival and thanks to her nursing and the sulphonamide pills, he'd made giant steps back to health.

It was true, Maggie thought. Nevil could now more or less look after himself. He still needed his dressing changed, but as the infection was clearing up and the wound healing nicely, twice a day was sufficient.

'Go on, you might even enjoy it,' Nevil urged. 'And it'll give you something to do other than sitting around here with me all day long.'

'Does that mean you're getting tired of my company?' she jibed.

'It means nothing of the sort, as you well know. But you do have to admit we are getting somewhat under one another's feet.'

That was also true, she thought.

'And it'll give you a chance to help the cause,' Felicia further argued. She looked dog-tired, having just spent ten hours at her machine-gun.

'Are any of these prisoners dangerous?' Maggie asked.

'No, not in the least! They won't give you any trouble. It's just that they have to be guarded, that's all.'

'And you say half of them are children?'

'Toddlers up to early teens, I believe. The sons and daughters of the Fascist women.'

Maggie didn't see how she could refuse. And it would please Nevil that she was helping the cause and perhaps even detract a little from his mounting frustration at being inactive.

'I rather like the idea of the children,' Maggie smiled. 'That could be fun.'

'You'll do it then?' Felicia queried.

'When do I start?'

'No time like the present. I'll take you there myself.'

That shook Maggie. 'I didn't realize you meant right away,' she laughed. 'But why not!'

'That's the spirit, girl,' Nevil said, nodding his approval.

Felicia ran a hand over her face. She couldn't wait to tumble into bed and the welcome arms of oblivion. It wouldn't take long to get Maggie sorted out, then it was straight to her billet and blanket bay. She wondered if she'd see Andy before going back on duty, she hadn't seen him for several days now and hoped she would, as she thoroughly enjoyed his company.

It only took Maggie a couple of seconds to get ready. Nevil wished her good luck after she'd kissed him goodbye.

'If I'm late remember to keep me something to eat,' she called back from the door.

'I won't forget!'

It was a shock for her to be out in the street, as she hadn't left the Hotel Colon since she'd arrived. She gazed curiously about her as she and Felicia made their way to the convent.

Many buildings were badly damaged from the shelling. Others had been completely destroyed, being simply reduced to a pile of rubble.

There had been many fatalities, as Andy had predicted, both

212

among those living in the city and those defending it. Madrid was now completely encircled and cut off by Fascist troops, positioned in hastily erected barricades and dug trenches.

So far the threatened gas hadn't been used, but the rumour still circulated. Maggie and Felicia were both carrying gas masks with them, while Nevil had his in his room. They had been supplied by Andy, who'd been vague about where they'd come from. Most people in Madrid were without one.

They came to a street Felicia had intended using, but it was impassable due to a mountain of rubble totally blocking its entrance. Two large office buildings had been blown up and had fallen in on one another. They took an adjoining street that was clear instead.

'Tell me something, Felicia, what will happen to the militia inside Madrid if it falls?' Maggie asked as they strode along side-by-side.

'It won't fall,' Felicia replied, instantly, and with complete conviction.

'That's what Nevil says. But what if it does?'

Felicia's expression became extremely bleak. 'It's my belief that should the unthinkable actually happen any surviving militia would be summarily executed. Each and every last one of us would be stood up against a wall and shot.'

Maggie felt her heart sink when she heard this confirmation of her own worst fears. On the number of occasions she'd put the same question to Nevil he'd either refused to reply, or been evasive.

'They'll never stand me up against a wall. I promise you that,' Felicia said.

Maggie believed her.

The street they were now in was fairly busy. There was a long queue outside a milk shop and other people were either on the move or dotted about in small groups talking to one another.

Felicia heard the aeroplane first. She stopped in her tracks, and glanced up at the sky. But the fighter, appearing as though from nowhere, was already upon them.

Felicia moved with the speed of lightning as the plane

began firing. A bemused Maggie felt herself grabbed and pulled into the relative safety of an entranceway as twin spurts of bullets raced towards where she and Felicia had been only moments before. As the plane went past it was flying so low she actually caught a glimpse of the pilot's grinning face.

'Oh my God!' Maggie choked, realizing just how close she'd been to death.

The plane went as quickly as it had appeared, skimming away over the roof-tops.

'You all right?' Felicia asked in a dry voice.

'I eh . . . I . . . Thank you.'

'Come on,' replied Felicia, with a smile. She understood perfectly how Maggie felt – it had been a very near thing.

A scene of brutal butchery greeted them when they stepped back out into the street. The queue outside the milk shop had been mown down. Bodies lay writhing and jerking, in a huge pool of still-spreading blood.

Somebody was moaning piteously, while one woman was making a sound that was quite indescribable and Maggie knew it would haunt her for the rest of her life. A baby cried in its dead mother's arms. Other bodies and wounded lay strewn throughout the street. There were also a few shocked, but otherwise completely unscathed survivors like themselves.

'The pilot was grinning when he did this,' Maggie said. 'I saw him clearly. He was grinning as though this was some big joke.'

Felicia swore.

They helped as best they could until the services arrived.

Felicia and Maggie turned into the Plaza de Conde Toreno, and the convent was just in front of them. Both were splashed with blood from the victims of the Fascist plane.

'What order of nuns had the convent?' Maggie asked.

'Nuns of the Religious Order of the Capucines of the Most Immaculate Conception,' Felicia replied.

Maggie repeated that to herself. 'Rather a mouthful!' she joked.

'It's a church and convent together. The priests were

214

Fascists who sniped at workers in the street before being chased off by a band of militia.'

'Sniped! You mean with rifles?'

'Don't sound so amazed. The Church supports the Fascists, Nevil must have told you that.'

'He did say that members of the clergy have been witnessed loading weapons for Fascist soldiers and sympathizers, but not that priests themselves have actually fired upon the people.'

'Well, it's true, I assure you,' Felicia said.

'But how could a man of God do such a thing? That's what mystifies me.'

Felicia gave a bitter laugh. 'You've a lot to learn, Maggie. Many old beliefs and superstitions to be washed away. The Church, particularly in Spain, is rotten, cynical in the extreme, and only out for its own ends. If there is such a thing as God he certainly doesn't exist in the hearts of his Spanish clergy.'

'You don't believe in God then?'

'God, Odin, Zeus, Mohammed, Kali, whatever, all devices invented by the intelligent to keep the not so intelligent under control. Religion is nothing more than a confidence trick. If you've read Marx you'll know he described it as an "opiate for the masses". That's as good a definition as any, and better than most.'

She'd lost faith after Heymouth, Maggie thought. But her faith had returned. She disagreed totally with Felicia, but decided to keep that to herself. She liked Felicia enormously. But now she also felt sad for the sculptress, and a certain degree of pity.

They entered the convent through a pair of magnificent iron-studded and hinged wooden doors.

'Have you been here before?' Maggie asked, gazing about the dim interior.

'Only once. A while back when it was the billet for some of the 5th.'

They went through an arch and along a flagstone corridor that wasn't just dim, but positively gloomy.

'Where are the nuns?' Maggie queried.

'They had nothing to do with the sniping so were allowed to

215

go and stay in the private houses of friends. There are several here, but not belonging to this Order.'

They arrived at another iron-studded wooden door, which they opened with an iron ring that controlled a locking bar.

Behind this door was a well-lit room containing a number of tables and chairs and several sofas. Women of varying ages were sitting and lounging everywhere.

'Maggie Jordan?'

Maggie swung round to find herself staring at Evelyn Loup who was staring, just as dumbfounded, back at her. Evelyn was holding a revolver pointed down at the floor.

'Evelyn!'

They rushed towards one another, meeting roughly halfway, and embraced while Felicia watched in amusement.

'What are—' they both began at once. They stopped, then laughed in unison.

'You first,' Maggie said.

'What are you doing here?'

'I'm guarding these women and their children. What about you?'

'That's what I'm going to do. I only started about an hour ago when I was left here on my own. I was told I might have someone join me, but had no idea it was going to be *you*!'

'I take it the pair of you know each other,' smiled Felicia, coming over to them.

'Evelyn and I travelled to Madrid together,' Maggie explained.

'I said we might bump into one another again, and we have!' Evelyn said to her.

'I never thought we would. Just shows how wrong you can be. But why are you still in Madrid? I thought you meant to travel on to where your husband is fighting?'

'That was the plan,' Evelyn nodded. 'But once in Madrid I couldn't get out again. I've been trapped here since my arrival.'

'Your husband is fighting for the Republicans?' Felicia queried.

'Yes, he's a militiaman on the front around Siguenza.

216

At least that's where he was when last I heard from him.'

Maggie realized Evelyn and Felicia hadn't yet been introduced, so rectified that.

'Is that necessary?' Maggie asked, pointing at the revolver.

'I was told I had to have it, and that I'm to use it if any of the prisoners try to escape. Frankly, it terrifies the living daylights out of me.'

Maggie glanced over at the female prisoners, most of whom were regarding her and her two companions with idle curiosity.

'I'm sure neither of you will ever have to fire a revolver, at least not at any of this lot,' Felicia said.

There was a shriek of laughter, and a little girl appeared running along. A boy about her own age chased after her.

'I've Felicia to thank for being roped into this. What about yourself?' Maggie asked Evelyn.

'I was sitting at the hotel getting more and more bored. So when this was suggested to me I grabbed at it as a means of breaking the monotony. And also it does help the cause.' She indicated the blood on Maggie's overalls. 'What happened there?'

Evelyn listened grimly as Maggie recounted the story of the fighter plane in the street.

A shaft of light suddenly caught Felicia's face, highlighting her weariness.

'You look done in,' Maggie said sympathetically.

'I am. It was a long spell of duty.'

'Well, there's no need to stay here further on our account,' Evelyn said. 'I can soon explain to Maggie what little there is to know.'

'Will you be able to find your own way back to Fuencarral Street safely?' Felicia asked Maggie.

'That won't be a problem. Anyway, I've got my map, should I need it,' she replied, patting a pocket of her overalls.

'It really is terrific that we're working together like this!' Evelyn enthused after Felicia had gone.

'I couldn't be more delighted.'

'Come and I'll show you around – not that there's much to see.'

'How about food for these people? Were you told about that?'

Evelyn began putting Maggie in the picture.

Maggie found Nevil fast asleep, snoring, when she eventually returned to the Hotel Colon. A cold, congealed plate of food was on a chair with half a carafe of red wine on the floor beside it.

She stood staring down at Nevil, love and tenderness throbbing within her. Sitting on the bed she started to stroke his cheek.

'Uh! Uh!' he grunted suddenly, stirring.

'Hello, gorgeous,' she smiled, and kissed him.

'Hello, gorgeous yourself,' he smiled in return, and this time he kissed her.

'You taste of lemons,' she said. 'Why's that?'

'No idea. You taste of you. Nothing else, simply you.'

'Like it?'

'Adore it.'

She kissed him again.

'I brought you up something to eat,' he murmured.

'Happily I can forego that pleasure. I had a meal with the prisoners.'

He raised himself into a sitting position. 'How did it go?'

'Remember Evelyn Loup whom I told you about?'

'The woman you got friendly with coming over?'

'That's her. Well, she's been trapped in Madrid all this while, and now she and I will be working together. There are two sets of couples guarding the prisoners, each set operating an eight-hour shift. For the remaining eight hours they're locked in. Evelyn and I are one of the sets, the other is a Dutch and French girl, both of whom I'll meet tomorrow.'

'And what about the prisoners themselves, what are they like?'

'Most of them are wealthy women who were found to be either engaged in anti-Republican activity or concealing arms for Fascists. They're pleasant enough, in a condescending way. There's a fairly ancient marchioness who seems to think

218

we're servants and keeps trying to give us orders. Fetch me this and fetch me that – that sort of thing. The old goat is wearing a necklace that must be worth a king's ransom.'

'She's been allowed to keep that, eh?' Nevil queried. 'I would have thought something so valuable would have been confiscated.'

'No, they've been allowed to keep all the personal belongings they had on them when arrested. There are quite a few gold watches, expensive rings and suchlike.'

'And what do they do all day long?'

'Talk, read, play cards or board games, or else just generally laze about. There's a large area where the children play, which is fun. I much prefer looking at them than their mothers. I've already started to pick up a bit of Spanish. Evelyn says I seem to have a natural gift for languages.'

'I know something else you have a natural gift for,' Nevil said softly, a gleam having appeared in his eye.

She laughed. 'Whatever could you be referring to?'

'I think you know.'

She didn't reply.

He stared deep into her eyes, adoringly. 'Why don't you take your clothes off and come to bed?' he suggested.

'I thought I'd have a bath first.'

'The water's cold.'

'How do you know?'

'I'd be surprised if it wasn't. It nearly always is at this time of night.'

'And I'm surprised you haven't commented on something else yet.'

He frowned. 'What?'

'There's no artillery shelling.'

'Oh, that! They were talking about it earlier in the canteen. Everyone's hoping the Nats have run out of shells.'

'Do you think that's the case?'

'It seems the logical explanation. They're most probably waiting for a fresh supply.'

She took a deep breath. 'Whatever the reason it's lovely that the shelling's stopped. Albeit if it's only temporary.'

She went into the bathroom and turned on the hot-water tap, smiling when it stayed cold just as he'd predicted. She'd have an all-over wash instead of a bath she decided.

She filled the sink, then stripped. She shivered as she soaped herself, goose pimples appearing all over her body.

He turned up in the doorway to gaze at her.

'Voyeur!' she accused, tongue in cheek.

'Guilty m'lud,' he confessed in the same light tone. 'Know something?'

'What?'

'I could stand here for a week looking at you.'

'I'd get pneumonia long before then,' she joked.

He went to her, kissed her first on one shoulder, then the other. He slipped a hand round to cup a soapy breast.

'I love you,' he whispered. He made a growling sound as he pushed his face into her hair. 'I love you and want you.'

'I did get that impression,' she replied drily. 'But can you just wait a minute!' she went on, turning and pushing him gently away.

The blood on her overalls caught his eye. His mood changed completely as she told him what had happened.

'I don't know what I'd do if I lost you,' he choked when she finished.

'What about me? What would I do if I lost you?' And there was far more likelihood of that, she thought soberly.

'Will you do my dressing for me?' he asked.

'Of course. Get the things ready and I'll be right through.'

Nightie or not? she wondered as she towelled herself. Not, she decided. She applied a liberal amount of talcum powder before going through, where she found him naked as well.

'A new bandage tonight, I think,' she said, undoing the one in place.

'How is it?' he queried when the old dressing was off and the wound revealed.

'Improving all the time.' In a way she wished that wasn't so. For when it was healed he would definitely return to the front.

220

As soon as the second of the two small brass safety pins was clicked shut he caught her in his good arm.

'I could eat you,' he said.

'Lie back,' she whispered.

He did as he was bid, and groaned as her hands fluttered over him, touching, teasing, cajoling. Then she came on top, and slowly down.

'Magic,' he pronounced in a long exhale. 'Sheer magic.'

She couldn't have agreed more.

Maggie closed her eyes, enjoying the winter sunshine beating on her face. Her pleasure was further enhanced by the sound of childish laughter, the result of the game of tig she'd introduced to the Spanish children held at the convent.

'Concepcion is it!' Eladio shouted.

'No I'm not, you missed.'

'Yes you are, I didn't.'

'You missed,' Concepcion lied again, knowing full well he hadn't.

'No, I didn't. Cheat! Cheat! Concepcion's a cheat!'

'Ra ra ra ra!' yelled Pablo, José, Maria and Juan Luis together. Concepcion dashed after Eladio, but couldn't catch him. She managed to tig Pilar instead. Pilar was only four years old whereas Concepcion was ten.

'Pilar's it! Pilar's it!' Concepcion shouted, dancing away.

Maggie opened her eyes to stare at these children of whom she'd become so fond. She could understand a lot of what they said now, her Spanish having improved by leaps and bounds.

Pilar ran after José, who let her catch him because he was her brother. He immediately went after Concepcion, who shrieked as she raced away from him.

José tripped, and went tumbling. But instantly he was back on his feet again to resume his pursuit.

Evelyn appeared, smiled at the happy scene, and gave Maggie a brief wave before disappearing again. Neither she nor Maggie now carried the revolver. They had both decided that while they were on shift it was entirely unnecessary. The Fascist women had absolutely no intention of trying to escape, knowing they would only be found and brought back. Gaby and Françoise, the other couple who guarded the prisoners, locked the revolver away as well.

Manolo came waddling over to Maggie. He was just two, with an enchanting elfin face, and was her favourite, though she'd never let on, not even to Evelyn. She swept him into her arms and cuddled him tight, before releasing him again.

'You're beautiful,' she said in English.

'*Que?*'

'Nothing, *nada*,' she replied, shaking her head.

Manolo scampered off to a corner where he was playing with Chicuelo, the pair of them having made an impromptu game out of several cardboard boxes. Chicuelo had a bad cast in his right eye and had been nicknamed Little Fox by the other children.

Maggie listened to the faint crackle of far-off firing. The militia were continuing to hold out against the Fascists, though paying heavily for doing so. Their somewhat grim boast was that three Fascists died for every one of them.

From another direction came the sudden bang of an exploding artillery shell. She'd long since been able to distinguish between that and a bomb bursting.

The Fascists had started shelling again at night, and also occasionally during the day. The night-time shelling was continuous, the daytime shelling spasmodic, as if they only bothered when the mood took them. Knowing the Spanish as she now did, Maggie thought this could well be the case. There again they could be intentionally playing on the nerves of the beleaguered Madrilenos.

She would have loved a cup of tea, she thought wistfully. The Spanish could keep their coffee and wine. Tea knocked both into a cocked hat.

'Tired?' Renata asked her. Renata was thirteen and had already blossomed into ripe womanhood. She was a great help with the younger children.

'Not really,' Maggie smiled.

'Thinking of home.'

'In a way.'

'You miss it very much?'

'Some aspects of it, yes.'

'But not so much as you might if you didn't have your Nevil.'

Renata was wise beyond her years, Maggie thought. She had more insight and understanding than many women twice her age.

'That's right,' she agreed.

Juan Luis was it now, haring after Pablo whom he knew he would soon catch as he was a far faster runner. Pablo jigged and weaved as he ran, putting off the moment of being caught for as long as possible.

'Lunch should be along soon,' Evelyn said from where she was sitting playing cards with three of the prisoners.

Maggie glanced at her watch. It should, but you could never rely on the Spanish. Punctuality wasn't exactly a strong point with them. She'd noticed that the meals had deteriorated of late. The city was a long way from starving, but dwindling supplies were being eked out. Even the militia was having to tighten its collective belt.

She rose and made her way inside, stopping to gaze into the children's dormitory, a room she adored. All the beds belonging to the younger children had been painted by Gaby, a marvellous artist, with pictures from Walt Disney cartoons and other film characters.

All of a sudden an explosion knocked her off her feet and on to the corridor floor, where she lay momentarily stunned while dust and debris rained down on her.

We've been hit, she told herself. The convent's been hit. She choked and coughed, dust clogging her throat.

A scream rang out, followed by others. Shrill, piercing, agonized screams that stabbed the eardrums and tore at the heart.

Maggie regained her feet and, still choking and coughing, stumbled towards the screams.

A wall had come down, and a section of the ceiling. Several of the women were clearly dead, including the ancient marchioness, and a number were wounded. But the real horror lay beyond, in the outside yard where the children had been.

She stared at the sight before her, unable to believe her eyes.

'Oh sweet God!' Evelyn breathed, joining Maggie. Like Maggie, she too was unhurt.

Maggie turned away, and threw up.

'It's a new type of shell modelled apparently on the famous French 75mm shell,' Nevil stated quietly. 'Andy and I were talking about them just the other day.'

Maggie's face was white and haggard, with dark circles under her eyes. Every so often she trembled all over.

'Are you sure you won't have some of this wine?' Nevil queried.

'No,' she answered dully.

He had a swallow, and wished it was something stronger.

'Not one child was left alive, nor . . .' She hesitated, then said, 'Nor whole.'

'It'll do you good to talk about it. You must get it out of your system,' Nevil said.

She bit her lip. 'What I don't understand is why there were so many bullet wounds, and bullet holes in the walls.'

'I can explain that if you want to know.'

She nodded.

'The shell is not designed for the destruction of property, but killing the maximum number of people. When it detonates it . . .' He took a deep breath. 'Are you certain you want to hear this?'

She nodded again.

'When it detonates it only causes minor impact damage, but on the other hand the lateral explosion force is tremendous. The shells are also filled with bullets so that on impact these bullets spray in all directions. The shells are principally designed for use against troops moving across open country where the objective is not the battering down of heavy defences, but the mowing down of men.'

'They're certainly effective in that way,' she acknowledged. 'Only in this instance it wasn't men who were mown down, but children.'

224

Her face contorted. 'It was like an abattoir, Nevil. Legs, arms, torn strips of flesh. And blood, an ocean of that. Manolo was . . . Manolo was . . .' She placed a hand over her mouth, unable to describe what had happened to her favourite.

'What's become of the prisoners who survived?'

'They've been put in another part of the convent. If it's had this effect on me, imagine what it must be like for the mothers among them. The mothers whose children had been out there where the shell landed.'

Nevil could well imagine.

'After Heymouth I thought I could never be so affected again, but this . . .' She trailed off.

'Will you be going on shift again tomorrow?'

'I'll have to, until they can find someone else to replace me.'

'You're giving it up then?'

Tears glistened in her eyes. 'I have decided to join the militia, Nevil. I thought about it as I walked back this evening. I'm going to join the 5th. Initially I didn't feel part of all this, but now I do.'

He went to her, and clasped her hands which were freezing cold.

'It's my fight too now,' she went on. 'It became my fight when I saw what had happened to those children.'

'And I also must do something,' he declared earnestly. 'I've been out of action far too long.'

'You're not properly healed yet, Nevil. That wound needs more time.'

'There must be some job I can do though, some way I can make myself useful!' he argued. 'I'll report in tomorrow and explain the situation. I can't continue to lie and sit around here any longer.'

She began to cry, long drawn-out sobs that racked her body while bright hot tears poured down her cheeks.

Nevil held her close, anger erupting inside him. 'They're bastards, the Fascists!' he said vehemently. 'Bastards! Bastards! Bastards!'

'Bits,' she wailed. 'All that was left of those children were bits.'

Nor could she get it out of her mind that if the shell had landed a few minutes earlier she would have been where Renata was.

She would have vomited again if there had been anything left in her stomach. She dry heaved instead.

Evelyn was allowed to translate for Maggie as the comrade officer's Spanish was too quick and heavily accented for her to understand.

'He says we will have another half-day of learning how to march, then he will instruct us in the use of the rifle and bayonet.'

They were in the same Francisco Rodriguez Street Barracks where Nevil and the others from Templeton's had been trained, and it was just as large, ugly and draughty as he had described it. It also stank dreadfully, something he had failed to mention.

There were forty-eight of them in that intake, and a very mixed bunch they were too. Some of the boys were no more than fifteen, but judged old enough to fight, and die if necessary, for their country.

The comrade officer in charge was Major Gallo, a foreman steelworker who had distinguished himself early on. A nicer, more jolly man you'd go a long way to meet.

Maggie and Evelyn had joined the 5th together, Evelyn having been just as sickened and distressed by the death of the children as Maggie. It was understood however that Evelyn would be released from the 5th whenever it became possible for her to travel on to where her husband was fighting – in other words when the siege of Madrid was over, and the attackers repulsed.

Major Gallo shouted out an order, instructing the intake to form itself into columns of fours.

'Who, me? Me, too? Am I included with the others?' a young recruit queried, a twinkle in his brown eyes.

'Yes, you too. When I give an order it is for everyone!' Major Gallo replied.

The young man shrugged. 'How was I to know?'

Typically Spanish, Maggie thought. They loathed to think of themselves as belonging to the herd. It could be very trying, to say the least. There always seemed to be one objector when orders were given.

She grinned at the idea of someone trying that on while being trained for the British army. The sergeant or NCO in command would have come down on the poor sod like a ton of bricks. But Major Gallo was used to, and understanding of, this type of behaviour. It happened all the time.

'Left turn!' Major Gallo cried when they were under way. Then, seconds later, 'Left turn!' again.

The Spanish marching step amused Maggie. It was very short and rapid so that those doing it looked as if they were strutting rather than marching. It always reminded her of a parade of orderly excited geese.

Then she remembered the children, and the smile faded from her face.

She put renewed energy into her marching.

Nevil sat at his temporary desk working at the assignment he'd been given, the smooth distribution of arms and ammunition throughout the 5th.

What a mess, he thought for the umpteenth time. A complete cock-up! No wonder they'd been anxious to replace his predecessor, the idiot couldn't have organized a booze up in a brewery.

He slowly translated the chit in front of him, then ticked it off against a master list, deducting the amount of ammo requested from the amount held in the arsenal. It was simple enough really, and everyone knew where they were at a glance.

'*Camarada* Sanderson.'

Nevil looked up, then rose quickly to his feet. He gave the Red salute.

Colonel Rivero returned the salute. Then said to the man standing beside him, 'This is *Camarada Teniente* Sanderson, one of our British volunteers.'

'Ah!' The man's face lit up. 'British, eh!'

227

To Nevil the colonel said, 'Allow me to introduce *Camarada* Antonio Mije, Councillor for War on the Madrid Defence Council.'

'*Salud Camarada*,' Nevil said.

'*Salud Camarada Teniente* Sanderson,' Mije replied. Then, switching to English, 'I'm pleased to meet you.'

'And I to meet you.' Mije was one of the most important figures currently in Madrid, and had already become something of a legend.

'*Camarada* Sanderson is assisting here while he recovers from a wound he received fighting in the Sierra de Guadarrama,' Rivero explained, also now speaking in English.

'Where were you hit?'

'Shoulder,' Nevil answered.

'Badly?'

'I unfortunately had complications. But I'm almost better now.'

'Good,' Mije muttered, nodding. 'And then it's back to killing Fascists?'

'As many as I can.'

Mije grunted his approval. 'Did you come from Britain alone?'

'No, there were fifteen of us originally. We're down to thirteen, I'm afraid, including one who's lost a foot.'

'And is *Camarada* Sanderson a good fighter?' Mije bluntly asked Rivero.

Nevil looked away in embarrassment.

'An excellent one, *Camarada* Councillor. All the British fight well, they have an aptitude for it. Particularly the Scots. They are devils.'

Mije regarded Nevil strangely, as if he was contemplating some deep secret. He then wagged a finger at Nevil. 'I shall not forget you, *Camarada* Scotsman. You are now firmly in my memory.'

Nevil didn't know what to make of that. 'Thank you,' was all he could think of to reply.

Mije moved away, and immediately broke into a torrent of

Spanish which he spoke quietly and directly to Colonel Rivero. Nevil listened but couldn't make out a word of what was being said.

He sat again at his desk and picked up another chit, this one for mortar shells of which they were extremely short.

After due consideration he decided to allocate them a third of what they'd indented for.

Maggie came striding into their hotel room, her face flushed with success.

'The course may have been short and sweet, but that's hardly my fault. I'm now a fully trained militiawoman,' she announced.

'Congratulations,' Nevil said and kissed her on the mouth. He would have attended the short ceremony if it had been possible, but he had been on duty.

'Hmmh, more!' she murmured when the kiss was over.

'That's all you're getting for now. I have a surprise.'

'Surprise?'

'Three actually. At long last Stuart Borland is out of hospital and ensconced on the floor below this one. That's number one. Number two is that the lads have been given a forty-eight-hour stand down. And number three is that we're all going out to celebrate Stuart, the stand down, and your becoming a fully fledged member of the 5th.'

'What do you mean *out*?' she queried.

'Just that. A night on the town. We're going to paint Madrid red.' He laughed, realizing he'd inadvertently made a joke. 'Red! Get it?'

'Oh, I get it,' she smiled. 'But out where?'

'Wherever. We thought perhaps the Café Moka.'

She'd heard Andy mention it. Excitement flared in her. 'Sounds fun. We haven't had a night out since I came to Madrid.'

'Well, tonight we shall.' He suddenly frowned. 'You don't mind the lads and Stuart coming along, do you? We could go on our own if you really wanted to.'

'But you'd prefer it with the others?'

'To be truthful, Maggie, with them available it wouldn't seem right somehow.'

'One big happy family, is that it?'

'On the nail.'

'What time do we meet up?' she asked.

He glanced at his watch. 'Roughly an hour from now.'

'Well, that doesn't give much time to get ready!' she complained. 'Is the water hot?'

'I don't know. Try it.'

She rushed through to the bathroom and was delighted to discover the water was piping hot. She'd have hated to go out without a wash. It would also have been nice to wear one of the pretty dresses she'd brought with her, but of course that was out of the question. It would be her uniform with – she brightened a little – a dab or two of perfume. It was frowned upon for perfume to be worn during normal routine work, but this was an occasion and therefore qualified as an exception.

'We'll have a right good night of it,' Charlie Menzies said, rubbing his hands together. 'I just hope there are some spare female *camaradas* about, that's all.'

'He never changes,' Nevil smiled at Maggie.

Felicia was with Andy and Stuart Borland, Stuart swinging along on crutches. He was becoming most adept with them.

Leaving the Hotel Colon, they approached the Mercedes that Felicia had somehow come up with, and which had to be returned in the morning.

'I'll drive!' declared Andy as Stuart manoeuvred himself into the front passenger seat.

'No, I will,' Felicia told him.

'I'm not having a woman driving me!' Andy protested.

'Walk then.'

'You wouldn't do that to me, would you, Fliss?' That was the pet name he'd taken to calling her.

Maggie grinned at this good-humoured banter.

'You're darn tootin' I would!' Felicia retorted.

'Oh, she's hard,' Charlie joked, solemnly shaking his head.

'I don't care who drives. It's just lovely to be in a car again,' Maggie said, diving into the spacious rear.

'Can we hurry? Or the others are going to be there before us,' Stuart said. The other lads had gone on ahead.

'I'll drive,' Andy argued.

'*I'm* driving,' stated Felicia firmly.

'They're just like an old married couple,' Maggie whispered loudly to Charlie who'd joined her – so loudly that Andy and Felicia would hear.

'Oh, well, if you insist!' Andy said, pretending to be miffed.

'I do.'

Andy got in the back with Maggie, Nevil and Charlie. It was a fairly tight squeeze.

'I've driven with her before, she's completely mad!' Andy said to Nevil.

The Mercedes shot away, like a ball out of a cannon.

'See what I mean!' Andy screeched.

Felicia chuckled behind the wheel – she'd done that deliberately. She then made the tyres squeal going round a corner.

'If Mo Cairns was in the car with us I'd make him say one of his Popish prayers,' Andy declared.

'God's banned, don't forget you're a Republican now,' Charlie reminded him.

'Oh aye! I'd forgot.'

'How about a dirty song? Just like the old days,' Charlie proposed.

'No, thank you,' Maggie said.

'They can be a good laugh,' he went on hopefully.

'We don't need dirty songs to have a good laugh. We've got you,' Maggie retorted.

Charlie screwed up his forehead, thinking about that.

'I'm having a smashing time already,' Maggie smiled at Nevil.

'And so am I,' Stuart said from the front.

Maggie had never got back to see Stuart in the hospital as she'd promised. But it had been one thing after another; luckily he'd understood.

He was still plagued by the hospital cough, though

otherwise fine. If you could call it fine, that is, losing a foot, a great deal of weight and ageing ten years in a few months. He'd started to go grey at the temples, which was a development since Maggie had last seen him.

Felicia parked the car when they reached the Café Moka, and they all went inside. She did the talking, and they were shown to two large tables that were pushed together for them.

It was a nightclub as opposed to what the British call a café, Maggie thought, as she gazed about. There was a dance floor, and a band on a rostrum. The band wasn't particularly good, but that didn't seem to matter. What was most important to her was that she was with Nevil.

'One thing's certain, I won't be doing any dancing,' Stuart joked, which earned him a sympathetic laugh.

'If I held you up we could both do bunny hops,' Felicia told him.

'True enough. I hadn't thought of that!'

They ordered enough wine for their entire party. And not long after that the others arrived, making a boisterous entrance.

The newcomers clustered round the two tables, laughing and joking as they sat down. They were a noisy group, but inoffensive, causing no harm to anyone.

'I had a dream last night,' Andy confided to Maggie.

She could see it was a come on. 'What sort of dream?'

'Oh a lovely one! Know what I dreamt of?'

She smiled.

'I dreamt that you still had a wee hoard of cigarettes and that you gave it to me.'

'I'm sorry, Andy. Those Senior Services are long gone.'

He sighed wistfully. 'It was a nice dream nonetheless.'

More wine was ordered and soon enough Charlie and several others drifted off with the intention of chatting up some of the female camaradas present. Charlie 'clicked' with one almost right away.

Maggie stared about her, fascinated.

'See those four men over there,' Felicia whispered, indicating the men she meant with a nod of her head.

'Oh-huh!'

232

'High-ranking Russian comrades here to help. It's said the one with the Charlie Chan moustache is an agent of the Ogpu.'

'And what's Ogpu?'

'Obedinyonnoye Gosudarstvennoye Polititshskoye Upravleniye, which translated means Unified State Political Directorate. In other words, Russian State Security,' Felicia explained.

Charlie Chan moustache was as sinister looking a man as Maggie had ever come across. There was something about him which made her flesh creep.

'And see that chap by himself,' Felicia went on. 'The one slightly to the left of the Russians.'

'Yes.'

'His name is Robert Jordan and he's an American. He's an expert dynamiter, and friend of the well-known American writer, Ernest Hemingway. I met him and Hemingway here before the siege started. Hemingway is somewhere else in Spain, I believe.'

Maggie had heard of Hemingway, but never read any of his books. 'Is Robert Jordan one of us?' she queried.

'Most certainly. I have it on good authority that he's caused enormous damage to Nationalist installations. We could use many more with his skill and talent.'

A handsome man, Maggie thought. Lean, with a slightly cadaverous face, he reminded her of a bird of prey.

She shivered. The Café Moka positively reeked of intrigue. So many of its denizens were shifty-eyed, with a secretive air about them.

'Who are that lot?' she enquired, surreptitiously gesturing at a table around which a number of men sat.

'Foreign journalists. They come here quite a bit.'

A raven-haired, fiery woman who'd been at the bar laughed raucously, made a filthy remark and swayed over to a table where she joined a man and woman.

'She's the editor of *Solidaridad Obrera*, the Anarchist newspaper, and a well-known character,' Felicia whispered.

'Who's she talking to?' Maggie asked.

'They work for *La Batalla*, the POUM newspaper.'
POUM stood for Partido Obrero de Unification Marxista,
numerically a small party within the Popular Front Coalition
Government. It was considered important however because it
contained an unusually high proportion of politically conscious members.

Maggie smothered a laugh when two young men in their
late teens sauntered across the dance floor. 'What are they
supposed to be!'

Felicia was smiling broadly. 'Maricons, or nancy boys.
They're here looking for trade.'

Someone exclaimed in anger, and a fist flew. Instantly the
companions of the men arguing were on their feet trying to
calm matters down.

'French,' Maggie stated, recognizing the language.

'Lorry drivers trapped here same as your friend Evelyn,'
Felicia said.

Maggie had sent Nevil earlier to invite Evelyn to join them,
as she was now billeted at the Hotel Colon, but Evelyn hadn't
been there. She hadn't been in the canteen either. They
decided that she'd already gone out somewhere.

The band began playing 'The Girl With the Dreamy Eyes'
which was extremely popular in Madrid at that time, and
heard everywhere. Maggie adored it.

'Our dance, I believe, comrade?' Nevil smiled at her.

'I was beginning to wonder if you'd ever ask.'

They moved on to the floor, and into each other's arms.
Maggie closed her eyes, relishing the moment.

'What are you thinking about?' he queried softly.

'Of you. And me.'

He held her even closer. 'No matter what happens, we've
had some time together. That's something which can never be
taken away from us.'

She went cold all over to hear him say that.

'Let's only think about today, and forget about tomorrow,'
he went on.

'But tomorrow always comes.'

His lips thinned into a chilling grimace, and she realized

234

what was on his mind. Tomorrow did always come, but not always for the individual. Death ensured that.

When they returned to their seats they found Stuart entertaining the company with the story of a man in the next hospital bed to him who'd been given medicine that turned his urine emerald green.

'True!' Stuart protested when Norman Currie called him a liar. 'I swear it. Emerald bloody green!'

Half-drunk, as most of them now were, it sounded hilariously funny. They laughed uproariously, that is, with the exception of Nevil and Maggie. Their evening was never quite the same for them after that first dance together.

'Street patrol!' Maggie exclaimed in disappointment.

'That's what the notice says. You and I have to link up with a Comrade Lerroux.'

Maggie and Evelyn moved back from the notice to allow the other newly-fledged militia milling about to have a look at it.

Names started being shouted out as other militia began arriving on the scene.

One of their intake had a quick-fire conversation with Evelyn, then moved off.

'That was Comrade Nin professing himself to be pig sick. He's also on street patrol.'

'Jordan! Loup!'

'I think that's us,' muttered Evelyn, glancing about.

'Jordan! Loup!'

'Over there,' said Maggie pointing.

They made their way through the throng and reached the female who'd been shouting their names. They both gave the Red salute.

'*Camarada* Lerroux?' Evelyn said when they'd finished saluting.

'*Camarada* Jordan?'

Evelyn explained that she was Loup, and that Maggie was Jordan. She further explained that she was English and spoke fluent Spanish, Maggie Scots, with some Spanish.

235

'Me some Englis,' Lerroux replied with a nod.

She was about thirty, Maggie judged, though it was hard to get it right with these peasant Spanish females. They aged far more quickly than their British counterparts.

'We go!' Comrade Lerroux announced abruptly, and strode away. Maggie and Evelyn hurried after her.

First of all they went to the armoury where they were issued with rifles and ammunition which would now be permanently theirs. Up until now they had only been issued with arms on a daily basis. They were both given short Mausers, or mousquetons, which were popular because they were light and comparatively new, together with fifty rounds apiece. They would indent for further ammunition when necessary.

Under the critical eye of Lerroux they checked their weapons as they'd been taught, then they were on their way.

In a mixture of Spanish and English Lerroux told them she would spend one day with them showing them the ropes. She had been on street patrol for a month, and had now been reposted to the trenches and barricades.

They learned a lot from Comrade Lerroux that day, but wished she'd been able to stay with them a week rather than a single turn of duty.

The second day they were on their own.

Maggie and Evelyn paused to watch a flight of aeroplanes bearing Republican markings fly overhead. The planes were tiny and very fast moving.

It was Evelyn who saw the hand come out of a window above them and toss something down at them which was silver coloured and sparkled as it fell.

'Grenade!' she croaked.

Maggie's heart leapt. They both froze, rooted to the spot.

The grenade clattered on to the pavement beside them. Maggie could make out quite clearly that its pin had been pulled.

Seconds ticked by, but still neither of them could move.

'Dud!' Evelyn further croaked, slumping where she stood.

Life returned to Maggie. Her eyes swivelled to the doorway

from which the grenade had come. She didn't waste time, but blew the door lock apart with a single shot as she raced towards it.

She bounded up the rickety stairs that faced her, thinking that the person who'd thrown the grenade must be a fifth columnist, as there were many in the city.

The expression was a new one, coined by General Mola whose forces ringed Madrid. It was his boast that he had four columns outside the city, and a fifth within, composed entirely of civilian sympathizers whom the Republicans termed traitors and terrorists. These so-called fifth columnists had been causing a great deal of havoc and disruption of late.

Maggie, with Evelyn pounding behind her, left the stairs to enter a long room filled with racks of completed and semi-completed garments. Dotted about were clusters of industrial sewing-machines. The factory had been closed down because of the siege.

She stopped, her chest heaving. 'Sshh!' she instructed Evelyn, who stopped beside her. They both listened.

They heard a scuffling to their left, followed by the unmistakable sound of a sash window being lifted.

They ran off again, now side-by-side. A rack of clothes went spinning when Evelyn accidentally knocked it.

They bore left, and turned into a dog-leg. At the end of the dog-leg was a window leading on to an iron staircase.

At the window-ledge Maggie looked down, then up. She was just in time to see a pair of man's legs disappear from the top of the staircase on to the roof.

She took the lead, Evelyn following hard behind her. Both were ready to shoot at an instant's notice. And both were half anticipating another grenade to come flying their way.

At the top of the staircase Maggie went into a crouch and peered over the flat roof. Evelyn did the same beside her.

'There's the bugger!' hissed Evelyn, pointing.

Maggie caught a startled gaze, the man having been lurking behind a chimney-stack. And then the man was off again, running like billy-o, arms pumping at his sides.

Maggie had developed a stitch, and was wheezing badly. They'd covered a lot of ground in a very short while. They might have been sprinting in the Olympics the way they'd been going.

The man came up short, having reached the end of the roof. He glanced desperately back at Maggie and Evelyn bearing quickly down on him.

'Now we've got him!' Maggie said triumphantly. But she was wrong.

The man hastily retreated a few steps, took a deep breath, and then charged towards the end of the roof, launching himself out into space.

Evelyn swore in a most unladylike manner.

They halted at the end of the roof just in time to witness the man they'd been chasing vanish into a wooden doorway that was on another roof about eight feet below them.

They both gazed impotently at the second roof, and doorway through which their quarry had popped like a rabbit down a burrow.

'I'm not even going to consider it,' Maggie said, gasping for breath.

Evelyn shook her head. 'Me neither.'

'I doubt I could jump that far at the best of times.'

'Same with me.'

'Aaahhh!' exhaled Maggie, using her Mauser as a prop. 'Know something?'

'What?'

'When that grenade landed I wet myself. I'm absolutely soaking.'

A smile cracked Maggie's strained face. 'Know something?'

'What?'

'So did I.'

Evelyn started to laugh, and Maggie joined in – a laugh that became a combined roar.

After a while, arm-in-arm, they made their way back along the roof. In the garment factory they sorted themselves out and lifted a few minor articles, before continuing on down to street level.

Every so often throughout the rest of the day they chuckled about the incident.

Maggie stared at Nevil, shocked by his announcement, though knowing it had had to come.

'When?' she asked dully.

'Just as soon as Colonel Rivero can get a replacement to take over the job I'm doing now. Hopefully that shouldn't take long. A few days at the most.'

She turned away, not wanting him to see her face. 'Are you sure that wound's completely healed? That you're fit enough to fight again?'

'Maggie, you know I am,' he replied softly.

There was no point in arguing with him, she thought. The honeymoon period since her arrival was over.

'I'll be in command of a detachment of thirty-five men. A fair old responsibility,' he said, attempting a smile which didn't quite come off.

'Yes,' she agreed. 'I presume that includes what's now Andy's platoon?'

'It does.'

They fell silent.

'It's why I came here, Maggie. I came to fight, not be a glorified clerk.'

'I appreciate that.'

'Then stop making me feel guilty!'

'Am I?'

'You know damn well you are!'

Good, she thought. Served him right.

He swung the arm belonging to his wounded shoulder round several times. 'Right as rain! Thanks to the ministering angel who looked after me.'

'I raided a brothel today,' she said, changing the subject.

He stared at her in amazement. 'Did you really?'

'Yes, four of us were ordered to shut it down. You should have seen . . .' She sniggered. 'You should have seen the couple I found in one room. I never knew such things were possible.'

'What things?' he demanded eagerly.

Just like a man, she thought, dying to know the sordid details. He went wide-eyed when she told him.

Later, she went into the bathroom, locked the door, and wept silently.

'I wonder what this is all about?' Evelyn said to Maggie.

'Your guess is as good as mine.'

They'd just got back from duty to find a note asking them both to come together to Felicia's.

On the way, a barefoot child pitter-pattered past them, disappearing quickly into the night. Maggie hoped he wasn't off to loot. More and more children were breaking into what had been Fascist homes and business premises to loot.

The smell of warm olive oil hung heavily in the air. That and other specific odours were ones Maggie would forever associate with Spain.

She thought of Susan Lennox in Heymouth, and wondered how she was getting on. Then she wondered about Natasha, dear fat, cross-eyed Natasha who'd been such a friend to her. And what of her sister Laura, how was she? And the twins, Margaret and Rose?

How far away Glasgow seemed. As for Heymouth, that might have been in another lifetime altogether. So much had happened to her in such a short space of time. So many incredible things. Some wonderful, some horrendous.

She snapped out of her reverie when an aeroplane droned overhead. It was a large one, from the sound of it, and a few seconds later they heard the whistle of falling bombs off in the distance. Flashes from the following explosions lit up the sky.

'Down here,' Maggie said when they reached a dark and dingy alley-way. Walking gingerly over slippery cobbles, they managed to find the house they were looking for without any problem.

Felicia answered their knock. 'Come in. Did you find me easily enough?'

'No trouble,' Maggie reassured her.

'We're becoming dab hands at getting round Madrid in the dark,' Evelyn joked, referring to their spells of night-duty.

The room Felicia ushered them into was bathed in soft yellow light from two paraffin lamps. There was a double bed covered in a patchwork quilt, several Spanish rugs on the stone floor, a handsome pair of wooden chairs, a low coffee table and a tiny settee.

Felicia herself was wearing a brightly coloured Japanese kimono tied at the waist, and had her hair pulled back in a pony tail. She had rope-soled sandals on her feet, similar to those favoured by the Spanish hoi polloi.

'Is this a billet?' Maggie queried, gazing about.

Felicia laughed. 'Let's just say it's *my* billet.'

'You certainly get yourself organized,' Evelyn complimented Felicia.

'It's a talent of mine.'

Maggie's eyes fell on an object standing on the floor in a corner. She recognized Andy's likeness immediately.

'Can I have a closer look at that, Felicia?' she requested, pointing at it.

'If you like.'

Felicia picked up the bust and handed it to Maggie. 'It's not finished yet,' she explained as Maggie stared at the carving.

'It's fabulous,' Evelyn whispered.

'Hardly that. But it does have promise. I've been working on it during my time off.'

'You've certainly caught him,' Maggie said.

'He has such sensitive, curiously vulnerable features. The first time I met him I knew I wanted to sculpt his face. I'd love to do a bronze of him, but of course that's impossible in the present circumstances.' She smiled. 'Perhaps someday though, eh?'

Maggie ran a hand slowly all over the bust. It was the queerest sensation, she felt as though she might have been touching Andy himself.

'I'm very impressed, but not surprised. I'd already guessed you were extremely gifted.'

'Thank you.'

Felicia put the bust back, then turned to face Maggie and Evelyn. 'Now, before I speak to you about why I asked you here, how about some tea and cucumber sandwiches?'

'Tea!' Maggie exclaimed in delight. 'Real British tea?'

'Well, it's Indian actually,' Felicia replied, tongue in cheek. 'But I'll be making it in a proper teapot just the way we do in England.'

'I can't think of anything I'd like more,' Maggie breathed.

'Nor I,' stated Evelyn. 'And cucumber sandwiches?'

'The bread leaves something to be desired I'm afraid. But I promise it shall be cut thinly and spread with butter.'

'Spanish butter?' Maggie sounded disappointed. Spanish butter tended to be rancid.

'No, butter from Normandy. Will that be all right?'

'Oh, yes please!' said Evelyn eagerly.

Felicia laughed softly, thoroughly enjoying this. 'You two make yourselves at home. I won't be long.' She then left them, disappearing behind a curtain that hung on one wall, which obviously led into a kitchen.

'Tea and cucumber sandwiches,' Evelyn said to Maggie. 'Would you credit it?'

Maggie had another look about her. The room had a marvellous atmosphere – cosy but in a rather exotic way. She liked it tremendously.

Maggie sat on one of the chairs, Evelyn on the settee. They chatted until Felicia returned carrying a tray.

'Tell me, how on earth did you manage to get cucumber at this time of year?' Evelyn queried.

'The Botanical Gardens,' Felicia explained simply. 'There are only several old gardeners left, the younger ones all in the militia. The old ones can be very accommodating, especially for an English woman fighting for their cause.'

Maggie remembered that the first time she'd heard of Felicia, Andy had called her an amazing person. She couldn't have agreed more.

'What was Transylvania like?' Maggie asked.

'How did you know I'd been there? Andy?'

Maggie nodded.

'It's a strange, beautiful place, yet very backward. At one point when I was camping in the forest a group of Ruthenian villagers suddenly appeared, having traced me by the smoke from my fire, and threatened to lynch me.'

'Lynch you!' Evelyn exclaimed. 'Whatever for?'

'Ignorance mainly. They weren't used to foreigners and were convinced I was a witch.'

'So what happened?' Maggie demanded, fascinated.

'I talked to them in my halting Hungarian and eventually convinced them I was just an ordinary human being, that there was nothing satanic about me.'

'If you hadn't managed that, do you think they actually would have lynched you?' Evelyn asked.

'Oh, yes! They had a rope and seemed quite prepared to use it. I got the impression it was something they'd done before.'

Maggie stared at Felicia in open admiration – no wonder Andy was besotted by her.

Felicia poured tea from the slightly steaming teapot into matching cups and saucers, delicately painted with English spring flowers.

'Help yourselves to milk and sugar,' Felicia instructed. 'I'm afraid the milk is tinned, the best I could do.'

Maggie had a sip, then closed her eyes in appreciation. 'Magnificent!' she sighed.

'How wonderful!' breathed Evelyn, also having taken a sip.

'Just don't ask me where I got the tea from, because I'm not telling,' Felicia said, eyes twinkling mischievously.

They all had another sip, then Felicia passed round a plate of cucumber sandwiches.

'Scrumptious!' Evelyn pronounced.

'I always think cucumber sandwiches are frightfully decadent, but I do so enjoy them,' Felicia smiled.

'The bread's not bad either. I've eaten a lot worse since I've been here,' Maggie said.

They demolished the sandwiches and their tea in double-quick time, then refilled their cups.

'And now,' said Felicia, her mood changing, 'down to business.'

Maggie and Evelyn both paid attention, curious as to what was coming next.

243

'As you know I'm in charge of a machine-gun, with two loaders to help me. Due to recent losses, which have been fairly heavy, my loaders are being promoted, with responsibility for their own guns. It means I need new loaders and I thought of you.'

It was the last thing Maggie had expected, and had quite taken her breath away. 'I see,' she said.

'Interested?'

'What about our present assignment?'

'I'm not without influence in the regiment. A word in the right ear and you'll be reposted within hours if needs be.'

Maggie glanced at Evelyn who, even in that yellow light, she could see had gone pale. If they accepted they'd be right at the sharp end of things.

Maggie thought of the children at the convent and her insides tightened. 'When do I start?' she said.

Felicia nodded her approval.

'You can count me in too,' Evelyn declared, a harsh note having crept into her voice.

'Good. I'll have that word first thing tomorrow,' Felicia replied.

Maggie was suddenly fearful, filled with apprehension. An understandable enough reaction, she told herself.

'I just hope I don't let you down, that's all,' Evelyn said to Felicia.

'In what way?'

'It's only a short while ago that merely holding a revolver scared the daylights out of me. I know we've been through training, but when it actually comes to having to kill someone I—' She trailed off, and bit her lower lip.

'That's something none of us ever knows until the moment of truth,' Felicia stated softly.

Maggie gazed into her cup. She understood exactly what Evelyn was saying. Although they'd been on street patrol carrying rifles they'd never had occasion to fire directly at anyone. How was she going to feel when she had a man or woman in her sights and had to pull the trigger? She didn't know. Nor would she until the moment of truth. She hoped she wouldn't let Felicia or any other comrade down.

'With that out of the way, how about some more tea?' said Felicia, picking up the teapot and standing up.

Maggie and Evelyn nodded in unison.

'Back in a tick. The water's already boiling,' Felicia said, and swept from the room.

Maggie looked over at Evelyn who stared back. Neither realized it, but each had a sickly smile on her face.

The attack was sudden and vicious. Dusk was creeping up when a whole horde of screaming Nats burst from their positions to charge their section of the defences.

Evelyn was dozing, Maggie lost in thought when it happened. She was thinking how tired and filthy she felt.

Felicia, ever alert, wasn't caught unawares. Her machine-gun immediately chattered into life sending a spurt of bullets spitting into the light-brown clad figures bearing down on them.

Maggie fed the belt of ammo in at one side, Evelyn kept it untangled and not interfering with the gun itself as it came out the other.

Three soldiers tumbled over. Another shrieked and clutched his chest which was suddenly bright red with blood.

A little further down the line, soldiers reached the barricades and fierce hand-to-hand fighting developed. Bayonets flashed, as did officers' sabres.

Maggie winced as a bullet zinged past her ear. Over on the left there was the soughing of a mortar being fired. The resulting explosion sent several Nationalist soldiers flying through the air.

The first belt of ammunition rattled to a finish, and even as it was still going through the gun Maggie was calmly reaching for a replacement.

'Reload!' Felicia instructed as Evelyn pulled the used belt free, and tossed it aside making space for the new one to collect.

Maggie slotted the new belt in, and tapped Felicia on the shoulder. Felicia instantly resumed firing.

The mortar soughed a second time, the shell landing in the remains of a house. Bricks and masonry mushroomed upwards.

Felicia noticed a Nationalist soldier pull a pin from a grenade, and altered her aim. He died with the grenade still unthrown, his body subsequently blown to pieces.

Something hot and sharp sliced Maggie's lower cheek, drawing blood. She hastily wiped the blood away, and bent again to her task.

The order was shouted to retreat, and the badly mauled Nationalists began falling back.

One went down shot in the legs. He crawled almost a dozen feet before two of his companions caught hold of him and dragged him back with them.

Felicia continued firing, and was still firing when everyone else in the section under attack had ceased.

'Felicia?' Maggie queried. Felicia was firing at nothing now, the Nats had all disappeared.

Felicia paid no heed, her finger remaining tight on the trigger.

Maggie frowned, still feeding in the ammo belt. 'Felicia?' she queried again, this time more urgently.

The machine-gun chattered on.

It was then Maggie noticed there was an oddness about Felicia's expression. It had a blank, staring quality about it.

Without letting up on feeding the gun she placed a hand on Felicia's shoulder. 'Felicia, they've all gone!'

'Oh Christ!' said Evelyn softly, and dropped her side of the belt.

Maggie reached the end of the belt which rattled through and dropped to the ground. The machine-gun fell silent, but Felicia didn't move. She remained staring blankly ahead, her finger tight on the trigger.

Maggie twisted herself into a position so she could look straight into Felicia's face. Directly above the nose was a dark hole ringed with blood. The bullet had come out the back of the head but because of Felicia's thickly bunched hair the exit site wasn't immediately evident.

Felicia had been right about one thing. If the Nats did take Madrid they'd never put her up against a wall.

The service had been a simple one, conducted by a Lutheran minister. Maggie remembered the cucumber sandwiches and had gone to the Botanical Gardens where the old gardeners had given her some flowers for the English *camarada*.

It was a grey day, heavily overcast and far colder than it had been so far that winter. Maggie shivered.

'I'll have to see about getting us some heavy coats,' Nevil said as they trudged along the pavement.

Maggie nodded.

'Of course . . .' He gave a thin smile. 'If Felicia had been alive she would have found us some without any bother. She was marvellous at things like that.'

'Yes,' Maggie agreed dully.

Nevil took a deep breath. 'Where the hell is Andy?' Andy should have been at the service with them but had never turned up. He hadn't been in his room when they'd called for him, so they'd presumed he'd gone ahead. But he hadn't. The rest of the lads were on duty temporarily under the command of a Spanish lieutenant. The three of them had been released to attend the funeral.

'I just hope he hasn't done anything stupid,' Nevil went on, clearly worried.

'Like what?'

'I don't know! He's capable of anything the state he's in.'

Andy had taken the news very badly when Maggie had broken it to him. It was as though his inner light had been switched off.

They walked a bit further in silence, then Maggie said, 'What happens if he doesn't turn up for his next duty?'

Nevil shot her a sideways glance. 'That's what I've been thinking. I can cover for him for so long, but not forever.'

'Surely the powers that be would understand?'

'Maybe. Maybe not. The Spanish are so mercurial you can never tell what their reaction is going to be.'

247

'He could have gone on a bender,' Maggie said.

'Possibly. But why before and not after the funeral? And why miss the service?'

Maggie didn't have an answer.

Returning to the Hotel Colon they went straight to Andy's room, but it was empty. Stuart Borland hadn't seen him, nor had any of the other resident militia they questioned.

Once more in their own room, Nevil began pacing up and down. 'I think the best thing I can do is go out and try to find him,' he said, stopping mid-track.

'Where will you look?'

'There are several bars he frequents, or there again it is just possible that he's gone back on duty without you or I, or anyone round here, being aware of it.'

'Do you want me to come with you?'

Nevil considered that, then shook his head. 'No, you stay here and check his room every so often. If he does show up make him stay put.'

'Right,' she nodded.

He started for the door.

'Nevil?'

He halted and turned to face her again.

'How about a kiss before you go?'

His expression twisted into one of impatience. He wanted to be on his way.

She kissed him, then hugged him tight. 'Now off you go!' she said softly, releasing him.

When she was alone she slumped into a chair and closed her eyes. She should get some sleep, she thought. She seemed to be permanently tired. Nor was she sleeping properly, often waking just as tired as when she'd dropped off.

She wondered how Evelyn was coping with Juanita, their new loader, a girl of fifteen who was so slow she made a snail look fast. Evelyn was now in charge of the machine-gun, replacing Felicia. Poor Evelyn, being lumbered with Juanita!

Out of the blue it came to her where Andy might be. Of course! she told herself, sitting bolt upright. It was so obvious really. She'd hurry over there at once.

Just to be on the safe side she checked his room again before leaving the hotel.

When her knock wasn't answered Maggie knocked a second time, and then a third. Andy opened the door on to the alley-way.

'I thought I'd find you here,' Maggie said. 'Can I come in?'

She closed the door quietly, then followed him into the room she remembered so well from her previous visit.

Andy sat on the tiny settee and clasped his hands. 'I couldn't go to the funeral, Maggie. I wanted to, but couldn't.'

Maggie glanced over at the bed. Felicia's kimono lay across it, the rope-soled sandals beside it on the floor.

'I can't believe she's gone,' Andy whispered. 'I keep thinking it's all a nightmare, that I'll wake up and everything will be just as it was. That she'll still be alive and we'll continue to see one another.'

He wrung his hands in anguish. 'I loved her, Maggie. Oh, how I loved that woman! And although she never said, I believe she loved me.'

'We're all going to miss her,' Maggie said.

He shook his head. 'I'd give anything to bring her back.'

'She died fighting for what she held dear and was deeply committed to, try and draw some comfort from that,' Maggie counselled.

'There's no comfort, Maggie!' he suddenly wailed, tears springing into his eyes. 'No comfort at all. And never will be.'

He was riven with grief, she thought, and was reminded of the Heymouth aftermath.

'Nothing will ever matter to me any more,' he went on, tears now streaming down his cheeks.

She crossed and kneeled beside him, taking his hands in hers. 'You feel that way at the moment. But it'll change, I promise you.'

'Will it?'

'Of course it will,' she replied reassuringly.

He gave her a ghastly smile. 'It's easy to say that in your shoes. But just imagine if it were Nevil you'd buried today. If that had been the case would you believe me if I told you what you've just said?'

Maggie went icy cold, as she had done during the service when that grisly thought had run through her mind. What if she'd been there burying Nevil?

She squeezed Andy's hands.

'Freedom, democracy, they don't mean a thing to me any more. They're empty words now as far as I'm concerned. Empty words, and certainly not worth Felicia's life.'

'She didn't agree with you, Andy, and I know still wouldn't if she could speak from the grave.'

His shoulders started to shake while the rest of his body appeared to sink in on itself. A steady flow of tears dripped from his chin, down his neck and wet his front.

'It hurts, Maggie,' he whispered. 'It hurts so much to lose her. And I mean physical pain. It's as though someone has stuck a bayonet in me and is twisting it slowly.'

She put an arm round him, and held him close. There were tears in her eyes now.

'Shall I tell you something, Maggie?'

'What?'

'I don't want to go on. I want to take my rifle here and . . .'

'No!' she exclaimed sharply, alarmed. 'You mustn't do that. You mustn't even think about it!'

'I want to end the pain,' he explained simply.

'Time will do that, or at least dull it. Time, as they say, is a great healer.'

He reached up and dashed some of the tears from his face. 'I never thought I could have loved a woman as I did Fliss. I never thought it possible. And now she's gone, forever!' That last word came out as a strangled cry.

Still holding him close, she rocked him back and forth for a few moments.

'You mustn't kill yourself,' she repeated softly. 'That's the last thing Felicia would have wanted. You must continue forward, with life, for as long as it is granted you.'

'But how can I without her?'

'You'll just have to. And think how lucky you've been.'

'Lucky?' he queried with a frown.

'You've been truly in love. That doesn't happen to everyone, you know – but it has to you.'

He considered that, and as he did she sensed a change in him, an acceptance of the situation.

He sighed, then swallowed. His shaking faded away. 'You're a good woman, Maggie. Fliss thought the world of you, and so do I.'

'Thank you,' she smiled. 'Any idea where Felicia kept her hankies?'

'Over here. I'll get you one. And one for myself,' he said, rising.

The crisis was over, she felt. He would cope from here. It would be hard for him, maybe harder than anything he'd ever done in his life. But he'd cope.

She sniffed into the hanky he handed her, then wiped her eyes and cheeks. He did likewise.

'I want to pack her things so that they can be sent home to her family when the post is working again,' he said.

'Good idea. Do you have an address?'

'She kept a diary. It's in there.' He hesitated, looking uncertain, then asked, 'Do you think it would be all right if I hung on to the wooden bust she was carving of me? Or should I pack it to go to the family as well?'

'I know the bust you mean, I saw it when I was here with Evelyn. My advice is that you should keep it.'

His face lit up. 'It would mean an awful lot to me.'

'I can understand that.'

He went over to the corner where the bust stood, picked it up and cradled it to himself. 'You say you've already seen it?'

'But I'd like to again,' she replied, knowing that would please him.

He held the bust out in front of her, his expression a combination of love and fierce pride.

'She had enormous talent,' Maggie declared, nodding.

'Enormous,' he agreed. 'And for that and her to be cut off so young . . .' He trailed off. It seemed the tears might return, but they didn't.

'How about a cup of tea?' Maggie suggested. 'I know Felicia had some.'

'That would be lovely,' he murmured.

She placed a hand on his cheek. 'All right now?'

He sucked in a deep breath. 'I wouldn't exactly say that. But certainly better than I was.'

She removed her hand, and lightly kissed where it had been. 'And you'll report in for your next spell of duty?'

'I'll be there,' he confirmed.

'Good.' She glanced about. 'There's no need for you to do her packing before you go on duty. Take your time over it – a couple of days or more.'

'I think that's what I'll do,' he replied slowly. 'Yes, that is what I'll do.'

She smiled at him. 'Now come and show me where to find the tea and crockery.'

She took the remainder of the tea back to the Hotel Colon with her after Andy said he didn't want it. To have left it would have been a waste.

The Spanish lieutenant was the same one who'd substituted for Nevil when Nevil had attended Felicia's funeral, though this was the first time Nevil had met him.

After saluting the lieutenant introduced himself as Teniente Blanquet, then delivered his message.

'You are ordered to report immediately to Colonel Rivero at Regimental Headquarters,' Lieutenant Blanquet said in English, which he spoke extremely well, having been a waiter in London for a number of years.

'Do you know what for?' Nevil queried.

Blanquet spread his hands out wide. 'I asked him, of course, but he would not tell me.' Blanquet gave Nevil a knowing look, then went on in a whisper, 'That colonel is a son of a bitch eh? Who does he think he is just because he's a colonel.' Blanquet spat on the ground. 'That is what I think of him.'

Nevil wanted to smile, but didn't. He'd never known anyone as touchy as the Spanish male. Each thought himself the best man on earth, everyone else inferior. Even now they never failed to both amaze and amuse him.

Nevil called Andy over, and explained the situation. He then left the detachment and headed off towards the Regimental HQ.

When he arrived, he was asked to wait, which he did fully expecting to be there for some time, as was the usual custom. But he was lucky and within a few minutes he was shown into Colonel Rivero's office.

The Colonel wasn't alone. Antonio Mije, Councillor for War on the Madrid Defence Council, was with him. Nevil had met him already while working temporarily at a desk.

'Ah, *Camarada* Sanderson!' said Rivero, getting up from his chair.

Nevil gave the Red salute.

'You remember *Camarada* Mije, I take it. He certainly remembers you.'

Mije also rose, and smiled. 'How are you, *Camarada* Sanderson?' he enquired politely.

'I can't complain, *Camarada*. And yourself?'

'Wishing I could take a holiday.'

They all laughed at this joke. Though as far as Mije was concerned it was only partially one.

'I understand your shoulder is better,' Mije said.

'Oh, much better. I've been back in action for quite some time now.'

Mije nodded. 'So I believe. And doing well as a *teniente*. The reports on you are excellent. Excellent indeed. Glowing, in fact!'

The fulsomeness of this praise and the effusiveness with which it was delivered embarrassed Nevil. 'Why, thank you, *camarada*,' he mumbled in reply.

Mije had been jovial before, now his manner changed. It became cold, hard and authoritative. 'Tell me, *camarada*, what do you know about the Malaga fronts?' he asked softly.

Nevil considered the question before replying. 'Not too much. I've heard that Malaga and that strip of coastline are under heavy attack, and that fierce fighting is taking place. That's about it, I'm afraid.'

Mije grunted. He produced a long, thin cigar, bit off the end and lit up. 'Let me put it this way, *Camarada*, the rebel push for Malaga is a push for roads.' He paused, then repeated the word. '*Roads*. Particularly for roads running directly north from a suitable landing place for German and Italian troops, roads that cut the otherwise impassible Andalusian sierras. These sierras are huge barren plains which rise from clusters of almond groves at their base to thick snow caps at their peak.'

'And the rebels don't have complete control over those roads, I take it?' Nevil said.

'Exactly! As long as we hold the Malaga fronts the Germans and Italians are denied access to the south from the sea.'

'So the Malaga fronts mustn't fall,' Nevil said.

'If they do then the Government side would be dealt a blow from which it would never recover. We believe that the loss of Malaga and the adjoining fronts at Marbella and Estapona would be the beginning of the end.'

Nevil glanced at Colonel Rivero.

'Therefore holding the Malaga fronts is a matter of the utmost importance,' Nevil said softly.

Mije nodded, drawing deeply on his cigar.

Nevil then asked the obvious question. 'But how does all this affect me?'

Mije stabbed his cigar at Nevil. 'Six hundred British volunteers, an entire battalion, have been training in north Africa. This battalion will shortly be landed at Malaga to add weight and backbone to our defences there. We desperately need some fresh men to fight with the *camaradas* on the Malaga fronts.'

'A British Battalion!' Nevil exclaimed, eyes gleaming.

'From all over your country, and of whom we have high hopes. You will remember that on the last occasion we spoke the Colonel said that the British all fight well, and now we have an entire battalion of them!' Mije's excitement blazed.

'How well trained are they?' Nevil queried.

'The majority have received a far longer and more intensive training than you did here. They are also bringing a

254

considerable amount of much needed equipment with them.'

'British equipment?' Nevil asked.

'No, unfortunately not. The British government persists in its unfair policy of neutrality. The equipment is mixed, but of a high quality, I am assured.'

Rivero now chipped in. 'The situation at the Malaga fronts is a double-edged sword. As we have already said we believe that if the Malaga fronts fall to the rebels, it will be the beginning of the end for our side. But, should the rebels actually be beaten back and perhaps even routed then that could be the beginning of the end for Franco and his Fascists.'

'I see,' mused Nevil. 'But where do I come in?'

Mije looked at Rivero, then scrutinized Nevil steadily through a haze of blue cigar smoke. 'We want you to be battalion commander with the rank of major,' he stated baldly.

Nevil's jaw dropped open. When he realized what had happened, he quickly shut it again. 'Battalion commander! Major! *Me?*'

'Promotion is swift under war conditions,' Rivero commented drily.

'Even so! It's not that long since I was a corporal.'

'True enough,' replied Mije. 'You were an excellent corporal, and now an excellent lieutenant. So why not an excellent major?'

'There's a bit of difference between a lieutenant and a major,' Nevil protested.

'Of course. But you have three factors in your favour. First, I am convinced, as is the colonel, that you have the ability and sense of responsibility to carry out what would be required of you. Second, you have fighting experience, both in the field and under siege conditions, which none of these volunteers yet have. And third . . .' He paused to smile, 'Third, your countrymen have made it quite plain to us that they will only serve under British officers.'

'Surely there must be men among them of officer material?' Nevil queried.

'Most certainly. And they have already been given NCO

rank. But for the officers themselves we need experience, which brings us on to what was your platoon. Each and every one of them, unless you have any individual objections, is being raised to the rank of officer.'

Nevil laughed. 'Excuse me,' he apologized when he'd finished. 'It just seems so . . . ridiculous somehow!'

'I can assure you, *Camarada* Sanderson, we do not find it ridiculous at all. Unusual, yes, but hardly ridiculous. How is it you say in Britain? You have to cut your coat according to your cloth.'

'And we are an irregular militia not regular army,' Rivero added.

Major and in command of a battalion! Nevil didn't know what to think. His mind reeled at the prospect.

'And what about you, *Camarada* Sanderson. Do you consider yourself unfit for such rank?' Mije asked, his tone teasing yet at the same time deadly serious.

'Unfit?' Nevil echoed. 'To be honest I've no idea whether I'm fit or unfit. But if you two *camaradas* consider me to be fit, then I'll give it my best go.'

'You agree then?' Rivero demanded.

'I agree,' Nevil stated.

Rivero's face broke into a smile, as did Mije's.

'I was sure that would be your answer,' Mije declared, after which he said something in rapid Spanish to Rivero.

'We will drink to this,' Rivero announced, and crossed to a cabinet. When he returned, he was carrying three heavy crystal glasses brimming with brandy. He gave one to Mije, and another to Nevil.

'To *Camarada* Sanderson and the British Battalion!' Mije toasted.

They then fell to discussing the details.

'Major! The Malaga fronts!' Maggie exclaimed, absolutely stunned.

'That's right.'

'But . . . but how do you get there?'

'Myself and the platoon are to be smuggled out of Madrid

256

the day after tomorrow. Apparently there is a fair amount of coming and going, all clandestine, of course. You have to have a damn good reason, or be on an important mission, before they'll let you use one of these routes.'

'And once you're out of Madrid, what then?'

'We make our way to Malaga as best we can, then enter the city,' he replied.

'You mean infiltrate the Nationalist lines there?'

Nevil nodded. 'That's it.'

'And how far is it from Madrid to Malaga?'

'Roughly two hundred and fifty miles as the crow flies.'

She sat on the edge of their bed to stare at him. 'And you leave the day after tomorrow?'

'That's the plan. And how about all the lads being made officers! I'm having Andy as a captain, and Charlie Menzies. And I thought . . .'

'I'm coming with you,' she stated flatly.

He broke off, and their eyes locked. 'You're not part of the platoon.'

'That doesn't matter.'

'My orders were . . .'

'Sod your orders! If they need you as badly as you've just said, then you can do as you damn well please. You insist I'm going along, and that will be that.'

She glared at him when he didn't reply. 'I mean it, Nevil. I'm not being separated again from you at this stage of the game. I go where you go, and that's final.'

Their eyes remained locked as the seconds ticked by. 'And what if I say no?' he said eventually.

'I'll find a way of following you.'

'That's stupid,' he smiled.

She knew then she had won. 'Maybe so, but it's what I'd do.'

He put his arms round her. 'It's not going to be as easy as that. I need more convincing.'

'Convincing or bribing?'

'Call it what you will.'

She placed a hand on the inside of his thigh, then moved

257

it slowly upwards. 'I know what I call it,' she whispered.

Later, when they lay side by side, he smiled to himself. He'd already decided to take her with them, if she asked, before arriving back at the hotel. And he thought he'd promote her to lieutenant.

She squealed with pretended indignation when he confessed.

Paco, who didn't speak a word of English, signalled that they should follow him into the building he'd brought them to. He'd just unlocked the door and once they were all inside, he hurriedly relocked it from within.

It was a large wine shop, Maggie noted. There were racks everywhere, and many barrels, some marked wine, others sherry.

'You could have a right old hogmanay in here,' Jimmy Sharkey whispered to Eric Young, who sniggered.

Paco took them into a rear room and from there led them into an underground vault, filled with bottles of wine, sherry and brandy.

Maggie shivered, glad of the sheepskin coat she was wearing. They'd all been issued them, at Nevil's instigation, for the mission. The vault was cold and damp and led into another, and then onto a third. There was a whole series of them. There must be millions of bottles down here, Maggie thought. Clearly the shop was a major supplier.

At the end of the final vault was a tall wooden ladder standing against the wall. Paco climbed up it and disappeared through a hole at the top. Nevil instructed Andy, who was carrying a torch, to send the platoon up one at a time, and Andy would bring up the rear. Nevil and Maggie then followed Paco. They emerged into an empty warehouse where a second Spaniard was waiting for them.

'I leave you now. You go with him,' Paco said in Spanish, indicating the second Spaniard.

'*Gracias*,' Nevil replied, nodding that he understood.

Paco made a dismissive gesture, grinned revealing terrible teeth, and left.

'Ramon,' the new man stated, introducing himself.

Nevil shook hands with Ramon.

'Follow me, and quietly, please,' Ramon said.

The platoon went two abreast, Nevil with Ramon, Maggie with Charlie Menzies, and the rest followed suit.

The warehouse had a very large set of doors, with a smaller door inset. Ramon opened the inset and nervously peered out. Seeing that the coast was clear he stepped into the street where a dull brown van stood waiting.

'*Rapido*! Quick!' he hissed, throwing open the rear of the van.

The entire platoon, including Nevil, leapt inside. And the moment the last one was in, the door was swiftly shut. Seconds later the van rumbled into life, and moved off.

Maggie sat, as did they all, on the floor of the van with her rifle upright between her legs. Going through the wine vaults had brought them under the forward Nationalist positions. Now the van would hopefully transport them through the suburbs and out of the city.

They were stopped once by a security check, but the papers Ramon was carrying did the trick, and the van was allowed to proceed without being checked.

Half an hour later the van stopped again, and the rear was thrown open.

'South!' announced a beaming Ramon, pointing.

After Maggie had climbed out of the van she glanced about. They were on a main road surrounded by countryside. It was dusk.

'*Gracias! Gracias!*' said Nevil, shaking Ramon by the hand. He then gave him the Red salute, which Ramon returned.

The platoon camped for the night under an overhanging cliff about a quarter of a mile from the road. They began the long journey to Malaga at first light.

CHAPTER SEVEN

'Listen!' said Mike Cook, coming up short.

'What is it?' queried Ian Ireland, who'd been marching beside him.

'Shooting, in the distance.'

Ian Ireland cocked an ear. Mike was right. There was shooting. 'Nevil!' he called out.

Nevil stopped, and turned.

'Shooting,' Mike Cook explained, pointing ahead.

The entire platoon had stopped now. Maggie took the opportunity to place the butt of her rifle on the ground, and lean on it. Her legs were aching and it wasn't yet noon. She thought of Evelyn whom they'd sadly left behind. They'd have brought her with them if they'd been heading remotely in the direction of where her husband was fighting. But unfortunately they were going the opposite way completely.

'And smoke,' added Tom Currie.

A column of smoke rose into the air, followed shortly by another.

'What do you think?' Andy asked Nevil.

Nevil gazed about him. There was plenty of cover hereabouts, and it was the same ahead as far as he could see. 'We'll continue, but everyone keep their eyes peeled,' he said. He then repeated that loudly so that the whole platoon could hear.

They resumed marching, and Nevil fell back beside Maggie. 'You all right?'

'My feet are killing me.'

'So are mine. But it's going to get a lot worse before it gets better.'

'We need transport.'

'I know that. But I want to get well away from Madrid

before I do anything. Then it's a case of opportunity.'

Maggie cradled her rifle under one arm, unscrewed the cap from her water bottle and had a drink.

'Go easy with that. It might have to last a while,' Nevil counselled.

'It's thirsty work, marching.'

'I know, but eke the water out anyway.'

'You're a hard taskmaster,' she smiled.

He returned her smile, then trotted forward to catch up with Andy, now leading the platoon. A few minutes later the shooting ceased, but the columns of black smoke continued to rise.

About ten minutes after that a dust cloud appeared on the horizon, the sort the men all recognized from the Sierra de Guadarrama.

'Cavalry,' Teddy Agnew explained to Maggie when she asked him about it. 'And quite a few of them too.'

Nevil halted the platoon, not sure what to do. 'We'll stay here until I can ascertain which way that cavalry is going,' he declared after some thought.

Maggie dropped to the ground, and drew in several deep breaths. She still had a few ounces of Felicia's tea left in a tin that was in her knapsack. What she would have given for a cup!

She wiggled her toes, and wondered whether to take her boots off. Better not, she decided, they might have to move again quickly.

She looked over at Nevil who was peering into a pair of binoculars. She saw him say something to Andy, but couldn't hear what it was.

A sudden gushing sound caught her attention, and there was Mike Cook watering the grass. She swiftly glanced away. Nevil had warned her that as a member of the platoon there were certain things she would just have to accept.

'Over a hundred, regular army,' Nevil said to Andy. 'And they have trucks with them.' He counted. 'I can make out six. But there may be more.'

'According to this map there's a village ahead,' Andy replied.

Nevil regarded him grimly.

'So what do we do?'

Nevil dropped the binoculars on to his chest where they dangled at the end of a leather strap. 'Stay tight until they're out of sight. We need a break anyway.'

Andy passed the word for the platoon to stand down. He reckoned they would stop for about a quarter of an hour.

Hearing that Maggie removed her boots, sighing with relief when they were off.

'I'd be careful if I were you,' Charlie Menzies cautioned her.

'What do you mean?'

'Feet swell when you're marching. You might find you can get your boots off but not back on again. Then where are you?'

She thanked him for the tip, it was a point she hadn't thought of. How embarrassing not to be able to get her boots back on! She'd look a right fool.

She tried them, and they did slip back on, but not as easily as they had that morning. She wouldn't take them off again until they settled down for the night – and perhaps not even then.

When the time was up and the cavalry and trucks had disappeared, Nevil ordered them to continue.

Soon they were able to see the village Andy had mentioned to Nevil, or what remained of it. Houses had been set alight and they were producing the columns of smoke.

They came upon their first corpse just outside the village, an old man stabbed through the chest.

'Sabre wound,' Bobby Farquharson muttered to Maggie.

The next corpse was also of an old man, this one clutching a wooden hoe he'd used attempting to defend himself. He was nearly decapitated from a slice to the throat.

Maggie heard a keening, and then spotted a woman on her knees rocking backwards and forwards over a baby. She thought the child was wearing a red garment until she got closer and saw that the garment was stained bright red with blood.

Ian Ireland swore repeatedly.

A young woman came into view from round the side of a blazing house. Her expression was blank, her eyes glazed. She had streaks of dirt on both cheeks.

The village consisted of almost two dozen houses, most of which had been put to the torch. All the male corpses were of old men, the young ones having previously left to join the militia. A number of women had also been killed, these of varying ages. Some children had escaped, others hadn't. Outside one house a slaughtered mother lay surrounded by her brood of five.

'Why?' Maggie whispered.

Nevil stopped the platoon in the centre of the village, and gazed stony-faced about him. With a roar a roof caved in, sending a shower of sparks hurtling upwards.

The sound of crying and wailing was everywhere. When Maggie tried to speak to Bobby Farquharson she found her throat clogged with emotion.

'Maggie!' Nevil called out, beckoning her to him. They walked over to where a woman was sitting on the ground and squatted beside her.

'Your Spanish is the best of all of us. Ask her what happened,' he instructed Maggie.

She had to swallow and swallow again before she could get the words out.

The woman fixed her with dark, soulful eyes and slowly began to speak.

When the woman had finished Maggie turned to Nevil. 'The soldiers took their cows, their sheep, their goats and their chickens – loaded them all aboard trucks. And when the soldiers had done that they took every ounce of food and grain in the village.'

Nevil understood now. 'They're going round the countryside collecting food to feed the army besieging Madrid.'

'What is to become of us?' the woman asked.

Maggie had no answer. Instead she just shook her head. Then she had an idea. Opening her knapsack she delved inside.

'What are you doing?' Nevil queried.

'I'm going to give her some of my rations.' Maggie explained.

'No.' That came out as a terse command.

'But they've nothing left. Didn't I make that clear? *Nothing*. They'll starve.'

'Stand up.'

Maggie did as ordered, her expression a combination of puzzlement and incredulity.

'You keep your rations for yourself. I'm sorry for these people, but the mission comes first. I won't jeopardize its success for anything.'

'But surely we can get other food? Replace that which we leave here?'

'How do you know that? That company may be one of dozens systematically stripping the area. It may well turn out that we'll need every last crumb that we have.'

His logic made sense to Maggie, but not his ruthlessness. This wasn't the Nevil she knew and loved. 'We just can't walk away without leaving something. That would be inhuman,' she argued.

His eyes became hard. 'Walking away without leaving anything is precisely what we are going to do. We couldn't leave them enough to matter anyway.'

'But at least we would have done our best!' Hot bile churned in her stomach as she reached again into her knapsack.

'I order you not to give that woman or anyone else here any food,' he said. He shouted it out again so that every member of the platoon could hear.

He added, still shouting, 'No food is to be handed over. That is an order!'

'Not even to the children?' Maggie asked softly.

He brought his hard, unyielding gaze back to bear on her. 'Not even to the children,' he confirmed.

He glanced round, but no-one, not even Andy, would stare at him directly. They all either looked away or down at the ground.

Maggie felt sick as she refastened her knapsack, sick, bewildered, and for some reason fearful.

264

Nevil pointed at a nearby well, clearly the village's main water supply. 'All water bottles to be topped up before we move on, which we'll do just as soon as we can.'

The platoon clustered round the well, and Jimmy Sharkey operated the winch.

'That includes you,' Nevil said to Maggie, who hadn't yet moved.

She joined those at the well, all of whom were silent.

Nevil was the last to top up his bottle. 'Let's go,' he said, having screwed its cap back on.

A subdued platoon marched out of the village, the crying and wailing ringing in their ears.

It was almost an hour later before someone spoke to his neighbour.

Nevil sat behind a large rock with Andy beside him. The rest of the platoon were behind similar cover on either side.

The two Fascist soldiers were arguing with one another as they changed the lorry wheel. The impression was that each was accusing the other of doing less work than himself.

Nevil waited patiently. Why should his men change the tyre? Let the Fascists do it. It was to be their last act on earth.

He'd brought the platoon on to this subsidiary road because of the large volume of traffic on the main one. He'd wanted somewhere quiet to stage an ambush, which they needn't worry about now as they had come across this lorry with a very convenient flat tyre.

The taller of the Fascists was gesticulating wildly at his companion, whose reply was to violently shake his head.

Get on with it, you buggers, Nevil thought to himself. And as though they were obeying him they did just that.

He glanced up and down the road. There was nothing to be seen.

'You take the bozo on the right and I'll take the other,' he whispered to Andy as the Fascists finished the task.

Maggie watched Nevil and Andy sight their rifles, and fired as one.

The platoon rose and came down the bank, approaching

warily in case either of the Fascists remained alive. The taller soldier, Nevil's victim, was conscious, still breathing, but unable to move. He stared up at them in hatred, blood running from the corner of his mouth. Nevil's second bullet blew half his head away.

'Strip off their uniforms, we'll keep those, and get rid of the bodies,' Nevil instructed Andy, who detailed Maurice Cairns and Eric Young to do the job.

Charlie Menzies undid the lorry's rear flaps.

'Let's see what we've got,' Nevil said. He pulled himself up into the lorry and Charlie Menzies did the same.

There were sixteen long black metal cylinders with a red skull and crossbones stencilled prominently on each. These were the lorry's principal cargo.

'Gas,' Charlie whispered.

'Oh, the rotten bastards,' Nevil said.

'For Madrid, do you think?'

'The rumour has been going round there long enough that gas is going to be used. It appears the rumour is about to become fact.'

Charlie then noticed that the cylinders had something else stencilled on them. 'What's "*la mostaza*"?' he asked Nevil.

' "*La mostaza*"?' Nevil repeated. It wasn't a word he knew. 'Maggie!' he cried out.

'What does "*la mostaza*" mean?' he asked her when she appeared at the back of the lorry.

She didn't know either and had to consult her dictionary. 'Mustard,' she replied when she'd found it.

'Mustard gas,' Nevil said. It had been used in the Great War with terrible effect.

'Christ!' Charlie swore softly.

'Get rid of it. Stick it with the bodies,' Nevil said.

While Andy was organizing that Nevil found out what else was on board. There were two drums of petrol, six boxes of bullets (wrong calibre for their weapons), a cardboard container filled with soft drinks and three boxes of cigars.

'Cigars!' Andy exclaimed in delight when Nevil told him. 'A decent smoke at last.'

'See they get equally distributed,' Nevil said.

Within seconds most of the platoon were happily puffing away.

Maggie woke up stiff and sore. The floor of the truck wasn't terribly comfortable. Another member of the platoon was snoring, and beside her Charlie Menzies twitched and snorted.

It was pitch black in the back of the lorry. She wondered what time it was, and how close to dawn. Nevil had decided they would drive at night and camp during the day. His reasoning was that it was safer that way.

Her mind went back to the village. All those poor people who'd been murdered, and those left alive to starve.

How could Nevil have done what he did! It was callous in the extreme. This was a new side to him that she'd never seen before. And not one she liked. She closed her eyes, intending to doze off again. But visions of the village kept flashing before her.

The lorry backfired once, then again even more explosively. The engine faltered and sounded as if it might cut out altogether. But luckily it didn't.

Shortly after that she couldn't help laughing because they hit a deep pot-hole which brought the other sleepers grumbling and cursing awake.

'What's the verdict?' Nevil asked the Currie brothers, who were both excellent mechanics.

Tom tapped the filthy, oily engine with a spanner. 'Pile of junk,' he pronounced.

'And badly maintained,' Norman added.

'Look at that, would you!' Tom exclaimed, pointing the offending part out to his brother.

'Sheer bloody negligence,' Norman agreed.

Nevil bit a thumbnail – this was worrying. 'But it'll take us to Malaga, won't it?' he queried.

Tom glanced at Norman, who shrugged. 'With a bit of luck,' Tom replied.

'It really is a clunker though,' Norman said.

'However,' Tom went on, 'if you'd give us a couple of days to strip it right down . . .'

'At least a couple of days,' Norman interjected. 'I think that's optimistic myself.'

Tom stared at the engine, then at his brother. 'Aye, maybe you're right.'

'We haven't got time for that. Just do the best you can,' Nevil told them.

He left the Curries and joined Maggie, who sat huddled over a small fire. They weren't far from the main road, but in a secluded place where they'd never be spotted.

'It's a cold wind that's blowing,' she said.

He glanced at the leaden sky. 'Could be snow up there.'

Despite the warmth of her sheepskin coat she shivered. 'I hope not.'

'We made excellent mileage last night,' he smiled at her.

She nodded. 'Good.'

'The lorry's a problem though. It's old and, according to Tom and Norman, badly maintained.'

'I heard it playing up during the night.'

'It did on several occasions.'

'Perhaps it's God paying you back,' she said.

He frowned. 'What do you mean?'

'For not leaving some food at that village.'

'Don't be ridiculous!' he snapped angrily.

'Maybe if you'd left some food he'd have arranged it so that we got a better lorry.'

She recoiled in fright when, for a split moment, she thought he was going to hit her.

Then he relaxed. 'I must have a chat with Andy and Charlie,' he declared, and walked away.

Had he been going to hit her? Or was that merely her imagination?

She didn't know. But it was very sad indeed, for it meant she now believed him capable of hitting her, which would have been inconceivable before the start of the mission.

*

268

Nevil sat in the cab of the lorry peering out into the darkness. Tom Currie was driving, keeping the lorry at a steady thirty miles per hour. He and Norman had agreed between them that anything over that wouldn't be advisable.

'What time is it?' Tom asked.

Nevil glanced at his luminous wristwatch. 'Just coming up to midnight.'

'Sorry about that,' Tom apologized when they hit a rut that made the lorry bounce. 'These Spanish roads are diabolical.'

Nevil was about to reply when the engine faltered, then failed altogether. He swore instead.

Tom tried to restart the engine, to no avail. 'We'll have to pull in,' he said.

Panic bloomed in Nevil. If they didn't get the lorry going again within a few minutes, another vehicle would inevitably come along and possibly stop to see if they could help. And what then?

He and Tom were wearing the Fascist uniforms of the two dead soldiers, but only for appearance's sake. If they had to open their mouths the game would be up.

Tom stopped on the verge, and hopped out. Almost immediately he was joined by Norman.

Nevil went to the rear and ordered the rest of the platoon out, then ordered them to conceal themselves close by. When he returned to the front of the lorry, he found Tom and Norman with their heads under the bonnet.

'How serious is it?' Nevil demanded anxiously.

Tom swung his torch from one section of the engine to another. 'Norman?'

'Wait a mo.'

Nevil looked back the way they'd come, but there were no approaching headlights, nor were there any coming towards them. He swore again.

'If only I could see properly,' Norman complained, fiddling with a piece of the engine.

Nevil got furious with the lorry. 'Come on, come on,' he murmured, restraining an impulse to kick it.

Norman glanced up at him. 'We're both doing our best, all right?'

'Sorry. I didn't mean it like that.'

'Try the engine now,' Norman said to his brother a few seconds later. It seemed like an eternity to Nevil.

Tom leapt back into the cab and engaged the starter. Nothing happened.

'Wait!' Norman called out. He twisted something with his screwdriver. 'Now try it!'

Still nothing happened. The engine was completely lifeless.

'If only we could get the lorry off the road,' Norman said.

Nevil had already thought of that, but it was an impossibility. Each side of the road had a bank rising from it which was far too steep for them to push the lorry up and over. Nor were there any minor roads leading off adjacent to where they were.

Squatting behind a bush on the bank closest to the lorry Maggie gazed along the road in the direction they'd been heading. A faint light blinked, and vanished. Then blinked again.

'Something's coming,' she warned Nevil.

'Where?'

'From the south.'

'And the other way!' Bobby Farquharson added.

Norman paused in what he was doing. 'Well?' he asked Nevil.

'Once more!' Nevil said to Tom in the cab.

Tom engaged the starter, but the engine remained dead.

Nevil could see both sets of lights now, coming closer with every passing second.

'More lights in the south,' Maggie said. 'In fact it could be a convoy.'

That settled it for Nevil. 'Right, that's it! Over that bank and keep going,' he ordered.

'It seems a pity . . .'

'Do as I say!' he yelled at Norman, who shut up.

They all scrambled up the bank and down the other side, with Nevil bringing up the rear.

By now Nevil had decided on his next move. 'Follow me,'

he hissed, and ran southwards for about a hundred yards.

He halted the platoon there and said, 'Andy and Charlie, come with me, the rest of you wait here. And no talking.'

Maggie sank on to the ground beside Jimmy Sharkey. What next? she wondered.

Nevil, Andy and Charlie crawled up the bank and watched what was indeed a convoy begin to rattle past. The lead truck picked up their abandoned lorry, and slewed right across the road to park behind it.

'Buggeration!' Nevil said to himself.

The vehicle coming from the north also stopped when it reached their lorry, and soon voices could be heard discussing the matter.

They had lost the lorry, Nevil was certain of that now. But then he'd known that the moment the first lights had appeared in the distance. It was bloody awful luck, but it was unavoidable. The only thing to do now was to put a fair amount of distance between the lorry and themselves before daylight.

The three of them rejoined the rest of the platoon, and together they plunged deep into the night.

The rabbit was young, and curious. Its whiskers trembled in the early morning air as it stared at Maggie. It reminded her of someone, she thought, but couldn't put her finger on whom.

'Hello,' she said softly.

Abruptly the rabbit turned and bounded away. The white of its tail bobbed briefly beside a tussock of grass, then it was gone.

The pale grey sky shot through with streaks of red told her it wasn't long past dawn. Sitting up, she reached for her water bottle and had a drink.

They could only have covered about two or three miles after abandoning their lorry the previous night. And those few miles had been a horrendous slog for them. At one point Andy had fallen into a bog and had to be pulled out. If only there had been a moon to help them.

She spied Nevil, who was also awake. From the looks of things, he was poring over their map.

He glanced up, saw her looking at him, smiled and waved. She smiled and waved back.

He came over. 'Sleep well?' he asked.

'As well as could be expected. Yourself?'

He scratched a chin covered in dark stubble. 'I would have much rather been back in our bed in the Hotel Colon, I can tell you!'

They both laughed. 'It's funny how you take certain things for granted, until you have to do without them – like beds,' she said.

'You get used to it after a while. Baths are another thing you miss when you're living like this.'

'Oh yes! What I'd give for a piping hot bath.' She sighed. 'That would be sheer bliss.'

'Hopefully you can have one when we get to Malaga.'

If we get to Malaga, she thought, but didn't say so. 'I'm starving,' she said instead.

'Well, you're going to have to wait for breakfast. To be on the safe side I want to get further away from the truck. So we'll march for a few hours, and then have breakfast.'

He reached out and placed a hand on her arm, then moved it up to rest on her cheek.

'Shall I rouse the others?' she asked.

'We both will.'

When they started marching Mo Cairns led them on point, scouting ahead of the platoon, with Teddy Agnew and Mike Cook flanking.

'Over there!' Eric Young said to Maggie, pointing off to their left.

There was a column of thick black smoke similar to those they'd seen above the village.

The platoon halted, and they all stared at the smoke, rapt up in their own thoughts.

'We can guess what that means. Another village,' Eric said.

Maggie glanced ahead at Nevil gazing at the smoke. He

suddenly looked at her, his expression said 'I told you so.'

He might have been right, but he'd still been wrong, she thought. Nothing would ever convince her otherwise.

They continued marching.

'Are you going to try and find another vehicle?' Andy asked Nevil, having just trotted forward to catch up with him.

'I would if I could, but how? The main road is out of the question, with the volume of traffic on it, and according to the map there isn't a subsidiary one for miles. Not unless we go well out of our way, that is, which I don't want to do.'

'So we foot it?'

'For the time being anyway. Until I can come up with something else. Any suggestions?'

Andy laughed softly, and shook his head. 'You're the brains, Nevil. I just do what you say.'

Nevil playfully punched his friend on the shoulder. 'Don't underestimate yourself. If anything happens to me you take over. And I wouldn't have it that way if I didn't think you were up to the job.'

They marched a little way in silence, then Nevil said, his tone quite different to what it had been before, 'How are you managing?'

Andy glanced sideways at Nevil, then straight ahead again. 'You mean about Fliss?'

'Yes.'

'I'll never get over her, it's as simple as that. But at least I knew her, and loved her. I take great comfort from that.'

Andy then changed the subject.

Maggie moved stealthily forward, her ears straining, her eyes continually scanning from left to right and back again. It was her first time on point.

Nevil had been against her going on either point or flank, but she'd insisted she do her turn just like everyone else. It wouldn't be fair on the others if she didn't.

She was a fully fledged militiawoman, she'd argued. Why should she get preferential treatment? She would hold her

273

own with the rest of them, and that was an end to it. Reluctantly Nevil had given in and posted her out to point.

God, she was hungry! Because of the weight problem they'd only brought a certain amount of rations with them, which were now finished. The idea had been that they'd acquire food as they went along, only there had been precious little food to be had, thanks to the Nats commandeering everything.

She thought of the young rabbit she'd woken to one morning. If that ever happened again and she could get to her rifle in time, the rabbit would be for the high jump. She could see the rabbit turning on a spit, and almost smell it. It was absolutely mouth-watering. She chuckled to herself. The power of the imagination, unbelievable sometimes. If she didn't know better she would have sworn she actually smelt roasting rabbit.

She sucked in a deep breath, and momentarily closed her eyes, delighting in the aroma teasing the inside of her nose.

Gorgeous, she thought. If only it were real.

A horse whinnied, which brought her up short, alarm bells jangling in her brain. And the smell persisted. It *was* real, she realized with a shock, and not a product of her imagination.

She dropped quietly on to the gorse, and listened. There were cold prickles all down her back and buttocks. She had two options: Return and warn the platoon, or investigate? Return would be Nevil's counsel. She decided to investigate and make a proper job of it.

She rose to a low crouching position, and went slowly on, watching every footstep, careful not to make the least sound herself.

The gorse gave way to bracken, which she glided through. Beyond that she came upon some trees, and was studying them when she heard male laughter.

'*No hace falta!*' an authoritative voice cried out. An officer?

A few seconds later the same voice said, '*Pues es muy raro.*'

Maggie's heart was pounding in her chest. She gripped her Mauser even more tightly, the palms of her hands sweating so profusely she could easily have dropped it.

There was no movement whatever among those trees within her line of vision, which meant the voices had come from deeper in.

She ran to the nearest tree, and shrank against it. Wraithlike, she flitted to the next tree, and the tree after that.

It proved to be only a very narrow strip of trees. Just before she could have broken out into the open again she went on to her knees then stretched full out. She inched forward till she could see what lay in the small valley below.

A group of Fascist cavalry were camped beside a meandering silver river. A fire had been lit and a spit constructed from branches. It wasn't rabbit she'd been smelling after all, but a far larger animal. As she watched a soldier went over and gave the roasting animal a quarter turn.

Four men were playing cards, others lounging here and there. One man, stripped to the waist, was shaving, his mirror hooked on to a bush.

She shifted her attention to where the horses were tethered, all fine-looking beasts. Starting at one end she carefully counted to the other.

Satisfied she could give Nevil a full report she silently turned and hurried back the way she'd come.

'You did what!' Nevil exploded.

'I reconnoitred the situation,' she retorted.

'That was bloody stupid!'

She regarded him angrily. 'If Ian had been on point, or Jimmy or Mo, wouldn't you have expected them to do precisely as I did?'

He wanted to say that was different, but knew it wasn't. 'How many men?' he queried.

'They were difficult to count, and perhaps all the men weren't visible. So I counted the horses instead.'

'Hmmh!'

'There were twenty-two.'

Nevil glanced at Andy, then at Charlie. He knew they'd be thinking precisely the same thing he was. Horses were the answer to their problem, slower than a lorry, but in many ways better, and safer.

'Twenty-two mounts, that would mean we would have spares,' Charlie said.

'I've never ridden before,' Andy mused.

'None of us have. But we can soon learn,' Nevil stated firmly.

'Twenty-two of them against thirteen of us,' Andy said, raising an eyebrow.

'But we would have the element of surprise on our side,' Nevil countered.

He looked again at Maggie. 'Now describe to us in detail where this camp is and its layout.'

They listened attentively while Maggie spoke, occasionally interrupting with the odd question.

They entered the narrow strip of trees with Nevil in the middle. Maggie had Bobby Farquharson on one side of her, Teddy Agnew on the other.

Charlie was with Mike Cook and Eric Young, the three of them having been assigned the horses. They were to ensure none broke free and escaped, or if some did they were to minimize the loss.

The smell of roasting meat was even stronger than it had been earlier. Maggie's tummy rumbled, which caused her to bite her lip.

She glanced at Bobby, but he didn't appear to have heard and nor had Teddy.

Through the trees they silently stalked. Then, at a sign from Nevil, they dropped to the ground and continued at a wriggle, rifles cradled across their arms.

Maggie glanced at her watch. It was almost forty minutes since she'd last been here.

The four men who'd been playing cards were still doing so. A number of soldiers were playing football using a makeshift ball of some kind. Two were feeding the horses while an officer sat on a large stone rhythmically whacking his right boot with a riding-crop. Others were lounging about talking and watching the football game. Several were at the river washing.

Nevil checked that everyone was in position, and that all eyes were on him.

He raised his rifle, which was the signal for those under his command to do likewise, and start counting to ten. On reaching ten they all fired simultaneously.

Maggie's target, one of the football players, threw up his arms and spun sideways. As she prepared to shoot him again he fell prostrate.

Soldiers died where they stood, or scrambling for their weapons. The wounded jerked and writhed upon the ground.

'We surrender! In the name of God we surrender!' went up the cry in Spanish.

The officer with the riding-crop lay backwards over the stone, his legs splayed wide apart. He'd died instantly.

There was no fight left in the survivors. The suddenness, and thoroughness, of the attack had knocked the stuffing right out of them. They were completely demoralized. They stood with hands raised in submission, fear and terror stamped across their faces.

Nevil glanced over at the horses who were milling about in agitation, but were still tethered. He glimpsed Charlie moving among them. Then there was some sort of commotion.

Nevil rose, and the others followed suit. They went down the incline and into the Fascist camp.

There were bodies everywhere, and some wounded. It was a terrible sight.

'What now?' Andy asked, joining Nevil.

Maggie counted the unscathed survivors – there were five of them. She now noticed that three of these were young lads, fifteen years old, if that.

'Boys,' she said to Nevil.

'Eh?'

'Three of those are boys.'

Tom Currie appeared pushing another unscathed survivor ahead of him. 'Found this bugger further along hiding behind a bush,' Tom stated.

'I wasn't hiding. I merely elected to stay where I was. Hell, I didn't want my ass shot off!' the man said in an American accent. He was wearing civilian clothes.

'If you weren't hiding, Nat, what were you doing?' Andy demanded.

'The bathroom if you must know. There I was, minding my own business when suddenly, without warning, all holy bejesus broke loose!'

Some of the platoon laughed to hear that. But not Nevil.

The smallest of the young Fascist lads sank to his knees, clasped his hands in front of him, and began to pray. Tears rolled down his cheeks.

One of the two older soldiers stepped forward. 'Do not kill me, for the sake of the Virgin of the Carmen,' he begged. His normally olive skin had turned a pasty green, his large brown eyes were bulging in their sockets.

'Nevil!' Charlie's voice called out. And there was Charlie striding towards them.

'I didn't see you lose any horses,' Nevil said when Charlie was by his side.

'We didn't. But we lost Mike,' Charlie answered.

Those of the platoon within hearing went very still. Several seconds passed while Nevil digested that. 'How?' he asked eventually.

'Somebody we thought dead came back to life again just long enough to stick a knife in him.'

Jimmy Sharkey swore. He and Mike Cook had been particularly close friends.

A wave of nausea swept over Maggie. She retched a couple of times, but thankfully wasn't sick.

'We'll bury him after we've attended to this lot,' Nevil said. He turned to stare stony-faced at the unscathed survivors.

Another of the young lads, who must have understood something of the conversation between Charlie and Nevil, also fell to his knees, and scrabbled in the dirt.

'Please! Please!' he pleaded in Spanish, his features contorted.

'Take these six away and execute them. Then finish off the wounded,' Nevil instructed Charlie.

The young lad scrabbling in the dirt howled in anguish.

'Godalmighty!' the American exclaimed, realizing he was included in the six.

'You can't do that, Nevil,' Maggie said quietly.

He turned on her. 'Keep out of this!'

'But you *can't*! You can't kill in cold blood people who've surrendered to you and whose surrender you've accepted.'

'Who says I can't?'

'Decency says so. It wouldn't be right.'

He barked out a bitter laugh. 'Right! Since when do the Fascists do things that are right! Or by the rules! Was it right to kill all those kids you were looking after! Eh? Is it right to strip folk of every last morsel of food and leave them to starve? Is it right to kill and maim those same folk while doing it? Is it right for Franco's Moors to violate every female they can lay their filthy hands on? Is it right for those same Moors to torture as they do? Don't talk to me of right or by the rules!'

'You could have given those villagers some food, but didn't,' Maggie argued.

His eyes became hard with fury, and took on a staring quality that she remembered only too well from the Hotel Colon. That look had scared her then, and it scared her even more now.

'I explained to you at the time, the mission came first. And I was correct in what I did. Subsequent events have proven that.'

Doggedly, she repeated, 'You can't kill people in cold blood who've surrendered to you, some of whom are mere boys.' She grasped him by the arm. 'What you've said about the Fascists is true. But please, for your own sake, don't sink to their level. Let's just take the horses and ride on.'

He took a deep breath. 'I can't do that, Maggie. It could possibly endanger the mission.'

'How?'

'Survivors could report where we attacked them, and in which direction we went off. The Nats could then pursue and

279

destroy us. Or they could telegraph, telephone or wireless ahead and have us intercepted.'

He shook his head. 'No, this entire troop must die and vanish. At least vanish for the time being. There's no other way.'

'Can I speak?' the American asked.

Nevil tore his gaze away from Maggie. 'What is it?'

'I'm not a Nationalist soldier, I'm a journalist. I've been sent over here on special assignment by *The New York Times* to cover the story from the Nationalist side, which is what I've been doing. I'm not involved in any way. So you can't kill me.'

Nevil rubbed a hand across his face. 'You're wrong. Being with them makes you involved. And I can kill you. And I shall. For the same reason I'm going to kill the others. I can't leave anyone behind who will tell which way we went.'

'I won't tell anyone. You have my word on that.'

'I'm sorry,' Nevil said, and turned away from him. 'Carry out your orders,' he nodded to Charlie.

Special assignment for *The New York Times*. That rang a bell with Maggie. And there was something familiar about the American's face. Especially those warm, light green eyes. Now where had she seen those eyes, and that face before?

'Mo! Tom! Teddy! Jimmy! Eric! Form a detail,' Charlie called out.

The young lad praying now began doing so even more furiously. The one scrabbling in the dirt threw himself on to his back and drummed his feet.

'Make it quick,' Nevil said to Charlie.

Charlie had already selected a spot down by the river. 'Take them over there,' he told the detail, pointing.

'But I'm a journalist, I tell you!' the American said tightly to Nevil, who ignored him.

Mo and Eric grabbed the boy lying on his back and hauled him upright. The one praying came to his feet of his own accord.

Teddy Agnew pushed the American in the direction he wished him to go. The American stumbled, swore, then staggered towards the river.

Suddenly Maggie recalled the American, and where

280

they'd met. 'Wait!' she said urgently to Nevil. 'I know him.'

'Know him? Who?' Nevil queried with a frown.

'The American. I know him from Heymouth. He interviewed me after the flood. His name's Howard.'

The American, who'd overheard this, had stopped to stare at Maggie in astonishment. 'Yeah, I remember you too. You gave me some excellent copy.'

She smiled. 'I thought you were a ghoul to begin with. Then you introduced yourself, explained why you were there and interviewed me.'

The American brushed past Teddy Agnew, who allowed him to do so, and returned to where Maggie and Nevil were standing. 'Howard Taft. And you were Miss Jordan. Miss . . .' He frantically searched his memory.

'Maggie Jordan,' she said.

'Yeah, Maggie Jordan. But how do you come to be here fighting with the Republicans?'

'That's a long story, I'm afraid.'

She confronted Nevil, and when she spoke there was steel in her voice. 'Shoot the others if you absolutely have to. But please, not him.'

'I can't leave any survivors,' Nevil replied.

'I know him. Can't you understand? I *know* him. And from Heymouth.'

'I can't, and won't, leave any survivors,' Nevil persisted.

'Then don't. Bring him with us.'

'Maggie, you don't appreciate that—'

'I'm asking you, Nevil,' she interrupted softly, but firmly.

Nevil glanced at Taft, then back at Maggie. He was clearly undecided.

'Or are you too small a man to be seen to change his mind?'

He winced. 'That's below the belt.'

'Perhaps. But is it also true?'

The other five unscathed survivors had gone now. Teddy Agnew hovered close by. Howard literally sweated, the beads appearing on his brow.

'He can remain alive for the moment. Until I've thought the matter through,' Nevil relented.

Howard gave a small gasp of relief.

Teddy Agnew hurried off to rejoin the rest of the detail. Less than a minute later a volley of shots rang out and for the hapless five it was all over.

Charlie checked they were dead, then left the bodies lying there for the time being. He and the detail began the grisly task of finishing off the wounded.

When that was done Nevil called the platoon together. 'Andy, take a couple of men and see if you can find somewhere we can bury the corpses. Charlie, go through the baggage and see what's what. Maggie, you organize a meal for as soon as possible. Meanwhile you, Jimmy, and you, Ian, can dig Mike's grave. We'll bury him after we've eaten.'

Nevil strode away, heading for the horse lines. When he reached Mike's body he slung it over his shoulder and went back to where he'd previously stood. Having laid Mike out he returned to the horse lines for a saddle-blanket, as he'd noticed a stack of them. He covered Mike with one.

Three of their number now dead, he thought grimly. Mike, Kevin McGee and Davey Law. Stuart Borland was still alive, if hardly kicking. Whether or not Stuart remained alive depended upon what happened in Madrid.

He gazed across at Maggie. She had a tongue in her when she cared to use it. Too small a man to be seen to change his mind! He wouldn't have taken that from anyone other than her. For he knew it was untrue, just.

He strolled over to where Charlie was rummaging through a pack. 'Anything useful?' he asked.

'A bottle of brandy for starters. Want a slug?'

Nevil considered it, then shook his head. 'Maybe later. See that anyone who wants a tot gets one with the meal.'

'And what about this, eh?' Charlie unrolled a beautifully stitched and embroidered cape. 'Must have belonged to the officer.'

Nevil took the cape. 'It'll do for me now.' He'd lost his sheepskin coat and uniform when they'd fled the lorry. So had Tom Currie.

Remembering the incident he said, 'Tom had better have

Mike's coat and uniform. We'll take them off before burying him.'

Nevil was walking away from Charlie and the horse when Andy fell into step beside him. 'We've discovered a small gully which should do the trick. We'll tip the corpses down there then cover them with rocks. There are thousands of those, all shapes and sizes, scattered thereabouts.'

Nevil nodded his approval. 'Do you want to do that before or after food?' he asked.

'Preferably after. But that's up to you.'

'Let's speak to Maggie then.'

They walked over to Maggie who was busy with a pile of tin plates and a large pot of beans that had been cooking by the side of the fire.

'Any time you like. The meat's done,' she replied in answer to Nevil's question.

'Roast pork. Delicious!' Andy said, savouring the smell.

'This was their carving utensil apparently,' Maggie declared, picking up a specially sharpened bayonet.

'You safe to do the honours?' Nevil queried with a smile.

She didn't smile back, that was the last thing she felt like doing. The deaths of the five unscathed survivors and the wounded had upset her considerably. It was one thing to kill soldiers as they'd done in the attack, quite another to execute – for whatever reason – people who'd surrendered or were wounded.

'I'll manage. You can tell the men to come over.'

Nevil nearly said something, knowing full well what was bothering her, but didn't because of Andy's presence. 'Fine then.'

Maggie started slicing the pork, the meat falling away from the bones. The pig had been a young one, and extremely well fed. When the platoon came to eat it the meat seemed to melt in the mouths.

Howard Taft was the last, bar Maggie, to be served, having purposely hung back to the end. He was still severely shaken by the closeness of his escape. Every so often he looked over at where the bodies of the five lay, and shuddered. It didn't take too much imagination to see himself lying there, spattered with blood as they were.

'Thank you,' he said when Maggie handed him a plate of pork and beans. Nor was it only the food he was thanking her for, as Maggie was aware.

He settled himself down and although the last thing he wanted to do was eat, he forced himself. It might be a while between meals.

'Like a tot of brandy?'

Howard glanced up at Charlie, who was holding a bottle and several tin mugs. 'Please.'

Charlie poured a hefty measure, and gave it to him. 'You were lucky,' he stated flatly.

'I know.'

Charlie was about to move away again when Howard said, 'Tell me something, are you all British?'

'Scots,' Charlie replied. 'We're all Scots and Glaswegians, except Maggie, that is.'

'You all joined together, huh?'

'We all worked in Glasgow, came over here together, and joined up together.'

Howard's gaze flicked to where Nevil was sitting with Andy. 'And the one called Nevil who appears to be in command, what's his last name?'

Charlie frowned. 'You're asking an awful lot of questions, pal.'

'Sorry!' Howard said quickly. 'As a journalist it's a habit with me. I'm only being curious.'

'Sanderson,' Charlie replied, seeing no harm in it. 'Major Nevil Sanderson.'

'Major! With so few men at his command?'

Charlie decided on a little teasing. 'Ah yes, but all officers.'

'All?'

'Every last one of us.'

Howard had a sip of brandy. The brandy was rough and fiery, but enjoyable nonetheless. 'Can I ask what rank you are?'

'Sure. I'm Captain Charlie Menzies. Would you care to write it down?'

Howard shook his head. 'No no, I was only . . .'

'Being curious,' Charlie interjected, finishing the sentence for him.

Howard took the hint and shut up. He stared after Charlie as he walked away. Just what had he fallen into? He couldn't help but wonder.

Directly after they'd finished their meal they buried Mike Cook. Tom Currie had already changed into Mike's coat and uniform. It wasn't something he'd been particularly keen to do, but then he hadn't wanted to continue wearing the hated Fascist uniform either.

'I know the Republican movement is anti-religious, but nonetheless I think we should say a few words,' Nevil told the assembled group. Several nodded in reply.

'I don't have a bible, so the best I can think of is the Lord's prayer. Please join me: "Our Father, who art in heaven, hallowed be thy name . . ." '

There were tears in Maggie's eyes when they reached the end of the prayer. And she wasn't the only one weeping.

As soon as the burial was over they started dealing with the Spanish corpses. All of them, including Howard but with the exception of Maggie, who'd been excused, dragged the corpses to the gully and pitched them in. When the last corpse had gone over the side they began heaving in rocks. In a surprisingly short time they were completely covered.

'How much food did you come up with?' Nevil asked Charlie as they returned to the camp.

'With what's left of the pig we've got enough to feed us for three to four days.'

That was good, Nevil thought. He had questions to put to Taft, but they could wait. He was anxious to get away from this place.

His immediate problem was the horses. Or to be more specific the men riding the horses, none of whom had ever ridden previously. And then he remembered that one of their number had. Taft.

Nevil assembled the platoon at the horse lines. 'As you'll be accompanying us you can start being useful right now and show us how to saddle up,' he said to Howard. They would have worked it out eventually, but why waste time?

The platoon watched intently as Howard placed a saddle-blanket on his horse, and followed that with a saddle. As he went through the various procedures Howard gave them invaluable tips. The rest then followed his example.

Howard paid particular attention to Maggie, choosing a horse and giving her the officer's saddle which, because of its quality, was the most comfortable.

'I don't think I like this!' exclaimed Norman Currie as his horse, with him aboard, reared up on to its back legs.

'All you've got to do is show it who's boss,' counselled Bobby Farquharson. The words were hardly out of his mouth when his horse bucked, sending him flying. He landed, amidst jeers and cheering, with a jarring thump.

'What was that again?' Norman said, trying to keep a straight face and failing.

'Very funny,' moaned Bobby, rubbing an elbow that had lost a patch of skin.

Nevil, who was also having difficulty staying in the saddle, began to wonder if this mode of transport was a good idea after all.

Howard could see that no-one in the platoon was going to be able to ride *and* hold on to a spare horse. He therefore made a suggestion to Nevil who, appreciating the sense of it, agreed.

While the platoon walked their horses up and down, gradually, getting used to them, Howard saddled up the remaining eight. He then tied them together by means of reins to the tail of the horse in front. He would be in control of the string by holding on to the reins of the first horse.

Nevil gave everyone a quarter of an hour to get in as much practice as they could. After that they dismounted and dismantled the camp, loading provisions and bits of gear they'd appropriated on to the spare horses.

When everyone was ready Nevil led off, Howard bringing

up the rear with the string of spare horses, himself flanked by Tom and Norman Currie.

As he rode, Howard thought the platoon a comical sight. Eric Young swayed wildly in the saddle, Ian Ireland hung on for dear life, while Major Nevil Sanderson looked completely at odds with his mount.

Then he remembered what had just taken place. The men who'd been alive that morning were now dead, buried under a pile of rocks.

And suddenly the platoon didn't seem comical any more.

It was going to be a bitter night, Maggie thought, warming her hands at the fire. She found the cold nights so debilitating. Even after a full eight hours' sleep she was still tired, and remained so during the rest of the day.

Her backside ached. And she knew it would be even worse in the morning. The morrow's travel on horseback promised to be sheer hell.

At least she felt she was making progress, beginning to get the hang of it. And it did beat marching, no doubt about that.

Andy sat beside her. 'Any more coffee going?'

She gestured to the pot by the side of the fire. 'Help yourself.'

He stared at her. Then refilled his mug. 'You?'

'No thanks. I've had enough.'

'What time shall we leave here?' Andy asked Nevil.

'Just after dawn.' He spread the map in front of him, and studied it.

'Same direction?'

'I don't see why not.'

Howard appeared out of the darkness. 'You want to speak to me, I believe, Major?' he said.

Nevil gestured him to sit.

When he'd settled, Howard pulled out a packet of Camel cigarettes. 'Mind if I smoke?'

'Not if you pass them round,' Andy growled.

Howard laughed. 'Be my guest.'

'You must have got cigarettes off the soldiers,' Howard said when those who smoke had lit up.

'We did. And good ones too. Though not British or American.'

'I understand the Republicans have been going short of tobacco?' Howard said.

Andy didn't reply to that. Nor did anyone else.

'Why was that patrol camped up as it was?' Nevil asked softly.

'The Lieutenant would do that every so often, when there weren't any Republicans in the vicinity, that was. They would spend an entire day eating, relaxing and generally enjoying themselves.'

'Well, on this occasion there were Republicans in the vicinity,' Charlie commented with a chuckle.

Andy looked contemptuous. 'And no-one on guard!'

'With all due respect to my previous hosts,' Howard said slowly, 'they could be extremely lackadaisical about certain matters. Posting guards was one of them.'

'What area were they patrolling?' Nevil queried, sliding the map across to Howard.

Howard indicated a small section of the map. 'They are, or were, one of several units patrolling between Andujar here, Aubeda to the east, and Jaen in the south.' The latter was on the perimeter of Andalusia, the province containing Malaga.

'Were they due to link up or make contact with another patrol at any time?' Nevil asked. This was his major worry.

Howard shook his head.

'You're certain about that?'

'Absolutely.'

Nevil, though he didn't show it, inwardly heaved a sigh of relief. If that were the case it might be years before the corpses in the gully were discovered. If indeed ever.

'What were you doing with them?' Nevil probed further.

'As I explained earlier, I'm a journalist on special assignment for *The New York Times*, my brief to cover the war. I've been here since the fall of Irún in September.'

'You must have seen a lot in almost five months,' Maggie said.

'Quite a bit,' he agreed.

'How about the siege of Madrid?' she went on.

'I watched it for a while. From the Nationalist position, of course, as I was outside the city.'

'A lot of women and children have died there since the siege began,' Charlie said.

Howard looked at Charlie, and their eyes locked. 'It hasn't exactly been a civilized war,' Howard replied.

'What are you implying?' Charlie queried softly, hackles up.

'Nothing at all,' Howard replied, matching Charlie's tone. 'I meant precisely what I said.'

'Why were you on this particular patrol?' Nevil enquired.

'I've been covering various aspects of the war, this is just another of them. And a mistake on my part. It had been deadly dull, no action whatever, until today. Everything had been perfectly routine until your fire cut the patrol to pieces.'

'And now you're with us bogeymen. At least that's how much of the foreign Press sees us Republicans,' Andy grinned.

Nevil glanced at Andy, his brow furrowing in thought. Then he brought his attention back to Howard.

'Do you deny the British and American Press, plus the Press of other countries, have been completely biased against the Republicans?'

Howard regarded Nevil steadily, his face impassive. 'I know the reports I have filed have all been factual.'

'That's not answering the question!'

'I think it does.'

'America is pro-Fascist, just as our own Britain is!' Charlie said vehemently.

'Do you truly believe that?'

'I do!'

Howard thought for a few moments, then said, 'I have to admit my country may lean a little towards Franco, as opposed to the other way. But that doesn't make it pro-Fascist.'

Andy exclaimed in disagreement, and drew heavily on his cigarette.

'And why does America favour Franco?' Maggie asked.

'I didn't say favour, I said lean towards. And the answer is, I suppose, that my country being ardently anti-Communist views Fascism as the lesser of two evils. Though that is simplifying matters.'

'Lesser of two evils,' Nevil mused, finding that funny.

'The British Press is certainly biased as regards this war. I cannot disagree with you there,' Howard stated.

'Ah!' said Andy, his face lighting up.

'But I must insist my own newspaper is neutral in its coverage. It sure as hell is as far as I'm concerned!'

'It's the British aristocracy, Press and Tory politicians who are against the democratically elected Popular Front here. Not the common people whom we represent,' Andy said.

'Regarding aristocrats, the French had the right idea with that guillotine of theirs,' Charlie muttered.

'You have the Russians on your side,' Howard said quietly.

'And Franco has the Germans and Italians on his,' Nevil countered.

'The Russians are a formidable ally. Particularly now that they have an army, and a large army, I'm told, on Spanish soil,' Howard continued.

'I've heard of this army,' Nevil said.

'Only heard of? Not actually seen?'

Nevil shook his head.

'There are a number of Russians in Madrid, mind you,' Andy said. 'Some fighting, others acting as advisers.'

'But only a number, not an army?'

'What's so important about this Russian army?' Nevil queried.

'It could make all the difference, don't you think?'

Andy flicked the remains of his cigarette into the fire where they crackled and hissed.

'I personally don't know anyone who's seen this army, though many people have heard of it,' Maggie said.

'Perhaps it's a secret army,' Charlie joked.

'Secret, or mythical?' Howard posed with a smile.

Charlie scowled at him. 'The Russians are our friends,' he stated emphatically.

'That is undoubtedly so. As we have said, the Popular Front's ally. The question remains, however, why don't they send more men and arms?'

When no-one answered that Howard went on. 'Stalin plays a deep and devious game. So deep and devious there are those who wonder if he knows what he's doing. Is his foreign policy diabolically clever? Or merely opportunistic and stupid?'

'Stalin's a great man,' Andy declared stoutly.

Maggie was enjoying this debate, though slightly worried that Howard might go too far. 'I think we should all turn in. It's getting late,' she said.

Nevil glanced at his wristwatch. 'You're right. We've an early start.'

Howard was aware that Maggie had stopped the conversation, and was grateful to her. But she needn't have concerned herself. He wouldn't have said anything that would have landed him in hot water.

'If I may be excused, goodnight then,' Howard said, rising.

'Goodnight,' Maggie replied. The only one to do so.

They exchanged smiles as they left the campfire.

She shook out the captured Fascist bedroll, thankful for its acquisition. It would keep her warmer during the night than she'd been up until now.

'Maggie!'

She faced Nevil, who joined her carrying his newly acquired bedroll. They hadn't made love since starting the mission. It would have been impossible, and unfair on the others.

'Can we talk?' he asked quietly.

'About what?' she queried, just as quietly.

'Us.'

She sighed, and sank down on to her bedroll. He shook out his, and lay down also. Reaching out he took her hand.

'Things don't seem to be the same between us,' he said, now speaking in a low whisper so as not to be overheard.

She didn't answer that.

291

'I don't want them to change, Maggie. I swear I don't!'

'You've become ruthless and hard, Nevil. I find that disconcerting and off-putting,' she replied in the same low whisper that the rest of their conversation would be conducted in.

'You have to be when in command,' he explained.

'But so much so?'

'I had to kill those men today, Maggie. My decision was the right one.'

'You pride yourself on making correct decisions, don't you?' she jibed.

'I let your friend live.'

'But only for the moment, until you've thought the matter through,' she said, reminding Nevil of his exact words.

'I have the platoon to consider. They're my friends, and responsibility. If killing Taft means saving their lives I'd have no hesitation in shooting him myself.'

'He's a journalist, a non-combatant,' she argued.

'That doesn't make any difference. If he yapped to the Nats we could all end up dead, our mission a failure.'

'He wouldn't yap. Not if I asked him not to.'

Nevil raised an eyebrow. 'Are you certain about that? Certain enough to stake your life on it? For that's what you'd be doing.'

'You think I'm too soft, don't you?'

He smiled thinly. 'Just as you think I'm too hard.'

Maggie removed her hand from his, pulled off her boina, her black beret, tossed it down then ran both hands through her hair. It badly needed a wash, she thought, scratching her scalp.

'What shall I do about Taft?' he asked.

'I can tell you what I *don't* want you to do.'

He grunted. 'It's the war, you know.'

She stopped scratching. 'What's the war?'

'What's happening between you and I.'

She considered that. 'It didn't happen in Madrid.'

'Madrid was different. To begin with I was wounded and you were nursing me. And then there was the hotel room where we could spend nights together. Nor were you ever part of the platoon there.'

'Madrid is only a short while ago, and yet already it seems so far away,' she said.

He wanted to place a hand on her cheek, to draw her to him, and hold her against his chest. But he couldn't because of those around them.

'The pork was good,' she said.

'Yes.'

'Just what everyone needed.'

'Have you fallen out of love with me, Maggie?'

'No,' she replied sharply. 'What made you ask such a thing?'

'For I haven't with you.'

She softened. 'I know that.'

'Nor will I ever.'

She glanced up at the bright stars twinkling down, a scattering of diamonds in a black velvet sky.

'A penny for them?' he asked.

'I was wishing.'

'For what?'

'If I tell you I won't get it.'

'Go on?' he urged.

'That things were as simple for us as they once were.'

He'd been smiling, now the smile faded. 'You can never go back, Maggie. That's a fact of life. You can never go back.'

'I know,' she replied somewhat forlornly.

'So we'll go forward together.'

She sighed a second time. 'I'm glad we've had this chat. I feel better for it.'

'Me too.'

'Now I'd like to get some sleep. I'm whacked.'

'Are you on guard duty tonight?' It was Andy's job to allocate the guard duties.

'No.'

'Neither am I. So we can at least sleep the night through, undisturbed.'

She slipped into her bedroll, which came all the way up to her chin. Nevil did the same.

'Maggie?' he whispered a minute later.

He got no reply, she was already fast asleep.

Maggie groaned, her backside even more painful than she'd thought possible. She was convinced that if she looked she'd find it to be a solid mass of bruises.

A horse cantered alongside, and there was Howard smiling at her. 'There are a lot of long faces in the party this morning,' he said.

'I can't think why!'

He laughed. 'It's like raging toothache of the butt, eh?'

Now she laughed. 'An apt description if ever there was one. No wonder you're a journalist.'

'It'll ease off after a few days. In the meantime you'll just have to suffer.'

'And suffering I surely am.'

He glanced ahead at Nevil, leading the platoon, then back at her. 'I want to thank you properly for what you did yesterday. You saved my life.'

She couldn't think of a suitable reply. So kept quiet.

'I'll always be in your debt.'

He had a nice voice, she thought. Once you got used to the American accent.

'It's a long way from Heymouth to here,' he said.

'More than miles.'

He smiled again. 'Yeah, I can imagine.'

They rode a little way in silence, then he asked, 'Am I safe now? Or is this simply a stay of execution?'

'I don't quite know what will happen, but I doubt very much that Nevil will have you killed. I've already spoken to him about that.'

'On my behalf?'

She nodded.

'You seem to have some influence with the major?'

'I should. He and I are engaged.'

Howard's eyebrows shot up. 'Engaged?'

'We worked for the same factory in Glasgow where I went after Heymouth. A carpet factory called Templeton's. We were all weavers there. The lads on the large setting looms, myself on the smaller weft loom.'

'Captain Menzies informed me yesterday that you all came over together,' Howard stated.

'Not exactly. The men did, while I followed on later. I came because . . .' She hesitated, then said, 'I came for several reasons, one of which was that Nevil had been wounded and I was worried about him. I got trapped in Madrid, and it was while I was there that something happened which made me decide to join the militia.'

'May I ask what that something was?'

She smiled at him. 'Always the journalist?'

'Of course. But I'd also like to know for my own information.'

She told him all about her job guarding the Fascist women and their children at the convent, and how those children had been blown to bits.

'I see,' he said when she finished.

'Did you go to the funeral?'

He blinked. 'I beg your pardon. What funeral?'

'At Heymouth.'

'Oh yeah, yeah I did!'

'I never saw you there.'

'I was there, I assure you,' he said, nodding. 'And you might not have seen me, but I saw you. You were with a man and a woman.'

'My sister and brother-in-law,' she explained.

'I did consider saying hello but . . . I decided not to. I didn't think you'd appreciate me intruding on such a private moment.'

Sensitive, she remembered that about him from their first encounter.

'Where did you go after Heymouth?' she asked.

'Edinburgh and London. Then it was back Stateside for a while. I believe I covered a story in Hawaii next, and one in Chile after that. If my memory serves me correctly, that is.'

'You certainly get around!' she laughed.

'Yeah, I most certainly do.'

'Is there a Mrs Taft?'

He shook his head. 'A wife and my profession don't

complement one another. Like oil and water they just don't mix.'

'So what do you have in New York, a house?'

'A bachelor apartment. It isn't enough, but I enjoy being there, which isn't often.'

'And what about your family. Where are they?'

He gave her a sideways glance in which his eyes were suddenly slightly hooded. 'They live upstate. I'm happy to say I get on with them and visit regularly.'

Nevil twisted in his saddle, and looked back. He frowned when he saw Howard with Maggie.

They continued talking, she delighting in Howard's company. He was one of the most entertaining men she'd ever come across.

Howard stared at Maggie now ahead of him, thinking of their earlier conversation. He hadn't really taken in how good-looking she was up until then. She'd hardly been at her best in Heymouth, and he'd been so rattled the day before he hadn't been taking in anything clearly.

Good-looking, and most attractive within herself. Once they'd started to talk there had been instant rapport between them.

And he owed her his life. If it hadn't been for Maggie Jordan and the fact he'd covered the Heymouth flood he'd be just dead meat under a pile of rocks.

His nostrils flared, remembering her scent. She had a gorgeous personal scent, reminiscent of wild flowers, he thought. Yes, that was it precisely – wild flowers.

The platoon continued, moving steadily southwards, towards Malaga.

Nevil stood, binoculars glued to his eyes, and trembled with a combination of fury and impotence.

The platoon watched bombs fall from the Junkers aeroplanes to explode among the troops on the ground, sending earth and bodies flying into the air.

'How many, do you think?' Andy asked, his voice tight. He

296

was referring to the Republican troops caught flat-footed by the Junkers on the open plain.

'Several hundred at least. Maybe more.'

Charlie, on the other side of Nevil, swore.

Planes that had dropped their bomb load now returned methodically to strafe.

Nevil tore the binoculars from his eyes. 'There's nothing we can do,' he said. That was obvious, but he'd felt the need to articulate it nonetheless.

'Death and blood. Ever since we came to Spain that's all it's been, death and blood,' Andy muttered.

'We'll wait here. Take a break until that's over,' Nevil said.

Charlie gave the command to dismount, then returned to watch the massacre on the plain.

'Poor buggers haven't a chance,' he said to Nevil.

'Stupid bastards for being caught out in the open like that. What the hell were their officers thinking of?'

It lasted a few more minutes. Then the Junkers, having used up all their bombs, sped off back to base.

Nevil stared grimly at the strewn corpses in the distance. The Nats had had a field day.

'Let's get started again,' he growled, and swung himself back up on to his horse.

Charlie gave the order to remount.

It was a little later that Bobby Farquharson urged his mount forward to catch up with Nevil.

'Someone there!' he said, pointing.

Nevil held up a hand, and the platoon reined in. A figure moved several hundred yards away. Then he saw it wasn't a solitary figure but four, two of whom were shouldering one between them.

'Militia,' Andy declared, recognizing their uniforms.

'Bring them here,' Nevil instructed. Andy, Bobby and several others went to their aid.

As the men neared Nevil, he saw that their faces were blackened from the bombing and burning. He guessed correctly that they were survivors from the massacre on the plain. Two of them had blood oozing from handkerchiefs tied round their wounds.

Nevil dismounted, as did the rest of the platoon, all of them gazing on in concern.

Finally the pathetic little group reached Nevil, and the one not helping to shoulder-carry collapsed to the ground. The militiaman on the right-hand side of the man being carried spat out a stream of Spanish.

Nevil waved up Maggie, and tried to speak to the man in his own language.

Water bottles were opened and three of them drank greedily. When Andy attempted to give water to the chap who'd been carried he found him to be dead already.

'Ask them what happened? How did they come to be out in the open like that?' Nevil said softly to Maggie.

She found the militiamen terribly difficult to understand, their accents were broad and totally new to her. However, with patience and her dictionary she finally put their story together.

'They'd been ordered to proceed at full speed to engage the troops besieging Malaga,' she explained to Nevil. 'Their job apparently was to try and relieve some of the pressure on the town.

'Their officers decided to take a chance by moving across the plain in broad daylight, but unfortunately when they were halfway over they were seen by a spotter plane which called up the Junkers. We witnessed the result.'

Matters at Malaga must have deteriorated even further, Nevil thought. It was imperative that he and his platoon got there as soon as possible. When he'd left Madrid no-one had known when the ship carrying the British Battalion would arrive in Malaga, but by now it could only be days away, a week at the outside.

'What are you going to do with them?' Charlie queried.

'Give them three of the spare horses, some water and food. The rest is up to them,' Nevil replied. They'd been alternating the horses so that all were periodically rested, and therefore kept relatively fresh.

'Right,' Charlie acknowledged, nodding.

'Explain it to them,' Nevil instructed Maggie.

'*Gracias*,' one of the men said after she'd done so.

'Tell them it's the best we can do,' Nevil added.

'I've already done so. They say they understand.'

A few minutes later the platoon had resumed its journey southward, leaving the three militiamen to bury their dead companion.

The following day the platoon again stumbled on a scene of human carnage, but this one had not been caused by bomb or bullet.

The corpses were unbelievably grotesque. Men on their knees clutching their throats, their eyes bulging as though about to burst from their sockets. An individual had clawed his face, ripping it to shreds in his agony. Another, who must have been in excruciating pain, had stuck the barrel of a pistol in his mouth and pulled the trigger.

A young militiawoman, roughly the same age as Maggie, lay on her back gazing at the sky through sightless eyes. She was clutching the shirt she'd ripped open to expose her breasts, something she'd clearly done in her desperate fight for breath.

All the faces of the dead militia were blackish in colour, and mottled. Everywhere dried blood was heavily encrusted below the ears and noses.

They all gazed at the scene in horror. It was somehow worse than anything they'd seen before.

'Gas,' said Jimmy Sharkey.

Mo Cairns slid from his horse and stumbled behind a tree from where the rest of them heard him throw up.

Nevil, eyes blazing anger, dismounted.

'Sorry,' Mo apologized, re-emerging from behind the tree. 'It's just that my da died from gas in the Great War. I suddenly saw him here with the rest of these.'

Something seemed to snap in Nevil. He ran at Howard, and dragged the journalist from his horse. 'Gas!' he yelled. 'Bloody gas. Will you print that in your newspaper?'

The last thing Howard intended doing was arguing. 'Of course I will.'

'Liar!' Nevil shrieked at him. 'You're as biased as the rest of the newspaper shits!'

'If I get a chance to file this story I swear to you I shall,' Howard responded quietly, and soothingly.

Maggie had already dismounted, and now hurried to Nevil's side. She bit her lower lip, unsure whether to intervene or not.

Nevil shook Howard the way a dog does a rat. 'Liar! Liar! Liar! You're all against us. All of you bastards!'

'Take it easy,' Maggie pleaded, grasping Nevil's arm.

Quick as lightning he partially released Howard to slap Maggie, who went flying. His expression was crazed, a man out of his wits.

Charlie went to Maggie, Andy to Nevil. 'Get a grip, Nevil!' Andy hissed in a low voice.

'I'm all right,' Maggie said in a similar low voice to a concerned Charlie. She couldn't believe that Nevil had actually hit her.

Nevil drew in a deep breath, then another, and appeared to regain control of himself. But he still didn't let go of Howard, who was doing his best to remain calm.

'I know now what I'm going to do with you,' Nevil told Howard.

'What?'

'I'm going to take you all the way with us to the Malaga fronts, where you'll get the greatest story of the war. You're going to be there when we rout the Nats and turn the tide of the war in our favour. You're going to be there to see the beginning of the end for Franco and his rebels. And you're going to send the story not only to your own newspaper, but put it on the wire services so that for once the whole world will know the truth and not the damned lies and half-truths that the British and International Press have been peddling to date.'

This was the first Howard had heard of their mission. 'If that's what you want me to do, Major Sanderson, then that's what I'll do. And not merely because you tell me to do it, but because it would be a tremendous scoop and huge feather in my cap.'

Nevil grunted.

'So I'll accompany you with pleasure.'

Nevil released Howard, and slightly pushed him away.

Howard knew he was chancing his luck, but his journalistic curiosity got the better of him. 'Can I ask a question, Major?'

'Depends what that question is.'

'Do you have any basis for saying that the tide of war will be turned in your favour on the Malaga fronts?'

Nevil smiled thinly, and somewhat chillingly. 'We are going there to take command of a British Battalion of well-trained volunteers who'll be landing from the sea. It's not only my hope, but my sincere belief; that such a battalion, with myself at its head and my friends here as officers, will both defeat and repel the rebels. We will become the instigation of what will become a general rout – the catalyst that changes impending defeat to victory.'

'A British Battalion,' Howard breathed. This was copy indeed.

'Lads from all over Britain who've come forward to fight the Fascists. And who'll fight like very furies out of hell when I tell them about things like that!' Nevil said, pointing dramatically at the gassed militia.

Maggie rose again to her feet, and dusted herself down. She was shaken by Nevil's slap, but otherwise unhurt.

Nevil turned to her, dismissing Howard. 'I shouldn't have done that. I'm sorry.'

She stared at him, and it was as though she was seeing a stranger. The figure and features were Nevil's, but not the Nevil she knew. He was not the Nevil she'd journeyed to Spain to be with.

'Let's ride,' said Nevil abruptly, making for his horse.

When the platoon moved off Howard was alongside Maggie.

Nevil glanced up from the map he'd been studying, and over at where Maggie, Howard and the Currie brothers were playing Pontoon for pesetas. They were sitting beside a campfire.

Maggie laughed, obviously thoroughly enjoying herself, and said something to Howard, who laughed in return.

Nevil frowned. Those two were becoming thick as thieves. Whenever he looked they were in each other's company. They rode together, they ate together. It was a wonder they didn't damn well sleep next to one another!

With a shock he realized he was jealous – jealous as sin. If he could have waved a magic wand and made the journalist disappear he would have done.

He laid the map aside. Slowly he crossed to where the foursome were playing cards. He was unaware that he was scowling.

'Who's winning?' he asked.

'I am,' replied Maggie with a smile.

That smile somehow, irrationally, infuriated him. 'Good,' he mumbled.

'She's taking us to the cleaners,' said Norman Currie.

Nevil stretched out a leg and tapped Howard with his foot. 'And how are you?'

The atmosphere surrounding the card game immediately changed to become tense. 'Fine, thank you,' Howard politely replied.

'Written your story about the gassing yet?'

Howard had foreseen that might come up. 'Yes, I have. It's ready to be filled through to New York. When next I'm in a position to do so, that is.'

'I'd like to read it.'

'Surely. It's in my saddle bag.'

'Then go and get it.'

Howard placed his cards on the ground, and walked off into the darkness.

'A cold night again,' Tom Currie said by way of making conversation.

'Yes,' Nevil agreed.

'At least there's plenty of water hereabouts. There's no danger of us running short of that,' Norman said.

'Yes,' Nevil further agreed.

There was silence until Howard returned holding a thick

302

notebook which he handed to Nevil. 'I've written about five hundred words which they'll no doubt edit. But not too much, I hope. The use of poison gas is an extremely serious business. Particularly as my article isn't just an allegation, but an actual eyewitness account.'

Nevil looked at Maggie. 'Have you read this?'

'I did so earlier today and thought it excellent.'

Jealousy again stabbed in him. Jealousy he tried to keep from his face.

He opened the notebook and read, aware that four sets of eyes were on him.

He would have liked to find fault, but couldn't. The article was a straight reporting job, stating the facts and no more. There wasn't a hint of bias, towards either side, in it.

'OK,' he said, and returned the notebook to Howard.

He left them to get on with their game.

They were well into Andalusia now, Nevil thought, when his horse suddenly stumbled pitching him from the saddle.

A sharp pain lanced through him as he hit the ground awkwardly, landing on the shoulder he'd already wounded. He knew instantly that he'd hurt himself.

Andy jumped down beside him. 'Nevil, are you all right?'

When he tried to move his arm it wouldn't respond.

He had to grit his teeth as he pulled himself up on to his bottom. 'I've damaged something,' he said to Andy.

'How do you mean?'

'I think I've broken my arm.'

Charlie and Maggie joined them, while others clustered round.

'He thinks he's broken his arm,' Andy informed Maggie.

'Let me see,' she murmured.

She gingerly felt his arm, which didn't bother him, then moved her hand up to the shoulder itself. He yelped like a stuck pig.

'Can you wiggle your fingers?' she asked.

He could.

'From what I understand that means your arm isn't broken. So the problem must be your shoulder.'

'It could be dislocated,' Howard suggested, standing just behind Maggie.

She swung on him. 'Could you tell if it is?'

Howard nodded, and knelt beside Maggie. Nevil winced, but didn't yelp as he examined the shoulder.

'It's dislocated, all right,' Howard pronounced.

'So what can we do?' Maggie asked him.

'We either take him to a doctor, or else one of us puts it back in place.'

'We can't go to a doctor,' Nevil stated firmly, his face a mucky shade of grey.

'Then one of us puts it back,' Howard said.

'Well, don't look at me!' Andy exclaimed. 'I haven't a clue what to do.'

'Have any of you?' Howard asked generally.

Some replied 'No.' Others shook their head.

'Maybe I can ride with it like this,' Nevil said.

'I'm telling you now you won't be able to,' Howard informed him.

Nevil glared at the journalist. 'You seem to know about dislocated shoulders.'

'I've seen it happen to a lot of guys while playing our American football. And it has even happened to me once.'

'Can you put it back in for him?' Maggie asked.

'I can try. At least I have the experience of having watched it being done.'

Nevil continued to glare at Howard, who stared benignly in return.

'It's entirely up to you, Major,' Howard said quietly.

Nevil was cursing inwardly. What a bloody stupid thing to happen! He grunted when he inadvertently moved and another sharp pain shot through the offending shoulder.

'Go ahead,' he instructed, his tone most unpleasant.

Howard wondered if he should make Nevil take off his top garments, then decided against it. Closing his eyes he recalled the occasion Coach Gerber had fixed his shoulder, trying to remember precisely what he had done and how he had gone about it. Like a loop of film he reran the scene a number of times in his mind before being satisfied.

'Come on!' Nevil urged.

Howard didn't manage it on his first attempt, but was successful on his second.

Nevil choked as his shoulder clicked back into place.

'That's it,' Howard declared. 'Now the arm needs strapping.'

'Maggie will do that,' Nevil snarled.

'Right,' said Howard, coming to his feet.

Maggie looked hard at Nevil, then at Howard. 'Strapped how?'

'Across his chest. And fairly tight to the chest.'

She nodded that she understood, but wondered what she could use for the strapping.

'A section of reins off one of the spare horses,' Andy answered when she asked for suggestions.

'Good idea. Can you arrange it?'

Andy left them, and the rest of the platoon dispersed to do other things, leaving only Charlie with Maggie and Nevil, Howard having sloped off as well.

'It would be this shoulder,' Nevil complained.

'You might have shown a little gratitude for what he did,' Maggie admonished.

'Who?'

'Howard, of course.'

He sneered. 'What did you want me to do, give the bugger a medal?'

'Don't be stupid!'

Nevil gave Charlie a flick of the head indicating that he should leave.

When Charlie had gone Nevil said, 'I don't like you two being together so much.'

'Why ever not?' she replied, genuinely surprised.

'I just don't like it. Truth is, I don't fully trust him.'

Maggie laughed. 'You're being ridiculous!'

'You'll do as I say, damn you!'

She stared Nevil straight in the eye. 'He's a good man, a laugh, and far better company than you've been recently,' she said.

'This is a war, not a bloody social event!' he hissed in reply.

There was a strained silence between them, then she said softly, 'I wish . . .'

'What?' he prompted when she trailed off.

She shook her head. 'Nothing.'

As soon as she'd securely strapped his arm across his chest he gave the order for them to resume their journey.

Nevil was about to call a halt for the night when a single shot rang out ahead. Mo Cairns was on point.

Had Mo run into a Fascist patrol, Nevil wondered? It was entirely possible. But if so why only the single shot?

'Take a couple of men and investigate,' Nevil ordered Andy, who was by his side.

Andy signalled to Eric Young and Ian Ireland to follow him, and kicked his horse into a canter.

Every passing day saw an improvement in the platoon's ability to handle their mounts. Without exception they'd reached a standard of amateurish competence. Individual styles left a lot to be desired, but then none of them were bothered about that.

Nevil felt terrible. The continual movement of his horse made his shoulder throb appallingly, which had earlier brought on a bad headache. And it was his turn for guard duty too! He could have excused himself, but didn't even contemplate doing so. Despite his shoulder he was determined to do his spell just like everyone else.

He glanced up at the sky. A falcon wheeled, and was joined by another. Its mate? The pair of them completed a complicated manoeuvre that he found fascinating, then flapped out of sight behind a group of trees.

A little further on Andy, Eric and Ian reappeared, and Mo with them. Mo had something slung in front of him. A body? No, it didn't seem the right shape for that. As they came closer Nevil saw that it was a beast of some sort.

'Deer!' a grinning Mo announced when he reached the platoon.

That was greeted with cheers. They hadn't had meat since the pig.

'We'll camp here,' said Nevil, then told Eric and Ian to ride out and bring in the flankers.

Wood was gathered, and fires lit. While this was happening Mo and Bobby Farquharson set about skinning and dismembering the deer.

Nevil, using one hand, shook out his bedroll, and then sat on it. He unscrewed the cap of his water-bottle, had a long drink, then screwed the cap back on again.

He made a mental note to speak to the platoon about water. After a rapid succession of streams they hadn't encountered one for a while, which could mean they'd entered a dry area with little or no water available. If that was the case the horses would have to be given preference over the men. A few minutes later Maggie joined him.

'How's the shoulder?' she enquired.

'Throbbing like billy-o! It's being constantly in the saddle that's causing it.'

She nodded that she understood. Then changed the subject. 'Have you ever had venison before?'

'No, I haven't,' he admitted.

'We used to get it in Heymouth. I was just thinking this will be the first I've had since leaving there.'

Her presence was beginning to relax him, just as it had of old. 'It's a strong flavour, I believe,' he said.

'Strong, and gamey. That one is a young deer so it should be tender, and not too strong. Venison that's been well hung can be something of an acquired taste.'

He rubbed his shoulder, which helped.

'Would you like me to do that for you? Give you a massage?' she offered.

'That would be smashing, Maggie.'

'Right then.'

She went behind him, and pulled aside his cape. He closed his eyes in appreciation as her hands began to move.

She kneaded gently, doing her best to soothe away the pain.

'How's that?' she asked.

'Sheer heaven.'

'You'd like me to go on then?'

'Please.'

She shifted herself, to get into a different position, but her hands never stopped.

A warmth rose up in him, and a mellowness. Not only was the pain in his shoulder going, but the throbbing in his head had lessened as well.

He opened his eyes to look at her. But she, smiling, was glancing elsewhere. He followed her stare and there was Howard Taft smiling back at her.

His stomach contracted into a tight knot, as though it had been punched hard.

'That's enough now,' he said, a sharpness in his voice that hadn't previously been there.

The interlude with her was completely and utterly spoiled.

The high sierras, capped with snow just as Antonio Mije had said they'd be, loomed before them. They'd been climbing for some time now, through the rocky hills that were the approach to the mountains.

'Halt!' Nevil called out, reining in his mount. When the platoon had stopped he told them to gather round.

'This is as far south as we can go by horse,' he said. 'Our next move is to cut back across to the main road where, somehow or other, we'll have to acquire a vehicle to take us through the Nationalist lines. It isn't going to be easy.'

'Roadblocks?' Teddy Agnew queried softly.

'Bound to be,' Nevil replied. He paused, then went on, 'It's been relatively easy up until now. But from here things get difficult.'

'Can I ask a couple of questions?'

Nevil looked at Howard who'd spoken. 'What are they?'

'You actually intend trying to pass through the Nationalist lines and roadblocks, and all that entails, while none of you speak fluent Spanish?' His tone was one of incredulity.

Nevil nodded. 'We've no choice.'

Howard pointed to the sierras. 'Of course you have. Go over the top.'

'My information, from a Spaniard, I might add, is that those sierras are impassable.'

Howard took a deep breath, and sat back in his saddle. 'That's not entirely true.'

Nevil resisted the temptation to give a mocking, derisory, laugh. 'Explain yourself?'

'These sierras might be impassable to wheeled traffic, or large groups of people, but there are trails over them that would accommodate our number.'

'And how do you know that?'

'I read a comprehensive article about the Andalusian sierras in the *National Geographic* magazine. Trails exist, narrow and dangerous, I admit, but exist nonetheless, which the locals know of, and use. In this article the American who crossed over was guided by a local, the pair of them on mountain ponies. It was summer admittedly, and we are handicapped by the snow, but I certainly think you should consider the matter, and ask the advice of the locals before committing yourself to the road route.'

Nevil regarded Howard. Uncertainty had appeared where only seconds previously there had been a steady resolve.

'And why should you help us?' he asked.

'Because I'd like to live to file that scoop you've promised me.'

A plausible enough reason, Nevil thought. 'Andy, what's your opinion?'

'There's no getting away from the fact that we'll be up against it trying to get through the Nationalist lines by road. And to be honest, I don't rate our chances all that high. Though I have to say, if anyone can pull it off you can.'

Nevil grunted, pleased by that praise which he knew was genuine and not sycophantic. 'Charlie?'

'I agree with Andy. If there's the possibility of an alternative route then let's find out about it.'

309

Nevil looked at Maggie and could see she went along with Howard, as did the men if he was interpreting their expressions correctly.

'We'll dismount for half an hour while we talk this through,' he announced, and stepped down from his horse. He wanted to hear more about this *National Geographic* magazine, and consult their map.

When they moved off again they were heading for the village of Ermita situated several miles to the east.

Roque Ballaster was the equivalent of the village mayor, and Maggie judged him to be in his early to mid-fifties. He had leathery skin that was tanned dark brown by the sun, and eyes that were very close together. His eyebrows were a straight black bar of hair.

The Ballasters' house was a mean construction of lime-washed stone. It did have floorboards, however, which Maggie hadn't expected, and the furniture was made entirely of hand-carved wood.

Maggie finished her explanation, which had necessitated quite a few references to the dictionary, then glanced at Nevil who gave her a reassuring nod that she'd done well.

Ballaster considered what Maggie had told him, then fastened Nevil, whom he now knew to be the platoon's leader, with a gaze that was both penetrating and appraising.

Roque Ballaster might be a peasant and uneducated, but was nonetheless keenly intelligent. As the Andalusian proverb went, he knew how many beans made five.

'Is it possible at this time of year?' Nevil asked. Maggie translated.

Ballaster's gaze went from Nevil to the others present, then back to Nevil. '*Si!*'

'So will you, or one of your people, guide us?'

Ballaster sighed, and rubbed his work-worn hands together after Maggie had translated that.

'It is for the Republic,' Nevil added.

'Many of our young men, the hotbloods, have gone to fight for the Republic,' Ballaster answered slowly.

310

'So you will help us as you would hope others would help them.'

The hint of a smile creased Ballaster's lips, then disappeared again. He didn't reply.

'We need to get to Malaga. It is very important for the town and Republican cause that we do.'

'Malaga!' Ballaster exclaimed. Screwing up his face in contempt he hawked into the fire.

'I don't think I need translate that,' Maggie joked quietly, which made Charlie, Andy and Howard, the others of their party present, smile. But not Nevil.

'It is very important,' Nevil repeated.

'To you,' Ballaster said.

'And the Republican cause.'

Ballaster fell silent again, and studied the fire.

Nevil looked at Andy, and shrugged.

They all sat in silence, a silence that stretched endlessly, while Ballaster continued to stare into the fire as though he were alone.

Nevil opened his mouth to break the silence when Ballaster suddenly said, 'How much?'

'How much? You mean money?'

'Pesetas.'

Nevil was shocked. 'You want money! But I've explained to you, this is an important matter to the Republican cause. How can you ask for money for such a thing?'

Now it was Ballaster who shrugged. 'War is business same as anything else.'

That shocked Nevil even more. 'Surely you've translated it wrongly?' he said to Maggie.

To be certain she asked Ballaster to repeat himself, which he did.

'No,' she informed Nevil. 'That's correct.'

'My God!' he exclaimed. He couldn't believe that he, a foreigner, who'd come to Spain to fight for the Republican cause was being asked for money by a Spanish peasant to further that cause – a cause completely in the Spanish peasant's interests.

Naïve, Howard thought, staring at Nevil. But then he'd guessed that already. Charlie was clearly angry, but keeping his anger under control. Andy just looked sad.

Ballaster picked up a stick, poked the fire and waited.

'We have very little money with us, I'm afraid,' Nevil said to him.

'How many pesetas?'

'I've no idea. But not a lot.'

Ballaster poked the fire again.

Maggie thought of the cash she had in her money belt. The last thing she wanted to do was part with it, but would if it meant saving lives.

'Horses,' Howard said. 'Offer him horses instead of money.'

The obvious solution, Nevil thought. But it annoyed him that the American had come up with it rather than himself. He corrected that, *before* himself. The damn Yank always seemed to be one step ahead of him.

'*Si!*' smiled Ballaster.

That was what Ballaster had been after all along, Nevil suddenly realized. He glanced at Howard and saw that Howard had already worked that out. A step ahead of him again!

'How many horses?' Nevil asked.

Ballaster held up five fingers, a full spread of hand.

They could easily spare that. And anyway, what use were horses to them after they reached Malaga? None at all.

'Five,' he agreed.

'Of my choosing,' Ballaster added.

Nevil laughed. The Spaniard was a cheeky bugger right enough! 'Of your choosing,' he further agreed.

A beaming Ballaster came to his feet and shook hands with Nevil, after which he shook hands with all the others including Maggie.

When that was concluded he called for wine and coffee which his wife hurried to fetch.

Maggie couldn't remember ever having been so cold. Her body, despite the sheepskin coat, was frozen through. She shivered as she rode, dimly aware of her teeth chattering.

312

Snow had been falling for hours now, huge swirling flakes that had reduced visibility to mere yards.

They emerged from the narrow track they'd been riding along in single file on to a far broader one. Instantly Howard urged his horse forward so that he could catch up with Maggie.

'How are you doing?' he asked when he was alongside.

'Tired. Terribly tired.'

'You mustn't sleep!' he warned her. 'That could be fatal.'

'I know. But it's so tempting just to doze off.'

He reached over and slapped her arm. 'Come on, keep those eyes open!'

'So hard,' she mumbled.

'Goddamnit woman, do as I say!' he positively roared at her.

She shook herself, and sat upright. 'Wish I could breathe more easily,' she said.

'Yeah, we're high up.'

'At least there isn't a wind. We can be thankful for that.'

'You know something, Maggie?'

'What?'

'I'd give anything for a steaming bowl of clam chowder. I adore clam chowder!'

She laughed. 'I've heard of it, but never tasted it.'

'But surely, having lived in Heymouth, you've eaten clam?'

'Mussels yes, but not clam. They didn't exist round our part of the coast.'

'What is your favourite soup, Maggie?' He was trying to get her to talk, and thereby keep her awake.

'Homemade leek and potato.'

'Vichyssoise. I like that too.'

'That's something we have in common then,' she said, giving him a bleak smile.

'I'm sure we have a lot more in common than leek and potato soup,' he replied lightly.

'I'm sure.'

Their horses plodded on.

'You know I'd love to go to America some day. It must be a marvellous country,' she said.

'It is. And B-I-G. And very diverse.'

'Tell me about it,' she requested.

'Only if you tell me all about Scotland afterwards. That was one place I took a shine to, and to which I've promised myself I'll return.'

'You have?'

'You bet I have!'

And as they spoke the hours and miles slipped by unnoticed.

Two things happened simultaneously: they heard the sound of artillery fire, and the snow abruptly stopped as though switched off.

Seconds later the path they were on twisted and began to descend.

Malaga lay revealed below them, a huddle of houses and buildings between the sierras and the sea. Their destination at last.

As they continued downwards church bells began to ring, giving the alarm. And with the bells came a swarm of Fascist aeroplanes to bomb and strafe the hapless city.

CHAPTER EIGHT

They entered Malaga under escort. They had been stopped by the militia, who had barricaded their entrance to the city. A Political Commissar, Prieto Viltron, had then been hastily summoned to accompany them through.

Maggie, who was riding beside Nevil as interpreter, gazed about her at scenes of utter devastation. She had witnessed a great deal of damage in Madrid, but nothing compared with this. But then, Malaga was a far smaller town, and easier to destroy. Evidently Nationalists were trying their hardest to raze it to the ground.

The faces of the people she glimpsed were stark with fear and hopelessness. The smell and feel of impending defeat was everywhere.

Eventually they came to the Hotel Caleta Palace, where they stopped. Nevil signalled the platoon to gather round.

'We're being billeted here. I want you all, with the exception of Maggie, to go in and get yourselves sorted out. I'll be back in a while and will hopefully be able to tell you exactly what's happening.'

'Where do we stable the horses?' Andy asked.

Nevil gave him a thin smile. '*Camarada* Viltron has already spoken about that. The kitchen staff will be attending to them.'

'Jesus Christ!' exclaimed Ian Ireland. 'Does that mean what I think?'

'Food is at a premium,' Nevil explained.

'Horse meat though. Yuch!' Mo Cairns added, pulling a face.

'They've been eating worse than that, I've been told,' Nevil said softly. He didn't elaborate, nor did Mo or anyone else ask him to.

Viltron barked out some orders to the rest of the escort, who immediately gathered up the horses' reins, while one of their number dashed inside to inform the kitchen staff.

'Look after my belongings, will you?' Maggie asked Andy.

Nevil momentarily closed his eyes. He looked very drawn and exceptionally tired, Maggie thought. But there again, they were all feeling the strain of what they'd been through.

She glanced up as an artillery shell screamed overhead. Thankfully it exploded quite some distance away.

'Just like being back in Madrid,' she joked to Nevil, who smiled – a smile that suddenly turned to a wince.

'What's wrong?' she demanded.

'This shoulder is giving me gyp. But it's nothing to worry about.'

'Well, there's bound to be a doctor here. He can have a look at it,' she said.

'I think the dislocation must have disturbed the old wound. However, given time I'm sure it'll settle down.'

'You should still consult a doctor,' she told him.

'Have you forgotten about Spanish doctors? You may have, but I certainly haven't.'

She bit her lip. He was right, she had temporarily forgotten.

'This way, *camaradas*. Follow me!' Viltron said breezily to Nevil and Maggie, waving a hand in the air. He strode quickly off, Nevil and Maggie hurrying to keep up.

Viltron took them to a building about a quarter of a mile away.

'*Camarada* Major Sanderson to see *Camarada* General Fenellosa,' he declared to a militiaman sitting behind a make-shift desk.

The militiaman's bored expression didn't change. 'The General is busy,' he replied.

'The General is anxious to speak with Major Sanderson,' Viltron went on.

The bored expression became one of disbelief.

'And that is the truth,' Viltron added.

'Sit down then,' the militiaman said to Nevil. 'I will have a word with the General by and by.'

Maggie was appalled by this procedure. And yet, she couldn't help thinking, how typical of the indolent Spanish.

Viltron rounded on Nevil. 'I have duties elsewhere, *camarada*, and must go.'

Maggie translated this, along with the rest of the conversation.

'Thank you for your assistance, *camarada*,' Nevil said, and gave Viltron the Red salute.

Viltron returned the salute. Glancing at the militiaman, he muttered something under his breath, and strode away.

'Do you think this chap's just being awkward?' Nevil asked Maggie, indicating the militiaman.

'Exercising his little bit of authority. He'll probably keep us waiting a couple of hours before letting the General know we're here.'

'And probably keep us waiting longer than anyone else because we're foreigners,' Nevil said slowly.

The militiaman tilted his chair back on to its rear legs, and stuck his own on top of the desk in front. He then clasped his hands behind his head.

The situation might have been saved if the militiaman hadn't done what he did next. He smiled insolently.

Maggie saw the change come over Nevil.

'Shall we sit down?' she said.

'Translate for me,' Nevil instructed her, his voice tight and crackly, as he desperately suppressed his fury.

'I have been admiring that fine pistol you are wearing, *camarada*. May I look at it?' he asked the militiaman.

The militiaman shrugged. '*Si!*' Removing the pistol from its cutaway holster he arrogantly held it out by its barrel.

Nevil accepted the pistol, and the next second that self-same barrel was pointing up the militiaman's nose.

The transformation was instantaneous. The militiaman's face drained of colour while his eyes popped out like organ stops.

'I want to see General Fenellosa, and I want to see him *now*. Do you understand?'

'*Si! Si!*' croaked the militiaman.

'General Fenellosa *ahora*!' Nevil repeated, and withdrew the pistol several inches, which allowed the militiaman to scramble to his feet and rush off.

'That's one way of making your point,' Maggie said.

'And a most effective way.' He stuck the pistol into the waist-band of his trousers, having decided to keep it.

Within minutes the militiaman was back asking them to please accompany him and he'd take them to the general. His manner was cringing, like that of a whipped dog.

The room they were shown into contained a huge desk which was as ornate and sumptuous as the militiaman's had been makeshift. The General, dwarfed by it, sat behind the desk.

Nevil gave the Red salute. Maggie considered doing so, and decided not to. The general rose to his feet – he was tiny – and returned Nevil's salute.

'Welcome to Malaga, *Camarada* Major Sanderson. Welcome!' he said in strongly accented English.

Coming out from behind his desk he crossed to Nevil and shook him warmly by the hand, after which he shook hands with Maggie.

'I was beginning to think you weren't going to make it,' he said to Nevil.

'We travelled as fast as we could, *camarada*.'

'A difficult journey. Tell me, how did you get through the Nationalist lines?'

'We came over the sierras,' Nevil replied.

Fenellosa nodded. 'That is what I would have attempted myself. Did you have a guide?'

'A man from Ermita. He charged five horses to bring us over.'

Fenellosa scowled. 'Scum! Some people have no respect or sense of duty.' He pointed at Nevil's strapped arm. 'You are wounded?'

'No, I dislocated my shoulder, that's all. Nothing serious.'

'It has been attended to?'

'It has,' Nevil stated emphatically.

'Good. And what about the officers you brought with you? Have they all arrived safe and sound?'

318

'We lost one chap unfortunately,' Nevil replied.

'A pity. Worse than none, but better than two, heh?' He swivelled round to stare admiringly at Maggie. 'And who are you, *camarada*?'

'*Camarada* Lieutenant Jordan,' she replied.

'Ah so! A very pretty lieutenant too, if I may say.'

Maggie blushed.

'Maggie has been interpreting for us,' Nevil explained. 'She didn't know any Spanish at all when she came over only a few months ago, but has picked up the language very quickly. I use her as an interpreter as she's far more fluent than any of the rest of us.'

'You speak extremely good English, *camarada*,' Maggie said.

'I have often been to England, and have many friends there,' Fenellosa beamed, clearly pleased by this compliment.

'As you don't need me, do you want me to wait outside?' Maggie asked Nevil.

'I won't hear of that. You will remain and have some wine with me,' Fenellosa answered instead.

A ladies' man, Maggie thought. But then weren't all Spaniards! At least so they liked to imagine.

Fenellosa produced an already opened bottle of Rioja and three glasses. He filled the glasses and handed them round.

'Bottoms up!' Fenellosa toasted.

Maggie and Nevil both smiled at the seeming incongruousness of a Spanish general saying that. 'Bottoms up!' they repeated.

After he'd had a gulp of wine Fenellosa's expression altered to become sombre in the extreme. 'I have been anxiously awaiting your arrival, Major Sanderson. And the arrival of the *Dolphin* carrying the British Battalion plus the equipment and supplies we so desperately need. Together you represent Malaga's last hope.'

'It's as bad as that, then?' Nevil said softly.

'Our ammunition and our food are almost gone, while our casualties are calamitous! We are on our knees, and only a miracle can get us back on our feet again. I am hoping that you, your men, the British Battalion and what they bring with them will be that miracle.'

This wasn't the situation Nevil had anticipated. A city under heavy siege, yes, but not one as far gone as this.

'When is the *Dolphin* due in?' he queried.

Fenellosa spread his hands. 'She is under radio silence and will only contact us shortly before she docks. All I can say is that we expect her at any time.'

He crossed to a map hanging on the wall and jabbed at it. 'And yesterday the worst possible news from our spies. The Nationalists are massing for a new push which could also come at any time now.'

'Malaga mustn't fall,' Nevil said grimly. '*Camarada* Mije in Madrid is convinced it would be the beginning of the end for us.'

'I am afraid so,' Fenellosa agreed.

'He also believes that if we could beat back the besiegers it could be the beginning of the end for Franco.'

Fenellosa's eyes shone with fervour. 'This too I believe. If only it would be so!'

'The turning point of the war,' Nevil murmured. 'The question is, though, which way?'

'Morale here is low,' Fenellosa said. 'But the arrival of the British Battalion would give new heart to my troops, and to the Malagans themselves. And with new heart, plus the replenishment of food and ammunition, who knows what may still be accomplished!'

'They must arrive before the new push,' Nevil declared passionately.

'Today, tonight, tomorrow, they must come soon,' Fenellosa said.

He raised his glass in a second toast, and they all drank to that.

'Soon,' Fenellosa repeated.

The Hotel Caleta Palace was full of militia, some rooms that had been designed to sleep two now sleeping as many as sixteen. The platoon had been assigned a section of corridor on the third floor.

Maggie stared at her filthy, and much stained, cot in

disgust. The blanket on top of it smelled of rotten fish.

'Disgusting!' she exclaimed.

'Not exactly the Savoy, is it?' said Andy from the next bed.

'At least it's a bed,' commented Bobby Farquharson from his cot where he was lying stretched out.

'There are beds and beds,' replied Maggie.

'Aye, well, these are the latter,' jibed Bobby, which made her grin ruefully.

'I think I'd prefer my bedroll on the ground,' she said.

'You can always sleep on the floor. But I wouldn't recommend it,' Andy retorted.

'Why not?'

'It's concrete underneath that carpet. A very *thin* carpet, I may add. There's nothing worse to sleep on than concrete. It's not only hard and totally unyielding, but cold. Cold that will seep right through that carpet at night.'

Maggie sighed. The cot it would have to be, but not the blanket. Picking up the blanket she disdainfully tossed it aside.

'Hi!' said Howard, coming up to her. 'How did it go?'

'How did what go?'

'Whatever it was you and the major went off to do? Or whoever you went off to see?'

'Fine.'

'What do you think of your new billet?'

She raised an eyebrow. 'Do you really want to know?'

He laughed. 'The same as the rest of us, I imagine. But listen, I'm here to ask you a favour.'

'What's that?'

'Are you busy just now?'

She shook her head. 'No.'

'Then how about coming with me while I file the gas and other stories I've written? I could manage on my own of course, but it would be far easier having someone with me who speaks the lingo as well as you do.'

She thought of Nevil, who'd gone off with Charlie. He hadn't said he'd need her in the immediate future so she presumed she was free. She had been hoping for a bit of sleep, but could defer that. 'All right,' she agreed, 'but I must go to the bathroom first.'

'It's along there,' he told her, pointing. 'Shall I wait here for you or down at the main entrance?'

'I'll meet you at the main entrance in fifteen minutes, providing the bathroom's free. How's that?'

'Ace!'

'Right then.' She left him, wondering if there would be any hot water available. The bathroom was free, and there wasn't.

Punctual, she joined him at the main entrance in just under fifteen minutes where he greeted her with a smile.

What they didn't know as they walked away was that Nevil had been in the foyer when Maggie had turned up, and had seen her link arms with Howard.

'That's that,' stated Howard as they emerged from the main post office, where he'd managed to wire his copy to *The New York Times*.

'You didn't really need me,' she said.

'But it's so much nicer and fun to arrange it with you!' he retorted.

It was nice and fun for her too, she thought.

'Do you ever miss the sea?' he queried.

'Sometimes. But why do you ask that?'

'I was wondering if you'd like to go down and have a stroll along the beach?'

'Know something? I would absolutely love to do that. I haven't strolled along a beach since . . .' She trailed off.

'It's this way,' he said quietly.

Maggie was about to step off the road on to the sand when she had a sudden thought. 'What if it's riddled with mines?'

'It isn't,' Howard informed her.

'How do you know?'

'I asked at the hotel.'

She turned to stare at him, amusement reflected in her eyes. 'Are you telling me you planned this before we left?'

322

'It had crossed my mind,' he replied straight-faced. 'Anything wrong with that?'

'No.'

'Well then!'

'You're devious, scheming and manipulative, Howard Taft,' she accused.

'I'd deny it, except it's true. But then, in my defence, journalists have to be. These are traits you're required to develop if you're going to get what you are looking for.'

'And do you always get what you're looking for?' she queried softly.

'Most times. But not always. That's because I persevere. I have a lot of perseverance. A trait you missed out.'

They both knew precisely what they were talking about. So far it had remained unspoken between them.

Maggie ran to where the waves were brushing the shoreline. Memories came flooding back to her that made her smile, and at the same time clogged her throat.

'If it were summer we could go for a swim,' Howard said, coming to stand by her side.

'Without costumes?' she teased.

'We could've improvised.'

'I bet!'

She gazed out over the water. ' "I must down to the seas again, to the lonely sea and the sky . . ." '

He interjected. ' "And all I ask is a tall ship and a star to steer her by." '

'You know your John Masefield then?' she said.

'I took English literature at college. I read all the great English poets.'

'And what about Burns?'

'The great *Scottish* poet,' he said, emphasizing the word Scottish. 'Yeah. I read him too. Very popular in Russia, I believe.'

'Very popular all over the world,' she told him, feigning indignation.

'When we met at Heymouth I remember instructing you on the difference between English and Scottish,' she went on.

323

'A lesson I've never forgotten. Just as I now know I'll never forget you.'

There it was, out in the open at last.

'Don't, Howard!' she whispered.

'I know it's only been a short while, but in that time I've come to feel an enormous amount for you. Hell, it's as if I've known you and been in love with you all my life!'

'I told you I'm engaged to Nevil. I never made any secret about that.'

'I recognize the way you look at me, Maggie. I know what it means.'

'You're mistaken,' she protested.

'No, I'm not.'

She turned to face him, forcing herself to stare deep into his eyes. 'I'm engaged to Nevil and I love him. That's the truth.'

'It's certainly true that you're engaged to him, and you may have loved him once . . .'

'And still do!' she cut in.

He could see it was a hopeless case. Evidently she'd thought about this beforehand, and made up her mind to stay with Nevil. He shook his head. 'Oh, Maggie!'

Reaching out he placed the palm of his hand against her cheek. 'If only things had been different,' he said softly.

'But they're not, Howard. They are as they are.'

'Can I kiss you? Just once? To remember you by?'

She should have refused. But in truth, she didn't want to. She'd like a kiss to remember him by as well.

'All right,' she whispered.

Using the hand already on her cheek he pulled her to him and their mouths met.

Back on the road, watching them, was Nevil, who'd followed them since they'd left the hotel.

Anger, self-pity, and hatred for the American suddenly exploded within him. All his suspicions were now confirmed.

'She's mine, and going to remain so. I promise you, Yank,' he said to himself, his tone a chilling one.

He didn't want to see any more. It would hurt too much. He began retracing his steps, leaving them kissing.

The platoon had been summoned to the hotel dining-room for a meal, sitting at several tables which had been arranged together to accommodate them. Nevil had been the last to arrive and had taken a seat across from Maggie and Howard, who had Jimmy Sharkey and Mo Cairns between them.

'I'm starving,' Andy declared. 'I could eat a . . .' He stopped abruptly, realizing what he'd been about to say.

'And you're going to, me old son. You're going to,' Charlie told him, which produced a roar of laughter.

Nevil was the only person present who didn't laugh. His face remained impassive, his eyes strangely glittering.

'Here we go then!' said Teddy Agnew as three females approached them carrying large trays laden with steaming plates.

'Stew,' muttered Ian Ireland as a plate was plonked in front of him.

'What does it smell like?' Mo Cairns asked in mock trepidation.

Ian had a sniff. 'Rather nice actually.'

'But what does it *taste* like?' Mo then queried.

Maggie was enjoying the banter, though was apprehensive about the meal. She reminded herself that food was food and better a full stomach than an empty one.

'The French eat horse all the time,' stated Norman Currie.

'And look at the bloody French!' his brother Tom added, which raised another laugh.

Maggie suddenly became aware that Nevil was looking at Howard, a look which was downright unfriendly, not to mention sinister.

One of the females thanked them all in Spanish for providing the food, the first decent meal they'd been able to cook for some time.

'It's not all that bad,' announced Ian Ireland. 'A bit tough and stringy, but nonetheless, not bad.'

'Hunger's good sauce,' said Charlie Menzies, regarding a piece of meat he'd speared on a fork.

'I wonder which one this was,' Jimmy Sharkey mused, studying his plate.

Howard tapped his meal with his knife, and went on tapping.

'What are you doing?' Norman Currie asked.

'Flogging a dead horse,' Howard instantly replied, which raised the biggest laugh yet.

'Very funny,' said Nevil in a voice that cut right through the laughter.

Howard stared quizzically at Nevil. There had been no mistaking the iciness in Nevil's tone.

Antagonism towards Howard seemed to flow from Nevil, which was so strong it was almost tangible.

'You know what they say, don't you?' Nevil queried.

'What's that?'

'He who laughs last, laughs longest.'

Smiling crookedly, Nevil started eating his meal.

The atmosphere round the tables was never the same again after that short exchange.

Maggie woke up to the urgent clamour of church bells, the warning that Fascist aeroplanes had been sighted. Seconds later the first bombs fell.

Somewhere orders were being shouted in Spanish, and then other voices joined in with further orders. Judging from the quality of the light in the corridor, Maggie guessed it was shortly after dawn.

'Something's out of the ordinary,' said Andy, swinging himself out of his cot.

More and more orders were being shouted. Everywhere doors were opening and militia, all of whom slept fully clothed, tumbled out.

Perhaps it's the new push, Maggie thought.

Militia raced past them as the hotel rapidly emptied. The platoon remained where they were. They were not to become involved in Malaga's defence immediately.

The confusion was beginning to settle down when a corporal appeared asking for Major Sanderson.

'That's me,' said Nevil, signalling Maggie to join him.

She listened to what the corporal had to say, then translated for Nevil. 'General Fenellosa has ordered you to go to him straight away. This man will take you there.'

'Right.'

Nevil was about to stride off when he spotted Howard sitting on his cot staring at him.

'You'd better come as well,' he said to Maggie. And without giving her the opportunity to argue, he continued on his way.

She hurried after him.

They found Fenellosa behind the barricades where intense fighting was taking place. He was surrounded by a group of other high-ranking officers.

A Stokes mortar from their side soughed sending its deadly missile flying towards the enemy. The noise was so loud Maggie didn't hear the resulting explosion.

Fenellosa motioned Nevil to wait, and went on talking to his officers whose heads were only inches from his in order that they could make out what he was saying.

A car drew up, and parked a dozen feet from the general, its driver a young militiawoman.

Abruptly Fenellosa's business with the other officers was over. They dispersed, while Fenellosa walked smartly to the car, waving to Nevil and Maggie to join him.

The three of them climbed inside and the car sped off.

They travelled a short distance, allowing the noise to diminish a little, before Fenellosa spoke.

'As you've probably guessed, the new push has begun,' he said. 'We are resisting as best we can, and will continue to do so for as long as we are able.'

'Any news yet of the *Dolphin*?' Nevil asked anxiously.

Fenellosa's face lit up. 'That is why you are here. She made radio contact several hours ago to inform us she will be coming in tonight.'

'Marvellous!' Nevil exclaimed.

'Not in Malaga itself, however, we now consider that

would be too dangerous. She will come in at Marbella further down the coast.'

'What time?'

'Around midnight. Your platoon's immediate job will be to meet the ship in local boats. Owing to its draught and the shallow waters in Marbella the *Dolphin* will have to stand slightly off-shore. The British Battalion will disembark with all their equipment and supplies. You will arrange to rush everyone and everything back to Malaga.'

'I understand,' Nevil nodded.

'Meanwhile I shall put it around that we are about to be reinforced by six hundred fresh British fighting men and that they will be bringing a large amount of ammunition, food and supplies with them.'

'How do we get the battalion and other things back to Malaga?' Nevil asked.

'Using a fleet of trucks which I will arrange to be on standby. Once this car drops me at my office, it will take you back to your hotel where you will wait. Be ready to leave for Marbella the moment you receive instructions.'

'Right,' Nevil nodded.

Fenellosa ran a hand wearily across his face. 'If you don't mind me saying so, *Camarada* General, you look done in,' Maggie said sympathetically.

'I am under enormous pressure. The responsibility weighs heavily on me.'

'I'm sure,' Maggie smiled.

When they arrived outside the general's office he got out, gave the driver new instructions, then turned again to look into the back of the car.

'Good luck, Major Sanderson. To a large extent what happens to Malaga and the fronts is now in your hands. I have no doubt you will not fail us.'

'Thank you, sir,' Nevil replied, so momentarily emotional he used a form of address he shouldn't have.

If Fenellosa noticed that he didn't comment. 'Till later then, heh?'

'Till later,' Nevil answered.

Fenellosa slammed the car door shut, straightened himself to his full height, and hurried inside.

'He may be tiny, but that's a big man,' Nevil commented quietly.

'And a desperately worried one,' Maggie added.

The car moved away from the pavement, heading for the Hotel Caleta Palace.

The trucks and lorries were a hastily assembled ragtag of all sorts, without one proper military vehicle. But what did that matter, Maggie thought? The only thing that mattered was that they worked.

Spanish drivers had been provided, but Nevil dismissed a number of these as some of the platoon would be able to take their place.

The vehicle Maggie chose was ancient, painted a deep shade of green. She clambered into the cabin hoping she was still competent at driving after all this while.

The other cab door opened and Howard peered in. 'Can I come with you?' he requested.

'I don't see why not.'

He leapt up beside her, while all around them the other trucks and lorries were bursting into life.

Maggie turned the key in the ignition and soon she was falling in behind one of the Spanish drivers. They were to travel in convoy.

'I'm surprised Nevil didn't rope you in to drive,' Maggie commented.

'I didn't volunteer, and he didn't ask.'

She glanced at Howard, pleased that he was with her. He smiled, and she smiled back.

'It sounds like the Nats are throwing everything including the kitchen sink at the defences,' Howard said.

'I was at the barricades with Nevil. It was absolutely incredible. You could hardly hear yourself think.'

'A lot of lives will have been lost by this evening,' Howard said.

'That's not the Republicans' fault. We didn't start this

329

war!' she retorted. Then, softly, 'But I know what you mean.'

They wound their way out of Malaga, and on to the coastal road running southwest. They passed mile after mile of golden sand, and then went by a long stretch of rocky coastline.

'Look!' said Howard, pointing.

She followed his arm and there, out at sea, was a large warship.

'I suppose it's theirs,' Maggie said.

'Undoubtedly. A cruiser, I'd say, and probably German. If it's not German then it's Italian.'

Maggie risked another glance. 'And steaming towards Malaga.'

'Probably with the intention of lending its fire-power to the push. And if it is a cruiser, considerable fire-power at that.'

The truck hit a hole in the road and they both bounced on their seats.

'You won't fall asleep driving on this road,' Maggie laughed.

To which Howard, also laughing, agreed.

Maggie was about to speak again when from the distance came a new noise, the boom of heavy naval guns going into action.

The cruiser had opened fire.

A Spanish driver waved Maggie to the spot where she was to park. She saw that Nevil, who'd been in the lead vehicle, was standing on the edge of the harbour wall staring out over it.

The ancient truck seemed to sigh with relief when she switched off the engine, as if to say, 'Thank God for that!' The notion made her smile.

She jumped down from the cab, then went round to the other side where Howard was waiting for her. There was a feeling of expectancy in the air.

When the last vehicle was parked and its driver on the ground Nevil shouted for them all to gather round.

The fishing boats in the harbour were sleek-lined and gaily painted. As there was something of a swell running, they

330

bobbed and danced where they rode. It was a pretty sight.

Nevil turned to the platoon and Spanish drivers. 'Two things,' he said. 'Number one is that I only want to make a single trip out to the *Dolphin* and back, which means we need more boats than these here.

'Andy, I noticed other boats hauled up on the shore as we came into Marbella. You will requisition them, and any others you can lay your hands on, and bring them to the harbour.'

'How do I do that?' Andy queried.

'That's your problem. Solve it. If you can't, let me know and I'll get someone else who can.'

Andy swallowed hard at this tough speaking.

'As for you, Charlie, you will take another detail and do the same in the opposite direction. Right?'

'Right!' Charlie agreed.

'The second thing is this, we aren't enough to man all the crafts we'll need, which means we'll have to find people to complement our numbers. Maggie and I, plus the Spanish drivers, will go from door to door asking for help.'

Nevil looked at Maggie. 'Just translate that last bit to the Spaniards so they know what I want.'

The Spanish drivers, not one of whom spoke a word of English, listened attentively to Maggie while she explained what was needed.

'Let's get going then,' Nevil said after that.

Nevil and Maggie strode towards the nearest houses with the Spanish drivers following behind, chattering among themselves like a bunch of agitated parrots.

Arriving at the houses Nevil instructed Maggie to tell them to split up, some to go off to the left, others to the right. Age or gender was irrelevant – what they needed were competent hands to crew the boats.

'You and I will work together,' Nevil said to her when the Spanish drivers had left them.

'Did you see the cruiser?' she queried.

'Saw and heard it,' he replied grimly. 'And how do you know it was a cruiser?'

'Howard identified it. He accompanied me.'

331

'Did he now! I wondered which truck he went in.'

'He said it was either a German or Italian cruiser and as such would have considerable fire-power. I just hope the *Dolphin* doesn't run up against it.'

'That's why the *Dolphin* is coming in under cover of darkness, so she'll hopefully avoid any Fascist vessel in the immediate vicinity.' His face creased with concern. 'We could have done without a bloody cruiser though. And who knows what's out there? As I understand it the large warships tend not to operate on their own, but with support satellite vessels.'

'I hadn't thought of that,' she replied slowly.

'Nor did Howard presumably,' he sneered.

'I don't know why you dislike him so much!' she said.

'Don't you?'

'No, I don't.'

It was on the tip of his tongue to tell her he'd seen them kissing, but he fought back the impulse. For the time being it was better for her to be unaware of the fact. Perhaps he would never let her know.

He knocked at the door facing them.

Maggie knocked at yet another door, and glanced sideways at Nevil, who was looking very strained and worried. She saw the tic leap under his left eye, then leap again.

'Are you all right?' she asked softly.

'Of course I'm all right!' he snarled in reply.

'I'm sorry,' she said, thinking she shouldn't really be apologizing, as it was he who was being so rude. But it was best to keep the peace. He was under a lot of pressure, after all.

Nevil checked his wrist-watch, and wondered how Andy and Charlie were doing. Time seemed to be flying by, whenever he looked another hour had gone.

He thought of the *Dolphin* and the task of taking off six hundred men plus supplies and equipment in the dark. That was going to be a nightmare.

Then he remembered what Fenellosa had said to him. To a

large extent what happened to Malaga and the fronts was now in his hands! That made him go cold all over, and his stomach knot with a combination of fear and apprehension.

Control, he told himself. That was the secret. He had to be in total control of himself, his men and the operation. He must think calmly and clearly, and *never*, no matter what happened, panic. If he did that, what could be a success might quickly turn into failure. And if he failed the entire war could be lost!

'Jesus!' he breathed.

'Pardon?'

He glared at Maggie. 'What?'

'You just said something?'

'Did I?'

'Yes, you did.'

'It doesn't matter,' he said dismissively.

The door opened to reveal a gnarled old woman bent over a stick.

As Maggie began to speak she noticed Nevil's tic leap again.

It might have been a grasshopper embedded underneath his skin.

It was late afternoon when Maggie returned to the harbour. It had been a long day, and promised to be an even longer night.

She paused to watch the Currie brothers and two older Marbella men carry a small boat towards the harbour. Despite the chill all four were sweating profusely as they laboured.

'It feels as heavy as a damned dreadnought!' Tom Currie called out to her, which made her smile.

One of the older Spaniards cursed as he stumbled, but they didn't drop the boat. Maggie watched them continue on their way.

'How are you doing?' Charlie said behind her.

'Fine,' she replied, as he came round to be by her side. 'And yourself?'

'Managing.'

'Are we going to have enough boats to do it all in a single trip?'

'I think so. And hope so. Nevil's idea of doing it in a single trip is a good one. The less time we spend on the sea the safer for all concerned.'

'Yes,' she agreed.

'He's in a bit of a state, though, isn't he? I've never seen him so worked up before.'

'There's an awful lot at risk here, Charlie. As he's only too well aware.'

Charlie nodded.

She spied Howard, who gestured towards her truck. He indicated he would meet her there.

'I'll get on then,' she said.

'I'll tell you one thing, Maggie.'

'What's that?'

'I'll be glad when tonight's over.'

'That goes for me too.'

Charlie left her, and she headed for the truck, where she found Howard sitting in the cabin holding a plate of food. An opened bottle of red wine and two glasses stood by his feet.

'Chow appeared from somewhere a little while ago so I thought I'd better keep some back for you,' he smiled.

'That was kind!'

'Can't have my favourite militiawoman going hungry now, can I?'

She accepted the plate, which she now saw contained sardines, a portion of boiled rice and haricot beans.

'It should still be warmish. I kept it close by a fire.'

She wanted to kiss him for being so thoughtful, but didn't. 'I'm ravenous,' she confessed.

'Then fall to!'

He filled the glasses and placed hers on the area behind the steering wheel.

'How do you find it?' he asked as she swallowed a mouthful of sardine and rice.

'Delicious.'

'Better than horse?'

'Any day.'

They both laughed.

'Your vino, madam,' he said, pointing to her glass.

'I don't want to sound ungrateful, but I would have preferred coffee.'

'Wine with the meal, coffee after. It's all arranged.'

'You're sweet, Howard,' she said.

'You're not too bad yourself, kid. But then I've already told you that.'

She ate more of her meal.

'I wonder how they're getting on back in Malaga?' he mused. Every so often, according to the wind, they heard faint sounds of the far-off battle.

'Our side will be holding on for dear life, and desperately awaiting our return, I should imagine,' she eventually replied.

Howard sipped some of his wine. 'I was just thinking earlier, for such a young woman you've certainly been through a lot.'

'You mean Heymouth and now this?'

He nodded.

'That's true enough. A great deal crammed into a relatively short space of time. I suppose it happens that way sometimes.'

'Like Alexander the Great. He'd conquered the then-known world by the age of thirty-two. There's shifting for you.'

She smiled at that expression. 'You haven't done so badly yourself. How old are you?'

'Twenty-six.'

She thought back. 'Yes. I seem to remember you telling me your age in Heymouth. Well, you haven't done so badly yourself for a twenty-six-year-old. You too have shifted.'

He studied her, looking puzzled. 'Why is it I enjoy your company so much? Being with you is . . . is like completing the circle. If that makes sense at all. I know it does to me.'

'The Magic Circle,' she joked.

But he didn't take it as a joke. 'Yeah,' he replied, nodding. 'That's it exactly. A magic circle. The magic of you and me, and how we somehow interact together.'

'Interact?' she said. 'A very American word.'

'Oh, we have lots of words in the States that you don't use in Eng . . . in Britain.'

She smiled at him correcting himself, knowing that she would have done so if he hadn't.

'And not only different words, but different meanings to words. For example, what do you call a cookie?'

She explained to him what she understood by that.

'Not for us. In the States we call a cookie what you call a biscuit. Same with candy. What we call candy you call sweets.'

'Except for puff candy. We call that candy although it's a sweet.'

'Most confusing,' he said.

'Isn't it! But go on, teach me more American while I finish this off.'

Which was precisely what he did, both of them thoroughly enjoying every second of the lesson.

'Listen, may I make a suggestion?' Howard asked as she drained her coffee cup.

'Depends what the suggestion is,' she replied, tongue in cheek.

His eyes twinkled mischievously. 'If I suggested that, I know what your answer would be. So there's no point.'

To her surprise she felt herself blushing. And other things happened that surprised her even more.

'No, seriously,' he went on, 'what I was going to suggest was that you climb into the back of this truck and grab some shut-eye. I shall certainly try and get my head down.'

'I'll have to ask Nevil first. In case he wants me.'

'If he doesn't want you, I'll gladly have you,' Howard said softly.

She blushed again. 'Stop it! And stop being suggestive.'

'Is that what I'm being?' he replied, feigning innocence.

'You know you are.'

'Suggestive . . .' His face suddenly changed to match what he said next, 'but serious.'

'Now don't start that nonsense again!' she admonished, reaching for the cab door handle.

As she walked away from the truck to search for Nevil she was aware of Howard's gaze burning into her back. It made her shiver.

The floor of the truck was hard, but Maggie had become accustomed to hard beds recently. She pulled the lapels of her sheepskin up round her ears and closed her eyes.

The inside of the truck smelled delicious, for it was normally employed carrying vegetables and other garden produce. All manner of herbs had left their mark. Garlic of course, and an odour she thought was chives. There was a faint whiff of mint, and the unmistakable scent of sweet basil. She sighed with contentment, feeling herself drop off.

Then the wind must have altered, for now it was a sea smell dancing in her nostrils, a smell she'd grown up with on another shoreline in another country.

Salt, and seaweed. And there, the raucous cry of a gull, followed closely by the cries of other gulls.

She heard two Spaniards talking, something about the boats and fishing. She didn't try to translate what they were saying, all she wanted was sleep.

Deep, beautiful sleep was now rushing to envelop her.

'Nevil,' she murmured as sleep claimed her.

But it was of Howard she dreamt.

Howard had been watching Nevil for some while, now he decided to approach him. Nevil was at the harbour wall, gazing anxiously out to sea.

'You've got a good night for it,' Howard said when he reached Nevil. 'No moon and only a few stars. Visibility, but considerably restricted. All in all, ideal.'

Nevil glanced at the luminous dials of his watch. Earlier time had been flying. Now it was dragging. Every passing hour was a seeming eternity.

When Howard didn't get a reply he said, 'It's going to be tricky for you.'

'We'll cope.'

'I hope you do.'

Nevil swung on Howard to regard him through slightly slitted eyes. 'Do you?'

'Of course. I've come to know the guys in the platoon quite

well. I'd hate to see anything happen to any one of them.'

'The guys *and* the girl.'

'And Maggie,' Howard nodded. 'I'd particularly hate to see anything happen to her.'

'We're going to be married after all this, you know.'

'She's told me you're engaged.'

Nevil went back to gazing out to sea, though in fact he could make out very little.

'A big night,' Howard said.

The American was irritating him even more than usual, Nevil thought. By rights he should have been killed with the rest of that cavalry patrol. What an extraordinary thing that Maggie had met him in Heymouth.

'A big night,' Howard repeated.

Probably the biggest, most important, night of my entire life, Nevil thought. His tic leapt, and leapt again, but he didn't realize it. He was still quite oblivious to the fact he'd developed one.

'How far in to shore can the ship come?' Howard asked.

'I'm not sure. But it will come as close as is possible. That I do know.'

'And how will you know that the ship's arrived, when you probably won't be able to see it? A signal light maybe?'

Nevil turned again to Howard. 'You ask a lot of questions, don't you?'

'That's a journalist's job.'

Nevil reached out and tapped Howard on the chest. 'Just you make sure that you file tonight's story not only with your own paper but with the wire services as you promised. For this *will* be the night the war turned in our favour. And the beginning of the end for that bastard Franco. I swear it will be so!'

'Don't worry,' Howard replied, 'I'll keep my promise to you. I'll file the story of whatever happens tonight with my own newspaper plus the wire services – every last goddamn one of them, starting with Reuters.'

'What do you mean *whatever* happens?' Nevil asked softly, but with underlying anger in his voice.

'Exactly that. It's what I thought you wanted? The truth to be reported.'

'I'll also want to read that story before you send it,' Nevil hissed.

'To censor it?' Howard knew he was stupid to say that, but couldn't help himself.

'Merely to ensure it doesn't contain any bias.'

'I assure you there won't be, Major. You have my oath on that. Just as you have my oath that none of my Spanish articles have been biased.'

Why did he feel the American was always somehow out-smarting him? He was always one step ahead of him. It was infuriating. He was about to open his mouth to reply when they both heard the tramp of many approaching feet.

Old men, middle-aged men, women of all ages, and children, down they came *en masse* to the harbour to man the boats. It was still some time till the boats put out, but they'd been asked to come early.

Nevil stared at these people and felt his eyes moisten. Emotion welled within him. This was a night he would remember in vivid detail till the day he died.

Maggie appeared at Nevil's side as the Marbellans gathered silently round.

'We are here,' an old man said simply. His face was so weath-erbeaten and lived-in, it might have been as old as time itself.

'*Gracias*,' Nevil replied.

'*Viva la libertad!*' a young lad exclaimed, pumping a clenched fist into the air.

'*Viva la libertad!*' many voices echoed.

'With liberty and justice for all,' Howard said to himself, quoting from the American pledge of allegiance.

The minutes continued to tick slowly and interminably by.

Nevil glanced at his watch for the umpteenth time. Twenty-six minutes past midnight. Where was the *Dolphin*? Where in hell was the bloody ship?

Worry gnawed at his insides, like a pack of rats trying to eat their way out.

Had something happened to the *Dolphin*? He glanced down at the short-wave radio transmitter they'd brought from Malaga, and on which the *Dolphin* would be contacting them. If something *had* happened surely the *Dolphin* would have let them know? Unless, of course, there hadn't been time to do so.

A Spaniard spoke quietly to another – and was immediately told to shut up by a third. In the harbour the boats floated serenely. The water inside the harbour, and the sea beyond, was a deathly calm.

Nevil glanced at Maggie, unaware that his tic was now leaping non-stop. He wanted to smile reassuringly at her, but couldn't.

Damn this arm strapping! he suddenly inwardly raged. Maggie had used a reinforced bandage to replace the original section of horse reins. His shoulder was still sore, but he'd had enough of the strapping.

He fumbled with the pins, and began unwinding the bandage. When it finally fell free, releasing his arm, he tossed it scornfully aside.

He bit his lip as fresh pain stabbed his shoulder. Pretend it isn't there, he told himself. Ignore it. Wipe it right out of your mind.

What time now? Twenty-seven minutes past.

He gazed again out to sea, straining into the darkness, desperately hoping that it would reveal its secret.

Maggie had nearly gone to Nevil when she'd seen him undo the strapping. But she had stopped herself. It would have been quite wrong.

The tension was almost unbearable, Howard thought. Everyone's nerves were stretched to breaking point.

Howard cocked an ear, listening. But there was nothing, nothing at all. Nothing but silence.

Nevil realized his mouth had gone bone dry, and tried to generate some saliva. He finally succeeded, but it wasn't easy.

Andy had found a long piece of string which he was busy knotting. When he finished knotting the entire length, which he'd already done innumerable times, he pulled it apart and started all over again.

340

Twenty-eight minutes now! Nevil saw, staring at his watch. Where was the *Dolphin*!

'Maybe the transmitter isn't working. Maybe it's broken,' Charlie said tersely, glaring at it.

'I was assured it was working when it was given to me,' Nevil replied.

'Maybe it's broken since then?'

Nevil shook his head. 'No, that's not it. And it's switched on correctly. That isn't the problem either.'

'Hmmh!' Charlie muttered. Then, 'It's on the right wavelength, I take it?'

Nevil could have hit him. 'Yes!' he hissed in reply.

'You're su—'

'Yes!' Nevil interjected. A tiny niggle of doubt sprang up. So he decided to check it, just to be completely on the safe side.

'*Dolphin* calling Sanderson. *Dolphin* calling Sanderson. Do you read me? Over.'

Nevil sighed with relief. At last! He snatched up the microphone and operated it as he'd been shown. 'This is Sanderson. I repeat, this is Sanderson. I hear you clearly, *Dolphin*. Over.'

'We are approximately one mile off shore. We are approximately one mile off shore. Over.'

'I understand, *Dolphin*. You are approximately one mile off shore. Are you coming closer? Over.'

'Steaming slowly, Sanderson. Steaming slowly. We can come to five hundred yards off harbour. Over.'

Excitement was racing in Nevil. His hand holding the microphone was trembling when he spoke again. 'I understand, *Dolphin*. You can come to five hundred yards off harbour. Shall we meet you there or wait until we drop anchor? Over.'

'Safer from your point of view to wait until we drop anchor. I will contact you again then. Over.'

'I understand, *Dolphin*. Over.'

'Everything ready for disembarkation and unloading this end. Over.'

'Everything also ready our end. We will be meeting you with fishing boats and assorted small craft. Repeat, fishing boats and assorted small craft. I hope to do only single journey. Over.'

'That will suit us, Sanderson. The sooner we are underway the better. Will contact again shortly. Over and out.'

Nevil took a deep breath. 'Right! Everyone into the boats. I will be in the lead boat with Andy. Maggie . . .' He glanced over to make eye contact with her, 'translate that.'

When she'd done so they all hurried down the several sets of stone steps cut into and leading out from the harbour wall, and on to the boats. They clambered from boat to boat, each boat rapidly being assigned a crew.

Maggie guessed that Howard would want to be with her. They settled into a boat close to Nevil and Andy, Andy having humped the transmitter with him.

When Nevil judged that everyone was in place he called out, 'Release the boats and move towards the harbour mouth.'

Maggie translated that to the Marbellan in the boat next to her, and he passed it on. Within the space of a few short minutes the fleet was clustered at the harbour mouth, waiting for the word to head seawards.

'I think I can hear something,' Howard muttered to Maggie.

She listened. And yes, she thought she could hear something as well, but couldn't have identified exactly what it was.

'There!' whispered Howard, pointing.

The darkness did seem a little more dense at that spot, as if there was an actual object there.

Then Maggie felt the boat rock a little as sudden waves lapped against it. As the sea had previously been dead calm, the waves could only have been caused by the incoming *Dolphin*.

Nevil jerked as if he'd been gaffed when a bright orange explosion lit up the night. For a handful of seconds the *Dolphin* was illuminated, reeling under the impact of what had just occurred.

Maggie stared in disbelief. They were all completely stunned by this turn of events.

'Holy Harry!' Howard swore softly.

Then came the second explosion, which, from the way

the ship reacted, appeared to have taken it in the stern.

Maggie saw figures running and scrambling along the deck, which was already tilted.

'She's been mortally hit,' Howard whispered.

Maggie placed a hand across her mouth and kept it there. Had the *Dolphin* struck mines or what? The answer was soon forthcoming.

A dozen fires were raging aboard the *Dolphin* whose tilt had now increased considerably. It was clearly going to go down stern first.

Men were throwing themselves off the deck into the water. Agitated British voices could be heard shouting and yelling to one another.

'Must help them. Must help them,' Nevil muttered. He was about to issue the order for the fleet to head seawards when a large object surfaced.

'Stay!' exclaimed Andy, grabbing Nevil by the arm.

'But we have to . . .'

'That's a submarine,' Andy hissed.

'Submarine,' Howard said to Maggie.

She knew then it hadn't been mines that had done for the *Dolphin*, but torpedoes.

Somewhere near Maggie a female voice began to pray softly in Spanish.

'I can't swim!' a Geordie voice cried out in anguish.

And figures continued to jump from the stricken ship, whose stern had now vanished. Fire inside the ship's stern could be seen underwater, an extremely eerie sight.

Nevil literally held his breath, waiting to see what the submarine was going to do next. If it submerged again he would take the fleet out as quickly as he could.

Now they could hear German voices, one in particular issuing orders. A bright white light lanced out from the submarine as a spotlight snapped on.

The spotlight played on the men in the water, hundreds of them struggling and swimming, an impossible feat, as they were wearing such heavy clothes. Some of those struggling were attempting to rid themselves of their outer garments.

The U-boat's for'ard machine-gun opened up, chattering viciously as it began to spray the water where the men from the *Dolphin* were.

'Oh my God!' Maggie choked, transfixed by what she was witnessing.

The U-boat's rear machine-gun also opened up to add to the carnage.

Nevil twisted his hands into fists, while hot tears crowded his eyes. There was nothing he could do. He and the rest of the fleet were as helpless as babes in arms. To venture out beyond the harbour mouth would be tantamount to suicide.

Some died silently, others shrieking and howling their impotence and fear. Bodies twisted and contorted as the bullets smacked into them.

A Liverpool voice screamed obscenities at the German butchers, until it too was silenced.

The *Dolphin* slid under water, sending out a wake that made the fishing fleet bob violently. Boats knocked and banged into one another.

And still the spotlight continued to play, and the machine-guns to fire. The entire operation was carried out with German ruthlessness and efficiency.

The worst moment of all for Maggie was when she heard a Glaswegian shout defiance, his accent unmistakable. Then he too was no more.

The machine-guns were relentless, until at last they abruptly stopped. The spotlight remained playing over the water, seeking any survivors. There was not one.

The British Battalion and crew of the *Dolphin* had been wiped out, slaughtered in the water. Bodies were everywhere. Some were floating face upwards, others face down, a few in the vertical position.

A German command rang out and the spotlight flicked off. There was the clang of feet on metal, followed by the bang of a hatch being closed.

They didn't see the U-boat resubmerge, but somehow they all knew when it was gone.

'Are you all right?' Howard asked Maggie gently.

She nodded.

Nevil sat down, and dropped his head into his hands. He couldn't believe what had just happened. All those men. And more importantly, what they represented.

'How?' he croaked.

'How did the Gerries know it was there? Christ alone knows!' Andy answered. He too was emotional in the extreme.

'German bastards!' Nevil swore vehemently, momentarily lifting his head out of his hands.

'There was at least one Glasgow lad among them. Did you hear him?' Andy queried.

'I heard him.'

'Poor sod,' Andy whispered.

Nevil had never known such pain, loss or bewilderment. He felt as though he could fly apart into a million pieces.

Charlie climbed into their boat, having made his way over from his own. 'What now?' he asked in a tone that betrayed how thoroughly shaken he was.

Still holding his head, Nevil shook it. He didn't answer.

'Let's get this lot back to shore,' Charlie said, taking command.

When Maggie tried to translate she couldn't. The words just wouldn't come.

The Marbellans and Spanish drivers understood anyway.

Nevil sat in the cabin of Maggie's truck staring blankly ahead. His eyes were glazed, his complexion ashen. The tic had vanished.

'There was absolutely nothing you could have done,' Maggie said, giving him an anxious sideways look.

'But how, Maggie? How?'

'I don't know. The submarine might simply have been lurking around and picked the *Dolphin* up on its instruments. It's entirely possible. And don't forget you yourself said that cruiser was bound to have support vessels in the area.

'There again, it could have been the work of spies. Each side is riddled with them.'

'It was a nightmare,' Nevil stated simply.

'Yes.'

'All those helpless men. They didn't have a chance.'

Maggie shuddered. It didn't bear remembering, though she knew she'd never forget what she'd witnessed earlier. It would haunt her for ever.

'Malaga's lost,' Nevil said, biting his lower lip.

'You can't blame yourself in any way, Nevil. We were ordered down here, we came, and were ready. It just wasn't to be, that's all. It wasn't on the cards.'

'But our cause is right,' he retorted fiercely. 'Our cause is right while that of the Nationalists is evil.'

The right side doesn't always win, she felt like saying, but didn't.

'If that submarine was there merely by chance then it's scuppered any chance we had left of winning the war.'

And probably the death of all of them, she thought grimly.

'Damn Franco and all Fascists to everlasting hell,' Nevil whispered.

'And those Germans tonight in particular,' Maggie qualified.

Nevil fell silent after that, a silence full of agonized despair.

And the closer they got to Malaga the louder became the sound of what earlier the previous day had turned into a full-scale, bloody battle.

Maggie sat in the hotel room listening to the cruiser's big guns firing off shore. Other artillery, mainly from the Nationalist side, was also firing. But the cruiser's guns had an unmistakable sound all their own.

The platoon were the only ones in the lounge, everyone else was either hiding or fighting. They were waiting for Nevil to return, as he had gone to report to Fenellosa.

She glanced over at Andy, who was sitting with his eyes closed and a peculiar lop-sided smile on his face. He was thinking about Felicia, she guessed. And if she'd asked him he'd have told her she was right.

Charlie was in a comfy chair holding a bottle of beer he'd

acquired from somewhere. Every so often he gave a deep and heartfelt sigh.

Mo Cairns, the Currie brothers and Ian Ireland were playing pontoon. They were laughing. But the laughter had a forced, strained quality about it.

Jimmy Sharkey lay stretched out on a sofa fast asleep. From the way he tossed and turned, and occasionally moaned, he was having a bad dream.

Eric Young was engrossed in an English novel he'd found on a table. His lips moved, mouthing the words, as he read.

Bobby Farquharson and Teddy Agnew were talking together about Scottish football, the pair of them dedicated fans. Bobby supported mighty Rangers, Teddy humble Partick Thistle.

Maggie looked out of a window. Dawn had come up about an hour previously. Malaga had hung on through the night. But for how much longer?

Nevil strode into the lounge. His eyes were wild, staring and dangerous, resembling those of a cornered animal who knew there was no way out.

Maggie took him by the arm, and asked, 'What did the General say?'

Nevil seemed to have trouble focusing on her. 'Say? What could he say?' His voice rose to become a shrill scream. 'What could he fucking say!'

Charlie laid his beer aside and rose. 'I presume it's the barricades for us now?'

Nevil ignored him, having spotted Howard sitting writing in a corner. He wrenched himself free from Maggie and lurched towards the American.

'What are you doing?' he demanded on reaching Howard.

Howard glanced up at him, thinking Nevil looked ghastly. 'Writing my story,' he replied.

'You mean about the *Dolphin*?'

'And what that entails.'

Nevil held out a hand. 'Let me see it.'

'Sure.' Still sitting, Howard gave Nevil the notebook in which he'd been writing.

Nevil frowned in concentration as he began to read. His shoulder was hurting again, and there were pains inside his head.

He read silently to start with, then aloud. 'In the opening minutes of this morning more than a ship carrying six hundred British volunteers was sunk. So too was the Republican cause.'

Nevil paused. 'Oh, you bastard!' he spat at Howard.

'It's true though, isn't it?' Howard replied softly.

Hysteria enveloped Nevil, causing him to tremble from head to toe. 'I'm going to tell you something, Yank. In fact I'm going to tell you two things.

'The first is you'll never get Maggie. She's mine and going to remain so.

'And the second is you'll never have the satisfaction of filing this story. Nor receive the plaudits for the scoop it undoubtedly is. Know why?'

Howard shook his head.

'Because I'm going to kill you, that's why.'

And having said that Nevil produced the pistol he'd taken from the militiaman outside Fenellosa's office and pointed it at Howard's head.

'No!' shrieked Maggie, while everyone else looked on in stunned amazement.

Nevil's lips curled into a smile as his finger tightened on the trigger. Howard stared into the black hole of the barrel, believing his last moment had come.

The sound of the explosion was far greater than Howard would have thought. He was overcome by a huge roar and then felt himself thrown violently across the room.

There he lay, surrounded by a cloud of swirling dust and other debris. Everything had turned white.

Was this heaven?

He coughed and spluttered as some dust lodged in his throat. Funny thing to happen in heaven, he thought.

And if he was dead why was Maggie peering at him? Nevil hadn't shot her too, had he?

'You all right?' she gasped.

He succeeded in clearing his throat. And as he did she touched him. Her flesh was as warm on his as living flesh had ever been. That jerked him back to reality.

'What happened?' he queried.

'The hotel's been hit by a shell.'

He struggled to his feet, his mind functioning again. Nevil lay sprawled on the floor about a dozen feet away, the pistol still in his hand.

'He's been knocked out,' Maggie explained. 'You must get away from here before he regains consciousness.'

'I thought I was a goner,' Howard said.

'You very nearly were. Now hurry!'

He caught her to him, aware that others of the platoon were watching, and not giving a damn. 'Maggie, I . . .'

Nevil stirred.

'Run, for Christ's sake, before he does kill you!'

Nevil's breaths were shallow and intermittent.

'Goodbye, Maggie.'

'Goodbye. Now go!'

Howard fled, jumping over upturned furniture and debris, leaving what remained of the hotel, and Maggie's life.

When Howard had gone Maggie took a deep breath, and ran a hand through her now filthy hair. 'Anyone injured?' she called out.

'Bobby's got a smashed leg,' Teddy Agnew replied.

'And I've got a headache you wouldn't believe,' said Eric Young.

'I need help!' cried Norman Currie. 'Tom's buried under here.'

Instantly others of the platoon were hurrying to his side to assist. Tom was covered by a mound of bricks and plaster which they immediately began tearing away.

'Maggie!'

She turned to face Nevil, who was trying to pull himself into a sitting position. With a soft exclamation of pain he fell on to his back, the pistol spinning away.

Maggie grasped him by the lapels, and heaved him upright. She then kneeled beside him.

'A shell hit the hotel and you were knocked out,' she explained.

'Kiss me,' he said in a cracked whisper.

'Eh?' That seemed an odd request in the circumstances.

'Kiss me,' he repeated, this time more urgently.

She closed her eyes as their lips met. And suddenly it was Nevil of old she was kissing, the Nevil who'd captured her heart, and whom she'd come to Spain to be with.

'That was lovely,' she murmured when the kiss was over. Smiling at him.

He too was smiling. A strange, fixed smile. While his eyes . . .

'Nevil?' she queried, fear in her voice.

He didn't answer.

She stared into those eyes where Nevil had once been, and wasn't any more.

'Nevil!' she commanded. But she was commanding someone who couldn't hear. He was dead.

'Oh no!' she exclaimed as the truth hit home.

For the space of several seconds she gazed at his face, then gathered him into her arms and bosom.

Slowly she began to rock back and forth, tears streaming down her cheeks. And as she rocked the first of the barricades was being over-run.

PART THREE

A Second Adam

'A second Adam to the fight
and to the rescue came . . .'

From a hymn by Cardinal J.H. Newman
(1801–1890)

CHAPTER NINE

The sound of Andy busy at the sink and stove woke Maggie up from a deep sleep. He sometimes hummed as he made the tea, however, that morning he was quiet. Beside her Liss lay snuggled, her young arm thrown casually over her bosom.

Maggie opened her eyes, and yawned. 'Hello,' she said.

'Good sleep?' Andy asked, setting out the cups.

'Hmmh. Liss was restless and muttering at one point, but that passed.'

Andy stopped what he was doing to face the cavity bed containing his wife and eight-year-old daughter. 'Do you think she's sickening for something?' he asked anxiously. Liss was the apple of his eye. He absolutely doted on her.

'I shouldn't imagine so. She was probably dreaming, or had a little bit of indigestion.'

Andy grunted, and continued making the tea, which he did every morning when he arrived home from work. He was a nightwatchman with the Glasgow Corporation, spending his working hours on site guarding the materials there.

'Was it cold last night?' Maggie enquired, lifting herself on to an elbow. It was coming up for mid-September.

'Colder than it's been. I was glad of my fire, I can tell you.'

'And what about wind? Have they fixed that hole in your hidey?' The hidey she was referring to was a part wood, part canvas hut where he spent his time when not touring the site. His coal-filled brazier was kept at the door of the hut, which was lit inside by several oil lamps. Other oil lamps, the red warning variety, were dotted strategically round the site and it was his responsibility to fill and maintain them all.

'Aye, it has been fixed. There was a wind, but nothing to worry about.' There had been a lot of wind recently, some of it gale force. He'd gone to work complaining that wind whistling through the hole in his hidey was the last thing he needed.

He poured out her tea and handed it to her. 'And how's my wee lass this morning?' he queried of Liss who was still fast asleep and snoring gently.

'Just don't tickle her awake or this tea will be all over the place!' Maggie warned. It was just the sort of thing Andy would do.

Andy stroked his daughter's chin instead. 'Come on, Liss, wakey wakey. Time to get up!' he crooned.

She wriggled in protest.

'You have to go to school,' he added.

'Don't want to go,' she said, without opening her eyes.

'But you have to, darling.'

'Want to stay here.'

'I'm afraid you can't.' Leaning over Maggie he kissed Liss on the cheek.

'And what about me?' Maggie demanded, pretending indignation.

He kissed her on the cheek as well. Then Liss again, this time on the tip of her nose.

Pouring himself out a cup of tea, Andy crossed to the room's solitary window and stared out. He watched as grey smoke streamed from a multitude of chimneys and vanished into an equally grey sky. Grey smoke coming out of grey chimney pots attached to grey tenements, he further qualified. Grey, the colour of life. With the exception of Liss, that was! She, his darling daughter, was all the colours of the rainbow.

Maggie finished her tea and swung herself out of the cavity bed that was slotted into a wall of their one-room apartment. There was no bathroom, while their toilet was out on the mezzanine landing and communal, shared with five other families.

She stood in front of the range, still warm from the night before though the fire had gone out hours previously. There she threw on her clothes as quickly as she could. When she was fully dressed she went to the sink and washed.

'Come on, Liss!' she called out.

'Oh Mummy, do I have to?'

'You know you do. Now stop being a lazy monkey and get yourself dressed this instant!'

'School's horrible. I hate it,' Liss declared, pulling the bedclothes up to her chin.

'There are lots of things in life which are hateful but just have to be put up with. You'll learn that,' Maggie said, beginning to busy herself with breakfast.

'Maybe she could have a day off? It wouldn't hurt,' Andy proposed.

Maggie shot him a withering look. 'Don't be so soft! She's going to school and that's the end of it.'

Andy glanced at his daughter, and shrugged. His expression clearly said, 'I did my best.'

'You don't have to worry about the po' this morning. It wasn't used,' Maggie told him. The po' she was referring to was the chamberpot kept by the side of the bed and which he usually emptied in the lavatory while she prepared breakfast.

Andy nodded, relieved. It wasn't a task he enjoyed, but it was one that had to be done.

As Liss reluctantly got out of bed Andy sank into his chair by the range and opened the morning *Record*.

'What's for brekky?' Liss enquired as she struggled into her uniform.

'Porridge and bread,' Maggie replied.

Liss pulled a face. 'I'd prefer scrambled egg.'

'So would I, but we can't afford it.'

A strange expression came over Andy, and his eyes wavered slightly as he switched from reading the paper to being introspective. His lips curled into a bitter smile.

'Can we have scrambled egg on Sunday then?' Liss asked.

'I had planned kippers. But if your dad doesn't mind we'll have that instead,' Maggie said.

'Dad?' Liss demanded eagerly.

Andy looked at her. 'Scrambled egg is fine with me, angel.'

It was precisely the answer Maggie had expected him to give. He denied Liss nothing that was within his power, much to her exasperation sometimes. She'd often said he should be stronger with the girl and not completely spoil her as he did. But Andy dismissed any such accusations, saying that it was impossible to spoil anyone as adorable as Liss.

'Get washed now,' Maggie instructed Liss when she was finally dressed.

Liss skipped to the sink where she did as she'd been told.

'And teeth,' Maggie reminded her.

While Liss was doing that Maggie glanced over at Andy, whose eyes were again unfocused in introspection. There was an air of worry and concern about him.

'You all right?' Maggie enquired.

He immediately snapped out of his reverie. 'Fine! Fine! Just weary, that's all. Nothing a decent turn in that bed won't cure.'

'Well, get straight in there after we've gone,' she said.

He didn't reply, but went back to reading his newspaper.

His complexion was paler than usual, Maggie now noticed. But was it her imagination or did it have a somewhat waxy sheen to it? Maybe it was he who was sickening for something. Flu had been doing the rounds, it could be that. However, she'd wait and see how he was after his sleep.

Andy continued to read his newspaper through the hurried breakfast, then it was time for Maggie and Liss to leave. Maggie stacked the dirty dishes in the sink while Liss got into her school raincoat.

'Goodbye, lass, have a good day,' Andy beamed to Liss, who'd come to him for a kiss.

'And you a good sleep, Dad,' she replied as he gave her a big juicy kiss on the cheek.

'I don't know what I'd ever do without you,' he said, tweaking her chin.

'Come on, we'll be late!' Maggie urged.

Outside in the street she turned her collar up against the cold. The colder night had given way to a colder day than it had been recently. She took Liss's hand in her own as they hurried off down the street towards the school.

Maggie let herself in quietly, expecting Andy to be fast asleep in the cavity bed. He wasn't. He was standing staring out of the window, smoking.

'I thought you were tired?' she accused.

Seconds ticked slowly by, then he replied in a soft voice, 'I was just saying that because Liss was listening.'

She knew then it was bad news and not that he was ill. 'What happened?' she asked in a tone that matched his.

'I got the sack.'

She should have guessed. The old story. The same old story! 'What went wrong this time?'

'The gaffer did a spot check and found four of the warning lamps out, two bags of cement gone, and me asleep in the hidey. That was that.'

She sighed, and slumped into the nearest chair. Three and a half months he'd held this job, which was about average for him of recent years. 'Why did you go to sleep?' she queried. Not that it mattered, the damage was done.

He shrugged. 'I don't know. Boredom, I suppose. It gets bloody boring sitting there night after night. I didn't mean to, but I must have just nodded off. It's easily done.'

'Oh! You've nodded off before, have you?'

He didn't reply to that.

'You're a fool! A fool to us, and most of all to yourself. They were paying you to stay awake. Didn't you realize that?'

Again he didn't reply.

'So, what are you going to do now?'

'There's plenty of work about.'

'Not for a cripple with your work record!' she retorted scathingly. And instantly regretted it. Andy wasn't really a cripple. It was just that he hobbled badly from the loss of one complete heel, which had been blown away by rifle fire during their escape together from Spain.

'I'm sorry,' he mumbled, and dragged heavily on his cigarette.

So he should be, she thought. He just couldn't seem to hold down a job. How many was it now since he'd left Templeton's a second time? She couldn't remember.

'When's your last night?' she asked.

'Friday. That's their week if you remember. My replacement will start Saturday night.'

He turned to face her. 'I am sorry, Maggie. Honestly I am. It was sheer rotten luck the gaffer came round when he did.'

'Was it? What about the two bags of cement? How would you have explained them this morning?'

He bit his lip. 'I hadn't thought of that.'

That was his trouble, he rarely did think. She could have slapped him.

'The boredom gets to you after a while,' he explained. 'Most of the time you're just sitting there waiting for the hours to pass.'

'It wasn't exactly a brilliant wage, but between yours and mine we got by,' she said. She had a part-time position as a dinner lady at the school Liss attended.

'I'll get something else soon enough. You'll see,' he replied defiantly.

'Your work record is against you. You know that, Andy.'

He couldn't argue with that, for he knew it was true. 'I'll sign on the Labour first thing Monday. And start looking directly after that,' he said.

The Labour! she thought scornfully. It was hardly worth signing on for what they doled out. All it was was a few miserable shillings that went nowhere.

'It was the wind that blew out the lamps,' he said.

'I thought you told me earlier there wasn't much of one?'

'Aye, well, neither there was,' he replied lamely. 'It must have been gusting, though, while I was asleep for there was still plenty of oil in the lamps when I checked.'

God alone knew how long he'd slept for, she thought. It must have been quite a while for the wind to gust up then die down again.

'Perhaps the gaffer will give you another chance?' she queried.

'No, he did that . . .' Andy broke off, looking sheepish.

She regarded him frostily. 'So last night wasn't the first occasion it's happened?'

'The first occasion I've had materials stolen off the site,' he countered.

'But not fallen asleep?'

He dropped his eyes, unable to meet her gaze.

Pathetic, she thought.

'I'm sorry,' he repeated yet again.

There was no use going on about this, she told herself. The damage was done and couldn't be undone. 'You get to bed and I'll see to the dishes,' she said, rising from her chair.

Her mind was racing, but at the same time numb. It was going to mean cutbacks again, she thought. Though they'd have that scrambled egg on Sunday for breakfast, she was determined about that.

'Maggie?'

She glanced at Andy, now in bed staring at her. 'What?'

'Come here,' he whispered.

'I'm busy.'

'Please?'

She crossed over to stand in front of the bed. 'What is it?'

'I feel awful about letting you and Liss down again.'

'And so you should.'

'You've always regretted it, haven't you?'

'Regretted what?' she queried.

'Marrying me.'

The anger and disappointment seemed to flow out of her and were replaced by tenderness and other emotions. She sat on the edge of the bed, reaching out to touch his cheek. 'I've never regretted it, Andy. I give you my word on that.'

'I've often thought you have.'

'You've never mentioned it before?'

'No. But I have thought it.'

She shook her head. 'Not regret, but I have to say you haven't exactly made it easy for Liss and myself. And by that I mean never holding down a job for long and all that entails.'

'You know why, Maggie,' he said in a cracked whisper.

She fought back tears that were suddenly threatening. 'Yes, I know,' she said softly.

He smiled at her, and she at him. Both smiles were pained.

When the dishes were dried and put away she put the kettle on again to make herself a cup of tea. Andy had long since dropped off, occasionally emitting whistling noises through his mouth, which was a habit of his when asleep.

She went to the mirror hanging above the mantelpiece with the intention of combing her hair. The face that stared back at her made her wince.

'Oh, Maggie!' she sighed. How decrepit and haggard she looked. Years older than the thirty she was. She would have described herself as completely worn down by the hand Fate had dealt her.

She took a hank of hair and rubbed it with her fingers. The hair was dry and lifeless, just like she felt herself. Closing her eyes she recalled the girl who'd gone to Spain. How vital she'd been then, blooming with health and exuberance, fresh-faced, sparkly-eyed and glowing from within.

She compared herself to a flower at its peak. Now the flower had prematurely withered, its colour faded. Age and hardship had taken their toll.

Glasgow was grinding enough, but to be saddled with a man like Andy on top of that made everything a hundred times worse. There were times when, if it hadn't been for Liss, she could easily have . . .

She banished that thought from her mind. It was wrong, evil. She mustn't think it. But, oh, what she would have given for a sweet escape. And that would be her eventual escape, though no doubt later rather than sooner.

'Hateful!' she said quietly to her reflection. 'That's how you've come to look, Maggie, hateful.'

She threw her comb down in disgust beside the bust of Andy that Felicia Browne had carved, and which Andy had left in Madrid with money and instructions for it to be sent to his home in Scotland after the war.

She tied a scarf round her head before leaving to go shopping.

What remained of that week flew by, and all too soon it was Saturday morning and Andy was once more unemployed.

'There you are,' he said to Maggie when breakfast was over, tossing his pay packet on to the table.

She picked it up, wondering how long it would be till she was given another from him.

'I'll cut my cigarettes down to five a day,' he promised.

She nodded.

'And I won't meet Teddy for a pint this dinnertime.'

It was Andy's practice to have a drink with Teddy Agnew every Saturday dinnertime. Teddy was one of the four survivors of the original platoon that had set out for Malaga. The other was Jimmy Sharkey, who'd emigrated to New Zealand. The rest had been killed.

'Go ahead and see Teddy, but tell him it'll be your last Saturday get-together until you get another job,' she said.

'I don't have to go!' Andy protested. 'Better we save the money.'

He was right, she thought wearily. It was better for them to save the money.

'As I won't be working tonight there's no need for me to sleep this morning. So how about I take Liss for a walk in the park?' he suggested.

'Oh please, Daddy! Please!' Liss enthused, clapping her hands together.

'We can watch them sailing their wee boats on the pond. You always like that,' he smiled.

She clapped her hands again. This was a treat.

'And I'll buy you a . . .' He trailed off, realizing what he'd almost promised.

'A what?' she demanded eagerly.

'Nothing,' he shrugged. 'Not today anyway.'

She pouted.

'Another day though. And what do you say we leave straight away, eh?' He turned to Maggie. 'If that's all right with you, love?'

'Of course it is. Off you go, the pair of you.'

As Maggie saw them to the door she didn't bother to tell them to enjoy themselves. They always did when they were together.

That night, shortly after eight o'clock, Maggie said to Andy, 'I'm going to pop out for a little while. All right?'

He glanced up from the jigsaw he was doing with Liss.

'I want a word with Mrs Rubin in Sauchiehall Street,' she explained.

Andy's face coloured slightly. Mrs Rubin was someone Maggie had done housework for in the past. She was a good employer, if a demanding one.

'Liss and I will be just fine,' he replied.

'Right then.'

Outside it was a thoroughly miserable evening, raw and raining.

Maggie hadn't gone far when she realized her left shoe was letting water in. 'Damn!' she muttered, despair welling up within her.

By the time she arrived at the Rubins her left foot was thoroughly awash.

Mrs Rubin was a sympathetic Jewish woman who listened attentively to Maggie's tale, nodding every so often, causing the heavy gold necklaces she was wearing to clink.

'I'm sorry I can't help you, Maggie,' she said in her strangely accented English when Maggie had finished. 'But the lady "doing" for me now is very nice and satisfactory. I can't just fire her because you are available again.'

'Oh!' Disappointment crippled Maggie. 'I must have got it wrong. I heard that Mrs Emmerslie had left you.'

Mrs Rubin gave Maggie a fat smile. 'She nearly did, true. But I offered to increase her hourly rate and that persuaded her to stay.'

Increased hourly rate! That was a real sickener. She couldn't bring herself to ask how much Mrs Emmerslie was now earning.

'I'll just have to try elsewhere then,' Maggie said.

'I'll tell you what, Maggie. How about if I ask round my friends? Perhaps one of them needs someone for the housework. And I will give you my personal recommendation.'

Maggie brightened to hear that. It was a ray of hope at least. There weren't all that many part-time housework jobs going in Glasgow, the vast majority of women did their own.

'That's kind of you,' she acknowledged.

'I have your address. If anything transpires I'll drop you a line.'

The rain was now falling in sheets as Maggie squelched her way back home again.

The school dinners were over for the day, and now the dinner ladies were doing the washing and clearing up. Maggie was at one of the three huge sinks, up to her elbows in hot soapy water. She was chatting to Hattie McGuire who had a lassie in the same class as Liss.

'Here, listen to this, you lot!' called out Lena Gardiner. Then, 'Go on, Chrissie, tell them your joke.'

Chrissie McDougall needed no second bidding. She launched into a filthy joke that brought shrieks of raucous laughter when she delivered the punchline.

'Oh, that's terrific, so it is!' said May Dunwoodie, the head dinner lady, wiping a tear from her eye.

Maggie was smiling as she brought her attention back to the sink. You needed a broad sense of humour to work with this bunch. You just never knew what they'd come out with next.

'Is it right that your man is out of work again?' May Dunwoodie asked Maggie, coming to stand beside her.

There was disapproval in May's voice which wasn't lost on Maggie. 'Yes,' she admitted.

'And what was it this time?'

The general chit-chat had ceased, everyone else listening, Maggie realized. She muttered something inaudible.

'What was it?' May demanded.

Maggie could have sloshed her. 'The stupid bugger fell asleep on the job so his gaffer rightly sacked him,' she replied, knowing anything other than the truth would have rung false.

May grunted her sympathy. She was genuinely fond of Maggie, but thought Andy a wastrel and skiver. 'He'll be looking for something else then, I take it?'

Maggie laid aside more plates for Hattie to dry. 'He's looking,' she confirmed.

'Well, here's wishing him luck,' May said gruffly. Privately she was of the same opinion as Maggie, Andy's reputation was against him. If he didn't mend his ways soon he'd become unemployable, if he wasn't that already.

May came closer to Maggie. 'There's a nice bit of steak pie left over, and vegetables to go with it. You take those home with you for tea, they'll easily reheat.'

Maggie's face flamed with embarrassment. There was no insult meant by this offer, only kindness and caring. But how it hurt her. Pride, she told herself, swallowing hers, can be a terrible thing.

'And there's some apple crumble. Take that as well,' May went on.

Seeing Maggie's humiliation May further added, 'For the bairn's sake.'

'Thank you,' Maggie mumbled, dropping her head to hide her expression.

'Any more jokes, Chrissie?' Lena Gardiner queried.

Chrissie had. The second even filthier, and funnier, than the first.

One night the following month, as Andy was reading to Liss, there was a knock on the door. Maggie automatically assumed it was a neighbour come to call. The people up the close and round about were forever in each other's houses.

She opened the door to find a well-dressed man standing there. He had a large bunch of flowers in one hand, a brown paperbag in the other. His face was vaguely familiar.

'Yes?' she asked.

He didn't reply, merely stared intently at her.

'Can I help you?'

'Don't you know me?' he asked softly in an American accent.

The penny dropped immediately. Her eyes widened in shock, and she went stiff all over.

'It's great to see you again, Maggie,' said Howard Taft.

She swallowed, then swallowed again.

'Aren't you going to invite me in?'

She stood aside and he walked past her.

'Hope I'm not intruding,' he said. 'I did consider writing to

364

warn you I'd be visiting, but in the end decided to give you a surprise.'

Surprise wasn't the word for it, she thought as she closed the door behind him. She couldn't believe what she was hearing and seeing.

'Hello, Andy,' Howard said to Andy, who was sitting staring quizzically up at him, Liss on his lap.

'Christ!' Andy swore as he recognized Howard. 'You!'

'In the flesh,' Howard smiled. His gaze flicked round the single room, taking in its meanness.

'And who's this?' he queried, bringing his smile to bear on Liss.

'Elizabeth, our only child. We call her Liss,' Andy explained.

'Pleased to meet you, Liss,' said Howard. He laid the flowers and brown paperbag on the table, then solemnly shook hands with Liss, who giggled.

Maggie had a hand over her mouth, still struck dumb. How well and successful Howard looked, she thought.

'Can I take your coat?' she asked, finding her voice at last.

'Is that all right? I'm not breaking in on anything?'

'Don't be daft!' she admonished, aware she was blushing. If only she'd had some warning she might have put on a decent dress, and done something about her appearance!

Andy lifted Liss off his lap, and rose to his feet. Like Maggie, he could hardly credit this turn of events.

'I brought the flowers and candy for you,' Howard said as Maggie bore his coat away. 'But I didn't know you had a daughter. Your sister Laura never mentioned that. Perhaps Liss can share the candy with you!'

'You've spoken to Laura?'

'Yeah! That's how I found out that you and Andy were married, and where you both lived.'

'This is incredible,' Andy said.

'I'll put the kettle on,' Maggie declared, still flustered. Her insides were churning like billy-o.

'I told you I'd taken a shine to Scotland and would return to it one day, and here I am!' Howard said to her.

'How long are you here for?' Maggie enquired as she filled the kettle.

'A couple of years. Maybe more.'

Maggie glanced at him in astonishment.

'I've been posted here, to Glasgow, with my job,' he explained.

'*The New York Times*?' Andy asked.

Howard shook his head. 'Naw, I left *The Times* early in '42 when I joined up. Nor did I go back into journalism after the war. But we'll come to that. I want to hear about you two and the platoon?'

'Sit down first,' said Andy, indicating the chair he'd just vacated, the best in the house.

Maggie lit the gas with fingers that were shaking, then plonked the kettle on top of it. She had no cakes or shortbread in. There wasn't any coffee either, as that was something else that had gone by the board with Andy's job.

Liss stuck a thumb in her mouth, and pushed herself against her father's leg. She peeped shyly at Howard whose appearance and accent both fascinated and awed her.

She took after Andy, Howard was thinking. He could see Maggie in her, but she was mainly Andy. 'My name's Howard,' he said to her.

'Hello, Howard,' she replied in a shy whisper.

'I'm an old friend of your mommy and daddy. We knew each other in Spain years ago.' He glanced at Andy, wondering if he'd made a mistake. 'She does know about Spain, I take it?'

'Oh aye!'

'Daddy and Mummy were soldiers there. They fought against horrible General Franco,' Liss stated.

'That's right,' Howard nodded.

'Did you fight against horrible General Franco?'

'I'm afraid not. I was a journalist at the time. I wrote for an American newspaper.'

'Daddy takes the *Record* in the morning,' she informed Howard.

'The *Daily Record*, a good read,' Andy elaborated.

'Is it all right if we talk in front of Liss?' Howard asked.

Andy glanced at the clock on the mantelpiece that stood to one side of his bust. 'She'll be going to bed soon anyway. Won't you, darling?'

'Aw, Daddy, do I have to!'

'You know you do. Early to bed, early to rise, makes a young lassie . . .'

'Healthy, wealthy and wise,' Liss finished for him.

Andy laughed, delighted. 'Clever, isn't she!' he said to Howard.

'Very.'

Andy ran a hand through Liss's hair. 'And she's going to be a right cracker when she grows up. She'll break a thousand hearts.'

Howard smiled at this exaggeration. Liss was pretty, but hardly a budding beauty. She did have exceptionally nice eyes, though, Maggie's eyes.

'You saw Laura?' Maggie prompted.

'I remembered you mentioning her and her husband when we were in Spain. It wasn't too difficult for my secretary to trace the right John McNair and for me to go there and ask your whereabouts. I caught them on their way out, and in a hurry, which is presumably why they failed to tell me about Liss.'

'How was Laura? We don't meet up all that often, though always exchange Christmas cards.'

'Looked fine to me. As did the rest of the family. Her husband and the two girls.'

'Margaret and Rose, they're twins,' Maggie smiled. Mentally she calculated how old they now were; they'd been born in 1933, and it was now 1948, so that made them fifteen.

'My cousins,' Liss piped up.

'You have a secretary then?' Maggie probed. She remembered that she had mentioned Laura and John to Howard, but wouldn't have told him about John's attempted rape of her. She'd only confided that to Nevil, and Andy after they were married, when he wanted to know why she was so cool towards the McNairs.

'I've got several actually,' Howard admitted.

'Several!' Andy exclaimed, impressed. 'You must have an important position?'

'I'm the Vice-Consul at the United States Consulate in Hope Street,' Howard informed him.

'I didn't know we had an United States Consulate in Glasgow!' Andy replied.

'You most certainly do. And a busy consulate it is. A lot of tourists come over here nowadays, and of course there's a great deal of business between our two countries.'

'Vice-Consul,' Maggie mused. 'Does that mean you're the big cheese there?'

Howard laughed at the expression. 'No, the Consul-General is what you'd call the big cheese, our top-ranking official at the consulate. Beneath him is the Consul. With me, the Vice-Consul, beneath that.'

'And beneath you?' Maggie asked, intrigued.

'Lesser staff. Messengers, secretaries, pool typists, filing clerks and such like.'

'Well, well!' Maggie smiled. 'Imagine you a diplomat.'

'A far cry from being a journalist,' Andy said.

'Indeed,' Howard agreed.

'And you enjoy it?' Maggie asked.

'Very much so. I feel I'm contributing to the world at large, and the United States in particular, in a way that I never did as a humble scribe.'

Maggie nodded to hear that. 'You'll take a cup of tea with us?' she said, wiggling their pot at him.

'Certainly.'

Andy shifted uncomfortably. 'I'm sorry we have nothing harder in,' he apologized.

Maggie thought about that. It was terrible to only offer Howard tea. Scots hospitality was always generous in the extreme. And Howard was a foreigner after all, and a friend they hadn't seen in years.

'Perhaps you'd like to pop out to the off-licence and get a half-bottle,' she suggested to Andy. The cost of that was going to make a big hole in what she had for the week, but she felt it was a gesture they had to make.

'Aye, right,' he agreed.

'You don't have to go to any trouble on my account,' Howard protested.

'No, no, we insist!' Maggie told him.

'We do,' Andy agreed.

Maggie went to her handbag and took out her purse. In her purse she found a single pound note, the only paper money it contained.

'Here you are,' she said to Andy, handing him the pound.

Howard missed none of this interplay, he could see how much the cash meant to them. It was written plainly on both their faces.

He had another quick glance about him, shocked at the poorness of his surroundings. Here was breadline living right enough.

'I'll only be a few minutes,' Andy announced. 'You be a good girl now while I'm gone,' he added to Liss.

Howard looked across at the cavity bed, the first he'd ever seen. But where did Liss sleep? There was no other bed in evidence. Did that mean she slept with her parents? How awful for them all if she did.

'There's so much to catch up on I hardly know where to start,' Maggie said nervously.

She'd aged, he thought, but so had he. Except his lifestyle had been quite different to what she'd had to endure. His heart went out to her.

He'd often contemplated what it would be like meeting her again. Now he knew. It was as if they'd never been apart. Maggie was still the same despite the time gap. In a curious way they were resuming their relationship precisely where it had left off. But then, wasn't that the way it should be with true friendship?

'It's good to see you again, Maggie. I can't tell you how much,' he stated simply.

'And you, Howard. You don't look all that different, whereas I . . .' She trailed off, and gave a small shrug.

'You look just fine, Maggie. And I don't lie.'

'You're being kind, Howard. But you always were kind and sensitive.'

'Why don't you put those flowers in water?' he suggested.

She picked up the blooms, now aware of the several dozen gorgeous red roses. 'These must have cost a fortune, being out of season,' she said.

'Do you like them, though?'

'Very much. Thank you.'

The only trouble was, she thought ruefully, she didn't have a vase. The few flowers they'd had in the house she'd stuck in milk bottles and she could hardly do that with these.

Then she had a brainwave. Mrs Brownlee across the landing had a vase and it was a cut Edinburgh crystal one at that. She'd ask to borrow it, certain she wouldn't be refused. The neighbours hereabouts were forever borrowing things off one another.

'Won't be a tick!' she said, laying the flowers back on the table, and hurried from the house.

That gave Howard a better opportunity to gaze about him. Everything was cheap and tawdry, he noted. The linoleum underfoot was rubbed bare in many places, and cracked in others. The wallpaper must have gone back to before the Great War.

'You talk like people in the pictures,' Liss said coyly.

'You've been to the movies?'

She nodded.

'Who's your favourite star?'

'I don't know,' she replied, shaking her head.

He crooked a finger at her. 'Come here.'

She didn't move.

'It's all right, come here.'

He groped in his pocket for change. 'Take these,' he said when she was standing in front of him, and gave her two half-crowns. 'But don't tell Mommy and Daddy until after I'm gone. OK?'

She stared at the money, never having had so much before. 'All of this?' she queried.

'All of it,' he confirmed. 'To spend as you like.'

Her small hand curled over the two half-crowns, while her eyes shone with pleasure and excitement.

Howard put a finger across his mouth. 'Now remember, not a word until after I'm gone. Promise?'

'Promise,' she answered, matching his conspiratorial tone.

Maggie breezed back in holding Mrs Brownlee's vase. 'Sorry about that,' she said.

Howard stared at the vase, realizing why Maggie had suddenly left the house. He didn't comment on what a nice vase it was as she arranged the flowers.

'How many of the platoon came home again?' he asked.

He blanched when she told him.

'Stuart Borland also made it eventually, but you never knew him. He wasn't with us when we met up with you.'

'God!' Howard whispered. 'All those guys.'

'Yes, all good men,' Maggie said, a choke in her voice.

'Do you mind talking about it?'

She shook her head.

'What happened to Nevil?'

She paused in what she was doing. 'Remember the hotel was hit by a shell just as he was about to shoot you?'

'Yeah, the explosion knocked him unconscious.'

'It did more than that. He revived, but died in my arms minutes later.'

'Of what?' Howard queried softly.

'I've no idea. It was all so confusing at the time. There didn't appear to be a wound on him. But there again, we didn't exactly strip him to look either. It could have been something internal. Whatever, it killed him.'

Howard thought about that. It was probably blast. 'May I smoke?'

'Go ahead. There's an ashtray by the range.'

Howard glanced at the door, then back at Maggie. 'When I went to your sister Laura's I fully expected her to tell me you were Mrs Sanderson.'

Maggie wished Andy would hurry up with that whisky. She wasn't much of a drinker, but she could use one now.

'The same shell also killed Tom Currie. He was buried under a mound of debris out of which we dug him. He was already dead, though, a steel fragment having severed his windpipe.'

Howard pulled a face as he lit up.

'And Bobby Farquharson, remember him?'

'Of course.'

'His leg was smashed in the same explosion. But it didn't stop him fighting alongside the rest of us later. He ended up being bayoneted in the back.'

Howard glanced at Liss who was standing listening to all this. What a bloodthirsty conversation for her to be party to, he thought. He wished she'd go play by herself in a corner.

'What about Charlie Menzies?' Howard queried. 'I always thought he didn't like me.'

Using her kitchen scissors she snipped a piece off a rose stem that was longer than the others. 'Charlie got shot by a machine-gun while trying to drag Eric Young to safety. The machine-gun riddled them both.'

'And Norman Currie?'

'Norman went berserk when he realized Tom was dead. The first opportunity he had he charged the Fascists. Once he committed himself he never had a chance.

'There,' she said, completing her arrangement. 'How's that!'

'What do you think, Liss?' Howard queried.

'Nice,' she smiled at him.

Maggie placed the flowers in the centre of the table, where they were a colourful sight against their drab surroundings.

'But you and Andy got out?' Howard prompted.

'With Charlie gone Andy was put in sole charge of what was left of the platoon, and he decided we'd make a run for it. Malaga and the fronts were lost anyway, our staying and dying wouldn't have made a blind bit of difference to that.'

'I quite agree,' Howard said quietly.

She attended to the kettle which had been boiling its head off. 'Did you know before visiting Laura that I had survived?' she queried.

'I always believed you had, though I had nothing to substantiate that belief. I just felt it here.' And with that he patted his heart.

She looked at him, her brow creased quizzically.

'So how did you escape?' he asked.

'Via Gibraltar.'

'Ah!' That made sense.

'You will recall that when the Nats broke through they swept straight down to the sea, thereby dividing the city's defences?'

He nodded.

'Well, luckily, we were in the western sector. Which meant we could try for Gib. That would have been impossible if we'd been trapped in the eastern sector.'

'Mummy?'

Maggie turned to Liss. 'Yes, darling?'

'Can I have one of the sweeties Howard brought?'

'You can indeed. Perhaps Howard will open them for you while I make this tea.'

'Delighted!' Howard said, jumping to his feet.

He took the box of handmade chocolates from the brown paperbag and then removed the tissue paper wrapped round it. He opened the box and placed it on the table in front of Liss.

'Oohhh!' she exhaled softly, staring at the chocolates as though she'd just been taken inside Aladdin's cave.

'That must have taken up quite a few of your points. Or aren't American diplomats affected by our rationing?' Maggie said.

Liss selected a chocolate that was oval in shape and had whorls on top. She popped it into her mouth, then closed her eyes in appreciation.

'Nice?' Howard smiled.

'Hmmh!'

Maggie came round to where the box was, and gazed down at its contents. 'They look so lovely it seems a shame to eat them,' she commented.

'Go on, force yourself!'

She chose one. 'Scrumptious!' she declared, savouring the orange filling.

Liss helped herself to another. This one contained marzipan.

'Wherever did you come by such chocolates? I've never seen or tasted anything like them.'

'They're Swiss. But go on with your tale.'

'Well, Andy said we needed transport, so we went back to

where we'd left the trucks we'd taken to Marbella. We appropriated what we thought would be the fastest, topped up the tank from some petrol cans that were available and off we set.'

'Wait a minute,' said Howard, going over in his mind what she'd told him so far. 'That would be you, Andy, Jimmy Sharkey, Teddy Agnew, Ian Ireland and Mo Cairns?'

'Right.'

He nodded for her to continue.

'We got out of Malaga safely, and on to the Marbella road. Only this time we never made it as far as Marbella. We hit a mine, that had been newly laid by our own side, which blew the truck right off the road and killed Mo and Ian.'

She paused, then said, 'Ian was killed outright, but not Mo. It took him more than an hour to die during which he was in terrible pain. The four of us left stayed with him until it was over.'

Howard ground out what remained of his cigarette and placed the ashtray on the floor. 'What happened after that?' he queried.

'Sugar and milk?' she asked, having poured out two cups of tea.

'Please.'

She went on. 'We had to walk as far as Marbella, where we picked up some rusty old bikes. They served their purpose, however, and were better than walking. We were only a few miles from Gib when a sniper got Andy. Shot his heel right off.'

'Did you kill the sniper?'

'Jimmy and Teddy went after him, but he'd fled. While they were doing that I bound Andy's foot, which nonetheless continued to bleed profusely. They then carried Andy the rest of the way on their backs, taking turns to do so.

'At Gib, where they had to let us in because we were British citizens, Andy was immediately whisked off to hospital, where he remained for nearly a month.'

'And you?' he asked.

'Jimmy, Teddy and myself were fed, watered, given a change

of clothing and sent home on the first available ship. I think the authorities wanted to get rid of us as quickly as possible, which is precisely what they did.'

'But not Andy?'

'His foot became infected and he developed a high fever, which meant he couldn't be moved. During his entire stay in the hospital he was kept apart from the other patients, and warned not to tell anyone where he'd been or what he'd been doing. When he was well enough to travel he was shipped home.'

Maggie rounded on Liss. 'I think that's enough for now, don't you? Any more and you'll be sick.'

Liss stared guiltily at her mother, having just eaten her sixth chocolate.

'Besides, sweets as good and expensive as those should be relished, not wolfed down as if there's no tomorrow,' Maggie added.

'Sorry,' Liss muttered, her expression so contrite and hangdog it made Howard want to laugh.

Maggie put the top back on the box, and placed it in a drawer of the sideboard. While her back was turned, Howard gave Liss a subtle wink.

'Lovely cup of tea. Nobody makes tea like you British,' he said.

Maggie was pleased he liked it, for it was cheap tea, the cheapest you could buy.

'So what about when you got home to Scotland?' Howard asked.

Maggie sat facing him, holding her cup in her lap. 'I'd lived with the McNairs before going to Spain, but didn't want to do so again. I thought about finding myself a place in Glasgow, then decided to go back to Heymouth. There, I stayed with friends called the Lennoxes, but couldn't settle. There were ghosts everywhere I went, ghosts of my family, friends and people I'd known. So after a few months I packed my bags and returned to Glasgow and Templeton's.'

'And met up with Andy again?'

'I went to see him several times, of course, then he too started back at Templeton's. Somehow it just seemed the most natural thing in the world for us to get together.'

'And he's still working there, I take it?'

Maggie glanced down into her tea. 'No, he left eventually. He's had a number of jobs since, but is currently unemployed.'

'I see,' Howard said softly. This was bad news. 'And what about yourself?'

'I had to leave when I was expecting Liss. A full-time job was out of the question after that, but since she's been at school I've been able to take on part-time work. It doesn't pay much, but every little helps.'

They both looked at the door when it opened and Andy hobbled in. 'There was a queue a mile along,' he explained, brandishing the half-bottle.

'I've just been bringing Howard up to date with us,' Maggie said.

Andy's expression instantly changed to one of wariness. 'Oh aye?'

'She's been telling me the events that befell you after we parted at the Hotel Caleta Palace,' Howard said.

'I left your tea in the pot,' Maggie smiled at Andy.

'Ach to hell with tea when there's whisky in the house! I'll pour us all drams, eh?'

'Spoken like a true Scotsman,' Howard said.

'Aye, true enough,' Andy chuckled, going to the sideboard from which he ferreted out three glasses.

'Aren't those lovely roses,' Maggie said to him.

'Very pretty.' He stooped over them for a sniff. 'And they smell lovely too.'

Howard finished his tea and laid his cup down beside the ashtray. 'Cigarette, Andy?' he asked, pulling out his packet. Offering cigarettes round was something he'd had to learn to do in Britain. It wasn't a custom in the States.

Andy's eyes gleamed. 'Camels! I see you haven't changed your brand.'

Howard flicked his Zippo, and he and Andy lit up.

'Sheer bliss,' Andy pronounced, smoke streaming from his mouth and nostrils.

'My dad smokes like a lum when he's able to,' Liss informed Howard.

'A lum?'

'Scots word for chimney,' Maggie explained.

'A lum!' Howard smiled. 'I'll have to remember that.'

'A lum is a chimney and also a hat,' Andy added mischievously.

'Any particular sort of hat?'

'The old-fashioned stovepipe ones.'

'Like Abe Lincoln wore?'

'The very hat!' Andy said, laughing.

Maggie accepted her whisky from Andy, and Howard his. 'Can I have some water with it?' Howard requested.

Andy pretended to be mortified. 'You're joking, surely! You're not going to spoil fine whisky by diluting it?'

'An awful American habit,' Howard replied, tongue in cheek. He would have asked for ice cubes also if he'd thought there was any chance of them being available.

'Oh well, if you insist!' Andy sighed.

'I'll do that,' Maggie said, coming to her feet. She wanted to use a beautiful wee jug she had that she'd bought in a junk shop for coppers.

'I think I'll have water also,' she said after Howard had helped himself from the jug.

Andy raised his eyes to heaven. 'God save us from Yanks and their corrupting ways!'

Maggie and Howard laughed at that.

'A toast is in order,' Andy then declared.

He cast about in his mind for a suitable toast, and as he did his mood changed to become sombre. 'To old friends and comrades we won't see again this side of the grave. Never forgotten!'

'Amen,' Maggie mumbled, and sipped her drink.

Andy pulled a wooden chair out from the table and sat down. 'Now how about telling us all about you? How did you become a diplomat?'

'It was a decision I made somewhere during the Second World War, when I was in the Pacific,' Howard replied.

'Don't start in the middle, but at the beginning. Directly

after you left us at the Hotel Caleta Palace,' Maggie insisted.

'OK! When I left the hotel I ran like hell thinking Nevil might be right behind me. I dodged from street to street, until suddenly I was surrounded by Nationalist soldiers who'd broken through. I quickly explained to one of their officers that I was an American journalist, and showed him my papers to prove my story.

'I stayed with those Nats for the rest of that day and all of the next. Fighting was fierce and bloody, in some pockets of resistance the Republicans fighting heroically to the last.

'When it was finally all over, and Malaga had fallen, I wrote and filed my story. Then I checked with the prisoners, thinking I might find members of the platoon. But I didn't.'

'Did you remain in Spain till the end of the war?' Maggie asked.

Howard shook his head. 'I left just before the Brunete offensive in July, and was replaced by a guy called Chuck Aronson. I went back to the States, where I had an extended vacation before being handed another assignment.'

He took a sip of his drink. 'Chuck told me afterwards that he had a real sticky time of it in Catalonia, where different Republican factions turned on one another.'

'I heard about that. It was a vile business,' Andy commented.

'The POUM suffered badly, with many of their people shot by fellow Republicans,' Howard continued.

'It was a deadly power struggle,' Maggie said bitterly.

'Anyway, Chuck came out of it all right. And with some damned fine copy that delighted the paper.'

Maggie glanced at the clock on the mantelpiece to see it was later than she'd thought. 'Before you go on, Howard, I want to put Liss to bed,' she said.

'Oh mum!'

Maggie smiled at this protest. 'As we have a guest you can sleep with us tonight. How's that?'

Which informed Howard that the child did normally sleep in a bed of her own. But it was a bed not in evidence. A shakedown of some sort, he surmised.

'You can listen to us talking so you won't miss anything,'

Maggie said, knowing full well that Liss would soon fall asleep.

Maggie laid her drink aside and crossed to a chest of drawers from which she took a clean pair of child's pyjamas. 'If you change behind Howard's chair he won't see anything he shouldn't,' she suggested, much to Liss's obvious relief.

'Let me give you a top-up there,' Andy said to Howard.

'I believe you're out of work. That's rotten luck,' Howard commiserated with him.

Andy's eyes flicked to Maggie, then away again. 'I'll soon get something else. There's plenty of work about,' he replied.

'I'm sure,' Howard said as Maggie and Liss disappeared behind him.

'What sort of job are you looking for?' Howard asked, genuinely interested.

Andy shrugged. 'Whatever's going, it doesn't matter. I'm afraid I'm not exactly ambitious. A quiet life is all I want nowadays.'

'To each his own,' Howard said.

The two men made small talk until Liss was ready, which she was in a matter of a few minutes.

'Will you kiss Howard goodnight?' Maggie asked her.

Liss went all coy, clasping her hands in front of her and dropping her head. Howard wondered what she'd done with the half-crowns.

'I'd love a kiss,' he said.

'All right,' she replied hesitantly, but not reluctantly.

Going to Howard she offered him her cheek.

'Thank you,' he said when he'd pecked it.

'And what about your mum?'

Maggie got a smacker on the lips.

'And your dad?' queried Andy, having risen again.

Liss squealed and threw herself into her father's arms, Andy lifting her right off her feet and into a tight embrace.

'Oh, my bonnie!' he enthused, squeezing her, which caused her to squeal even louder.

'Thick as thieves, those two,' Maggie smiled to Howard.

'I can see that.'

'Come on and I'll tuck you in,' Andy told Liss, hobbling to the cavity bed.

He sat her upright. 'But first your prayers.'

'But Dad, Howard's there!'

'That doesn't matter. He says his prayers as well. Don't you, Howard?'

'Every night.'

'I'll bet you don't!' Liss grinned.

'I most certainly do. I swear.'

'Right then, let's get on with it,' Andy urged her.

'Will you say them with me, Dad?'

'If you like.' He paused, then began, Liss joining in, ' "Our Father, who art in Heaven, hallowed be Thy name . . ." '

When it was over Liss snuggled down and Andy tucked her in as he'd promised. He kissed her on the forehead, cheek and finally mouth before moving away.

'Another cigarette?' Howard asked.

'Have one of mine.'

Andy crossed to the mantelpiece to pick up his packet of five. 'Only Woody Woodbines, I'm afraid,' he apologized, opening the packet and offering its contents to Howard.

Howard stared at the two remaining cigarettes and wondered if he should help himself or not. The last thing he wanted to do was offend Andy.

'We'll smoke mine after this to save you going out again,' he said, slipping a Woody from the green packet.

'Aye, I should have got some when I was buying the whisky. But I clean forgot,' Andy lied.

Maggie's throat and neck burned with embarrassment. Poverty wasn't a sin, she reminded herself, though in their case it could be called that for it was self-inflicted.

'So, where was I?' Howard said, settling back into his chair.

'You'd returned to America, had an extended vacation and were now on a different assignment,' Maggie reminded him.

'That's right! An assignment that took me down to Alabama, I recall, and was to do with the Ku Klux Klan. Anyway, that's unimportant. Nineteen thirty-seven became

380

thirty-eight. Which in turn became thirty-nine, the year war broke out. The big one.'

His eyes misted in reflection. 'Later I came to London for a short while – a matter of weeks only. And then went back again to the States. I was based in our Washington office, covering the domestic political situation, when the Japs bombed Pearl Harbour. Two months later, February 1942, I joined up.'

'That surprises me,' commented Maggie.

'Why?'

'I would have thought you'd have covered the war for your newspaper.'

Howard shook his head. 'That was something I personally had to get involved in.'

'As the lads from Templeton's felt about matters in Spain,' Andy said.

'Did you go into the Army?' Maggie asked.

'No, I became a Navy pilot. I flew Hellcats for Combat Air Patrol, our principal job to provide air cover for our own vessel and any other accompanying vessels.'

'Did you see much action?' Maggie queried softly.

'I certainly did. Both aboard the *White Plains* and the *Suwanee*, the two carriers I was attached to during my service.'

'Were you ever shot down?' Maggie further queried.

'Yeah, once. When I was with the *Suwanee*. We tangled with a flight of Mitsubishi A6M Zeros, and in the resulting scrap I ended up in the drink. Luckily I was fairly close to the *Suwanee* and they managed to get to me before the sharks did.'

'Sharks!' Maggie breathed, and shuddered, thinking that must be an awful death.

'Not a pleasant way to go,' Howard confirmed, correctly reading her thoughts.

They fell silent for a few seconds, then Howard said, 'As I mentioned earlier, it was while in the Pacific that I decided I didn't want to return to journalism after the war. What I did want was something more constructive, and hit on the idea of joining the Diplomatic Corps. When I was discharged I applied, and much to my delight they accepted me. And so here I am!'

'This isn't your first posting, though, is it?' Maggie asked.

'No, my second. The first was to Bolivia.'

'Bolivia,' Maggie mused. How exotic that sounded.

'Did you enjoy it there?' Andy enquired.

'It wasn't bad. And an excellent introduction to the Corps. I learned a lot in Bolivia.'

'And from there you were posted to Glasgow?' Maggie said with a smile, finding that amusing.

'It was time for me to be promoted, and moved on. Three posts were available at my new level. Glasgow, Rangoon in Burma. And Adelaide, South Australia. I chose the Consulate in Glasgow.'

'Because you'd always wanted to come back here one day,' Maggie said.

He nodded. 'Exactly. It seemed like the perfect opportunity.'

'Well, well, well,' Andy muttered.

'You've certainly seen the world, and will continue to do so in the Diplomatic Corps,' Maggie said.

'And let's hope it becomes a safer world after what we've been through.'

Maggie sipped what remained of her drink. There was one subject Howard hadn't yet touched on, and which she was dying to hear about.

'Whereabouts in Glasgow are you living?' Andy enquired.

'I have a consulate apartment in Clairmont Gardens. That's off Sauchiehall Street, near to Charing Cross.'

'Uh!' said Andy. 'Sounds posh.'

'Bound to be,' declared Maggie. Then, innocently, 'And are you there by yourself?'

Howard frowned. 'How do you mean?'

'Is there a Mrs Taft? I've always thought diplomats have to be married.' She hadn't at all. She'd just made that up.

'Marriage isn't a prerequisite,' he informed her. 'And yes, there was a Mrs Taft. But no longer – we're divorced.'

'I'm sorry to hear that,' Maggie fibbed.

'Her name is Dawne Marie, and we met in Washington. Our divorce was finalized just weeks before I left the Navy.'

It was impolite, but she'd ask anyway. 'Did you divorce her, or was it the other way round?'

'She divorced me, actually, but that was by mutual agreement. She's married again to a lawyer, and blissfully happy, she tells me.'

'Did you and Dawne Marie have any children?'

'Unfortunately, or fortunately, as the case may be, we didn't. Maybe if we had . . .' He trailed off, and shrugged. 'Who knows!'

Andy drained his glass. 'That's slipping down a treat and no mistake. We'll have another.'

Howard eyed the half-bottle, which wasn't going to last much longer at this rate. Should he leave when it was finished, or offer to buy a replacement? He really should go, but there again was tremendously enjoying being reunited with Maggie.

He looked deep into her eyes. But she didn't, or couldn't, hold his gaze. She broke contact by glancing down.

'What about you, Andy? What did you do during the war?'

'Me! My injury exempted me, so I spent it as an ARP Warden. Nor was I sorry to miss it. I had a bellyful of war in Spain. Enough to last me a lifetime.'

'Andy took Spain very hard,' Maggie stated quietly.

'Aye,' Andy agreed.

'Spain, prelude to the main event,' Howard mused.

'Some bloody prelude,' Andy muttered darkly. For a split second his expression was one of tortured anguish. Then it vanished as quickly as it had appeared. It was as though it had never been there.

'You had some laughs as a warden, though, didn't you?' Maggie prompted, attempting to lighten the suddenly strained conversation.

Andy brightened, and began telling Howard about these incidents. One in particular, which involved an unexploded bomb and a wooden crutch, was extremely funny.

Later, when Howard returned with the bottle of whisky he'd bought at the off-licence, he found that Maggie had changed her clothes, put on some make-up and tidied her hair.

It was well after midnight before he finally left for Clairmont Gardens, and when he went he contrived to leave a full pack of Camels behind, a pack he'd picked up from his car while out for the whisky.

Maggie lay in bed not in the least bit tired, her mind whirling and leaping like a dancing dervish. She still couldn't believe that Howard had turned up on their doorstep after all these years. Or that he was now working in Glasgow. It was simply incredible.

The clock on the mantelpiece chimed two a.m. Beside her Andy stirred. Then turned his back on her to cuddle up to Liss, who was right inside the bed.

If only Howard *had* warned them he was coming, she thought. She'd felt a proper mess for most of the evening. At least she'd been able to tart herself up a little when he went to the off-licence.

How smart he'd looked, and successful. A vice-consul with the American Diplomatic Corps – imagine that.

'Dawne Marie,' she whispered. What a ridiculous name that was. Nothing real about it at all.

And what had Dawne Marie been like, she wondered? Jealousy consumed her. Beautiful? Probably. With the most fabulous figure – a real stunner.

She was no doubt pampered too. With all her orders, as the saying went. One thing was certain, she thought bitterly. Dawne Marie hadn't had to go to work as a dinner lady, or down on her hands and knees to skivvy for someone else.

Oh Nevil! she wailed inside her head. If only he'd never agreed to go to Spain with the others, how different her life might have been. If only . . . If only . . .

But Nevil had agreed to go. And even if he had survived he would have been a completely changed man, just as Andy was. She'd witnessed that change taking place on the journey between Madrid and Malaga, a change that had already been happening before her arrival at the Hotel Colon.

She closed her eyes and tried to envisage Dawne Marie. A blonde? Brunette? Redhead? Fay Wray? Claudette Colbert?

Rita Hayworth? The faces that leapt into her mind all belonged to film stars.

This was stupid, she berated herself. Why should she be concerned about Howard's ex-wife? The woman was nothing to her, or to Howard any more, she thought with satisfaction.

What had happened between them for the marriage to break down? Could it be that they hadn't really loved one another? Just as she and . . .

She drew in a deep breath, and sighed. Howard Taft! Like a jack-in-the-box. She smiled. How marvellous it had been to see him again, and terribly exciting.

She hoped Andy would get another job soon. She prayed he would. He'd been after any number since he'd lost his nightwatchman's one, without any success. Glasgow might appear to be a big city, but in many ways it was very small. Word got round. Good things and bad. Good *reputations* and bad.

The evening had cost them the price of a half-bottle which they could ill afford, but it had been worth it. Worth every farthing for the pleasure it had given her.

And hadn't it been nice of Howard to buy that full bottle when the half-bottle had run out! He'd done that just like a Glaswegian. He'd get on very well in Glasgow and Scotland.

And what about his pretending to leave those cigarettes behind? He'd done that deliberately, he couldn't fool her.

She sighed again, this time softly as her mind quietened and sleep began to steal upon her.

When she did fall asleep she dreamt Howard was kissing Rita Hayworth, with Fay Wray and Claudette Colbert also there, begging him to kiss them.

Then they were somehow joined by Nevil and Andy. And the whole thing became three couples: Howard kissing Rita Hayworth; Nevil kissing Claudette Colbert; and Andy doing the same to Fay Wray.

They were still kissing when, with a thunderous roar, a huge flood appeared to sweep them all into oblivion.

★

'Maggie!'

She turned to find Howard grinning at her from the driver's seat of an enormous left-hand drive American car.

'I was just on my way to see you. Hop in!'

She was suddenly all flustered, aware of people staring at her, him, and most of all, the monster he was driving.

'Come on!' he called out again, and leaning over opened his front passenger door.

'This is very kind of you,' she said, somewhat breathlessly, as she slid on to a tan-coloured leather seat.

'As I said, I was on my way to see you. So bumping into you like this was a stroke of luck.'

She pushed a stray lock of hair into place. Damn! He'd caught her again looking a right sight.

'I've just come from work,' she explained, as he engaged gear and the car moved off.

He frowned. 'Your school dinners must have been late today.' It was almost five p.m.

'No, that was earlier! I've been to a Mrs Epstein for whom I do housework.' Mrs Epstein was a friend of Mrs Rubin, who'd recommended Maggie to her.

His frown deepened. She'd mentioned her dinner lady job the other night but not this. 'You mean you work for her as a maid?'

Maggie laughed. 'Hardly that! Well, certainly not what we call a maid. I dust, polish and scrub the floor, those sort of things.'

His lips pursed in what she took to be disapproval.

'It isn't so hard,' she said, feeling the need to justify her skivvying. 'And it's only till Andy finds something else. Though perhaps I will keep it on after that. I don't know yet. It would depend upon whether or not Mrs Epstein would let me bring Liss along during the school holidays.'

'And I suppose like the school dinner job it isn't exactly highly paid?'

'I get the going rate,' she replied defensively.

He hated to think what that was. Less than peanuts, he

imagined. He fought to keep the combined anger and sadness he felt from showing.

Maggie decided to change the subject. 'What an enormous car! What make is it?'

'It's a Buick Roadmaster, and belongs to the consulate. It's permanently at my disposal.'

'It must gobble up the petrol.'

'It surely does!' he agreed. 'But then that's all part of my general expenses. The petrol doesn't cost me a dime.'

'What's a sawbuck?' she asked.

He blinked in amazement. 'Where did you hear that?'

'Not hear, but read. I read it in a book set in America which didn't explain what it meant other than the fact it was a reference to money.'

'A sawbuck is five bucks, or dollars,' he explained.

'Ah! Well, now I know.'

'Now you know,' he smiled, his anger and sadness melting into a loving warmth towards her.

He drew up in front of Maggie's close, his the only car in the street. Two scruffy boys, eyes popping, stopped to gaze at the car as if it was something newly arrived from Mars.

'Jings!' breathed one of them.

While Maggie waited on the pavement Howard took a very large parcel from the rear seat which he held in his arms.

'Lock and close that door for me, will you,' he asked Maggie.

She stared curiously at the parcel. 'What's that?' she questioned.

'I'll show you upstairs. Is Andy in?'

'He should be. Unless he's taken Liss out somewhere.'

It transpired Andy was home, and he got to his feet when Howard staggered into the room.

'What's all this then?' Andy queried as Howard dumped the parcel on the table.

'Have you got a knife?'

'Aye, in the drawer,' Maggie replied, and hurried to get it.

'I hope you're not going to take offence by this, but I don't see why you and your family should miss out,' Howard told Andy.

'Miss out on what?' asked Andy, mystified.

'I'll show you.'

Howard accepted the well-honed knife Maggie handed him and proceeded to open the parcel. String had to be cut, sticky tape sliced through, and brown paper removed. Inside was a cardboard box bearing in various places the legend A&P.

'What's A&P?' Maggie enquired.

'The name of an American supermarket chain. I believe it stands for Atlantic and Pacific.'

Howard pulled out a tangle of straw packing to reveal a multitude of tinned goods and other foodstuffs.

'Good God!' Andy exclaimed softly.

'And . . .' said Howard, rummaging in the box until he found what he was after. 'A carton of cigarettes for you, Andy! These parcels always contain a carton of cigarettes.'

Andy stared at the two hundred Lucky Strike Howard had given him. 'Is this from you?'

Howard shook his head. 'Folk in the United States believe you people in Britain are starving and so send these parcels over in their thousands. One of my tasks at the consulate is to distribute the parcels allocated to us by our embassy in London. Normally I send them to institutions, old people's homes and the like, but I don't see why you shouldn't share in the largesse.'

'Peaches!' Maggie gasped, gazing at a can she'd picked out. 'I can't remember the last time I ate canned peaches.'

'And salmon!' she further exclaimed, delving back into the box.

There was a netting of chocolate bars which Howard picked from the box and opened. 'Try that!' he smiled to Liss, handing her a Hershey bar.

'What's jello?' Andy queried.

'What you call jelly. As in ice-cream and . . .' Howard informed him.

'Oh!'

'I haven't seen food like this in . . . well, years!' Maggie declared in wonder.

'I'll drop you by one of these parcels every week for as

long as I'm here and they keep coming,' Howard smiled.

'What a feast we'll have tonight,' Maggie said, her face filled with gratitude.

'I . . . We can't thank you enough,' a subdued Andy told him.

'We're friends, aren't we? And that's what friends are for.'

'Ham!' Maggie cried in delight. 'I absolutely adore ham.' The tin she lifted from the box had a label on its front stating it contained three pounds of prime Canadian ham.

'And you can really get us one of these boxes every week?' Andy queried.

'No problem at all.'

Andy held the carton of Lucky Strike to his chest. Two hundred American cigarettes! He couldn't believe his luck. And two hundred a week from here on in. He was speechless.

'Talking of feasts, that's another reason I came today. I wondered if you'd allow me to take you out for a meal? Say Saturday night?'

'A meal?' a bemused Maggie echoed.

'Yeah, I know a place on the banks of Loch Lomond. It does a thing called a dinner-dance which can be quite enjoyable.'

He had a sudden thought. 'You don't have to dance of course. That isn't obligatory.'

Maggie realized why Howard had made that qualification. 'Andy can dance all right. Can't you, darling?'

'Let's put it this way, I can get round the floor. I don't claim to any more than that.'

They all laughed.

'Well, what do you think?' Maggie asked Andy. It was his place to answer for them.

Andy looked uncertain.

'Completely my treat,' Howard said. 'I'll even pick you up and drop you home again in my car.'

'And wait till you see that!' Maggie told Andy.

'A night out would do us both the world of good,' Andy said hesitantly.

'That's it settled then!' stated Howard.

Maggie glanced at Liss still chewing the Hershey bar she'd

389

been given. 'You wouldn't mind staying the night with Granny and Grandpa, would you, love?'

Liss shook her head. She adored staying with Granny and Grandpa Ramsay. Grandpa was almost as much fun as her dad.

'I'll call for you at seven?' Howard suggested.

'Fine,' Maggie nodded.

'OK then, I'll be on my way.'

Maggie saw him to the door. 'Thanks again for that parcel, Howard. It's . . . well, extremely appreciated.'

'I know that,' he smiled.

'Till Saturday then.'

'Till Saturday.'

She watched him run down the stairs, closing the door only when he was out of sight.

'There's even chewing gum in here. Things called chiclets,' Andy said, nosing around inside the box.

'How do you fancy salmon and chips for tea?' she proposed.

He growled approvingly.

'What does salmon taste like?' Liss asked.

She adored it when she found out.

'Everything all right?' Mrs Epstein asked Maggie, who'd been going around with a self-occupied expression since her arrival half an hour previously.

'Sorry?' replied Maggie, snapping out of her reverie.

'I said, is everything all right?'

'Fine, thank you! Sorry, am I being slow today?'

'Not slow, but not your usual self either. You seem to be away with the fairies.'

Maggie laughed. She liked Mrs Epstein, who was only a few years older than herself. The pair of them, though very different in looks and temperament, got on well together.

'To be truthful I do have a problem. But one I'll no doubt sort out somehow.'

'Your husband?' Mrs Epstein queried, knowing something of Andy from Mrs Rubin.

Maggie shook her head. 'No, not him. It's . . . well, we've

been asked out to dinner by the American Vice-Consul who's an old friend and I don't have anything suitable to wear.'

Mrs Epstein's jaw had literally fallen open. 'Say that again?' she demanded.

Maggie repeated herself.

'The American Vice-Consul in Glasgow is an old friend of yours?'

Maggie smiled. 'I know it does seem unlikely that a couple living in the Cowcaddens should have such an elevated friend, but it's true nonetheless. We met in Spain when Andy and I were fighting for the Republicans and Howard was a journalist for *The New York Times*.'

'You fought in the Spanish Civil War?'

'As a militiawoman.'

This was a new and fascinating Maggie. Mrs Epstein was intrigued.

Maggie went on. 'We hadn't seen Howard for years. And now suddenly he's been posted to Glasgow, has contacted us again, and asked us out on Saturday night for a meal.'

'Did he say where he's taking you?'

'Some place on the banks of Loch Lomond that does dinner-dances.'

Mrs Epstein put a finger to her lips and thought about that. 'It could be the Lochside Hotel, or else the Hotel Lomond. Both do dinner-dances.'

'And probably very swanky as well,' Maggie said.

Mrs Epstein could see how troubled Maggie was about this. 'They're both lovely, well-appointed hotels which cater for a certain class of clientèle. But not in the least bit snobbish. Each has a very relaxed atmosphere.'

Maggie's face fell. 'I used to work in an hotel, and can guess exactly what they're like.'

Mrs Epstein regarded her sympathetically. 'Have you nothing at all you can wear?'

'Not that's really suitable.'

'You could buy if you had the ration points?'

'I have the points, but not the money,' Maggie replied.

Mrs Epstein had an idea. 'What about your friends and

391

neighbours? Isn't there one of them you could borrow a dress from?'

'My friends and neighbours!' Maggie laughed. 'They're not quite the cocktail set, you know.'

Mrs Epstein smiled, thinking it had been ingenuous of her to suggest that. Then she had it, the ideal solution. 'Put that polish down and come with me,' she instructed.

'Come where?'

'Just come!' said Mrs Epstein, crooking a long-nailed finger.

She led Maggie through to the master bedroom where she threw open her fitted wardrobe door. 'I judge you to be about the same size as me. Correct?'

Maggie nodded, wondering what this was all about.

Mrs Epstein went through her clothes till she found the dress that had come to mind. Taking it from the rack she held it in front of Maggie.

'What do you think of that?' she asked.

The dress was black and extremely chic. It was close-fitting, with full sleeves which tapered to a point.

'It's gorgeous,' Maggie stated.

'Then it's yours.'

Maggie gaped at Mrs Epstein. 'I can't take this from you! It must have cost a fortune.'

'It would, if you bought it in the shops. But I got it free.'

Seeing Maggie's puzzled expression she explained, 'We're in the trade, Maggie. Mr Epstein is in the clothes business.'

'I didn't know that,' Maggie replied truthfully.

'So here, take it with my blessing. I'd give you shoes to go with it, but my feet are much larger than yours.'

Maggie crossed to a full-length mirror and held the dress against herself. 'Are you quite certain?' she asked over her shoulder.

'Totally. I can't have you going out with the American vice-consul not looking your best.'

'You're very kind,' Maggie said, turning to Mrs Epstein. 'And honestly, when I told you what was worrying me I wasn't trying to . . .'

'I know you weren't,' Mrs Epstein interjected. 'You're just not that sort of woman.'

Mrs Epstein paused, then added, 'There is a price though.'

'Oh?'

'You must tell me all about the evening. I shall love to hear.'

'It's a bargain,' Maggie told her.

Maggie and Andy were ready when Howard knocked their door promptly at seven p.m. Andy answered. 'Come away in,' he said.

Howard halted when he saw Maggie standing at the far side of the room. She was looking positively radiant and her dress was quite stunning.

'Will I do?' she asked.

'You'll more than do. You'll be the belle of the ball.'

Maggie was thrilled to hear that. How marvellous to be thought of as a possible belle of the ball after all the drudgery she'd been through in recent years.

'Thank you, kind sir,' she replied.

'An angel descended, eh?' Howard said to Andy.

'Now don't get carried away!' Maggie chided him, but secretly relishing the compliment.

'It's a beautiful dress,' Howard stated, thinking but not as beautiful as the person wearing it. He would have said so if Andy hadn't been present.

'And thereby hangs a tale,' she replied.

'Oh?'

'Which I'll tell you later.'

He nodded. 'Right then. Shall we go?'

Out on the landing Howard gave Maggie his arm while Andy locked the door. 'I found out about those two half-crowns you gave Liss. It was very naughty of you.'

'It was the least I could do, not having brought her anything.'

'But five shillings was far too generous.'

'I'm afraid I said she could spend it on whatever she liked.'

Maggie wagged a finger at him. 'Naughty again!'

'I was always a naughty boy,' he replied in a tone that made Maggie wonder just what he meant by that.

'I'm looking forward to this,' Howard said to Maggie as they proceeded down the stairs, Andy following on behind.

'Me too.' She was, now that she had a decent dress to wear. Her shoes were an old pre-war pair that she'd redyed herself, her coat something she intended leaving in the car when they got to the hotel.

The suit Andy had on was also pre-war, and tight. But it would simply have to do, as it was all he had. His shirt appeared new, but wasn't. Maggie had turned the collar and cuffs for the occasion.

Maggie was laughing at a remark Howard had made when they reached the street, but her laughter died in her throat when she saw there was a young woman sitting in the Buick's front passenger seat. As they approached the car the young woman rolled down her window.

A blonde, and a very pretty one at that, Maggie now saw, gazing into a dazzling smile.

'Maggie, I'd like you to meet Fiona Kilgour, my date for the evening,' Howard said.

Maggie forced a smile on to her face to match Fiona's. She could have scratched the bitch's eyes out. 'Pleased to meet you,' she lied.

'And I'm pleased to meet you.'

Fiona extended a hand through the open window which Maggie shook. She'd much rather have shaken her neck.

'And this is Andy, Maggie's husband.'

'Hello, Andy,' said Fiona in a sultry, smoky voice.

'How do,' Andy replied with a broad beam.

The evening was completely ruined, Maggie thought. It had never crossed her mind that Howard would bring some-one with him. She'd just presumed it was going to be a three-some. For two pins she'd have turned right round and gone back up the stairs, but of course she couldn't.

Howard opened the rear door for Maggie and she climbed inside behind Fiona. There was a strong smell of perfume in the car, a musky smell that made her nostrils flare. She could just imagine the effect it had on men.

Sex, she thought. That's what the perfume made her think of – sex. She already hated Fiona.

Andy slid in beside Maggie. 'It's some car this!' he enthused.

Maggie glanced at her husband, irritated by his fulsome tone.

'The Buick is a very popular car in the States,' Howard replied. 'I'd prefer a Mercury myself in this price range. Its zippiness is more to my taste.'

Always a naughty boy! Maggie thought bitterly. Well, what Howard had meant by that was now evident. He was having an affair with Fiona.

'Is this Buick what they call a V8?' Andy asked.

'That's correct,' Howard answered as the car eased away from the kerb.

'And what about you, Fiona? Are you from Glasgow?' Andy enquired.

'No, Dalry. I only came to Glasgow a few years ago.'

'Fiona is one of my secretaries at the consulate,' Howard explained.

How convenient, Maggie thought. Pushing herself further back into her extremely comfortable seat, she wished she was a witch with a magic wand. She'd make Fiona disappear in a puff of smoke or better still, turn her into a toad.

'What are you chuckling at?' Andy queried.

'Nothing.'

Maggie fell silent, and only spoke when she was spoken to.

Eventually they arrived at the hotel, a splendid baronial-type building overlooking the cold waters of the loch. The Hotel Lomond, Howard informed them. So Mrs Epstein had been right.

'I'll drop you at the front entrance, then park the car,' Howard said.

When the car had stopped Maggie got out, took off her coat and tossed it on to where she'd been sitting. She shivered, for it was a chilly night.

Entering the hotel Maggie saw that Fiona was even prettier than she'd thought. The blond hair was natural, framing an oval face dominated by sparkling intelligent eyes. Her figure was slim, enhanced by a pert bottom and full bosom. She was about twenty-one, Maggie estimated, feeling positively ancient.

'Where's your coat?' Fiona asked, realizing Maggie wasn't wearing hers any more.

'I left it in the car.'

'Oh! Well, if you'll just hang on a second I'll hand mine in.'

Maggie's heart sank even further as she watched Fiona walk away, a walk that was seduction incarnate. She spotted a middle-aged man staring at Fiona, a look that left nothing to the imagination.

'Very nice,' commented Andy, gazing around.

'Oh, shut up!' she snapped softly in reply.

Andy was completely taken aback, wondering what he'd said.

Fiona soon returned. 'Let's go to the bar and wait there, shall we?' she suggested, taking command.

'Let's,' echoed Maggie, her voice tinged with a combination of sarcasm and mockery.

Fiona frowned fractionally, then led the way. Maggie and Andy brought up the rear.

'Now what would you like?' Fiona enquired when they reached the bar.

'Shouldn't we wait for Howard?' Maggie said. 'That would be polite after all.' In her mind she pictured herself sticking out her tongue at Fiona, and immediately felt better.

Fiona was about to reply, when Howard reappeared, resolving the matter. 'What's it to be then?' he said, rubbing his hands.

'I told them we're here, so we can go through after we've had this drink,' Howard stated after having given a white-coated barman their order.

Andy glanced about him. Tartan and ancient weapons featured everywhere. There were also a great many brass and pewter pieces.

Howard paid when their drinks appeared, then raised his whisky and soda in a toast. 'Here's how!' he said.

Being in an hotel like this brought back so many memories of The Haven for Maggie. The dear old Haven, and Lawlers who'd owned it. New shops now stood where The Haven had been, while the Lawlers had retired completely away from the area.

'Have you been here before?' Andy asked Fiona.

'No, never.'

'First time for us too.'

'You get a marvellous view across the loch during the day,' Howard said.

From the bedroom window, Maggie wondered? Was Fiona lying when she'd said she hadn't been here before? She had seemed to hesitate before replying. Or was that merely her imagination running away with her?

A waiter approached them with a wine list. 'Would you care to order your wine now, sir?' he asked Howard.

Howard glanced at the list, then at Maggie. 'How about a Spanish wine? I see they have some.'

'I'd rather you didn't,' Andy said quickly.

Howard looked at him in surprise. Then, when Andy didn't give an explanation, said, 'Right, we'll stick with French. A bottle of sauterne, I think, and another of claret. That meet with everyone's approval?'

'Most certainly,' Fiona replied, giving him a warm smile.

'To start with,' Howard informed the waiter, returning the list.

'Certainly, sir. I understand.'

She should have been feeling happy, uplifted, looking forward to a good night, Maggie told herself. Instead her mood was quite the opposite. She wasn't enjoying this one little bit; the presence of Fiona Kilgour had seen to that.

'Are you all right?' Howard asked.

'Yes, thank you.'

'You're very quiet.'

She was aware of Fiona and Andy also staring at her, but particularly Fiona. 'Am I?'

'Yes, come on, cheer up!' Andy urged.

She could have slaughtered him for saying that. She didn't reply, but sipped her drink instead.

'Have you been to America yourself?' Andy asked Fiona, whom he was clearly taken with.

She shook her head. 'Not yet. But I hope to next year. Howard is arranging that. Aren't you, Howard?'

'I surely am.'

Maggie hoped she went and never came back.

They continued making small talk until they had finished their drinks, then headed for the dining-room where the dinner-dance was taking place.

The four-piece band was already well into its stride, with a number of couples on the floor. A waiter showed them to their reserved tables where Maggie sat facing Fiona, Andy and Howard on either side of her. The wine was already on the table and opened, the sauterne in an ice-bucket.

'White or red?' Howard smiled at Maggie.

She shrugged. 'Whichever.'

'Well, do you think you'll have meat or fish?'

'I don't know. I haven't seen the menu yet.'

'Perhaps you'd prefer to wait then?'

'I'll have red,' she said contrarily.

Maggie watched the various waiters and waitresses at work, assessing their performances. She decided they weren't at all bad.

'How about a dance?' Fiona proposed to Howard.

'I'd love to. But we'd better order first.'

'I simply adore dancing,' Fiona said to Andy, also trying to include Maggie.

'Then maybe you'll give me one later. I'm not much of a partner, I'm afraid, as I can only hobble about, but I enjoy it nonetheless.'

'You're on!' promised Fiona. She didn't enquire about Andy's hobble as Howard had explained its cause before they'd picked up the Ramsays.

'And you'll have one with me?' Howard said to Maggie.

'How could I refuse?'

He wasn't at all sure how to take that. What was the matter

with her tonight? She'd been fine to begin with, then had suddenly changed.

A waitress came over and gave them all menus which they studied. The waitress meanwhile left them to give them time to choose.

Howard laughed. 'There's no doubt what I'm having for my entrée.'

'What's that?' asked Fiona.

'Leek and potato soup,' he replied, but looking straight at Maggie, grinning from ear to ear.

Maggie failed to see why that was funny.

'Are you ordering it as well?' he asked her.

'I rather fancied the prawn cocktail myself.'

He nearly commented on that, but didn't. He'd keep it till they were alone together, but he had to admit he was disappointed she'd forgotten.

When they had ordered, Howard immediately got up with Fiona, the dance a slow waltz.

'Not yet,' Maggie replied, when Andy asked if she wanted to take the floor.

'What's wrong with you?' Andy demanded.

'There's nothing wrong with me,' she replied tartly.

'Yes, there is. You're being very off.'

'Maybe I feel off.'

'But why?'

She certainly couldn't tell him that she was jealous of Fiona. 'Women's troubles,' she whispered confidentially.

That explained it. 'Is there anything you want?'

She shook her head. 'I'm sure it'll soon pass.'

They drank their wine in silence, Andy glancing about him, taking everything in, as Maggie watched Howard and Fiona moving round the floor, never taking her eyes off them.

Howard and Fiona returned to the table at the end of the next dance.

'You're very good,' Andy complimented Fiona.

'Thank you.'

'You can't say the same to me. Fred Astaire I'll never be!' Howard joked.

399

'As Maggie won't get up, will you do me the honour?' Andy asked Fiona.

'Of course. I'd be delighted.'

'You're in for an experience, I can tell you,' he said, rising to his feet.

Howard topped up Maggie's glass. 'I'm surprised you'd forgotten,' he said.

'About what?'

'The leek and potato soup. Don't you remember, we spoke about it crossing the Andalusian sierras? Liking it was something we discovered we had in common.'

Her face flamed. 'You know I had forgotten that! But then whole sections of that part of the journey are no more than a haze in my mind.'

'It was one hell of a crossing, but we made it.'

'I remember I wanted to fall asleep and you wouldn't allow it. You positively roared at me to stay awake.'

'It would have been fatal to have fallen asleep,' he said.

'You probably saved my life.'

'You'd already saved mine when I was captured. And I believe did so again after the shell hit the Hotel Caleta Palace.'

'No,' she replied, shaking her head emphatically. 'The others wouldn't have shot you. Nevil would if he'd survived the shell, but in the event he didn't.'

'I never *forgot* you,' Howard stated simply.

'Yet you got married.'

'So did you.'

'That was different.'

'How?' he queried.

She sipped her wine, and didn't reply. 'Fiona is a very attractive young woman,' she said after a while.

'Indeed.'

'How long has she been your girlfriend?'

Suddenly Howard knew what was wrong with Maggie. How stupid of him not to have realized before! 'She's not my girlfriend.'

Maggie stared at him in disbelief.

'I swear it. I only brought her along to make up the numbers

400

tonight. She's nothing at all to me, other than a damn good secretary.'

'I thought . . .' She trailed off in confusion, and bit her lower lip.

'You were wrong.'

Maggie's heart hammered inside her chest. Fiona *wasn't* Howard's girlfriend! Elation suddenly filled her, and her spirits soared.

'I'm sorry, I just assumed—' she apologized.

'It's my fault. I should have made the position clear.'

'No, it's mine. I shouldn't have assumed.'

They grinned at one another.

'Well, I'm glad that's out the way,' Howard said.

'Me, too.'

'You look gorgeous tonight, Maggie. Truly gorgeous.'

'I felt my age when I saw Fiona. She made me acutely aware of every wrinkle and line.'

He looked thoughtful. 'Maybe I did blunder in bringing Fiona along. You would probably have been happier if I'd brought our Miss X.'

Maggie was intrigued. 'Who's she? A spy?'

'No, the office cleaner. Or one of them anyway. She's fifty if she's a day with a backside on her the size of a Sumo wrestler's,' he teased.

Maggie laughed. 'I presume that's large?'

'Positively gross.'

'And why Miss X?'

He shrugged. 'God alone knows. She's been at the consulate longer than anyone else there and none of the present staff I've asked have any idea where the initial or nickname came from.'

She stared into his eyes, the warmth she saw there washing over her. 'It's so good to have you back in our lives, Howard. I can't tell you.'

'And I feel the same about you and Andy.'

Together they glanced over to where Andy and Fiona were dancing, if you could call Andy's peculiar movements that. Andy noticed them looking, and waved. Maggie waved in return.

'Do you want to get up now? Trip the light fantastic, as they say,' Howard asked.

'There's nothing I want more. But I'd better have a dance with Andy first. It's only proper.'

It wasn't lost on Howard how Maggie spoke about Andy, or the words she used. It told him a great deal.

'I hope we'll be seeing a lot of you,' Maggie said quietly.

'If you'd like that.'

'Yes, I would.' She paused, then added, 'And I'm sure it's the same with Andy.'

When Andy and Fiona rejoined them they found a quite different Maggie to the one they'd left. And from there on the evening sparkled.

At one point Maggie did something she'd never normally dream of doing, and told one of Chrissie McDougall's filthy jokes.

Howard laughed so hard he choked from it and had to be pounded on the back by Fiona and Maggie.

Andy was struck dumb by such hilarity, finding the joke even funnier because it had come from the usually strait-laced Maggie.

Andy and Maggie were both extremely tiddly as, with arms round one another, they staggered up the stairs, after Howard had dropped them off. Without the others being aware of it Howard had contrived to drink far less than them because he was driving.

Andy cried as a leg buckled under him.

Maggie held him up, and he found his feet again. 'They don't seem to be functioning properly any more,' he giggled.

Maggie knew exactly what he meant. Hers weren't too clever either.

'A nice man, that Howard,' Andy muttered.

'Lovely.'

'And I thought Fiona nice, too.'

'I noticed,' she replied drily.

'Aw, come on, I wasn't that bad!' he protested.

'No, you were fine, Andy.'

'Know something?'

'What?'

He stopped. 'I haven't enjoyed myself so much in a long time – in fact in a very long time.'

'It was a smashing evening, right enough.'

'Too true.'

Andy belched, then swallowed, making a sound in his throat as he did.

'You're not going to be sick, are you?' she asked anxiously. He'd had a great deal of alcohol.

'Nope!'

'You're sure?'

'Sure, positive.'

They continued on until they arrived at their door which Andy, after a bit of fumbling and cursing, finally managed to open. As the door swung open a letter was revealed lying just inside.

'Late for the post,' Andy said.

Maggie picked up the letter, which she saw had been hand-delivered and was addressed to Andy. 'For you,' she told him, passing it over.

She snapped on the light while Andy tore open the envelope. He had to screw up his eyes in order to read the single sheet of paper the envelope contained.

'Well, what is it?' Maggie queried, wondering who would hand-deliver a letter to them on a Saturday night.

He dropped the letter to his chest, and beamed at her. 'Remember that job as a labourer I went for at Stroud's Engineering, and which I didn't get?'

She nodded.

'Well, someone has let them down and they say that if I present myself first thing Monday morning they'll give me a start.'

'Oh Andy!' she exclaimed, absolutely delighted.

'I'm in work again!' he cried, punching the air.

It was the perfect end to a perfect evening, she thought.

CHAPTER TEN

'What!' Maggie exclaimed, aghast.

'I've been sacked. I'm sorry. Honest I am.'

Anger erupted in her. Her hand flashed to crack against the side of his face, knocking him sideways.

'Dad!' A horrified Liss ran to her father, and clutched at his clothes.

'I suppose I deserved that,' Andy mumbled, thinking it had been quite a slap.

Liss started to cry, bubbling as she pushed herself as tight as she could against Andy.

'How could you?' Maggie asked in a voice loaded with accusation.

He shook his head. 'It just happened.'

'How?'

He didn't answer.

'How?' she demanded, her tone steely.

'Mr Stroud never really took to me. I . . .'

'Andy!' she interrupted. 'The truth.'

'There, there, lassie, everything's going to be fine. Don't fret yourself,' he said softly to Liss, stroking her hair.

'The truth, Andy,' Maggie persisted.

He tried to stare her straight in the eyes, but couldn't. 'Mr Stroud said that my work wasn't up to standard – that I was lazy.'

If Liss hadn't been there she'd have hit him again. 'And was he right?'

Andy shrugged. 'He caught me day-dreaming a few times. This afternoon there was a wee bird I was watching, something foreign, I think, for I've never seen a bird like it round Glasgow before. Anyway, along came Stroud to find me watching the wee bird and that was that. He called me into his office and gave me my cards.'

'Watching a bird,' she whispered.

'Well, you know me,' he said lamely.

'Oh, I know you all right.' She paused, then said, 'How could you, Andy? How could you let us down like this yet again?'

'I didn't mean to, Maggie. I intended to hold down this job. It's just . . . Something I've told you often in the past. I just can't take things all that seriously after Spain. I don't see the importance and urgency in day-to-day matters that other people see any more.'

Her anger faded, leaving her drained, feeling like a washed-out rag.

Andy groped in a pocket to produce a handkerchief. 'Here now,' he said to Liss, wiping her face.

Maggie crossed to the nearest fireside chair, and slumped into it. What a mess! she thought. And what a terrible start to the new year, it being mid-January, 1949.

'We'll get by. We always have,' Andy said to her.

'Little thanks to you,' she snapped in reply.

'Please don't fight, Mummy and Daddy,' Liss pleaded.

'Mummy has a right to be angry,' Andy said.

'But not to hit you. You never ever hit her.'

'She just lost her temper for a moment, that's all,' Andy smiled.

Maggie closed her eyes and let her head droop. In her mind she saw herself standing on the edge of a bottomless black chasm. It seemed to her that unseen forces were trying to drag her over it.

'I'll get something else soon, you'll see,' Andy told her, trying to be encouraging.

How often had she heard those words!

'The money wasn't all that brilliant at Stroud's anyway. I'm sure I can do better.'

'You'll do well just to find another job. *Any* job. You know that,' she stated bitterly.

Andy returned the hanky to his pocket, and from another

405

brought out a packet of sweets which he gave to Liss. 'For after your tea,' he said.

'Thank you, Dad.'

He took a deep breath. 'You haven't started tea yet then?' he said to Maggie.

'Not yet. It's what's left of the shepherd's pie we had last night. It'll only take a few minutes to warm up.'

'Can I do that for you then?'

She shrugged.

He removed his jacket and hung it on the peg behind the door. 'I was thinking I might take Liss to the pictures tonight. It is a Friday, which means no school tomorrow, and Walt Disney's *Bambi* is playing all this week in town.'

'*Bambi!*' Liss squealed, clapping her hands together.

Maggie glanced up at him. 'Don't you think we should be saving that money now you're unemployed again?'

'Last fling, eh?' He hesitated, then said, 'And what about you, would you like to come?'

She noticed she'd been an afterthought. But then that was often the way when it was something involving him and Liss. 'No thanks, I'll stay home.'

'Are you certain about that?'

'Absolutely,' she replied wearily.

'Right then! The quicker we have tea the quicker we can be off. Liss, you help by setting the table and I'll get the shepherd's pie into the range oven.'

'What about your wage packet?' Maggie demanded.

'Oh, aye!' He came over and handed it to her. As usual it was unopened.

'I'll need some money for the pictures,' he said.

She tore open the brown packet and offered it to him. 'Help yourself,' she instructed.

When he had, he joked. 'Neat and tidy getting sacked on a Friday, eh? Meant I didn't have to go back for my pay.'

Only Liss's presence stopped her giving him a mouthful. 'Eat the shepherd's pie between you. I'm not hungry,' she said.

'I'll leave you some. You might get hungry later.'

'I won't,' she replied.

'But you just . . .'

'I said I won't,' she stated emphatically.

He let it go.

When the meal was over Andy stacked the dirty dishes in the sink.

'Leave those, I'll do them while you're out,' Maggie said. She was as keen for him to go out as he was. She wanted the house to herself, to have some time to think and grapple with the pain.

'Can I have my sweeties now?' Liss asked, bright-eyed.

'Why don't you save them for the pictures?' Maggie suggested.

Liss looked at Maggie, then back at Andy. 'Can I, Dad?'

'You heard what your mother said. Save them for the pictures.'

Her face fell.

'But I'm sure it's all right for you to have one or two on the way,' he added.

He spoiled her rotten, Maggie thought. He always had done and probably always would. As for Liss, she had him twisted round her little finger and knew it.

'Enjoy yourself,' Maggie said to Liss when it was time for her and Andy to leave. She placed her hands tenderly on her daughter's cheeks, then kissed her.

In a quick, ducking motion Andy bent and pecked Maggie on the forehead. 'I really am sorry, Maggie. Please forgive me,' he said quietly.

She wouldn't lie by saying she did. 'Get on, the pair of you. Off you go!' she said instead.

'Bye, Mummy!' Liss called out, skipping to the door, where she was joined by Andy.

Maggie sighed as the door clicked shut behind them.

She stared into the fire, wondering how all this was going to end. Time passed, and she was still pondering the situation when there was a knock on the door.

'Howard!' she exclaimed. He was holding a food parcel.

'This week's,' he stated, staggering into the room and dumping the parcel on the table.

He grinned at Maggie. 'I don't know what's in that one, but it's heavier than usual. That's why I chose it for you.'

'You're very kind.'

'Don't mention it!' He glanced about. 'No Andy and Liss?'

'He's taken her to the pictures. *Bambi*'s playing in town.'

'I see.'

She suddenly felt overwhelmed and broke down, tears spurting from her eyes as she sobbed.

An alarmed Howard gathered her into his arms. 'What is it? What's wrong, Maggie?'

She tried to speak, but couldn't. A huge lump of raw emotion choked her. Her upper torso heaved with her sobbing.

'It's OK. It's OK,' Howard said, patting her on the shoulder. Wild flowers, he thought. He'd once likened her personal scent to wild flowers. It was very strong at that moment.

After a short while she quietened and the sobbing stopped. 'Daft of me, that,' she mumbled.

'Come and sit down and I'll put the kettle on. That's the British remedy for everything, isn't it?' he joked as he guided her to the chair she'd been in.

'You don't have to explain if it's personal,' he said as he filled the kettle.

'Andy's lost his job again,' she stated simply.

Howard swore in that peculiar way that Americans do.

'His boss said that his work wasn't up to standard and that he was lazy. The final straw apparently was when the boss caught him standing watching a bird.'

It would be laughable really, Howard thought, if it wasn't so sad. 'What's wrong with that man?' he queried, anger in his voice.

Maggie wiped tear stains from her face. 'Spain gutted him, not to put too fine a point on it. The Andy who came back was completely different to the one who went.'

'You mean because he lost most of his pals over there?'

'That was certainly part and parcel of it. But in the main it was losing Felicia. Her death broke him.'

'Felicia?' Howard queried.

'She was someone he met in Madrid. An English sculptress

whom he fell madly in love with. And I mean *madly*. He worshipped the ground she walked on. I was right beside her when she got killed. She was in charge of a machine-gun, assisted by me and a girl called Evelyn.'

Maggie smiled at the memory. 'Even when dead, Felicia continued firing that damned gun until the belt was empty. That was typical of the woman. She was a tremendous character.'

'A sculptress?' Howard mused as he put the kettle on the stove.

Maggie pointed at Andy's wooden bust on the mantelpiece. 'She did that.'

Howard crossed to the bust and studied it. 'I've noticed it before. It's excellent.'

'Andy made arrangements for it to be sent back here after the war was over. It's his most treasured possession.'

'She certainly had talent,' Howard said.

'That's how Liss got her name, you see. Andy used to call Felicia, Fliss. When Liss was born Andy, without explaining why to me, insisted we call the baby Elizabeth, which in time became Liss.'

Howard stared at Maggie. 'I'm fascinated by all this. But I'm not sure how much I can ask.'

'Ask whatever you like.'

'Doesn't it bother you that he calls his daughter, your daughter, after his dead lover?'

'I don't know whether they were lovers or not. They might have been. Andy saw Felicia as quite a cut above himself, which may well have stopped him making any physical advances.'

'And he's never told you?'

She shook her head. 'Nor have I asked. That part of his life is very personal to him. I wouldn't dream of trying to pry into it. The same as he never pries about Nevil. Though in that case he knows Nevil and I were lovers.'

'Yours sounds a very sad marriage, if you don't think it impertinent of me to say so?'

'I suppose it is sad, or at least looks that way.'

'Why did you marry him?' Howard asked softly.

'I told you once before, it seemed the most natural thing that we got together. He'd lost Felicia whom I'd known and liked. I'd lost Nevil who was his great pal. It all added up to us having a lot in common.'

Howard glanced at the kettle. 'I could go out and get some booze if you'd prefer?'

'Not for me. A cup of tea, this fire and your company are just fine.'

Howard smiled to hear that.

'But go and get some for yourself if you'd like.'

'I won't bother. Your company is enough for me.'

She stared at him. 'You always make me feel so good inside. You're a joy to be with.'

'It's the same for me.'

She knelt down by the fire and stoked it into life. She wanted to get a good blaze going.

'Thank you for that parcel. With Andy unemployed we'll be relying on them heavily again.'

Howard's expression became grim. 'I take it this business of Andy losing his job is a regular occurrence? At least that's the message which comes across.'

'Yes,' she acknowledged in almost a whisper.

'Doesn't he realize, or care, about how hard he's making it for you?'

'Oh, he realizes and cares all right. But that doesn't make any difference. He never loses a job intentionally, and is always contrite afterwards. It's just the way he has been since Spain. Nothing really matters to him. Except Liss. He'd walk into the fires of hell for her.'

'And for you?'

'Andy and I understand each other. We have no illusions, or pretences, about our relationship.'

'So you don't love one another?'

She looked at Howard, and smiled thinly. But didn't reply.

'Well, let's hope Andy soon gets another job,' Howard said.

'To be truthful, with his record I was surprised he got the last one. After this his goose might be well and truly cooked.

410

Word gets around, you see. And I'm afraid Andy's reputation just gets blacker and blacker. However, I'm keeping my fingers crossed.'

'As bad as that, eh?'

She nodded. 'I'm afraid so.'

'And you can't take a full-time job because of Liss.'

'That's correct. She has to be taken to school and picked up again. We could get someone to do both tasks, but Andy wouldn't allow it.'

'It's quite a problem you've got then,' Howard said.

'And of our own making, that's what hurts.'

'Andy's making, not yours,' he corrected her. Why should she attach blame to herself when she wasn't at fault?

A thoughtful Howard returned to the stove where he warmed the teapot.

'The caddy is in the cupboard,' Maggie informed him. When he neither moved or replied she repeated herself.

'Sorry, I, eh . . . I've just had an idea. You could completely reverse the process.'

'How do you mean?'

'A spoonful for each of us and one for the pot. Is that right?'

'Yes.'

'What I mean is, why don't you forget about Andy going out to work? You get yourself a full-time job and let him stay at home in your place. A reversal of roles, in other words, with you becoming the bread winner.'

'Now why did I never think of that!' she exclaimed. Then her face fell. 'Probably because it wouldn't work.'

'Why not?'

'Wage differences. Women get paid less than men. I couldn't match his wage, low as it's been in his last few jobs.'

'I know a job going right now that might match his pay. In fact I'm certain of it.'

'Where? And doing what?'

The kettle was now boiling so he filled the teapot and set it aside to brew.

'At the American Consulate, being a clerk. One of our women handed in her notice earlier in the week.'

Excitement grew in Maggie. A clerk! She should be able to cope with that. And the job being at the American Consulate meant that she would see a lot more of Howard.

She looked into his eyes and saw he was also thinking that. She realized precisely what this job could lead to if she got it. She knew it, and so did he.

'Would Andy be agreeable to such an agreement?' Howard asked, a sudden tremor having crept into his voice.

She considered it. 'He might not be happy about it, and it would certainly put a big dent in his pride. And don't forget Glaswegian men are very long on pride. But, in the end, common sense would just have to prevail. I'd make sure of that.'

The possibility of seeing Maggie virtually every day made Howard's stomach tighten. When he stretched out a hand for the teapot he noted it was shaking slightly.

'How do I go about applying?' she asked.

'Leave that to me.'

Howard had only been gone about half an hour when Andy and Liss arrived back.

'You're home early?' Maggie said with a frown.

'Liss has had a funny turn. Haven't you, lass?'

Maggie saw now that Liss was pale, her features drawn. 'What sort of funny turn?' she demanded, going to her daughter.

'I felt sick and got an awful headache,' Liss replied.

'And went weak all over,' Andy added.

'Oh, my darling!' Maggie hugged Liss to her. 'Do you still have the headache?'

'Yes, Mummy.'

'I'll get the aspirins,' Andy said.

Maggie took Liss's coat off and drew her over to the fire. 'Maybe it's a cold coming on,' she said to Andy.

'Could be. Or there again, I wondered if it was something she'd eaten?'

Maggie thought of the shepherd's pie Andy had reheated earlier. 'Are you all right?' she asked him.

'Fine.'

So it wasn't that. Nor could she think of anything else she'd served up during the past twenty-four hours that might be tainted.

'I suddenly went all strange,' Liss told Maggie in a quiet, subdued voice.

Maggie stroked her cheek, thinking she didn't look at all well. 'Poor lamb,' she muttered.

'What about the school dinners today?' Andy demanded.

'They looked fine to me.' To Liss she said, 'Did you have the fish?'

'No, Mummy, the Irish stew with cabbage and boiled potatoes.'

The fish might just be suspect, you could never really be a hundred per cent certain with that. But she'd have bet her boots there had been nothing wrong with the stew.

'Only give her half,' Maggie instructed Andy.

'Right!'

He placed the aspirin on the table and cut it with a knife. Then he remembered there was an unfinished bottle of lemonade in the house. That would help it down.

'Here you are, darling,' he said, giving Liss half the tablet. 'And this to go with it.'

Liss drained the glass and handed it back to her father. 'Thank you, Dad.'

'Perhaps we should call the doctor?' Andy suggested to Maggie.

Maggie glanced at the mantelpiece clock. 'It's late to get him out considering it's not exactly an emergency. I think we'll just put her to bed and see how she is in the morning. If she's still unwell then I'll call him in.'

As it transpired a doctor proved unnecessary. When Liss woke after a good night's sleep she was as right as rain again.

Maggie was all twitchy with nerves as she waited for her interview with the Consul-General. She smoothed down the front of her skirt, part of a smart tailored suit she'd bought for the occasion. Howard had given her the money for it saying that if she were to land the job she was to look the part.

413

He'd also paid for the new blouse she was wearing, her shoes, and the coat lying folded on the chair beside her. Also she had been to a posh hairdresser where she'd not only had her hair done, but enjoyed the combined luxury of a facial and manicure. All in all a tidy outlay which Howard had laughed off, declaring he could easily afford it.

Relax, Maggie ordered herself. Mr Schuh, the Consul-General, wasn't going to bite. He was an extremely nice, charming man, Howard had assured her.

She grinned. Schuh! It was a strange name. She wondered where it originated from. Germany perhaps. Or further east? Definitely not Scotland. Who'd ever heard of the McShuhs!

'Something funny?' a friendly female voice asked.

Maggie realized that Fiona Kilgour had come up to stand beside her. 'No, not really.'

'I thought I'd come and wish you luck with your interview. It's a great place to work, I can tell you.'

'That's kind, Fiona. Thank you.'

'Have you seen Howard yet?'

Maggie shook her head. 'I expect he's busy.'

They chatted for a few minutes, then were interrupted by a woman who appeared to tell Maggie that the Consul-General would see her now.

As Maggie walked beside the woman taking her to the Consul-General she thought what a charming girl Fiona was. She'd quite misjudged her on their first meeting, but then anger and jealousy had been the cause of that.

They paused outside an ornately decorated door. 'Wait here a second,' the woman said, and vanished inside.

She was back almost immediately. 'You can go in,' she said.

Maggie's heart was thumping as she entered a palatially furnished and decorated room, dominated by a huge desk with a white-haired man sitting behind it. A large gilt-framed picture of President Truman hung on one wall.

'Welcome, Mrs Ramsay,' said Schuh, rising and extending a hand.

'Pleased to meet you,' she replied, shaking his hand, aware that he had a very firm handshake.

414

'Please sit down,' he said, indicating a chair in front of his desk.

She did, perching on it rather than sitting. Now that she was in the lion's den, so to speak, her nerves had subsided.

He smiled pleasantly at her, then looked down at her application form lying before him.

'Are you a Communist, Mrs Ramsay?' he asked, still smiling.

That was the last question she'd expected. 'No, why?'

'I see you fought for the Republicans in the Spanish Civil War.'

She'd declared that on her form on Howard's advice. 'All Republicans weren't Communists, sir.'

'But all were Left Wing?'

'Yes, you could say that.'

'If you're not a Communist what exactly are your politics, Mrs Ramsay?'

'Like the vast majority of people who live in Glasgow I vote Labour. I make no secret about that.'

'And what is your attitude towards the United States?'

'I have every admiration for America,' she replied.

He nodded his approval. 'So you bear us no ill will of any sort?'

'None whatever.'

He made a pyramid with his hands and studied her. Maggie had the feeling he was seeing into her mind and reading precisely what was there. It was like being on the other end of a microscope.

'I'm a Democrat myself . . .'

'Whose symbol is a donkey,' she interjected, and instantly regretted doing so.

The gimlet eyes bored into hers, and slowly narrowed.

That's it, big mouth, she told herself. Thank you and goodnight.

He laughed, a deep rumbling sound. 'I like that. Hell, yeah! I like a woman with wit.'

She hadn't meant to be witty. It had been merely a statement of fact.

She'd made a hit with the Consul-General, that became clear as he continued his questioning. When he made a sly dig at elephants, the American opposition party's symbol, she further endeared herself by picking that up and laughing at it.

On leaving Schuh's office she headed for the red-carpeted stairs that would take her to Reception. She was halfway down when Howard caught up with her.

'Well?' he demanded.

'Talk about questions! Mr Schuh really put me through the hoop.'

'But did you get the job?'

'That stare of his totally threw me to begin with. I've never come across such a penetrating stare.'

'Did you get the job?' Howard queried yet again.

She nodded. 'Subject to a security check which won't come up with anything, other than Spain that is, which he already knows about.'

'That's wonderful!' Howard breathed.

'And I'm to get seven pounds ten a week, which is considerably more than what Andy was earning.'

'I said we paid well. It's a policy of ours. But listen, why don't we go and have lunch to celebrate?'

'That would be lovely.'

He positively ached to take her in his arms and kiss her. 'I know a restaurant that does marvellous food. We'll go there. By the way, when do you start?'

'A fortnight next Monday. That allows time for the security check and for me to give the school and Mrs Epstein a fortnight's notice, which is only fair.'

'Yes,' he agreed, wishing she was going to start the very next day.

'I'm terribly pleased and thrilled, Howard. Thank you for suggesting this job,' she said.

'I have to pick my coat up from the office, so shall I meet you outside?'

'You mean it's more discreet that way?' she teased.

He tapped her on the end of her nose with the tip of his right index finger.

'Give me two minutes,' he said.

Snow was flying as they hurried arm-in-arm along the road. 'Have you been to the Rogano?' Howard asked her as they turned into Exchange Place.

'No, but I've heard of it.'

'Tremendous restaurant by any standards, and one which boasts an oyster bar. Do you fancy that?'

'Oh, yes please!' She'd had oysters once in Heymouth, an experience she'd thoroughly enjoyed.

'And champagne?'

'Now you're spoiling me,' she almost purred.

'Why not! It probably gives me more pleasure than it does you.'

Glancing into his eyes she saw that was true. She shivered, and not from the cold either.

The main restaurant in the Rogano was done out in a Twenties style and smelled absolutely delicious. Howard steered Maggie to the oyster bar where they hung up their coats and sat down. Howard ordered a dozen oysters each and a bottle of Roederer Cristal.

'You look quite marvellous today,' he told her.

'Thanks to you.' She felt marvellous. The new clothes and visit to the hairdresser had done wonders for her self-esteem.

'I can't wait for you to start,' he confessed.

'Nor me. I didn't think I was going to land the job, mind you. Mr Schuh's first question was whether or not I was a Communist!'

'Well, you're not, are you?'

'Of course not. I simply mean the unexpectedness of it took me completely by surprise.'

'America is somewhat paranoid about Communists right now. They're Public Enemy Number One as far as we're concerned. We fear them and in my opinion rightly so. They're a dark force.'

'Isn't that a bit melodramatic?'

417

'Not at all. But let's not talk about politics,' he said as their champagne arrived.

'Shall I or will you do it, sir?' asked the girl serving them.

'I'll do it,' Howard answered. Then, to Maggie, 'I always get a kick out of popping the cork.'

'I'm glad to hear it.'

They both laughed, enjoying her joke.

They laughed again as the bubbling wine splashed and frothed into their flute glasses. Slowly this time, Howard now topped up the glasses.

'A toast,' he proposed.

'To what?'

'To your new job. May you be extremely happy in it.'

They clinked their glasses, and drank.

Maggie murmured in appreciation. 'You know I could get to like this sort of life.'

Howard had a reply to that, but kept it to himself. It was too early for him to make such a statement or proposal.

Maggie paused to stare up at the tenement where she and Andy lived. As Howard was due back at the consulate, he hadn't been able to give her a lift home, so she'd come by tram instead.

How dirty and dingy it looked, she thought. It was a different world entirely to the Rogano, champagne and oysters. The memory brought a contented smile to her face. The lunch had been one of the best, if not the best, she'd ever had.

An old man in a tattered coat and greasy cap slouched by. He was unshaven and smelled, his down-at-heel boots scraping the pavement because he wasn't lifting his feet properly.

A different world entirely, she repeated mentally to herself and with a sigh plunged into her close.

Andy was dozing by the range, the morning newspaper a tent on his lap. He came awake as she was hanging up her new coat.

'How did it go?' he yawned.

'I got the job and start a fortnight on Monday.'

'Congratulations! What's the pay?'

'Seven pounds ten a week,' she informed him.

He gawped at her. 'You're joking!'

'That's what the Consul-General told me himself.'

'But that's more than I've ever earned.'

He stared at Maggie, and felt himself grow small in front of her. Worse still, an unseen transference of power and dominance took place between them. Maggie was now figuratively wearing the trousers in their house.

'Seven pounds ten a week is terrific,' he said unenthusiastically, with a tinge of resentment in his voice.

'Yes, terrific,' she agreed. 'We're very lucky.'

One of Maggie's many tasks at the consulate was to keep an account of the weekly petty expenses. She was engaged currently on that, the ledger lying open before her.

But her attention wasn't on the ledger and various dockets which needed to be entered and filed. It was on Howard standing a dozen feet away in conversation with the Consul, a Mr Cheever.

She was acutely aware of Howard's presence, and knew he felt the same about hers. It was as if they were somehow joined by an invisible band of electricity which surged and sparked from one to the other, trying to pull them together like two magnets.

She was tingling inside, while the hairs on her arms and the back of her neck had become so sensitive it seemed to her she could feel every single one.

Her mouth had gone dry, and her breathing had become shallow. She daren't look directly at Howard in case someone saw her giveaway expression. She felt seventeen again, young, and desperately in love.

'Hello, Maggie,' Morag Fullarton said.

'Hello, Morag,' Maggie replied, amazed at how normal her voice sounded. Morag was from the typing pool and lived out in Battlefield.

'You're busy, then?' Morag said when Maggie didn't glance up.

'Terribly.'

'Ah well, see you later.' And with that Morag sauntered off.

Mr Cheever left Howard, calling out that he'd speak to Howard again later.

There were several seconds before Howard moved off. And in that time, though they didn't look at one another, each knew precisely what the other was thinking.

'Maggie, I'd like a word with you in my office,' Howard said to her at the end of her morning coffee break one day.

'I'll be right there.'

She watched him bustle away, wondering what it was all about. When she entered his office she found him at the window staring out over Hope Street.

He rounded on her. 'I've been given a special assignment and I want you to be part of my team of helpers.'

'Oh?'

'Strictly speaking, this isn't your province, but I'm allowed to rope in whoever I wish, and I immediately thought of you. I imagined that you would enjoy being part of it.'

She raised an eyebrow, waiting to be told what 'it' was.

He went on. 'Our Secretary of Defence is flying into Prestwick the Tuesday after next, *en route* to the Netherlands, where he is to have talks with their prime minister regarding the forthcoming North Atlantic Treaty.

'He'll be staying over at Prestwick for a few hours, ostensibly to have a meeting with the Consul-General, but really because he and Schuh are old buddies who go way back together.

'Apart from the clambake it's also a gesture to boost Schuh's career, and because of that the ambassador in London is not invited so that all the limelight will focus on Schuh.'

'I see,' Maggie nodded. 'And just what sort of clambake do you have in mind?'

'We've to organize full media coverage. That's United States, British and anyone else we can interest. Then there will be an informal reception at the Prestwick Airport Hotel, after which the secretary will fly on to The Hague.'

'Sounds frightfully exciting,' Maggie enthused. 'Will any of our government be there?'

'Well, I doubt it will be the minister of defence, Mr Attlee himself. He, like Churchill his predecessor, doubles that post with the premiership. But I'm sure they'll want to send somebody, possibly Bevin, the Foreign Secretary.'

'And how many helpers will there be in your team?' she enquired.

'Fiona, Cathy McColl and yourself, making four of us in all. I'm sure between us we can get everything suitably organized.'

'I'm sure,' she agreed.

He glanced at his watch. 'I'm going to call a meeting in this office for four-fifteen. We'll begin laying plans then.'

Maggie had a sudden thought. 'Will Mr Schuh and his party be staying overnight at the Prestwick Airport Hotel?'

'I shouldn't imagine so, if the secretary's schedule is adhered to that is. But I would think it will be necessary for the four of us to stay.'

She knew then why she'd been asked to help and it filled her with a warm, anticipatory glow.

'There it is!' exclaimed Fiona, pointing.

Maggie followed Fiona's finger to spot the incoming dot that was the Secretary of Defence's aeroplane. As she watched, the dot became bigger and bigger, sprouting wings and a tail.

'Right on time,' said a nervous Howard.

'Well, of course, son!' smiled General Ekstrom, who was standing beside Howard. Ekstrom was in command of all USAF installations in Scotland.

Consul-General Schuh turned his coat collar up against the light but biting wind. 'Okay, hon?' he asked his wife.

'Just fine,' Estella Schuh replied.

Schuh glanced over to where the media was congregated. It was an excellent turnout, Taft had done well. He unconsciously sucked in his stomach and stuck out his chest when he saw that the British Movietone News team were already shooting film.

In her mind Maggie went over all the things that were her

personal responsibility again. She then visually counted the line of waiting official cars, making sure it was the correct number. These would take the official party to the hotel.

The only member of the foursome not present was Cathy McColl, who was back at the hotel keeping an eye on matters and adding last-minute touches.

The incoming plane was now looming large in the sky, its thunderous drone getting louder with every passing second.

General Ekstrom shaded his eyes as he watched the plane come in to land, nodding with satisfaction when it made a perfect touchdown. God help the pilot if it hadn't.

Maggie held down her coat and skirt from a sudden blast of air. By her side Fiona was doing the same.

Howard gazed up at the sky. Rain was threatening and he could only hope and pray it held off until the speeches had been made, photographs taken and the party were in their cars. The weather was, of course, something he hadn't been able to fix.

The American plane taxied forward to where a set of steps was already in position. At the bottom of the steps was a length of red carpet that ran to a lectern where the speeches, one by the Secretary and another by Schuh, would be made.

The media broke ranks and surged forward, cameras and microphones at the ready. A wedge of journalists was the first to reach the red carpet, on the edge of which it heaved and jostled.

'Make way for the BBC!' a pompous voice cried out.

An American voice replied telling the BBC just what it could do with itself.

Fiona left Maggie to reposition herself where the waiting USAF band could see her. She raised her hand as the aircraft door began to open.

The moment the secretary appeared Fiona gave the signal and the band struck up 'The Star Spangled Banner'.

The Secretary, like all other Americans present, came to attention. And in his case he placed a hand over his heart.

At the conclusion of 'The Star Spangled Banner' the band went into a rendition of 'God Save the King'.

The British national anthem over, Schuh strode forward to meet his old friend, the pair of them shaking hands vigorously at the bottom of the steps. The Secretary then repeatedly patted Schuh on the shoulder, much to the delight of those with cameras.

Howard again glanced up at the sky, which seemed even darker and more ominous than it had been. 'Another ten or fifteen minutes,' he pleaded to the Almighty. 'That's all, just another ten or fifteen minutes.'

The band played 'Scotland the Brave' while introductions were taking place. The overall atmosphere was jolly in the extreme.

Maggie watched in admiration as Mr Bevin, the Foreign Secretary, had a brief chat with the Secretary of Defence. The two of them laughed at something one of them had said.

Maggie went over to Howard. 'So far so good.'

'So far,' he echoed.

Schuh, now at the lectern, gestured for quiet. When everyone was settled, he said, 'Ladies and gentlemen, it gives me great pleasure to introduce the Secretary of Defence for the United States, my good friend James V. Forrestel!'

Forrestel made a short speech during which he contrived to mention Schuh's name a dozen times or more. The main subject of his speech was the North Atlantic Treaty due to be signed in a few months and his country's high hopes for that treaty.

When Forrestel had finished Schuh delivered his speech, also a short one. When that was over they were off to the hotel where Forrestel and Schuh would make themselves available to the media for personal interviews.

As the Secretary and Consul-General's car whisked off, Maggie bore down on the media. She was now in charge of them.

'There will be plenty of hospitality,' she assured one anxious journalist, which raised a cheer. They'd expected nothing less.

Maggie travelled with a film crew from Belgium. On arriving at the Airport Hotel she directed everyone to the room that had been set aside for them, and where a bar had been laid out. The media personnel immediately fell upon the alcohol like vultures on a corpse.

Having lived in Glasgow for many years, Maggie was used to heavy drinkers, but what she now witnessed rocked her. Bottles appeared to just empty before her very eyes.

She made an urgent phone call and within minutes more alcohol was being carried in by the hotel staff.

'How long till we see Forrestel?' a young chap clutching an almost full tumbler of neat whisky demanded somewhat belligerently.

'He and the Consul-General will be here directly,' she answered.

The young man grunted. 'The Yanks do well for themselves, don't they!' he said, glancing at the bar and gulping down some of his drink.

'There are sandwiches and other things to eat at the other side of the room,' Maggie informed him.

'Sod that. I'll just stick with the booze.'

What a rude and unpleasant young man, she thought, moving away from him.

'*Express*,' declared a man, grabbing her arm. 'When will the Secretary show?'

'Directly,' Maggie repeated with a smile.

The *Express* journalist released her. Then leered at her bust before turning round to talk to someone else.

She saw a cameraman put a bottle of gin into his camera case, doing so quite blatantly. She fought back the urge to go over and order him to replace it. But honestly, what a cheek!

'Who are you?' a smartly dressed woman demanded.

'I'm with the consulate.'

'In what capacity?'

'I'm one of the helpers organizing this event,' Maggie explained.

'Oh, a nobody.' And with that she turned her back on Maggie.

Maggie couldn't believe the grossness and vulgarity of these people. They were all absolutely loathsome. Then she remembered that Howard had once belonged to their tribe. He may have belonged, but had never been like them. He'd been different, an exception to the rule.

She was nearly knocked from her feet in the rush of bodies when Forrestel and Schuh appeared. Somewhere a tray of glasses went crashing to the ground.

The interviews lasted almost half an hour, after which Forrestel and Schuh retreated to another part of the hotel.

'Everyone satisfied now!' said a smiling Howard in a loud voice.

Only a few people answered him, the rest were making a beeline to demolish what was left of the alcohol.

Howard signed Maggie over to him. 'Leave this lot now. Our business with them is done.'

'They're awful,' Maggie stated quietly.

One journalist started arguing with another. 'I'm telling you, as the Press we have the *right* to report what we see fit. Irrespective!'

'Come on,' said Howard, and together they slipped away.

Forrestel was being entertained in a functions room where a buffet and bar were available. From the looks of things, he was thoroughly enjoying himself.

'Can I get you a drink?' Howard asked Maggie.

'Do you think we should?'

He smiled. 'Perfectly normal that we do.'

'In that case I'll have a glass of red wine.'

Cathy McColl entered pushing a tray on which were heaped piles of hamburgers and hot dogs. Forrestel roared with appreciative laughter when he saw them.

'The real McCoy, compliments of Colonel Ekstrom,' Schuh said to Forrestel.

'Let's grab some samples then,' Forrestel replied, and the two men went over to the trolley where they helped themselves.

The hamburgers and hot dogs had been Howard's idea. It pleased him to see that it had met with approval.

As time passed Forrestel moved round the entire company, exchanging a few words with everyone present. Maggie found him a delightful man when he spoke to her. But she was thrilled, when she met Bevin, that he too was a charming man.

After a while Forrestel and Schuh retreated into an inner sanctum to be by themselves. And during their absence the reception continued happily on.

They all waved as the American aeroplane sped down the runway, and then took off. They'd been lucky with the weather, Howard thought. It had been dry for the arrival and departure, but had lashed down during the reception. He offered up a silent prayer of thanks.

'I'm relieved that's over,' he said to Maggie. 'The whole thing has been quite a strain.'

'Must have been a success. The Secretary stayed almost an hour longer than he was supposed to.'

'He certainly seemed to enjoy himself.'

The plane banked, turning in the direction of Holland and The Hague, rapidly gaining height as it disappeared off into the distance.

Schuh came striding across. 'Well done, Howard. Well done. It couldn't have gone better.'

'Thank you, sir.'

'And you, Mrs Ramsay. Thank you.'

'My pleasure, sir.'

'Lots and lots of photographers and the like. A great many pictures taken, eh?'

'A great many,' Howard agreed.

Schuh rubbed his hands together. 'Mrs Schuh and myself are about to start back for Glasgow. But you and your team are remaining on, I understand.'

'I considered that necessary, sir. But we'll be in the consulate at the usual time.'

Schuh held up a hand. 'Won't hear of it. Take things easy and don't come in till the afternoon. You've all earned it.'

'Thank you, sir,' Howard and Maggie said in unison.

Schuh playfully punched Howard on the arm. 'Yup, went extremely well. A feather in your cap, Howard. A feather in your cap.'

426

Fiona and Cathy McColl came over, and the Consul-General thanked and praised them as well, declaring their efforts to have been A1, OK.

'I'm shattered,' said Fiona, slumping where she stood after Schuh had left them.

'Me too,' added Cathy.

'The Consul-General said his thanks, and now I want to say mine. The three of you were marvellous,' Howard told them.

He smiled at each in turn. It might have been her imagination but Maggie was certain he smiled at her the longest.

'However, I'm afraid it isn't over yet. There's still work to be done as you know.'

Cathy giggled. 'Wait till you get the bar bill. It's astronomical!'

'Those media people were quite disgusting,' Maggie stated.

'You should see the shambles they left behind. That's going to cost,' Fiona said.

'Bad eh?' Howard queried.

'The manager took me aside after they'd gone. According to him the carpet in that room has been ruined by spillages and ground-out cigarettes.'

Howard pulled a face. 'Maybe it'll clean.'

They headed for their car, many of the other official cars having already left. Others were in the process of doing so. Once in the car they returned to the hotel.

Maggie had brought a new nightgown with her for the occasion. It was a flimsy number she'd thought a man would find highly sexy. Having removed her make-up, washed and cleaned her teeth she now put it on.

The four of them had had a wonderful dinner together that Howard had said they more than deserved.

On one hand the meal had been extremely enjoyable, on the other difficult. And the reason for this was Howard. There was a point where she'd found herself laughing far too shrilly, and promptly shut up.

She dabbed on perfume, then dabbed on some more. What

to do now? Stay up or go to bed? Lie on the bed and read a magazine, she decided.

He hadn't said he was coming, he hadn't even hinted he might. But she knew he was.

Then she had a terrible thought. What if he lost his nerve and didn't come? That would be awful. No, worse than that – a disaster.

She bit a thumb nail and worried about that possibility. If he didn't put in an appearance would she have the nerve to get dressed again and go to him?

It would be quite out of character for her to take the lead. It wasn't that she was shy, far from it. It was simply that in her world women just didn't do things like that.

There again, she'd gone to Nevil in Spain. But that had been totally different. He'd been wounded and they were engaged.

Minutes later she tossed aside the magazine she'd been trying to read, unable to concentrate on it. She'd read one paragraph four times and still hadn't taken in what it said. All she could see and think of was Howard.

She sat bolt upright when there was a tap on the door. 'Come in!' she called out.

It was Howard, as she'd known it would be. He closed the door behind him, then slowly crossed to the end of the bed to stare at her.

'Hello,' he said.

'Hello.'

'I, eh . . .'

He was dreadfully nervous, she realized, as she was herself.

'I, eh . . .' he repeated.

'I'm glad you came,' she said softly.

He brightened. 'Are you?'

'Yes.'

What a silly, childish conversation they were having, she thought. But in a way that was right. It would have been completely wrong if he'd been or attempted to be a smooth seducer.

He pointed at the bed. 'May I sit down?'

'Please do.'

When he was sitting on the end of the bed, he smiled, and so did she. 'That's a beautiful night-gown.'

'Thank you.'

'Yes, very beautiful.'

He reached out and placed a hand over hers. 'I love you, Maggie. You know that, don't you?'

She nodded.

'I fell in love with you in Spain. And have continued to do so ever since.'

'And I fell in love with you there as well. I couldn't tell you because of Nevil, but I did.'

'Oh, Maggie!' he whispered.

It was so amazingly good to be alone in his company and hear him declare his feelings for her. She was brimming over with love and happiness.

He pulled her to him, and put his arms round her. She closed her eyes as their mouths met.

He sighed with pleasure when the kiss was over.

Maggie ran a hand over one cheek, brought it down to his chin, then ran it up the other.

'I've dreamed of this moment a million times,' he said. 'And I'm somewhat stunned that the dream has become reality. I can't even begin to tell you what you mean to me. Simply everything.'

'Everything?' she queried.

'*Everything*. I swear it.'

She laughed with joy, and nuzzled him.

He took her face in his hands and kissed her passionately.

'Why don't you lock the door and come to bed,' she suggested when, panting, they broke for air.

They lay together, entangled in one another's limbs, stroking each other sensuously.

'From the moment you reappeared back in my life this was inevitable,' Maggie said.

'No regrets then?'

'None whatsoever. You?'

'The only regret I've got is that we can't stay in this room forever.'

She smiled. 'You'd soon tire of me if we tried that.'

'Never!'

All of a sudden his brow furrowed slightly. 'Life's been empty for so long, Maggie. I never thought I'd see you again. As far as I was concerned our paths had briefly crossed and that was that. When I fled the Hotel Caleta Palace the day Nevil was killed I believed you'd gone out of my life forever. And now here we are, you and I. Lovers.'

'Can't life be strange and full of surprises.'

'Strange, full of surprises and fabulous!' he smiled.

'Oh, Howard!' she said, as he began making love to her again.

Maggie was in the consulate basement searching out a file she needed when she was suddenly caught round the waist.

'Got you!' Howard said, and drew her to him.

'Not in here!' she protested when she realized he was going to kiss her.

'There's no-one else about. I've checked.'

'But . . .'

Her words were stifled as his lips met hers. The kiss was passionate, urgent, yet tender at the same time.

'God!' he breathed when it was over.

'Let me go now!' she ordered him, which he did reluctantly.

'When can I see you again?' he asked.

'It's difficult.'

'Why don't you phone Andy and tell him you're working late tonight, and we can go to my place?' The consulate had paid for a phone to be installed in Maggie's house shortly after she'd begun work there. This was standard practice, for their mutual benefit, with all new employees who didn't already have one.

It was almost a week since Prestwick, and they hadn't been alone together since.

'I'm desperate for you,' Howard pleaded.

And she for him. 'I've never worked late before. Never had to.'

'So tonight you start. Andy will never know you're lying. Say the extra money will come in handy.'

'But there won't be any money!'

'If you need to prove the extra to him I'll give it to you.'

She arched an eyebrow. 'You know what that would make me, don't you?'

He laughed. 'Don't be ridiculous! It wouldn't make you that at all. Will you ring?'

How could she refuse when she wanted it just as much as he. 'I'll ring,' she agreed.

Maggie gazed along the length of Clairmont Gardens which was bathed in soft yellow gaslight. The pavement and gutters were scrupulously clean, a complete contrast to her own street forever strewn with rubbish.

They got out of the car and she waited while Howard locked it. A well-dressed, well-cared-for couple strolled by. The man was wearing a smart coat boasting an Astrakhan collar, the woman with a silver fox stole round her neck.

Maggie thought about the people who lived in her street and smiled. You didn't see many of them with an Astrakhan collar or silver fox stole. An old cloth cap and moth-eaten feather boa was more usual.

'Up here,' said Howard, taking her by the arm.

The handsome front door was painted maroon and had gleaming brass fittings. The fancy wrought-iron railings guarding the short flight of stone steps they'd just climbed were the same maroon colour.

Howard opened the door. Then he stood aside, ushering her in.

'How many of you live here?' she asked, stepping inside.

'There are four apartments, mine on the left here. My next-door neighbour is a university lecturer and his wife, while there's a veterinary surgeon and his family upstairs, with a bachelor like myself facing them.'

The carpet in the hallway was plain and deep pile. A small occasional table stood with an ornate lamp on it. There was some mail neatly laid out beside the lamp.

Howard stopped to go through the mail, pocketing one letter which was for him. 'From a friend in the States,' he explained to Maggie as he opened the door to his apartment.

The breath caught in Maggie's throat when he snapped on the light.

'Shall we have a drink?' Howard suggested, taking her coat from her.

'Please. And then I'd like you to show me around.'

'Of course.'

'It's very grand,' she commented as he hung her coat in a cupboard.

'All our apartments have to be, as they're used for entertaining from time to time. Uncle Sam has to be seen at his best. It would hardly do for the rest of the world to think of us as a bunch of cheapskates!'

'I see what you mean,' she replied.

He stared at her. 'It's good to have you here, Maggie.'

'And it's good to be here.'

He kissed her, a long lingering kiss that was sheer bliss for both of them.

'Drink,' she whispered afterwards.

'Drink,' he nodded.

The room he took her into was large and high-ceilinged. The furnishings were of the finest quality. Antiques were everywhere, and there were a number of gilt-framed paintings on the walls.

'Whisky, gin or brandy?' Howard asked.

'Whisky, please.'

He lifted a crystal decanter and poured her a liberal measure into a matching crystal glass. 'Single malt,' he said, handing it to her.

'I know it's sacrilege, but can I have some water?'

'Sure.'

He strode from the room, and she gazed about her. She couldn't help comparing this room with the one in which she and her family lived. The difference was so vast it made her laugh.

'What's funny?' Howard queried, re-entering the room.

She told him as he added water to her malt.

'Yes, I must say it was quite a shock to find you both in that sort of poverty,' he admitted frankly.

'Not pleasant,' she murmured. 'But let's look on the bright side. With my new job at the consulate I'm hoping we can move into something bigger soon and in a better area.'

Howard didn't reply.

'What size is this apartment?' Maggie enquired.

'Two receptions, a kitchen, a toilet and two *en suite* bedrooms. Being on the ground floor I also have a small yard at the rear which is exclusively mine.'

Two *en suite* bedrooms! Maggie thought enviously. Even the private toilet he mentioned was more than they had. One thing was certain, when they moved it would be to a house with its own toilet. She was determined about that.

'I'll give you the tour,' Howard said.

He led her to a kitchen which was square-shaped and decked out with every possible amenity and appliance.

'Do you cook yourself?' she asked.

'Yeah. I'm pretty fair at Italian. Do you like Italian?'

'I've only ever had spaghetti bolognese.'

'Then I'll have to educate you. I also do pretty mean steaks. You'll have to sample one of those as well.'

'Fillet or sirloin?'

'I do both. But my speciality are T-bones. I can get T-bones through our friend General Ekstrom any time I want.'

Maggie opened the oven door and peered inside. Her second-hand stove and range were dinosaurs by comparison.

'What's that?' she enquired, pointing.

'Electric skillet,' he explained.

She next went to the refrigerator, an American make, that was positively colossal. Beside it was a chest freezer.

She exclaimed softly, gazing into the fridge's interior which was done out in a pastel shade. Included among the many items the fridge contained were half-a-dozen cartons of fresh orange juice, something you never saw in the Glasgow shops.

'I like orange juice,' Howard said, when she mentioned the cartons.

'So it appears.'

'We get whatever we want through our own sources. I have a delivery made once a week that takes care of my needs.'

From the kitchen they progressed to a superbly appointed guest bedroom. The bathroom leading off it had a bath, separate shower unit, bidet and washbasin with wall mirror above. All the taps were gold-plated.

'Central heating throughout, of course,' he said when she placed a hand on a radiator that was warm.

'Of course,' she smiled mockingly in reply.

'And now the holy of holies. My bedroom.'

The bed was a four-poster and a genuine antique. Sixteenth-century Flemish, Howard informed her when she asked him about it.

On the bedside table was a silver-framed photograph of an older couple smiling into the camera. 'Your parents?' Maggie asked, picking it up.

'Yeah. How did you know?'

'You look like them. Your mother in particular.'

As she continued staring at the photograph she became suddenly acutely aware of his breath on her neck. Her skin there, and elsewhere, burst out in tingling gooseflesh.

'How long have we got?' he murmured.

'A couple of hours. I want to say goodnight to Liss.'

'Not long. We'd better not waste any of it.'

They didn't.

'That's the twentieth time,' Maggie sighed, stretching languorously between silken baby blue sheets.

Howard heaved himself on to an elbow to gaze at her. 'You mean you've been counting?'

'I have. That's the twentieth time we've made love together. And I'm happy to report that the twentieth time was every bit as delightful and satisfying as the first.'

He laughed. 'You're crazy. And I'm crazy about you.'

Maggie had been coming to Howard's apartment on a

weekly, occasionally twice-weekly, basis. Her excuse to Andy was always the same, that she was working late, and he never questioned her.

Howard sat up and reached for his cigarettes and Zippo lighter. 'I've got news,' he announced.

'Which is?'

'I'm going to London for a month. Schuh wants me to do some special duty there.'

'A month,' she repeated dully. A whole month without seeing or going to bed with Howard. The prospect was grim.

'The C.-G. only told me this morning. And before you ask, I can't explain what it's all about. I'm to travel down on Sunday.'

Maggie was well aware that there were matters handled at the consulate to which only the Americans were party. The local employees were most definitely excluded.

'I'm sorry,' he said.

'It's not your fault.'

'No, part of the job, I'm afraid.'

He drew on his cigarette, and blew out a long thin stream of smoke. 'I wish you could come with me?'

She thought about that, and shook her head. 'Impossible for all sorts of reasons. I wish it was otherwise, but it's not.'

'Oh well!' he shrugged. 'A month will soon fly by.'

He couldn't have been more wrong.

Eight days to go, Maggie thought, chewing the end of her pencil. Eight days and then Howard would be back again. On the pad in front of her she began making various calculations. Eight days were a hundred and ninety-two hours, or eleven thousand, five hundred and twenty minutes. Or six hundred and ninety-one thousand, two hundred seconds. Eight days was by far the best, she decided. It sounded shorter.

The past three weeks had been absolutely awful. The first couple of days hadn't been too bad, then the rot had set in. She craved Howard's presence the way a desperate smoker craves a cigarette, or an alcoholic a drink. She wanted to see him, touch him, sleep with him.

She longed for the moment when the two of them would be alone, and they could delight in one another's presence.

Eight days, she repeated mentally to herself. How was she ever going to get through them? She was filled with a terrible anguish that continually gnawed at her insides, and kept her awake at night.

They did manage to speak every so often on the telephone, which was a life-saver. Without that comfort it would have been far worse. Unfortunately their conversations, taking place as they did between embassy and consulate, couldn't be very intimate. Discretion, and coded language, were the twin names of that game.

She threw her pencil down and chewed a thumb instead. This is silly, she admonished herself. You're a grown woman, for God's sake. Act like one.

But no matter how hard she tried she couldn't put him out of her mind. He just wouldn't shift.

'Are you all right?' Fiona Kilgour asked, stopping beside Maggie's desk. 'You look quite odd.'

'Do I?'

'Yes, you do.'

Fiona didn't know about her and Howard. No-one in the consulate did. They'd managed to keep their affair completely secret.

'Well, I do have a bit of a headache,' Maggie lied.

'Have you taken something for it?'

'Not yet. But I will.'

'Perhaps you should go and lie down for half an hour?'

'No, I won't bother, thanks. It's best I try and get on.'

Maggie placed a hand on Fiona's arm. 'I appreciate your concern but I'll be all right. Honestly I will.'

Back to work, Maggie ordered herself to concentrate. Then the telephone rang, and it was Howard. It transpired he too was counting the days.

Maggie pushed her plate away.

'Something wrong with it?' a hostile Andy immediately demanded.

436

'I'm just not hungry, that's all.'

'Are you sure?'

Liss's gaze flicked from side to side, from Andy to Maggie and vice versa, as though she were watching a tennis match.

'Quite sure.'

Andy grunted. 'I do my best, you know. I'm a man, for Christ's sake, not a bloody woman.'

She was finding him irritating, but then that was happening more frequently of late.

'Not a bloody woman,' he repeated.

'The mince was fine,' she said.

'And what about the mashed potato?'

He might say he wasn't a bloody woman but he was rapidly beginning to sound like one – and a nagging one at that. 'It was a little lumpy.'

He threw down his knife and fork. 'Some people are never satisfied no matter what you do. The mince might possibly be slightly undercooked, but the potato most certainly isn't lumpy. I put nearly a full bottle of milk in, so it can't be!'

He could have put an entire crate in, it was still lumpy, she told herself.

'And butter,' he added. 'I didn't forget that. Do you find the potato lumpy, princess?'

'Don't involve the child,' Maggie snapped.

'I'm only asking for her opinion. What's wrong with that?'

'Just don't involve her, that's all.'

'Why? Scared she might bear me out?'

Maggie had an almost overwhelming urge to pick up her plate and ram it into his face. 'If you must know, as you persist, the mince *is* undercooked, and not just slightly, but considerably.'

'Ah!' he exclaimed. 'Now the truth.'

'But I kept quiet about it as I was trying to save your feelings.'

He leered at her, his expression twisted and ugly. 'That's a laugh! You were being patronizing, then just couldn't keep it up and had to accuse the potato of being lumpy. Which it isn't!'

'I was not patronizing you, there was nothing further from

my mind. And I wouldn't have mentioned the potato if you hadn't nagged.'

'Nagged! *Me!*'

'Yes, you!'

He jumped to his feet. 'Now listen to me—'

'Please stop it,' Liss pleaded quietly, tears in her eyes.

'Now, see what you've done!' Andy raged at Maggie.

She bit back her reply. Liss was right, this was rapidly getting out of hand.

'There, there, pet,' said Andy, squatting beside Liss.

'Please don't argue any more, Daddy.'

'I won't. I promise you.'

'So do I,' said Maggie.

'I've got some lovely tinned pineapple for sweet. How do you fancy that?' Andy smiled at Liss.

That cheered her up, and the tears ceased. 'Yes please. Heaps and heaps for me.'

'I'll get it,' said Maggie, rising.

'No, I will. I'm the housewife round here after all,' Andy told her waspishly.

They were growing further and further apart, Maggie thought as she watched Andy dole out the pineapple, which was from one of the consulate's food parcels, which they continued to receive.

Maggie changed the subject, asking Liss what had happened that day at school.

Howard answered her ring. 'I came straight from work, as quickly as I could,' she said.

'Come in.' He closed the front door behind her, then hurried her along the hallway to his apartment. The moment that door was closed he grabbed her and kissed her fiercely. As they kissed their hands were all over one another.

'Been so long. So long,' he murmured, burying his face in her neck.

They were both aflame with desire. She threw back her head as he unbuttoned her blouse, so quickly, and feverishly, he almost ripped it.

438

She closed her eyes when he pulled her bra up, freeing her breasts. His mouth fell on them, kissing them, going from one to the other.

'Oh, Howard! Howard!' she crooned.

He kicked off his shoes, and began slipping out of his jacket. 'Let's go to the bedroom,' he said.

Her coat and blouse dropped away. And then her bra. They were both already half-naked when they reached the bedroom. Seconds later they were completely so.

Howard rolled off Maggie, and gave the deepest sigh imaginable. 'That was simply glorious.'

She agreed.

He sought, and found her hand. 'I love you, Maggie Jordan.'

She smiled at his using her maiden name. 'And I love you, Howard Taft.'

'You were never out of my thoughts night and day while I was away.'

'And it was the same for me.'

She turned over so that she was partially lying on his chest. 'I was quite demented without you.'

'And I without you.'

She caressed that part of him which so recently had been part of her. 'I'm hoping for an encore before I go home.'

'Give me a breather and I'll do my best.'

She smiled again. 'You always do, for which I'm grateful.'

They were silent for a few moments, then he said, 'Maggie, marry me.'

She went very still. 'Say that again?'

'Will you marry me? I'm proposing.'

'But I'm already married.'

'To a man you don't love, and whom you're having to work to support. Leave him, get a divorce and marry me.'

It was as if a doorway had opened, a doorway through which she could glimpse paradise. She found she was holding her breath.

'Well?' he prompted.

'What about Liss?'

439

'I'll treat her as my own. She'd have the very finest of everything, including schooling. I'll love her as if she were my own daughter.'

Leave Andy, get a divorce and marry Howard. Those words throbbed in her brain.

'What could the situation be between my leaving Andy and marrying you?' she queried.

'That is the one fly in the ointment, though one I have a way round.'

Maggie sat up, and so did Howard. 'And that fly is we can't live together before our wedding. Not if I wish to remain with the Diplomatic Corps, that is. They take a very strong view about such matters. Our diplomats have to be squeaky clean, without flaw. Living with someone would most definitely not be tolerated.'

'So what's your solution?'

'I doubt I would be able to find you an apartment quite like this, but I could get you the very best available, and stock it with all the household appliances and gadgets you so admire. You and Liss could live there until your divorce comes through, and the moment it does we would get married. At which point you and Liss would move in here.'

'And when would I see you?' she queried.

'Every single day, I assure you. It would be just as though we were living together, except I would have to sleep here at nights.'

She thought about that. 'But I would need to take Liss to school and pick her up again when it's over. And what about school holidays?'

'That's easy. You could give up your job at the consulate.'

'And live on what?' she demanded.

'Me, of course. You could open a bank account and I would arrange for a sum to be paid into it monthly.'

'Can you afford to do all this?' she asked, frowning.

'I have money of my own, Maggie. More than enough to deal with whatever outgoings are involved.'

'And you're certain that having a relationship with me in these circumstances wouldn't affect your career?'

He shook his head. 'You'll have officially left Andy and be in the process of getting a divorce. And I would make it known, after a suitable time, that I was courting you and that we were planning to marry once you were free. Our Diplomatic Corps wouldn't take exception to that. They could, however, if I moved you in here and lived openly with you.'

'You've really thought this all the way through,' she smiled.

'And have been waiting till the moment was ripe to put it to you,' he replied.

She threw her arms round him, and hugged him tight. 'You're the most gorgeous man alive!'

'Does that mean "yes"?'

'It does.'

He let out a great exhalation of relief. 'I can't tell you how happy that makes me.'

'I think I know,' she whispered, and nibbled his ear.

'When will you tell Andy?'

'Tonight, I suppose. The sooner I get it over and done with the better for all concerned.'

Howard nodded his approval. 'What I suggest is this. Take Liss to school yourself tomorrow, then come to the consulate and explain to Schuh that you've left your husband and because of that have to give him instant notice on account of Liss. He won't be pleased, but will understand.

'I, in the meanwhile, will have been to the bank and withdrawn some cash which I'll give to you for general expenses and in case the hotel wants a deposit.'

'What hotel?' she queried.

'It's going to take a week or two to arrange your apartment, so you'll need someplace to stay in the meantime. Book into whatever hotel you like.'

'That's sheer extravagance!' she protested.

'I think you're worth it.' And with that he pecked her on the nose.

'Do we eat in this hotel?'

'Of course. You can use the restaurant, room service, laundry, bar, hairdresser, whatever!'

441

'I'll be living in the lap of luxury,' she breathed.

'Exactly. That's what I want.'

'I think I'd better go home after seeing Schuh to collect my things and Liss's. That way I can turn up at the hotel with luggage which will look better than if I do it the other way round.'

He pointed a finger at her. 'There's no need to bring too much for either of you. I intend seeing you both get completely new wardrobes.'

The thought of that quite dazzled Maggie. What fun it was going to be kitting herself out anew and doing the same for Liss. What a marvellous new world the pair of them were about to step into.

He smiled at her. 'I think that about covers everything. Any questions?'

'Yes. Is it encore time yet?'

'Let's find out, shall we.'

It was.

Liss sat on Andy's lap gazing spellbound at him as he read her a bedtime story. So magical was his ability to tell a tale you could clearly visualize what he was describing. It was as if the adventures of Peter Pan were taking place in that very room.

Liss's eyes widened at mention of the crocodile.

She bit her lip in concern. Then laughed at Captain Hook's reaction when he first heard, then spotted his old adversary.

'Come on, Peter!' she cried out a little later. And waved her right arm in the motions of sword fighting.

'And that,' said Andy finally, closing the book, 'I think is enough for tonight.'

'Oh Dad!'

'It's late, poppet.'

'But you finished at such an interesting bit.'

'Yes, wasn't it?' he agreed, eyes twinkling.

'You're teasing me.'

'You're quite correct. And I sit rebuked.' With that he bowed his head as though in disgrace.

'Am I forgiven?' he asked in a small voice.

'Of course you are.'

442

'Thank you!' he replied, lifting his head and beaming at her.

'You'll read me some more tomorrow night, won't you?'

He licked a finger, then traced the figure of a cross against his chest. 'Cross my heart and hope to die!'

Liss narrowed her eyes and pretended to glare at him. 'Worse than dying, you'll turn into a horrible slimy worm if you don't.'

Andy exclaimed in mock fright, 'Not a horrible slimy worm?'

'The horriblest and slimiest there's ever been.'

He took a deep breath. 'Well, that's that then. It's Peter Pan again tomorrow night and no mistake.'

They both laughed, while a frozen-faced Maggie watched on.

'You're the most wonderful daddy in the whole wide world,' Liss told him.

'And you're the most wonderful daughter. So wonderful, in fact, you should be in a fairy story yourself.'

'Would there be Red Indians and pirates in it?'

'There could be whatever you like, darling.'

Whatever you like, Maggie thought dully. A phrase Howard had used to her earlier when they were in bed together.

'Will you make up a story with me in it, Dad?' Liss pleaded.

'Oh, I don't know about that.'

'Please!'

'With Red Indians?'

She nodded eagerly.

'And pirates?'

She nodded again.

He sighed thoughtfully. He allowed a hiatus of a few seconds to develop, then said, 'All right, I'll try.'

Liss squealed with delight. 'Thank you, Daddy. Thank you!'

'I've never made up a story before so don't expect too much,' he cautioned her.

'But you will make one up?'

'I shall certainly try.'

Her eyes shone as she gazed at him. Then she turned to

look at Maggie, showing Maggie what was in those eyes.

'Bed now,' said Andy, laying the book on the floor.

'You'll tuck me in?'

'I'll tuck you in.'

When he'd done that he kissed her on the forehead and told her to get some good sleep. He'd see her in the morning. After which it was Maggie's turn.

'Good night, darling,' Maggie said, kissing Liss.

'Good night, Mummy. Isn't it exciting that Daddy's going to try and make up a story with me in it?'

'Very.'

'I can't wait to hear it. Do you think it'll take him long?'

'I shouldn't expect too long. Now you close your eyes, you've school in the morning.'

'Is it all right if I tell my teacher?'

'Of course. She'll be interested to hear.'

Smiling, Liss shut her eyes and turned her face to the pillow.

'I'm going to the toilet,' Andy announced, scooping up the evening paper.

Maggie returned to her chair and sat down again. There was a lump in her throat that seemed the size of a football. She felt like Judas Iscariot.

When Andy got back from the toilet, Liss was fast asleep.

'How was your day then?' he asked, sinking into the chair facing Maggie.

The moment she'd been dreading since leaving Howard's apartment had finally arrived.

'Enter!' Howard called out when there was a knock on his office door. It was Maggie.

He immediately leapt to his feet. 'I've got that money for you. Have you spoken to the C.-G. yet?'

She shook her head.

'He's tied up? Or you've come to see me first?'

She crossed over to him, her face taut and strained, her colour pale. 'We have to talk,' she said.

He caught her sombre mood, and went very still. 'About what?'

'It isn't going to work, Howard. I'm sorry.'

'But I love you and you said you love me.'

'I do. And always will. But it still won't work.' Tears welled in her eyes.

'Wait a minute,' he murmured. He went to the door and locked it, ensuring there wouldn't be any intrusions. When he returned to her she collapsed into his arms.

'I was going to tell Andy last night, but couldn't.'

He held her tight, her body vibrating in his arms. She was racked with emotion.

'Why not?'

'Liss. It would break her heart to be parted from Andy. And break his to be parted from her.'

'They'd get over it . . .'

'No!' Maggie interrupted. 'You don't understand. Those two are so close I just couldn't hurt either of them that much, particularly Liss. God alone knows what consequences it would have on her if I took her away.'

Howard thought about that. And all the while despair, and panic, grew keener inside him. 'You could always leave Liss with Andy. I'm sure we could come to some arrangement.'

She looked into his face, and smiled thinly. 'I can't give up my daughter, Howard, not in a million years. She's my own flesh and blood.'

'We'll have to think about this, discuss it at length. Perhaps with a little time . . .'

'I'll never change my mind,' she interjected. 'I won't give up Liss. Nor can I cause her the terrible hurt of being parted from her father whom she absolutely worships.'

Howard stared grimly at Maggie.

She went on. 'Furthermore if I did part them I know only too well what the result would be. That wrong would come between you and I, would eventually, and inevitably, sour our relationship.'

'You can't be sure about that!'

'Oh, but I am.'

'Andy would have full access to Liss. We would never deny him that.'

'And what happens when you're posted elsewhere? What then? He can't exactly go to Brazil, or the North Pole or Outer Mongolia or wherever we currently are to see her for the day. So he would have access, but be unable to use it.'

'He could visit during school holidays. I could help out financially.'

Maggie shook her head. 'That's not a solution, Howard. The pair of them seeing one another intermittently would only be aggravating an open wound. And I won't do that.'

He released her, went to the window and stared out. He'd arrived at work earlier feeling on top of the world, with everything now to look forward to. His joy had turned to ashes.

'I am sorry. You know that,' she whispered.

'You say you can't hurt them, but what about me? What do you think you're doing to me?'

She hung her head.

'You won't break their hearts, but you will mine.'

'It's the last thing I want to do.'

'But you will!'

'She's my daughter, Howard, please try and understand that. If you had been there last night and witnessed the pair of them together. When I opened my mouth to tell Andy the words simply wouldn't come out.'

'It's started to rain,' he stated quietly.

'You and I are both losers in this, Howard. I want to marry you, I want to with all my heart and soul. Nothing would make me happier than to spend the rest of my life with you as your wife. But I know now the price would be too high.'

'So that's that then,' he said.

'If you like we'll still go on seeing one another.'

'Our few hours a week?' he replied bitterly.

'A few hours are better than none at all.'

'But a poor consolation compared to what we might have had.'

'I am sorry,' she repeated yet again. 'But I know, without a shadow of a doubt, however much I might want it otherwise, that what I'm doing is right.'

'A few hours a week until, as you said, I'm posted on. Then we won't even have that.'

'No,' she mumbled, and shook all over.

An agonized silence fell between them during which the only sound to be heard was the patter of rain against the window.

Maggie had nothing further to say, and it seemed neither did Howard. She left his office, going straight to the lavatory where she washed away all the obvious traces of her crying.

When she'd gone Howard did something he'd normally never dream of doing at that time of the morning. He locked the door again, and opened his drinks cabinet.

CHAPTER ELEVEN

'I tell you she's losing too much weight!' Andy declared to Maggie. The pair of them were at home, sitting in front of the fireplace. Maggie had just come through from Liss's bedroom to say that Liss was fast asleep.

Their new house, which they'd moved into five months previously, was situated in Scotstoun. It was a huge improvement on the house they'd left in Cowcaddens. This house had two bedrooms, a kitchen, combined inside toilet and bathroom.

'I know she's losing weight but it's her age. She's growing,' Maggie replied.

'That's true,' he conceded. 'But she's getting as thin as a rake.'

'I was the same at her age. It's normal.'

He shook his head. 'I don't like it. It worries me. And what about these pains she gets?'

'Growing pains,' Maggie countered. 'They're normal as well. You're fussing like an old woman.'

His face clouded. 'I'm nothing of the sort. I'm just being a concerned parent. There's nothing wrong with that.'

'But you can be over-concerned.'

'Or not concerned enough!' he snapped.

Her lips thinned. 'That's not true and you know it, Andy Ramsay. I love Liss dearly. I simply don't go overboard with my love the way you do.'

'I do nothing of the sort!'

She didn't reply to that.

He lit a cigarette. 'You took in that tartan skirt of hers the other day, didn't you?'

'You saw me do it.'

'That's the second time you've had to take it in.'

'True enough. But as I said, that's because she's shooting up. She'll start filling out again when she's stopped growing, you'll see.'

Andy glowered into the fire. He remained unconvinced.

Maggie knew Andy too well to think he'd drop this. Once he got a bee in his bonnet, particularly where Liss was concerned, he'd worry at it till he succeeded in getting what he was after.

She sighed. 'In my opinion we're wasting the man's time. But still, to keep you happy, and be on the safe side, we can take her to the doctor's tomorrow night.'

Andy's glower vanished. 'I'd feel a lot better if we did. It worries me sick seeing her so thin, and getting thinner all the while. It's not as if she isn't fed well enough. Though it has to be said, she doesn't have much of an appetite.'

'Used to have, but not recently,' Maggie nodded. 'I've put that down to the growing thing as well. It's a stage she's going through. I'm sure the next stage will be her eating like a horse. I remember my mother mentioning that about my sister Pet. One moment she wouldn't eat, the next she was devouring everything in sight.'

Maggie laughed. 'I remember that especially because of devour, the word my mother used. Devourrr, she said. Rolling the r at the end. She made it sound like some wild beast devouring its prey.'

'So, we'll go to the doctor's tomorrow night then?'

'Right after I get in from work. That all right?'

'Fine,' Andy answered. 'You can never be too careful, that's my motto.'

Certainly where Liss was concerned, Maggie thought. Still, she'd much rather have Andy an over-concerned, over-protective father than one who didn't care at all.

Picking up a thriller she'd borrowed from Fiona Kilgour she started in on chapter four. Fiona had recommended it as a marvellous read, and so far she had to agree.

'Well, Liss, what do you think of all this?' Doctor McCrindle asked, having listened to what Andy and Maggie had had to say.

She wriggled in her chair, and smiled shyly at him. 'I don't know, doctor.'

'Mummy tells me you haven't much of an appetite?'

She shook her head.

'Why's that, I wonder?'

She shrugged.

'Are you just temporarily off your food?'

She shrugged again.

'What about if I gave you a big bowl of ice-cream. Would you eat that?'

She nodded vigorously. And the three adults laughed.

'She loves ice-cream,' Andy said.

'I'm quite partial to it myself,' McCrindle confessed, rising and coming round from behind his desk.

'My but you're a bonny girl. Would you like to sit up on my couch for me?' To Maggie and Andy he said, 'I think it best I give her a thorough examination and sounding.'

Maggie helped Liss up on to the couch where she sat with her legs dangling.

McCrindle took her temperature. Then he peered into her mouth and down both ears.

'Now if you'll just slip off that jumper and open your shirt, please,' he smiled.

An anxious Andy watched on.

'And can you pull your vest up,' McCrindle requested, warming the end of his stethoscope.

He sounded Liss's chest and back, but when he straightened up his brow was furrowed.

'She can get dressed again, Mrs Ramsay,' he said, and returned to sit at his desk.

'There, that wasn't too bad, was it?' Maggie murmured to Liss.

'No.'

'Quite fun really.'

Outside in the waiting-room someone coughed, a deep hacking cough followed by the wheezy, rattling sound of drawing in much-needed breath.

'A lot of bad colds around at the moment,' Andy commented, making conversation.

'And flu,' McCrindle told him, writing on Liss's notes.

'So what's the verdict?' Andy asked as soon as Maggie and Liss had resumed their seats.

McCrindle laid his pen down, and focused on Andy. 'I'd like her to go and have an X-ray. I'll write to the Western Infirmary tonight, and they'll make you an appointment. It'll be for during the day. I take it that won't be a problem?' He knew that Maggie worked and Andy didn't.

'Fine. We'll just have to keep Liss off school that day,' Andy replied.

'An X-ray,' Maggie said softly.

'What's wrong with her?' Andy blurted out.

'That's what we're trying to discover, Mr Ramsay,' McCrindle replied soothingly. 'I promised you a thorough going over, and that's what I'm doing. All right?'

'Nothing to worry about, though?' Andy said hopefully.

'Having an X-ray is common practice nowadays. It just gives us a clearer picture of what's going on inside,' McCrindle prevaricated.

Rising again, he showed them to the door.

Howard bumped into Maggie in one of the third-floor corridors. 'Hello,' he smiled, glancing casually round to see if they were in any danger of being overheard. They weren't.

'How about coming over to the apartment tonight?' he asked in a whisper.

Maggie shook her head. 'I can't. Must get straight home. It's today that Liss is having her X-ray,' she whispered in reply.

'Oh, of course!' He'd forgotten that.

'Naturally I can't wait to hear what was said and done.'

'Naturally. I quite understand.'

'Another night then?'

'Whenever you can make it, Maggie.'

They stared into one another's eyes, each wanting to kiss the other, but not daring to do so.

'See you,' Maggie said, and continued on her way.

Howard stared after her till she turned a corner and was lost to sight. Then, with a soft sigh, he continued along the corridor.

'So, how did it go?' Maggie demanded, bursting into the house.

Andy was cooking their evening meal. 'Very well,' he replied. 'Didn't it, Liss?'

Liss, playing with a battered doll's house that Andy had acquired from a church jumble sale, nodded.

'We weren't kept waiting too long either. Which can happen,' Andy added.

Maggie tossed her coat over the back of a chair. 'You mean they only took the X-ray and that was it?'

'They took several actually. But as you say, that was it.'

'Nothing was said? No result?'

'Nope,' replied Andy, *en route* to the sink where he was going to drain the sprouts.

'We met a nice nurse there,' Liss said.

'Nurse Moore. She and Liss got on like a house on fire,' Andy elaborated.

'So what happens now?'

'The hospital send the X-rays to Doctor McCrindle. And then he discusses them with us.'

Andy concentrated on what he was doing for several seconds, then went on in a light tone of voice. 'It was all very jolly actually. They gave the impression that the X-rays were being done simply as a matter of course. The last thing they appeared to be was worried.'

'And nothing was said?'

'Nothing,' Andy repeated.

'They put me on a weighing machine,' Liss informed Maggie.

'And measured your height,' Andy added.

'Nurse Moore said I was tall for my age. And thought I was going to grow into a very elegant young lady.'

'Well then, seems you two had a good time.'

'We did,' Andy smiled.

'I knew it was just a stage she was going through,' Maggie said with relief. 'And those pains are simply growing pains, nothing more.'

'They gave us tea and biscuits, didn't they, Daddy!'

'They did indeed, petal. And *chocolate* biscuits too. A real treat.'

Maggie went to Liss and cuddled her. 'Can I join in this game?' she asked.

'If you do it'll have to be after tea. I'm just about to serve up,' Andy announced.

During tea Maggie heard all about Nurse Moore, who came over as something of a cross between Florence Nightingale and an angel descended.

Liss's face was screwed up as the syringe slowly filled with the blood Doctor McCrindle was taking from her arm. Maggie was standing beside Liss, steadying her, Andy sitting half a dozen feet away biting a nail.

When McCrindle had the amount he required he slid the needle free and asked Liss to place the tip of a finger over the point of penetration, where a small blob of blood was already in evidence.

'Brave girl,' he congratulated her, laying the syringe aside.

Maggie smoothed Liss's brow, which was damp with cold sweat. 'All over and finished with,' Maggie crooned.

'You can remove your finger now,' McCrindle said. And he placed a strip of Elastoplast over the blood blob when she did.

'Didn't really hurt, did it?' he smiled.

Liss shook her head.

He'd been very gentle and professional, Maggie thought. Nor could he have been more sympathetic with Liss.

McCrindle took the syringe across to a table where he had laid out several small bottles of varying sizes. These he proceeded to fill with blood from the syringe.

Andy squatted beside Liss. 'How do you feel, lass?'

'All right, Daddy.'

'That was certainly a new experience for you,' he said, making something of a joke of it.

'And now the reward,' stated McCrindle, coming back to his desk and opening a drawer. 'A peppermint or toffee?'

'Peppermint, please,' Liss replied quickly.

McCrindle offered her an open tin, and she selected one which she promptly popped into her mouth.

'Have another for your pocket,' McCrindle said quietly and conspiratorially to her.

Liss didn't need to be told twice. A second peppermint vanished into her cardigan pocket. She pulled down the left sleeve, along with the sleeve of her shirt, and covered the Elastoplast.

'Do you think you could wait outside for a few minutes while I speak to your mummy and daddy,' McCrindle smiled at Liss. 'She'll be safe enough,' he added to Maggie.

McCrindle personally escorted Liss out to the waiting-room and made sure she knew where the children's books and comics were before returning to Andy and Maggie.

'As I mentioned to you on the telephone when I rang I've received the X-rays and radiologist's report,' he said, sitting again behind his desk.

Andy and Maggie leaned forward expectantly.

'We now know what's wrong with Liss. The reason I wanted her to have the X-rays was because I detected an irregular heartbeat. The X-rays have shown us the cause of that irregularity.'

He'd been looking at the buff coloured file in front of him when he'd said that. He now looked directly at them.

'It's bad news, I'm afraid. Liss has a congenital abnormality of the aorta, which is the major vessel leaving the heart.'

Andy swallowed, and swallowed again. 'How bad is that, doctor?'

'It's very serious, Mr Ramsay. Extremely so.'

Maggie felt herself go all strange. It was as if she had suddenly, somehow, stepped outside her body.

'But they can operate?' Andy queried. 'I mean, they can fix it?'

'There's no operation unfortunately,' McCrindle replied, his gaze unwavering.

'Please be specific. Spell it out for us,' a female voice ordered. Maggie realized with surprise it was her own. She hadn't been aware of speaking.

'The condition is inoperable. It's only a matter of time.'

Andy seemed to shrink in on himself. His expression was a combination of horror and disbelief.

'I truly am sorry,' McCrindle said softly, and dropped his eyes.

'No,' croaked Andy, shaking his head. 'You're wrong. Have to be!'

'You're perfectly entitled to seek a second opinion, Mr Ramsay.'

'I will. You're bloody right I will!'

Andy laughed, a hysterical laugh that had the tinge of a cackle to it. 'It's nonsense – preposterous – I've never heard the like. Not Liss. Not our Liss!'

Maggie, still with the out of the body sensation, glanced down to see herself wringing her hands. Her mind had gone numb, and icy cold. 'How much time?' she asked.

'That I can't say, Mrs Ramsay. The end could come tomorrow, next month, next year . . .' He trailed off, and shrugged. 'I wish I could be more specific, but I can't.'

Liss, her daughter, her darling Liss was going to die. What had she done, what crime had she committed, for death to constantly dog her heel, Maggie wondered? First her family and friends at Heymouth, then Nevil and the others in Spain, now this.

'I don't accept your diagnosis. I simply don't accept it,' Andy spluttered.

'As I stated, you do have the prerogative of a second opinion,' McCrindle replied.

Maggie found herself drifting back into her body again, the queerest of sensations. 'What about Liss, will the physical symptoms get worse?' she asked.

'Yes,' McCrindle nodded. 'She'll probably continue to lose weight, while her pains will increase in their intensity, though for that I can prescribe pain killers. There will also be other symptoms which will manifest themselves.'

'Will she have to go into hospital?' Maggie demanded.

'That depends. I think it best we play that one by ear.'

Andy jumped to his feet. 'Come on, Maggie. I'm not staying here a moment longer. We're going.'

'Mr Ramsay!' McCrindle said sharply, his voice ringing with authority. 'Please remain here until you've composed yourself. Don't forget Liss is outside waiting for you.'

'He's right,' Maggie said. 'We'll have to calm down before we go out there.'

Despite his distress and agitation Andy could see the sense in that.

'Would either of you like a glass of water?' McCrindle enquired.

Andy declined, Maggie agreed. McCrindle went and got it for her. 'I can give you a sedative to go with that if you want?'

She seriously considered the sedative, but in the end refused. As did Andy.

'I never expected anything like this. I was convinced she was just going through a stage,' Maggie said in a hollow voice.

Andy sucked in a deep breath. 'Well, I'm composed now. What about you, Maggie?'

'A few minutes more,' she answered. If she stood up now she was certain she'd keel over.

'Do you wish me to arrange the second opinion for you?' McCrindle asked.

Andy stabbed a finger at him. 'You do that, McCrindle. But listen to me, I want Liss to be seen by the best there is. None of your GPs or whatever, I want the top heart man in Glasgow.'

'That's perfectly understandable, Mr Ramsay. Leave the matter with me. I'll arrange for your consultation to take place as soon as possible.'

'Congenital abnormality of the heart,' Maggie repeated with a frown.

'Congenital abnormality of the aorta,' McCrindle corrected her.

Maggie rose to her feet. She felt wobbly, but able to leave now. 'Ready,' she said to Andy.

She forced herself to relax and managed to raise a weak smile. She quietly told Andy to do the same as they started for the waiting-room.

She said goodbye to McCrindle, but not thank you. What could you say after the bombshell he'd dropped?

Andy didn't say anything at all.

Maggie woke out of a troubled sleep to discover Andy was no longer by her side. They'd gone to bed late but still it had been hours before she'd finally dropped off. Andy's place when she felt it was cold. He'd been out of bed a while.

She got out herself, and slipped on her dressing-gown. If he'd made some tea and it was still warm she'd have a cup. She doubted very much there would be any more sleep for her that night.

She heard him as soon as she stepped into the hallway. He was in the kitchen, crying his eyes out.

It wasn't a loud sound, more the contained, intense sobbing of a man who was suffering profoundly.

She put a hand to her mouth, and wondered whether or not to go to him? She glided noiselessly to the kitchen door, which was partially ajar, and stopped outside it.

She glanced through the space between the door and its frame. A full moon illuminated the scene. He was sitting hunched forward, with his head in his hands.

He suddenly twisted violently to one side, and curled into the foetal position. She momentarily glimpsed his face, ravaged with pain and terrible anguish.

Turning round, she went back up the hallway as silently as she'd come down it. She checked Liss's bedroom was closed before returning to her own.

Having thought about it she'd decided he wouldn't thank her for intruding – not when he was in that sort of state.

When, much later, he reappeared in their bedroom she pretended to be asleep and maintained that pretence until it was time to get up.

★

'What!' Howard exclaimed, appalled. He and Maggie were in an out-of-the-way pub they occasionally used for a rendezvous. She had asked him to join her there for their lunchbreak, and had just told him about Liss.

'We're hoping, praying, that the second opinion will contradict Doctor McCrindle's diagnosis.'

'And who are you going to for this second opinion?'

'Andy's instructed him to get the best heart man in Glasgow.'

Howard nodded his approval. 'You must get the best, anyone or anything you need. I'll help out.'

She touched his hand in gratitude. 'That's kind of you, Howard, thank you. I've no idea yet what sort of outgoings are going to be involved, if any. But if I need help I'll come to you.'

'Christ!' Howard breathed. This was a shock indeed and so completely unexpected. He'd wondered why Maggie had looked so haggard when she'd come to work that morning. Now he knew.

'We're continuing as usual for the time being. At least until we've seen the second doctor,' she explained.

'And when will that be?'

'As soon as possible, McCrindle said.'

Maggie stared into her soft drink. Although it was a beautiful day outside she felt dreadfully cold. Lack of sleep was the obvious explanation, she thought.

She brushed away several wisps of stray hair. Please God let McCrindle be wrong, she silently prayed. It was a prayer she'd offered up frequently since leaving McCrindle's surgery.

'How's Andy taking it?' Howard asked.

Her grim expression intensified as she told him what she'd witnessed the previous night.

'Poor guy,' Howard commiserated.

Maggie pushed her drink away. She didn't want any more.

'Did McCrindle say how long Liss would have? If he's right, that is.'

'Years if we're lucky. Tomorrow if we're not. It's one of

458

those things, you just never know. All you can be certain of is that the condition is terminal.'

Tears bubbled into her eyes. 'Oh Howard!' she softly choked.

He tugged out his breast pocket handkerchief and offered it to her. 'Use that,' he said, as she started scrabbling in her handbag looking for one.

'I want you to take the rest of the day off. I'll square matters with the C.-G.'

'To be honest with you, I didn't do any work this morning. I just sat there and went through the motions,' she replied.

The bright, vibrant Maggie of late had completely disappeared, he thought. She'd gone back to looking the way she had when he'd first turned up at her door. His heart ached for her.

'Apart from the financial side, if there's anything I can do, and I mean *anything*, you only have to say.'

She nodded, for the moment too choked with emotion to be able to speak.

They left the pub shortly after that, and Howard insisted on driving her home.

Maggie and Andy were both ashen when they emerged from Doctor Leishmann's rooms. Andy had been convinced that McCrindle was wrong, Leishmann had confirmed him to be correct. Liss did have a congenital abnormality of the aorta. And it *was* only a matter of time.

'Nice man,' Maggie said as they went down a flight of stone steps.

Andy didn't reply.

At the bottom of the steps they turned in the direction of their tramstop, and began slowly walking towards it.

Maggie thought back to their meeting with Leishmann. He'd placed Liss's X-rays on a light device and pointed out the abnormality to them. Unfortunately there was no mistake, and absolutely nothing could be done about it.

'Do you want to go for a drink?' Maggie asked Andy.

He shook his head. 'Do you?'

'Not particularly.'

459

They continued on in silence after that, each wrapped in their own thoughts, until they reached the tramstop.

'I'd like to walk on. You can wait for the tram if you'd prefer,' Andy said.

'I'll walk with you – if you don't mind, that is?'

He gave her a strained, sickly smile. 'I don't mind in the least.'

He surprised her then by hooking his arm through hers and drawing her close.

'It isn't fair, is it?' he said.

'Life isn't. Someone said that to me once, but I can't remember who.'

'Nevil?'

'Could have been. I honestly can't remember.'

'I wonder what would have become of Nevil if he'd come home from Spain? He might have taken up his old job again, but I doubt he'd have stayed on at Templeton's.'

'Yes, I wonder,' she mused.

'Spain,' Andy breathed. 'There are times when it seems just like yesterday.'

'I know what you mean.'

'I'd always planned to take Liss there some day. To Madrid, and Malaga. Now . . .' he trailed off in despair.

'You never mentioned that before.'

He glanced sideways at Maggie, and gave her another sickly smile. 'Haven't I? I thought I had.'

'Was I included in this trip?' she queried.

'Of course. It was to be the three of us. You, me and . . .' He choked. 'Liss.'

They walked on a little further, then Maggie asked, 'And how was this trip to come about? How was it to be paid for?'

Andy shrugged. 'I don't know. It was just something I'd intended we'd somehow do.'

A tram rattled past them, clanking and swaying. Maggie thought that Liss loved tram rides. She always wanted to go upstairs and sit on the front seat. Two years previously they'd taken her to Paisley and back on the tram as a birthday treat. It had been a dreadful day, but Liss hadn't minded.

She'd had a long trip on a tram, that was all that mattered.

'It could be years and years before anything happened, Leishmann said,' Maggie murmured to Andy.

'And what does that mean? Three, four, five, six? Even six would only make her fifteen when she died. And what's fifteen, for Christ's sake? Nothing at all.'

Perhaps they could get to Spain, Maggie thought. Howard would lend her the money. But would travelling be harmful to Liss? Leishmann had said she should lead a relatively quiet life. Certainly sports and gym were out at school from now on. And vigorous exercise or labour of any sort was a thing of the past.

'Are you going back to work now?' Andy asked.

'I should.'

'You know what I'd like to do.'

'What?'

'Go for a walk in Kelvingrove Park. It's years since I've been there. And it's only a short distance away.'

'Then why don't you? You'd enjoy it.'

He hesitated, then said, 'Would you come with me, Maggie?'

She knew she didn't have to go back to work. They would understand perfectly if she didn't.

'Why not!' she smiled at him.

They spent quite some time strolling, sitting, talking in the park. And after that went to a café for a cup of tea.

When they finally returned home they were closer than they'd ever been.

Arriving at Howard's flat Maggie had gone straight to the toilet. Re-emerging from there she went into the reception room he tended to favour, where she found him with glass in hand. This was her first visit to his flat since the shock about Liss.

'I've poured myself a drink,' he said. 'How about you?'

She fancied something, but not whisky or gin. 'Do you have any port?'

'A bottle of vintage which I can personally recommend.'

'That would be lovely.'

He had to leave the room to find the port, and while he was

461

away she sat on a couch. She felt guilty at being with Howard when she should have been at home. She tried to put it out of her mind.

'Here you are,' he said on his return.

'Thank you,' she smiled, accepting the glass. She adored the colour of port, so warm and rich. She enjoyed looking at it just as much as drinking it.

Howard leaned over and kissed her on the lips. She responded, but nowhere as eagerly as he was used to.

'I don't want to go to bed,' she said when the kiss was over.

'OK. I understand.'

'I'm just not in the mood.'

'We don't have to go to bed. As I've told you before, I'm content simply to be in your company.'

She relaxed inside, glad that was out the way.

'Would you like me to play some classical music? That can be very soothing.'

'I'd much rather talk, Howard.'

'Then talk it is.'

He sat beside her, but left space between them so she wouldn't feel she was under pressure. Her smile told him that was the right thing to have done.

It soon transpired that Maggie didn't want to talk, but to speak. She did so at length while an attentive Howard listened, Liss her sole topic of conversation.

'Maggie! How are you!'

The voice was unmistakably that of Natasha, her old chum at Templeton's. Natasha Riggins now, as she had married a policeman during the war.

Maggie was delighted to meet Natasha, who hadn't changed one iota over the years. She was still cross-eyed, and as fat as ever.

The two women hugged each other. 'Oh it's great to see you, right enough!' Natasha beamed.

'And you. How's Sandy?' Sandy was Natasha's husband. The Prince Charming she'd always believed would never appear, but who had one night, when she was least expecting it. He was as thin as she was fat, though tall with it, standing well over six feet, which was unusual in Glasgow. She frequently referred to him as 'her big skinnymalink'.

'Sandy's terrific. And he's been promoted to Sergeant now, which means more money coming in.'

'That's good news,' Maggie nodded.

'And Andy, what about him?'

Natasha's face hardened a little, though she was doing her best not to let her feelings show, as Maggie explained about her going out to work full-time at the consulate while Andy stayed at home and took care of the house and Liss. Natasha thought it despicable that a man condoned that set-up. Lazy good-for-nothing bugger was what she thought of Andy.

'And how's Liss?' Natasha asked when Maggie had finished.

She'd been trying to avoid doing so, but she glanced down at Natasha's two daughters standing smiling by the fat woman's side. Eleanor was seven, Irene five, both pretty as pictures with beautiful temperaments. Natasha always said it amazed her how good-looking they were considering they had her for a mother and Sandy, who was plain, as a father.

Maggie found she simply couldn't tell Natasha about Liss. Perhaps another time, but not now. It would hurt too much to do so, particularly in front of Natasha's children.

'Liss is the same, growing like a weed,' she replied, which was partially true. 'And how are you girls?'

'Well, thank you,' Eleanor said shyly.

'And are you well too?' she asked Irene.

Irene nodded, and clung even more tightly to Natasha's coat.

Maggie realized there were tears in her eyes. 'That's good,' she mumbled.

'Is something the matter?' Natasha queried in sudden alarm, as she noticed the tears and heard the thickness that had crept into Maggie's voice.

Maggie shook her head. 'Nothing. I was just thinking to myself what gorgeous children you have. You must be very proud.'

'I am,' Natasha replied with a frown. 'Prouder than most, I suppose, as for years I never thought I would have children.'

'I wonder what they'll be like when they grow up?' Maggie mused. 'Being so pretty they'll no doubt have hordes of young men running after them.'

This was all very odd, Natasha thought. Maggie might say she was fine, but she certainly wasn't acting it.

Maggie stared, mesmerized, at Eleanor and Irene, imagining them in their late teens and early twenties, visualizing them at parties, dances, eventually having children of their own.

All of this was denied to Liss. The thrill of being asked out for the first time, or that first, clumsy, teenage kiss, or ... A thousand things ran through her mind.

'Here,' said Maggie, fumbling in her handbag.

She produced a pair of florins and gave Eleanor and Irene one each.

'That's terribly generous. Are you sure you can afford it?' Natasha said.

Maggie nodded. Suddenly she was desperate to get away.

'Would you like to go and have a cup of coffee somewhere?' Natasha asked.

'Can't, I'm afraid. I have an appointment,' Maggie lied.

'Right then,' a mystified Natasha replied. She couldn't for the life of her think why Maggie was acting so peculiarly.

'You must come over and see us sometime and we'll have a good chinwag together,' Natasha suggested.

'I'll do that.'

'I know it's a long trail out to where we are ...'

'Oh, it's not that bad!' Maggie interrupted, the desperation to be away from there mounting in her.

She glanced at her wristwatch. 'I really must fly! 'Bye, Natasha, lovely to have bumped into you.'

'And to have bumped into you.'

Maggie kissed Natasha on the cheek and then the girls.

'You don't know how lucky you are,' she said to Natasha, then fled away up Sauchiehall Street where she was soon swallowed by the crowds. The centre of Glasgow was always extremely busy on a Saturday morning.

Natasha shook her head, wondering what that had been all about. Something was wrong with Maggie, that was certain. Probably to do with that lazy bugger Andy, she decided. And hoped he wasn't knocking her about. She hadn't seen any signs of abuse, but you never knew.

She looked down at Eleanor and Irene, and for some sudden inexplicable reason, shuddered all over, as she was gripped by an awful fear. Quickly she gathered them to her, and hugged them tight. At which point she found there were tears in her eyes, just as there had been in Maggie's.

Only hers were tears of happiness.

Andy and Maggie were listening to a play on the wireless, as Maggie was darning a pair of Andy's socks, when a sound from outside the room caught Andy's attention. 'What's that?' he queried, drawing himself upright in his chair.

'What's what?'

'Listen!'

She laid her darning on her lap. 'It's . . .'

But before she could complete what she'd been about to say Andy had shot out of his chair and was heading for the kitchen door.

Maggie put her darning aside, and followed Andy into Liss's bedroom, where she found him, having switched on the light, staring in consternation at Liss.

Liss had pulled herself up into a sitting position. She was clutching at her chest while she alternately coughed and wheezed. Her wheezing caused her eyes to bulge in their sockets.

Maggie brushed past the transfixed Andy to sit beside Liss. 'There, there,' she crooned, placing a comforting arm round Liss's bony shoulders.

Liss gazed at her mother, panic in her face. She tried to speak, but couldn't. When she coughed her whole body convulsed.

Maggie's mind was whirling. All she could think of was croup, and the home treatment for that.

465

'Put the kettle on, we need lots of boiling water,' she said to Andy.

Andy swallowed, but didn't move.

'Boiling water, Liss needs steam,' she explained.

Still Andy remained rooted.

'Move, damnit!' she shrieked at him, which produced the desired result. He ran from the bedroom.

'Mummy,' Liss managed to gasp.

'You must try and take it easy, Liss. The more relaxed you can make yourself the easier it will be.'

Liss gave another long-drawn-out wheeze which caused the veins on her forehead to stand out like cords.

'I'm with you, Liss. I'm with you, darling. There's nothing to be frightened of,' Maggie soothed, as she thought she would have to make some sort of tent to cover Liss. One of the spare sheets would do the trick, she decided.

Andy returned. 'The kettle's on,' he announced.

'And pans?'

'You never mentioned pans!'

'Fill some pans and put them on the other three burners.' Then she had a brainwave. 'You'll find the big preserving pan under the sink. Use that.'

'Right,' said Andy, and dashed away again.

'I'm going to give you steam to inhale. It'll help a lot,' Maggie explained to Liss, who promptly burst into her fiercest bout of coughing yet.

When Andy reappeared with the kettle Maggie told him to place it on the floor and go back for the basin which they'd need. She then got Liss out of bed and on to a chair.

'I'll only be a moment, lass. Try and stay as calm as you can.' And with that she strode swiftly from the bedroom to fetch the sheet.

Andy was waiting with the basin when she returned. 'Now then,' she said, shaking out the sheet.

'Do you want a hand with that?' Andy asked.

'I can manage.' To Liss she explained, 'I'm going to drape this over your head so we can contain the steam. All right?'

Liss nodded that she understood.

When the sheet was in place Maggie poured the contents of the kettle into the basin and then took the basin underneath the sheet. She squatted in front of Liss, holding the basin as close to Liss as possible, and instructed her to breathe in deeply.

'Put the kettle back on,' she said to Andy, hovering outside the sheet.

It was difficult work, as Maggie had to be exceptionally careful not to scald Liss who continually moved about as a result of her coughing and wheezing.

Sweat was running down Maggie when she refilled the basin for the sixth time. It was like a hothouse inside the sheet, and highly uncomfortable, to say the least.

'How's it going in there?' an anxious Andy demanded.

'How are you now?' Maggie quietly asked Liss.

Liss sucked in a deep breath, then another. 'Better, Mummy.'

'Did you hear that?' Maggie called out.

'I couldn't make out what she said. Her voice was muffled.'

'She says she's better.'

Andy gave a sigh of relief.

'But still keep that water coming for now,' Maggie added.

Eventually the coughing subsided altogether, then the wheezing also died away.

'Back to bed, I think, for you,' Maggie said, and kissed Liss tenderly on the cheek.

'So tired,' Liss mumbled, eyelids drooping.

'Of course. That will have taken a great deal out of you.'

Maggie emerged from under the sheet which she then wrapped round Liss. Once Liss was in bed she removed the sheet and tucked Liss firmly in.

'I'm thirsty,' Liss said.

Andy hurried off to get her a glass of cold water. Liss greedily drank that down, and asked for more.

Maggie smoothed her daughter's wet hair away from her forehead, which was beaded with a multitude of tiny droplets. Maggie was wiping these away with the sheet when Andy

467

reappeared clutching the second glass of water. Liss drained that as well.

'Have I got a cold?' Liss asked wearily.

Maggie and Andy looked at one another, then back at Liss. 'I think you've had a dose of croup. Children get it all the time,' Maggie replied.

'Did you used to get it?'

'No, but my brother Charlie did. That's how I knew what to do. And my mother always gave him a cup of tea with honey in it afterwards. Would you like that?'

Liss shook her head.

'Well, you don't have to have it.'

Liss stared into Maggie's eyes, her own so trusting and vulnerable they made Maggie want to weep. 'Do I have to go to school tomorrow, Mum?'

'I think it best you stay off. Don't you?'

She smiled, a pale wan smile that tore at Maggie's heart. 'So I can sleep in?'

'You can sleep in as late as you like. And when you wake Daddy will cook you a really smashing breakfast. Anything you wish.'

'French toast with jam on it?'

Maggie laughed. That was Liss's favourite. 'As much of it as you can eat,' she promised.

Liss snuggled further down into the bed. She coughed, but only once, it wasn't a repetition of her attack.

'Get some good sleep now,' Maggie said, and kissed Liss on both cheeks.

'And don't let the bugs bite,' Andy added in an attempt to be jocular.

Liss was sound asleep before they'd even left the bedroom.

Maggie cradled her phone, having just rung home to speak to Andy. Doctor McCrindle had been to see Liss, who was now asleep again.

According to McCrindle Liss hadn't had croup the previous night, the coughing and wheezing had been brought on by her congenital defect pressing on the trachea. The bad news was this wasn't a one-off event, it would happen repeatedly. And probably more and more frequently as time went by.

McCrindle had also said that Maggie's home croup cure was a good idea, and one they were to employ with every attack. Maggie had then asked how Liss had enjoyed her breakfast, disappointed to hear that although Andy had made her several slices of French toast she'd only managed half of one. Andy had tried to coax her into eating more than that, to no avail. The half was enough, she'd insisted.

God! Maggie thought.

She turned back to her work. But in her head, she only saw and heard Liss coughing and wheezing.

Life had somehow degenerated into a nightmare. A nightmare getting rapidly worse with every passing night and day.

Howard, stark naked, was sitting up in a completely dishevelled bed when Maggie came out of the en suite bathroom where she'd just had a quick shower. She was wearing one of his dressing-gowns that was now put aside in the bathroom for her exclusive use.

She laughed at the sight of his hairy legs sticking out towards her. She'd always found men's bare legs funny, and the hairier the funnier.

'What's so amusing?' he asked.

'Nothing.'

'Something obviously is.'

He smiled when she told him. 'They don't look at all funny from where I am.'

'You should see them from here. And through a woman's eyes.'

His smile broadened a little. 'I hope that's *all* about my body you find funny?'

She twigged instantly to what he was referring. 'Oh I don't find *that* funny at all.'

'Glad to hear it.'

'Now I must get dressed and go home,' she said, giving him a kiss.

Howard watched her pick up her bra from the chair it had been thrown over, then drop her dressing-gown to the floor.

'Stay like that, just for a moment,' he said.

She turned to him in surprise. 'Why?'

'I adore seeing you in your birthday suit.'

She flushed with pleasure thinking how lovely it was to be appreciated by a man.

'Moment's up!' she declared, cupping her breasts into her bra.

Howard continued to watch in contemplative silence as she dressed, occasionally puffing on his cigar.

'I meant to ask you,' she said, pulling up her slip. 'What happened between you and the C.-G. this morning? You looked quite upset when you left his office.'

'Did I?'

'Well, I thought so.'

Howard took a long draw on his cigar, then knocked a thick band of ash off into the ashtray. 'Schuh offered me a new post at our consulate in Gothenburg in Sweden.'

Maggie stopped what she was doing and stared at Howard. The atmosphere between them was suddenly tense. 'A promotion?' she queried, her voice quavering ever so slightly.

'Uh-huh. The post is that of consul. Quite a compliment really, considering my relatively short time in the Corps.'

She had to force herself to ask the next question. 'And have you accepted?'

'No.'

She couldn't control herself, but burst into uncontrollable tears, the sudden relief of his not going flooding over her. She needed him so much, but felt such deep guilt at being with him when Liss was so ill.

He immediately went to her, and put a comforting arm round her. 'Come on now,' he whispered, and waited patiently till she regained her composure.

'I'm sorry,' she said, wiping tears from her cheeks.

'So am I, Maggie. You know it's almost two years since I arrived here,' he said. It was now late August 1950.

'Is it really? How time has flown,' she replied dully.

He kissed her tenderly on the forehead, but she broke away to continue with her dressing.

'I told Schuh I'd prefer to stay in Glasgow for a while longer. But it is only a matter of time. Another year at the very most. And that would be stretching it to the absolute maximum.'

'There's something in your voice which tells me you don't think it'll be that long?'

He shook his head. 'I can delay for a bit, but there is a limit. I'll have to move before they force me to. That would be bad for my career.'

'I understand.'

He stubbed out his cigar, which he wasn't enjoying any more. Then Maggie was back in his arms, resting her head against his chest.

'I know, I know,' he crooned.

Love and guilt gnawed at her insides.

Andy heard the telephone ringing as he reached the landing outside their front door. Hastily he grabbed for his keys thinking it would be Maggie. He was wrong. It was Mr Forsyth, the headmaster of Liss's school.

'I've been trying to ring you, but you've been out,' Mr Forsyth said.

'Yes, I've just this moment arrived back in. What's wrong?'

'It's Liss. She started going a peculiar colour round about milk break, so I thought it best to contact you and ask your advice. When we couldn't get hold of you we eventually decided the safe and proper thing to do was take her into hospital. Mr Tammes, our senior gym master, drove her there.'

Forsyth and the other teachers at the school knew all about Liss's condition, as Maggie had told them about it early on. Liss, on the other hand, was still ignorant of the true situation.

Andy found his mouth had gone dry, and had to salivate in order to speak again. He was furious with himself at being out of the house when Forsyth had tried to contact him.

'What sort of colour?' he asked.

'Blue, Mr Ramsay. A sort of greyish blue. It gave her and everyone else a fright, I can tell you.'

'Blue!' he exclaimed incredulously. 'You mean all over?'

'No, her extremities, Mr Ramsay. Hands, ears and different parts of the face. Toes too, presumably, though we didn't look at those.'

'And what did the hospital say?'

'They were adamant about keeping her in for a few days. I told them you'd no doubt be there shortly after I'd been in touch.'

'Was there any pain?'

'She said not, though she did complain of having difficulty in swallowing.'

'Thank you, Mr Forsyth, you did the right thing. Now if you'll excuse me I'll rush to the hospital. It was the Western Infirmary Mr Tammes took her to, I presume?'

'That's correct.'

'Right then, bye-bye.'

'Goodbye, Mr Ramsay.'

Andy hung up, then almost instantly picked up the receiver again. He rang the American consulate and spoke to Maggie.

Andy went behind the screens surrounding Liss's bed, and the first thing that struck him was the greyish blueness of her hands lying outside the covers, and different parts of the face. It was particularly evident around her mouth.

He stared at her, aghast. Then, realizing he was betraying his feelings, quickly transformed his features into a smile.

'Hello, poppet. In the wars again, eh?' he said, and kissed her on the cheek.

She watched him solemnly as he pulled the visitor's chair over to the bedside and sat on it.

'I've gone blue,' she said.

'Yes, I can see that. And you're having trouble swallowing.' She nodded.

'Have they given you any medicine?'

'Not so far. But the doctor has been to visit me.'

'And what did he say?'

'That they're going to put me on a glucose drip to give me strength and energy.'

'Anything else?' Andy probed gently.

'And I've to have more X-rays. They're going to do those before the drip.'

He reached across and stroked her sunken cheek. Her flesh was cold and not springy the way healthy flesh is.

'Daddy?'

'Yes, darling?'

'When are you and Mummy going to tell me what's really wrong with me? I know something is.'

He and Maggie had known Liss would have to be told eventually. Now it seemed that the crunch had arrived. To put it off would only be postponing the inevitable.

'I'm not stupid, you know,' she added.

'No, you're not. Far from it,' he smiled. Inside he felt sick, almost to the point of throwing up.

He was about to speak again when Maggie appeared. 'I came as quickly as I could,' she said.

They did the job together.

Maggie stared at the book she was trying to read, seeing nothing but a jumble of words. She hadn't turned a page in over an hour. Opposite her Andy was lying slouched back in his chair studying the ceiling. The clock on the mantelpiece ticked the seconds away, the only sound in the room.

'Captain Hook,' Andy said suddenly.

Maggie glanced up at him, and frowned. What on earth was he havering about?

'Captain Hook and the crocodile,' Andy explained. 'I've been listening to the clock and thinking about that.'

'Liss liked Peter Pan when you read it to her.'

'She didn't just like it, she loved it!'

'Why don't you take the book into the hospital when you go tomorrow and start reading it to her again?' Maggie suggested.

'Good idea! I'll do that.'

Maggie went back to her own book, but the words remained a jumble.

'I couldn't tell her what she had would kill her. I just couldn't do that,' Andy said softly.

Maggie bit her lip. She hadn't been able to either. They'd explained to her about having a congenital abnormality of the aorta and what that was exactly. They'd then explained it would cause her problems for the rest of her life as there unfortunately wasn't any operation to rectify it. The fact it would kill her in the foreseeable future had remained unsaid.

Maggie thought about what the hospital doctor had told them after he'd viewed the latest X-rays. A severe dilation had developed in the aorta, an expected degeneration of the abnormality, and this was causing many of Liss's symptoms.

Andy returned to studying the ceiling, then a few minutes later got up and hurried excitedly from the room.

What now? Maggie wondered.

When he reappeared he was carrying the battered doll's house he'd bought for Liss. He plonked it down on the kitchen table and stood staring at it, in deep contemplation.

'I dread to ask, but what are you doing?' Maggie queried.

He carefully opened a panel that swung out on hinges, and gazed inside. He grunted, then grunted again.

'Andy?'

'I thought I might do this up for her coming home. Or at least make a start on it. What do you think?'

'You mean paint it and such?'

'Replace those parts that are broken and the others that are the worse for wear. Then repaint it. A fiddly job, mind. But she gets so much pleasure out of it the way it is, just imagine how much more pleasure she'd get out of it if it were completely renovated!'

Maggie stared at him in admiration. 'Are you going to keep it a surprise?'

'If I can get it finished before she comes home I will. Otherwise the surprise will be that I'm doing it, but haven't yet finished.'

He took a deep breath. 'And there's no time like the present to get started.'

474

'If you intend using the table as a work bench make sure you put paper down,' she said softly.

'Will do!'

When Maggie eventually went to bed that night she left a whistling Andy still hard at work on the doll's house.

Liss was kept in hospital for ten days. Andy finally brought her home by taxi, as Maggie was working at the consulate.

'Want me to carry you up the stairs?' he asked at the bottom of their close.

'You can't carry me and that bag.' The bag contained items, pyjamas, toothbrush, teddy, that Maggie had taken to Liss in hospital.

'Want a bet?'

She grinned at her father. 'All right then.'

He picked her up and sat her on the crook of his left arm, while she put an arm round his neck. He then bent at the knees, and in one swift motion snatched up the bag.

Liss laughed, and kissed him on the cheek. 'You're as strong as Tarzan,' she teased.

'Tell me that after I've managed the stairs,' he replied, which made her laugh again.

'Owwowwwowwwowwwow!' he mouthed as he mounted the first flight. 'My imitation of Cheetah,' he informed her.

Outside their door he set her down, and groped for his keys. Couldn't carry her and the bag! He could have carried a dozen Liss's and the bag. It had shaken him to find out just how light she'd become. A sackful of feathers would have been heavier.

'Mum will be home as fast as she can after work,' he told her as they went inside.

Liss stopped and ran a hand across her forehead.

'Are you all right?' he asked anxiously.

'I'm fine. A little tired, that's all.'

'Come into the kitchen and put your feet up. Or perhaps you'd like to go to bed?'

'I'd prefer to sit down,' she said. 'I've had enough of bed for a while.'

He dropped her bag outside her bedroom door, and then

ushered her into the kitchen where the renovated doll's house stood proudly on top of the table.

Liss gasped when she saw it. 'It's beautiful!'

'A surprise for you, darling. Daddy did it for you himself.'

She ran to the doll's house and stared at it. 'It's painted and . . . everything,' she said.

He took off the roof. 'And I've put new wallpaper into some of the rooms, see, and painted others. And Mum recovered the three-piece suite for you which I was unable to do.'

Liss's eyes shone with pleasure, a sight that made Andy's heart sing within him. 'It's marvellous. Just marvellous,' she enthused.

'I'm glad you're pleased.'

She threw herself into his arms. 'Thank you, Dad. Thank you!'

'I had another thought while you were in hospital,' he said. 'As you know we didn't do much redecorating when we moved in here on account of most of the house being in fairly good order. But I've been thinking, inspired by the doll's house, I have to tell you, that maybe you'd like your bedroom totally done out. What do you say?'

She beamed up at him. 'Can I choose the colours?'

'Of course you can. Any colours of the rainbow you wish, just as long as I can get hold of them. I've spoken to Mummy and she's agreed you can have a new carpet. And I've also spoken to my friend Teddy Agnew, who's a first-rate carpenter, and he'll help me make you a new fitted wardrobe and bookshelves.'

Liss was dazzled by the prospect, unable to believe her luck. A fitted wardrobe all of her own. That was luxury indeed! None of the other girls at the school had a fitted wardrobe. They had the old fashioned free-standing kind which most of them had to share. Wait till she got back to school and told them about this! They'd be green with envy.

Andy went on. 'We'll move your bed into our bedroom while the redecorating is going on. That way you'll remain comfortable and not upset by the fumes.'

The look Liss now gave her father said it all, as did the look he gave her in return.

When Maggie finally got in from the consulate she found them both in Liss's bedroom stripping wallpaper and chattering together like a couple of magpies.

Liss was wide-eyed as she, Maggie, Andy and Howard entered the foyer of the Citizens' Theatre. It was six days before Christmas and Howard had booked them seats for the pantomime.

'The reviews were very good,' Howard said to Maggie as they passed through a set of glass doors.

'I'm looking forward to it. And so is Liss. Aren't you, Liss?'

'Oh yes!'

'It's very good of you, Howard,' Andy said.

'Don't mention it.'

Andy would have preferred to have paid for the tickets out of his own pocket, but that was impossible as the only money coming into the house was what Maggie earned. That was a state of affairs he'd come to terms with, though there were occasional times, like now, when it still rankled.

Liss gazed about her in wonder. The atmosphere was one of excitement and fun. Everywhere were happy faces, young and old, all expectant of a great night out.

Howard spotted the bar. 'How about a drink?' he suggested.

'I'll get them,' Andy said, having been given cash by Maggie earlier for just such a purpose.

'Please! The evening is on me,' Howard overraided him.

'But I . . .'

'I insist,' Howard stated firmly. 'Now who wants what? Lemonade or orange for you, Liss?'

Maggie and Liss remained outside the bar while Howard and Andy went in. Liss stared up at a framed bill of a previous production, *The Taming of the Shrew* by William Shakespeare.

'Maybe I'll be an actress when I grow up,' Liss breathed.

The smile froze on Maggie's face, and her stomach muscles contracted. She had to take a deep breath before replying, 'Well, you never know, do you! Though it's not quite the glamorous life it's made out to be, I'm told.'

'But it must be lovely to be an actress,' Liss persisted.

'Perhaps. And perhaps you will be one day. Who knows?'

Liss looked at another bill, then at a cluster of photographs of past production glories.

Lots of people were now arriving, the foyer and surrounding areas rapidly filling up. Being a pantomime there were many children in evidence, all clearly thrilled at what lay in store for them and on their best behaviour.

Howard and Andy returned with a tray. 'I'll take the coats and put them in the cloakroom while you have your drinks,' Howard said.

'No, let me.' Andy wagged a finger at Howard. 'Please, I insist!'

Howard laughed at Andy mimicking him. 'OK, Andy, the coats are all yours.'

Liss sipped her orange, then frowned, and rubbed her forehead. A dull throb had come on that she hoped would soon disappear.

'You look gorgeous,' Howard smiled at Maggie. She was wearing a new dress.

'Thank you.'

'Black really does suit you.'

'You mean it's flattering?'

'No, I mean what I said. It suits you.'

She knew he was also referring to some lacy black underwear he'd bought her as a present, and which she'd told Andy she'd bought herself.

She smiled back at him. Her twinkling eyes told him she was aware of what he was really on about.

Howard glanced round, saw there weren't any signs prohibiting smoking, and lit up.

'Where are we sitting?' Maggie asked.

'Quarter way up the stalls. Best seats in the house, I was assured.'

'Trust you,' Maggie nodded.

The atmosphere was building, and now had a sort of bubbling quality about it.

Andy reappeared with programmes, having been

determined at least to buy these. Howard didn't admonish him, but thanked him politely when handed his.

'I wonder who's playing the wolf?' Maggie mused, opening hers. The panto was *Little Red Riding Hood*.

'Terrific cast,' Andy commented. The cast were all well-known Scottish actors.

'These are for you, young lady,' said Howard, producing a single-layer box of assorted chocolates from an inside jacket pocket, and giving them to Liss.

'What do you say?' Maggie prompted.

'Thank you,' Liss said shyly.

'And another of the same for Mum,' stated Howard, producing an identical box from another pocket.

'You're very kind,' Maggie told him, and kissed him on the cheek.

'You'd better open them now to avoid making a noise in the auditorium,' Howard said to Liss, and squatted beside her in case she needed some help.

A bell rang informing them it was time to take their seats. They gulped down their drinks and went with the crowd into the auditorium.

Maggie held Liss's hand as Howard led them to their seats, which were, as he'd promised, some of the best in the house.

The orchestra were already in place, a few of the musicians giving their instruments a final tuning. They were all, including the conductor, wearing evening dress.

Liss sat between Maggie and Andy, with Howard on the other side of Maggie.

'The performance is sold out,' Howard informed Maggie.

Liss rubbed her left arm, which had become sore, frowning as she did. Nor had the throb in her head left her, if anything it was worse than before.

'Is this the first pantomime you've ever been to?' Maggie asked Howard.

He nodded. 'We don't have them in the States. A most peculiar British institution, I'm informed.'

'They're usually a good laugh – for adults as well as children.'

'Slapstick humour, is that right?'

'Very,' she replied.

She was thrilled when he contrived to surreptitiously touch her on the leg, letting his hand linger for a minute before removing it again.

'All right?' Andy asked Liss.

'Fine,' she lied.

Then the lights started to dim, and the band struck up. The audience sighed when the curtains parted to reveal the opening set, following that with an enthusiastic round of applause which would have warmed the designer's heart if he'd been present to hear it.

After that the jokes and gags came thick and fast, while the plot and action flowed smoothly from one scene to the next. They all became completely caught up in it, with the exception of Liss, who shrank further and further into her seat.

Halfway through the first act she began to cry soundlessly. Then she couldn't help herself and a sob escaped her now blood-less lips.

'What is it?' Maggie immediately queried. Her face flooded with concern when she realized something was wrong.

'Pain,' Liss choked.

Andy bent over her. 'Pain where?' he demanded in a whisper.

'In my chest, arms and head,' she replied.

Andy looked at Maggie, and bit his lip. They'd both been so enthralled by what was happening on stage they'd missed this coming on.

'What is it?' Howard asked, also in a whisper.

'Liss isn't feeling well,' Maggie explained.

Liss whimpered, and clutched at her head which she dropped forward.

'Do you want to go outside?' Maggie asked her.

Liss whimpered again, but didn't reply.

'Do you want to go outside, lass?' Andy repeated, now clearly disturbed and upset by the situation.

Liss moaned.

'I think we'd better take her,' Maggie said to Andy.

'Ssshhhh!' someone hissed behind them.

It was on the tip of Maggie's tongue to give a scathing retort, but she decided it wasn't worth it. 'Come on,' she said quietly, grasping Liss by the arm.

'Sore there!' Liss burst out.

'Ssshhhh!' the voice hissed again.

'Why don't you carry her?' Howard suggested to Andy. Then he turned around and said very politely and matter-of-factly, 'We're terribly sorry but this child is very ill.'

Andy gently pulled Liss to her feet. Then, half-standing, he scooped her into his arms and held her to him.

Howard and Maggie stepped out into the aisle. Andy strode past them towards the exit, and they hurried after him.

Out in the foyer Andy sat Liss on a leather seat. Tears were running down her face which was contorted with pain. 'Oh Daddy!' she sobbed. 'It hurts so much.'

'I've got the painkillers here,' Maggie said, rummaging through her bag.

Howard dashed off to the bar to get a glass of water. He was shaken by this turn of events, and the sight of Liss in such distress.

'Take these, pet,' Maggie urged when Howard returned with the water.

Liss accepted the two tablets, then swallowed them with some water.

'How long before this passes off?' Howard asked a distraught Maggie.

'I've no idea. Depends.'

'What do you say, Andy?'

Andy didn't answer because he hadn't heard. His full concentration was focused on Liss.

A concerned theatre employee came over and asked if he could help. Maggie replied that he couldn't, and asked how long it was before the interval. Once he'd told her, she glanced up at a wall clock to see how long they had to go.

'I think we should take her home. I'm sorry about that, Howard, but . . .' Maggie trailed off, and shrugged.

'We'll take her home if that's right,' Howard replied

481

instantly. 'I'll go and bring the car round to the front. Give me five minutes.'

An enormous roar of laughter came from the auditorium, which somehow seemed obscene in the circumstances. Once Howard reached the street he broke into a run. The Buick was parked relatively close by.

'Go and collect the coats,' Maggie instructed Andy.

'Is it still as bad?' she asked Liss.

'Yes,' came the anguished reply.

Maggie felt so helpless. It was awful enough to witness an adult in severe pain. But your own child was ten times worse.

When Andy came back he was wearing his coat, the others slung over an arm. Maggie slipped into hers and they put Liss's over her bony shoulders. Maggie carried Howard's, while Andy carried Liss.

They found Howard already waiting. Andy very carefully, and gently, placed Liss in the rear. Maggie got in the other side, while Andy then got in front with Howard.

Liss cried out, and arched.

'Dear God,' Andy muttered.

Liss arched again, after which she shook all over. Then she grabbed herself round the middle.

Maggie was at a loss as to what to do. She certainly couldn't give Liss any more painkillers, not for several hours at least.

Liss let go of her middle and clutched her head. Her eyes bulged as her head swayed from side to side. 'It's going to burst! It's going to burst!' she howled.

'No, no, it only seems that way,' Maggie hesitantly tried to reassure her.

Liss cried out again, then curled into a ball.

'We'll put her straight to bed when we get in and call the doctor,' Andy said, voice quavering.

'Yes,' Maggie agreed.

'Perhaps we should drive direct to the hospital?' Howard suggested.

Andy and Maggie considered that. 'I don't know,' Andy muttered, torn by indecision.

Maggie stared at Liss. This was by far and away the worst

482

attack Liss had ever experienced. It might well be that Howard was right.

'Oooohhhhh!' Liss moaned, a long-drawn-out moan that was heartrending to hear.

Maggie made up her mind. 'We'll go to the Western Infirmary.'

'Do you know the way?' she asked Howard.

Howard did.

Howard had gone to collect the cups of tea a nurse on casualty had offered to make for them to allow Maggie and Andy a few moments by themselves.

Leaving the office, he started back to where Maggie and Andy were sitting. When he caught sight of them he came up short.

Maggie and Andy were holding hands and she had her head on his shoulder. As he continued to watch, Andy reached up and stroked her hair.

They were a couple, Howard thought. A man and a woman bonded together, if not by love, by their child.

If not by love, by their child, he repeated to himself. Each word burning its way into his brain as though being imprinted there by a red-hot branding iron.

He could have wept at that point, for in those few seconds he'd come to realize that Maggie would never be his.

It just wasn't to be.

They were sipping their tea when a white-coated doctor approached them. 'Mr and Mrs Ramsay?'

The three of them stood. 'I'm a friend,' Howard explained.

The doctor stared at Maggie and Andy, his gaze sympathetic. 'I've given Elizabeth an injection of morphine which has sent her off to sleep ...'

'Morphine!' Maggie exclaimed.

'As the painkillers you gave her weren't having any effect the next step was morphine. Hopefully, by the time she wakens up the oedema of her head and arms, and the severe girdle pains that were brought on by pressure on her intercostal nerves will have settled down again.'

'Oedema?' Andy queried.

'That's an unusual accumulation of liquid causing abnormal swelling of the tissues,' the doctor explained. 'The oedema and pressure on the intercostal nerves, the nerves situated between the ribs, are common symptoms of a degenerating abnormality of the aorta.'

He paused, then said, 'It may seem strange that an abnormality of the aorta affects head, arms and middle but it does.'

'And will Liss continue to suffer these symptoms?' Maggie asked.

'I'm afraid so, Mrs Ramsay.'

Maggie slumped where she stood, her face drawn and grey.

'Are you keeping Liss in?' Andy queried.

'I think that wise, Mr Ramsay. That way she can be seen first thing tomorrow by the doctor who usually takes care of her.'

Andy nodded his agreement.

'I also suggest that when you visit tomorrow you bring her some night-clothes and whatever else she might need or want. I would imagine her regular doctor will wish her to be with us for a while.'

'Can we see her before we go?' Maggie asked.

'Of course. But as I did say to you she is asleep.'

'That doesn't matter. I'd still like to see her,' Maggie said.

'I'll take you to her myself.'

Howard waited till Maggie and Andy returned, then drove them home.

'Hey, what are you doing!' Maggie exclaimed as a camera clicked.

'Taking some pictures of you,' Howard replied. They'd arrived at the park only minutes previously, as he had suggested that they take a stroll there during their lunchbreak.

'Come on, give me a big smile,' Howard urged, peering into the viewfinder.

Click! went the shutter when she did.

'That's enough now,' she said.

'No, I want one more at least. This time give me a pose.'

'Hand on hip?' she teased.

'Something natural.'

She poked out her tongue at him, and immediately regretted it when there was another click.

'That's not fair!' she protested.

'Maybe not. But it'll teach you to be rude.'

She laughed, thinking what a glorious spring day it was. Bright sunshine was streaming down. 'Terrible man. What do you want photographs of me for anyway? We see each other almost every day.'

'They're to take away with me,' he replied, his tone suddenly serious.

It took several seconds for what he'd said to register. When it finally did Maggie stiffened with shock.

'Say that again?' she demanded quietly.

'I'm leaving Glasgow next month. A particular post has come up that I want enormously. Also I feel it's the last one I could turn down. Next time it wouldn't be an offer, but an order.'

Now she knew why he'd suggested the stroll. Getting together during the day where they might possibly be seen wasn't something they did very often.

'Where is this post?' she asked.

'Madrid.'

'Madrid! That's marvellous.'

'It'll be interesting to experience Spain in peacetime as opposed to when we were there. I'm extremely excited at the prospect. And I believe the embassy is especially keen on me because I already have some knowledge of the country and its people.'

'Returning to Spain just as you returned to Scotland,' Maggie commented drily.

'That's right.'

There was a long pause, during which they walked in silence, then he said, 'You knew it was on the cards, Maggie. I spelled it out clearly enough.'

Maggie stared out over the park. Flowers were coming into bloom and the trees starting to bud. A clump of daffodils caught her eye, their yellow bells nodding in the wind.

'Next month,' she said softly.

'I'm taking the train to London, where I have to attend to some business. Directly that is concluded, which should take a few days, it's straight over to Madrid by aeroplane.'

And out of her life, she thought.

Howard slipped his camera into a coat pocket, then lit a cigarette. 'Can I ask one question?'

'Go ahead.'

'It's a question I've tried to avoid asking, but I'm going to now. What happens when Liss dies?'

Maggie winced.

'Well?' he prompted when she didn't reply.

'I can't leave Andy. Knowing the state he'll be in I simply couldn't do that to him.'

She hesitated, then added, 'Ever.'

'I understand,' was said so softly it was almost a whisper.

She stopped, and put a restraining hand on his arm. 'When you asked me to marry you I wouldn't because of the hurt it would cause Liss to lose her father, and Andy to lose Liss. And now he is going to lose her, in a most horrible way. It would be the cruellest thing imaginable if I were to leave him after that. He'll need me more than he's ever needed me before. Because it's *our* daughter he'll have lost, whom we both loved dearly.'

'I said I understood,' Howard replied. 'And you don't have to justify yourself, Maggie. I knew the answer to my question before I asked it, but had to ask it nevertheless in case there was an outside chance I was wrong.'

They continued walking. 'I'm sorry,' Maggie said after a few steps.

'You've nothing to be sorry about. Neither of us has. Fate deals the cards, we can only play them to the best of our ability.'

'I'll miss you so much,' she mumbled.

'And I'll miss you.'

'Shit!' she swore, most unlike her, as she rarely used bad language. Then, 'What day next month?'

The date he gave her was less than three weeks away.

★

Maggie glanced at her wrist-watch. It was ten minutes till her lunchbreak during which she'd be seeing Howard off at the Central Station. He'd arranged his daytime departure specifically so that she could be there.

She thought of the previous night when she'd 'worked late' and gone to his apartment. What a disaster that had been. He'd been in a filthy mood when she'd arrived. And to be truthful, so had she.

The argument had flared suddenly, and very quickly blown out of all proportion. She'd never seen Howard so angry.

She'd nearly gone storming off, but had stayed and calmed down somewhat. Sadly the evening had been ruined for the pair of them, so much so they hadn't gone to bed. And it had been their last opportunity.

Maggie bit her lip. What a stupid thing to have happened! She realized now that the argument had been a result of the tension and extreme emotional stress they were both under. Maggie couldn't wait to say she was sorry for her part in it, something she hadn't been able to do the night before.

Oh Howard! she thought, glancing again at her wristwatch. Thirty-five minutes from now his train would leave Glasgow, bearing him away forever. Never again would they do all those marvellous and intimate things they'd done together. The conversations, the laughter, the lovemaking, the . . .

'Mrs Ramsay.'

She snapped out of her reverie to focus on the person who'd spoken. It was Mr Cheever, the consul.

She rose to her feet. 'Yes, sir, can I help you?'

'Have you got those figures that I asked for yesterday?'

Oh God, she'd forgotten all about them! 'I'm sorry, sir, but they're not quite ready yet. I'll have them on your desk early this afternoon.'

'That's not good enough,' he snapped. 'I need them for a call from the States that I'm due to receive shortly. You're normally reliable, Mrs Ramsay, but not on this occasion, it seems.'

'I'm sorry,' she stammered, looking down.

'Is there a problem with them? Something that's giving you trouble?'

'No, sir, they're straightforward enough.'

'Then I need them right away.'

Panic blossomed in her. 'But it's my lunchbreak coming up, Mr Cheever.'

'Change it, go later. But get those figures to me as quickly as you can.'

And with that Cheever stalked away.

Maggie stared after him in consternation. Of all days for this to happen! It was her own fault, mind, but nonetheless.

She tore open a drawer and took out the file containing the information that would give her the figures. She glanced again at her watch. It was possible, just possible if she flew at it.

And fly she did.

Maggie ran down Hope Street, her heels clacking on the pavement. A man exclaimed in annoyance when she bumped into him, but she didn't stop to apologize. Every second was vital if she was going to get to Howard's train before it left.

Damn Cheever and his bloody figures! And damn her for being so bloody stupid as to forget about them!

Please let her be in time, she prayed. Even a single minute would be enough. It would be awful if they parted without making up.

On reaching Gordon Street, and the station across the road, she paused for only the briefest of seconds before plunging into the traffic.

A horn hooted loudly. Hooting at her? She didn't know, or care. She stumbled at the far kerb, but swiftly recovered. Entering the station she didn't have to enquire which platform the train was leaving from. The London trains always went from either one or two.

A glance at the station clock made her heart sink, for it was several minutes faster than her own. It had to be wrong, she reassured herself, dodging in and out of the crowd.

Her chest was heaving when she arrived at the barrier, which she now discovered with a jolt was closed.

She stopped and grabbed hold of it, to stare along the empty track. The train was gone.

Wildly she looked at platform two, but that was also empty.

'Missed your train, missus?' a guard queried.

'I was supposed to be seeing someone off to London,' she gasped in reply.

'Too bad,' he commiserated, and walked away.

She gazed along the curving stretch of empty track, disappointment heavy as stone within her. Of all days for Cheever to insist she work into her lunchbreak! Of all days!

Letting go of the barrier she turned her back to it. Howard was gone and that was that.

She sighed deeply, a sigh that came from the very depths of her soul.

'The train now leaving . . .' the tannoy began to announce.

She could have wept.

Maggie was leaning against an iron pillar in the consulate basement, having come down there to get away from the other employees. It was nearly three hours now since Howard's train had left and she still felt sick at missing him.

'God,' she whispered for the umpteenth time.

'Are you all right, Maggie?'

She whirled round to find Fiona Kilgour behind her. 'I didn't hear you.'

'Well, I wasn't being particularly quiet. At least not that I was aware of.'

Maggie ran a hand over her face. 'I suppose I didn't hear you because I was deep in thought.'

Fiona's expression became one of concern. 'Is it about your daughter?'

'No, something else. Anyway, that doesn't matter.'

'Howard then? He left Glasgow today, I believe.'

'Why should—' Maggie broke off to stare at Fiona. 'How long have you known?'

'Some months.'

'Did he tell you?'

'No, I guessed. I saw the pair of you talking one day and it just clicked that there was more between you than mere friendship.'

'Does anyone else in the consulate know?' Maggie asked anxiously.

'Not that I'm aware of. I've certainly never heard it mentioned.'

'That's good. Because if it had got out it could possibly have harmed Howard's career.'

Maggie took a deep breath. 'I was supposed to see him off, and missed the train. And we had a fight last night.'

'Do you love him?'

Maggie then told Fiona the whole story, missing nothing out. It was a great relief to get it off her chest by confiding to a friend. For Fiona had certainly become a friend.

Fiona listened sympathetically. She was genuinely, and deeply, fond of both Maggie and Howard.

'Maybe it's for the best,' she said when Maggie had finished. 'Who knows about these things? The only thing to do is accept that it's over and consign it to history.'

'Not easy,' Maggie murmured.

'Love and men never are. Are they?'

Maggie smiled wanly. 'You can say that again.'

'Tell you what, I've got a gâteau upstairs that I had intended taking home. Why don't we go and pig ourselves on it instead?'

Maggie thought that was a terrific idea.

Andy lay in the darkness unable to sleep. Liss and her condition were tumbling round and round in his mind.

All these years there had been a timebomb literally ticking away inside her. And then one day the bomb had started to go off – an irreversible process to which there was only one end.

Maggie sighed beside him, and shifted her body. Then she shifted it again.

He smiled at the picture of Liss that popped into his head, Liss as she'd been before all this had started – lively, carefree, full of life!

Why her? he wondered bitterly. Why *her*!

'Oh!' Maggie moaned, and began rubbing her legs together. Dreaming, Andy told himself. And went back to thinking about Liss. He would take her in some fruit tomorrow. She adored fruit. He'd get her soft fruit, he decided, as she was having more and more trouble swallowing.

'Oh Howard! Oh darling!' Maggie breathed.

Andy turned to stare at her, just able to distinguish the outline of her head.

'Oh my love, Howard!' she said tightly, and shook all over in a way Andy knew only too well.

'Aaahhh!' she exhaled. And then went quiet again.

Andy's eyes were wide with shock. He couldn't believe that he'd just heard what he had.

Perhaps it was a dream, nothing more. A figment of her imagination?

Who are you trying to kid! he berated himself. That had been no figment, but the memory of something real. An actual event. She and Howard had been . . .

He drew in a deep breath, and tried to think clearly. This had stunned him, rocked him to the core. But was it really a complete surprise?

He knew full well she'd never loved him, just as she knew he'd never loved her. And how thick she and Howard had been since Howard's reappearance. It had been clever of Howard to organize their working together, and he was always at the house, or taking them out, being with them.

Howard and Maggie, having an affair. Or had been having one, for Howard had now gone, back to Spain and a new post there. So the affair was over. Which was probably why she was dreaming about him like she was. For she was missing him, and their physical relationship.

He knotted both hands into angry fists, then slowly relaxed them again. He had every reason to feel betrayed, hurt, but the affair was over so there was no need to confront her about it, none at all.

Anyway, and he smiled thinly, hadn't he cheated on Maggie many times since their marriage. Not in the flesh as she had him, but in the mind. How often had he made love to Felicia in his thoughts? Time without number. And wasn't imagined betrayal every bit as bad as actual betrayal? Some people might disagree saying it wasn't, but they were wrong.

And in truth, if Felicia had been still alive and available then the adultery most certainly wouldn't have remained in the mind. But there again, if Fliss had been still alive he wouldn't have been married to Maggie.

What a tangle, he thought. A passage from the Bible came into his mind: 'Let him who is without sin cast the first stone'.

And then he wondered if he'd ever said anything he shouldn't in his sleep. If he had, Maggie had never mentioned it.

His thoughts went tumbling on.

It was now October 1951 and Liss's condition continued to deteriorate. She had been in hospital since her admittance just before Christmas and Andy had long since stopped asking when she was going to be allowed home again.

He was only dimly aware of the man in the wheelchair, being pushed the opposite way along the corridor. The man, who'd been hunched, suddenly sat up straight. The strangest, and most unforgettable, expression on his face.

Blood shot from his mouth, a stream propelled as though by a high-powered jet. About a dozen feet in front of the man it spattered on the corridor floor.

Andy recoiled in horror, never having seen anything like it before. It was extremely gruesome to witness.

Someone screamed, and a middle-aged woman fainted, luckily caught by her male companion before she fell crashing to the floor.

And still the bright red sparkling blood flowed. Andy couldn't believe the human body contained so much.

The eyes of the man in the wheelchair started to glaze, while his face had gone a dirty white colour. His body underneath the tartan dressing-gown seemed to shrink in on itself like a deflating balloon.

The arc of blood finally began to lose force, retreating its way back to the man. The last dribble ran down his chin, then ceased altogether.

The young nurse who'd been pushing the wheelchair stood

rooted to the spot. As she now reached out to touch the man he slumped sideways, quite dead.

Andy swallowed hard – that had been horrible. And he couldn't help but wonder what had happened to the man to cause him to die like that.

Nurses and other hospital staff were appearing from everywhere, converging on the dead man and the young nurse, who was clearly badly shaken.

He left the bloody scene behind, and headed for the lifts.

'Hello, darling, how are you today?' he asked.

Her face, which with every passing day seemed more lined and wizened, now was screwed up with pain. 'So sore, Daddy, so sore,' she replied.

'I know,' he mumbled. 'When are you due for another injection?'

'Soon.'

She made a sound at the back of her throat, and rolled her eyes so that the pupils disappeared. She held her breath for a handful of seconds then slowly exhaled. As she did her pupils reappeared.

'It's that bad, is it?' he said in a cracked voice.

She started to nod, then stopped because that also hurt. Her head and neck were visibly swollen.

She looked a hundred years old, Andy thought. The illusion would have been perfect if her hair had been white.

'Daddy?'

'Yes, darling?'

'Remember you once wrote me a story, a story in which I was a fairy princess?'

He'd forgotten all about that, probably because it had been such a poor effort. He might be excellent at reading other people's stories, but wasn't so hot at writing them himself.

'That's right. You were a fairy princess and there were Red Indians and pirates in it just as you'd asked.'

The hint of a smile came on to her face. 'I'd like to hear it again.'

'I don't know if we still have it, but if it's in the house I

493

promise you I'll find it and bring it with me tomorrow. How's that?'

'Thank yo—' She broke off to cry out in agony.

Andy swore under his breath, but didn't touch her in case that caused her even further pain.

He glanced round, frantically looking for a nurse. But there wasn't one to be seen.

Liss cried out again, not a loud cry, but one with a terrible intensity to it.

'I'll get someone,' he said. Rising from the visitor's chair he fled up the ward.

He found a staff nurse coming out of the sister's office. 'Elizabeth needs another morphine injection right away!' he blurted out.

He grabbed the staff nurse by the arm. 'She's suffering dreadfully. Please hurry.'

'Just wait a second please, Mr Ramsay,' the staff nurse replied, and vanished back into the sister's office. When she re-emerged she had the sister with her.

'Now what's this all about?' the sister demanded.

'It's Elizabeth. The morphine has worn off and she needs another injection.'

'I understand your concern, Mr Ramsay, but she isn't due another injection for some time yet.'

Andy couldn't believe his ears. 'Are you saying you're not going to give her one? That you're going to leave her as she is?'

'We don't give morphine on demand, Mr Ramsay. The doctor has worked out a schedule for her, and we have to keep to that schedule.'

Something snapped in Andy. 'But she's in agony, woman!'

'I'm sorry, I can't help that.'

'Give her another injection now or, so help me God, I'll tear this fucking place apart with my bare hands!' he roared, having gone purple with fury.

Another nurse appeared from the sister's office, moving forward to stand supportively by her side.

Andy glared at her, his hands balled into white knuckled fists.

'I won't be spoken to like that,' the sister stated coldly, eyes flashing.

Andy took a deep breath, then said in a voice crackling with emotion, 'I don't care what your schedule is. That's my daughter in there, a wee lassie of ten. And she's in agony. Now please, please help her.'

He started to cry, large tears escaping from his eyes to roll down his cheeks. 'Please?' he pleaded.

The sister considered she'd won. Andy would have got nowhere with her if he'd continued shouting and using bad language. She addressed the staff nurse. 'Go and take care of Elizabeth, Staff.'

To the other nurse she said, 'Find Doctor Weir and ask him to come here as soon as he can. I'll need his authorization before I can advance Elizabeth's injection.'

'Yes, Sister.'

'Thank you,' Andy muttered, now alone with the sister.

Within minutes Liss had been given her injection and was fast asleep, at peace again.

As he left the ward, Andy went to the nearest gents toilet and washed his face. Feeling better, he caught a lift down to the ground floor.

He stopped at the spot where the man in the wheelchair had died. A woman cleaner, armed with bucket and mop, was just finishing washing the blood away.

She glanced at Andy, wondering what he was staring at.

'I saw it happen. It was awful,' Andy explained.

'He certainly made a mess.' She sniffed, then added, 'Which I've had to clear up on my own. We're shorthanded the day.'

Andy shook his head in sympathy.

'Still, there are worse jobs than this in a hospital, I can tell you. Some of the things we cleaners are expected to do would turn your stomach.'

'I can imagine,' he commiserated.

'When this is dried I'll come back and polish it,' the cleaner said, indicating the floor.

'I wonder what the man died of?' Andy mused. 'It was all so sudden and . . . well, gruesome. The sight of it made my own blood run cold.'

The cleaner came closer to Andy, and winked. She dropped her voice to a conspiratorial whisper. 'I know what the poor sod died of. I overheard a couple of the doctors talking about it.'

'Oh aye?'

She sniffed again. 'Rupture of a major vessel from the heart.'

The aorta was a major vessel from the heart. Did having a deteriorating abnormality mean the same thing could happen to Liss?

The cleaner frowned at Andy's reaction. 'You OK?'

'I'm fine,' he replied quickly. 'Are you certain about that?'

'I'm certain all right. As I said, I overheard a couple of doctors discussing it. Being a cleaner they don't take any notice, you see. It's as though you don't exist.'

'Thank you for the information,' Andy said, and moved off.

In his mind he could picture Liss in that wheelchair, and then . . .

Andy didn't know where the canal was, or how he'd got there. The canal itself was filthy with pollution, the bank littered with rubbish and other debris.

On the far bank was the rear of a factory. Black smoke belched from a cluster of chimneys on the factory roof, which rose steadily into a grey, lowering sky.

He loved Glasgow, but it wasn't the prettiest of cities. It was a place of hard graft, and hard living. Tough, uncompromising, grey as the sky above.

Bending he picked up a stone and threw it into the canal. When he looked up at the factory there was a lassie smiling at him from behind a window.

His tortured thoughts returned yet again to Liss. When she'd first been diagnosed he'd wanted her to live as long as possible. Not now. The longer she lived the more suffering she had to endure. Pain that was getting steadily worse, allayed by morphine injections that were getting stronger, and more frequent.

And what a physical effect it was having on her. Every time he looked at that lined and wizened face it was as though he'd been punched hard in the stomach.

Stopping, he raised his own face to the sky. 'Take her now, please?' he pleaded, his tone one of anguish.

'Please,' he repeated, and then hung his head.

And at that moment the idea, the solution, came to him.

He was using the underside of a spoon to crush into powder the remainder of the strong painkillers Liss had been prescribed before going into hospital.

When the last tablet was crushed he opened a bottle of American Cream Soda and began spooning the powder into the bottle.

He'd decided on cream soda because of its colour, similar to lemonade, only duller, and with something of an opaqueness about it. It also had a stronger taste.

When the last of the powder was in the bottle he restoppered it and shook it vigorously.

The cream soda foamed and bubbled, then gradually began settling down again. When it was back to normal Andy saw with satisfaction that there were only a few grains visible on the bottom of the bottle.

These vanished when he shook it again.

Liss was sitting up in bed and brighter than she'd been in weeks. She had a pink silk ribbon tied in her hair.

'Hello, poppet,' Andy said, and kissed her on the cheek.

'Hello, Dad.'

He placed the bag he'd brought with him on the floor, then pulled over the visitor's chair and sat down.

'You're looking better,' he smiled.

'I feel a lot better.'

'I like the ribbon.'

'Staff Nurse Lancaster gave it to me. She said pink suits me.'

'It does,' he agreed.

497

He glanced down at the bag on the floor. He had a bunch of grapes in it, and the cream soda.

It didn't matter what they did to him afterwards, he thought. Jail, whatever, it just didn't matter. Only Liss did.

'Any fruit for me today?' she asked.

'Seedless grapes. They cost a fortune, but never mind. You're worth it.'

She laughed, the first time in ages he'd heard her do so. 'Can I have them then?'

He took the grapes from the bag and placed them in front of her. He watched as she nipped a number off and ate them.

His hand was shaking when he reached back into the bag.

'Dad?'

He paused. 'What, lass?'

'I love you. You'll never forget that, will you?'

He stared into her eyes, and what he saw there melted his resolve. He simply wasn't going to be able to do it. Even if it was in her best interests, he couldn't. It wasn't in him, irrespective of the reason, to destroy someone he loved so much.

'I'll never forget,' he replied.

Removing his hand from inside the bag he rezipped it.

Maggie was combing her hair, preparing herself to leave for the consulate, Andy still in bed, when the telephone rang. It was the hospital.

Finishing the conversation she hastily cradled the phone again and ran through to the bedroom. 'We've to go to the Western right away, Liss has had a turn for the worse,' she gasped.

Andy shot out of bed. 'How do you mean, a turn for the worse?'

'The nurse didn't go into details. Just said we were to get there as quickly as possible.'

Andy began throwing on his clothes, hurrying as fast as he could.

While he was doing this Maggie slipped into her coat, then returned impatiently to the bedroom. There was no point in her ringing the consulate, there wouldn't be anyone there yet.

When Andy was finished he rushed out into the hallway, followed by Maggie, and grabbed his coat.

Luckily they managed to find a cruising taxi. During the drive to the infirmary they each quietly fretted.

The only time their eyes met they both swiftly looked away again.

'Could you come into Sister's office, please,' Staff Nurse Lancaster requested, the same staff nurse who'd given Liss the ribbon.

'What's wrong? What's happened?' Maggie demanded, her voice harsh and discordant.

Staff Nurse Lancaster closed the door behind them, then offered them a seat.

Maggie was nervous, her hands constantly moving. 'You said a turn for the worse on the phone. What does that mean exactly?'

'Elizabeth's condition suddenly worsened dramatically early this morning. Everyone did everything they could, but I'm afraid we lost her just before you arrived. I'm terribly sorry,' Staff Nurse Lancaster replied.

Maggie's mouth opened, then closed again.

'Lost her?' Andy said in a hollow voice. 'You mean she's dead?'

'Yes, Mr Ramsay.'

Tears welled in his eyes, blurring his vision. 'I'm glad for her sake,' he choked.

Staff Nurse Lancaster understood exactly what he meant by that. 'Yes,' she agreed.

He thought of the cream soda he'd so nearly given Liss the previous afternoon, and smiled wryly. God had heard his prayers after all.

'Can we see Liss?' Maggie queried. She too was now crying.

'Of course. We've put her into a single room where you can spend as much time as you want.'

'Thank you,' Maggie replied.

'I'll leave you here to have a few moments by yourselves, then I'll come back for you,' Staff Nurse Lancaster said.

Outside the office Staff Nurse Lancaster took a deep breath. That was a job which never got any easier, particularly where children were concerned. Just her luck to be in charge of the ward that morning. Just her rotten luck!

From inside the office came the sound of uncontrollable sobbing.

Andy placed fresh flowers on Liss's grave. It was now over a month since her funeral, and during that time he'd visited the grave every single day.

He lifted up the old, withered bunch and took them to a nearby bin. Having thrown them away, he returned to the grave.

How empty life was now that Liss had gone, he thought. How awfully empty.

There was Maggie, of course, but she'd become quite withdrawn since Liss's death. She would sit at home for hours on end and never utter a word – not a syllable.

There again, he wasn't doing too much speaking either. Most of the time that was simply because he had nothing whatever to say.

He stayed for half an hour, standing with his hands in his pockets, staring at the plot and stone. Then he walked slowly home.

He'd be back again the next day.

Every night was the same, Monday to Friday Maggie came home from work and they stayed in. They stayed in Saturday and Sunday nights also, the only difference being that Maggie didn't go to work during the day. Neither of them wanted to go out. Neither of them had any wish to do so.

Maggie had been knitting, but the knitting was now lying forgotten on her lap while she stared into space.

Andy was watching her from behind his newspaper thinking how incredibly sad she looked.

'It's surprising we never hear from Howard,' he said.

Maggie immediately flushed and looked guilty, which confirmed what Andy had suspected. She'd been thinking of

500

Howard. Something he was certain she frequently did.

'He's no doubt very busy in his new job,' she replied, picking up her knitting again.

'Have you written to tell him about Liss yet?'

Maggie shook her head.

'I'm sure he'd want to know.'

'I'll get round to it when I'm ready,' she muttered.

Another confirmation, Andy thought. She'd written to everyone else who needed writing to, with the exception of him. It could only be an indication of the depths of her feelings for him. At least that was how he read the situation.

Silence fell once more between them.

There was nothing left for him, Andy thought, but there possibly could be for Maggie. He was going to give her that chance, he decided.

There would be no regret on his part. He'd really died in Spain with Fliss and the others. Liss had been a much valued extension to his life, an extension that no longer existed.

His mind was made up. It was time to go. Best to go. But in a manner that would leave Maggie entirely free of guilt.

Andy lit a cigarette and threw the spent match into the fireplace. 'There's a big match on at Ibrox this Saturday. Do you mind if I go?' he asked Maggie.

She looked at him in surprise. Apart from his daily visits to the cemetery he'd hardly been over the door since Liss's death. 'No, not at all. Will you go with Teddy?'

'On my own, I think. I'm not really very good company of late.'

She understood that.

'So Ibrox on Saturday it is then,' he smiled. 'I'll be looking forward to it.'

The Subway platform, the Subway being what Glaswegians call their underground rail system, was thronged with football supporters, all off to see the game. Andy had worked his way through them so that he was now standing on the edge of the platform with a clear view up the tunnel along which the next train would come.

A group of supporters began to sing:

'We are, we are, we are the Billy Boys,
We are, we are, we are the Billy Boys,
Up to our knees in Fenian blood, surrender or you die!
For we are the good King Billy Boys . . .'

That they should sing that song amused Andy. He put his amusement aside, however, to concentrate on the task on hand. The supporters went on singing but he didn't hear them any more.

This shouldn't hurt a bit, he reassured himself. If he did it properly it should be all over in a second.

He steeled himself, resolute in his determination. It was the right thing to do, for him and Maggie. He was convinced of that.

A far-off rumble announced the imminent arrival of the train. All over in a second, he told himself again.

He wasn't scared. A little apprehensive, but definitely not scared. He poised himself, ready for action.

The red train flashed into view, hurtling forwards. Andy had intentionally positioned himself at the top end of the platform so that the train would only have begun to slow when he did what he intended.

He'd worked it all out so that witnesses could report what he wanted them to.

Now! he commanded himself.

He gave a cry and seemed to stumble, as though he'd lost his balance or been knocked off it. His arms were flailing frantically as he pitched headlong from the platform.

The group of supporters, unaware of what had happened, continued to sing.

They were halfway through the graveside service when Maggie saw him arrive. He gave the slightly flustered appearance of a man who'd been in a rush. Their eyes met, but neither smiled. It was hardly the time or place for that.

When the service was over he stayed apart, waiting for his chance to speak to her. A good ten minutes passed before she was able to excuse herself and go over to him.

'I'm sorry,' Howard said.

'How did you know?'

'Fiona rang and told me.'

She nodded. That explained it.

'We have to talk,' he said quietly.

'I'm having some people back to the house. You could join us and wait till they leave, or come round this evening when I'll be alone.'

'What time this evening?' he queried.

'Eight?'

'Fine,' he said.

'How long are you over for?'

'I have to fly back tomorrow morning. I'm booked on a flight from Prestwick.'

'I'll see you later then,' she said.

'At eight.'

Maggie left Howard to rejoin Andy's mother and father, who were among those going back to the house for a meal and drink.

'Hi!' Howard said when she opened the door to him. 'Have they all gone?'

'Long since.'

He followed her into the kitchen where he put the carrier bag he'd brought with him on to the table.

'A bottle of scotch in case you'd run out after your wake,' he explained.

She stood and stared at him. She wasn't wearing any make-up, and didn't care that she wasn't. She knew she looked fairly ghastly, and didn't care about that either.

'It's good to see you,' she said.

'And you. I've missed you.'

'I'll pour you some of that whisky.'

'And yourself?'

She nodded. 'I'll have some too. I didn't have anything when the others were here, but I could use it now.'

She poured them each a liberal measure. She put water in both, knowing that was how he liked his and it was how she wanted hers.

'An accident, according to Fiona?' he said after he'd had a sip.

'Yes, that was the verdict. He's never been all that brilliant on his feet since being wounded. He could easily lose his balance, which is apparently what happened.'

She paused, then added, 'At least, thank God, it was all over quickly for him. According to the doctor who examined him death must have been instantaneous.'

'And Liss,' Howard stated softly.

'Yes, last month.'

'Poor Maggie,' Howard said, aching to take her in his arms, but not doing so because he felt she didn't want that.

'Now she and Andy are buried together. Close in death as they were in life.'

Howard didn't know what to reply to that, so said nothing.

'I told Fiona about us, the same afternoon I missed your train.'

'I've often wondered about that,' he replied.

She gave him a weak smile. 'I had to work into my lunchbreak on something I had forgotten for Cheever, and which he was insistent I do there and then. I ran all the way to the station, but missed you by minutes.'

'You might have written and explained.'

'No,' she said. 'The break had been made, even if badly at the end, and it was best to leave it as it was.'

'Perhaps you're right,' Howard murmured.

She swept back a lock of hair that had fallen across her forehead. 'I still haven't really taken it in that Andy's dead. Liss was expected, of course, but not him.'

Fear began to invade Howard. Fear that he'd made a mistake, that things had changed between them. 'Was it wrong of me to come today?' he asked.

'I'm pleased you did. Your appearance earlier was like a ray of sunshine.'

The fear retreated. 'And what about us now that you're free?'

Anguish came into her eyes, and she went even paler than she'd been.

His fear rushed back when she shook her head.

'What does that mean?' he queried.

'I need time, Howard. Time to mourn, time to think, time to just be alone.'

'And then?'

'And then I'll know what I want to do.'

'I still love you, Maggie. Heart and soul, understand that.'

How lovely he was, she thought. 'And I still love you. At least I believe I do. But I've just buried a husband and a daughter shortly before that. At the moment my emotions are numb, and completely shattered.'

He crossed to the table and poured himself another whisky. He didn't ask her if she wanted a top up, she'd hardly touched her glass.

'Whatever you decide or happens, Maggie, I want you to know I'll always be your friend. There whenever you need me.'

'I appreciate you saying that, Howard, thank you. Now tell me about Spain and Madrid. How are they both?'

When it was time for him to leave she kissed him on the cheek, a kiss that was more of a peck really.

A peck as cold as charity.

Days went by to become weeks, which in turn became months. And during all this the healing process progressed within Maggie. Then one night, almost seven months after Andy's death, her telephone rang.

'It's Howard. How are you?'

'Howard!' she exclaimed in delight. 'I'm fine. Very well.'

Which was precisely what he'd wanted to hear.

'Where are you?'

'Madrid. Can't you tell by this awful line!'

She laughed, the connection was a bad one. There were various hummings and crackling to contend with.

They chatted for a few minutes, catching up on each other's news, then he said, 'How about letting me buy you dinner?'

'You mean here, in Glasgow?'

'No, Prestwick actually. I thought I might fly over and have a weekend at our old friend the Prestwick Airport Hotel. There are flights that arrive on Saturday morning and depart on Sunday evening that would suit me.'

'And you want me to come and have dinner with you there?'

'I was hoping you might spend the weekend.' He paused, then added, 'Your own room, of course. And without obligation. What do you say?'

'I say yes,' she replied without hesitation.

Then he told her all she had to do was show up. He would make all the arrangements.

Maggie gasped when she entered her hotel room. It was filled with masses of flowers and fruit. There were bouquets, baskets and arrangements everywhere.

On the coffee table was a card which simply stated 'Love from Howard'.

Maggie was sniffing some freesias when there was a knock on the door. 'Come in!' she called out. It was Howard.

'Glad you made it,' he smiled.

She went straight to him and kissed him on the cheek. It was far warmer and softer than the last one she'd given him.

'Thank you for all this. It's absolutely gorgeous.'

'My pleasure. Now, I thought we might have a walk along the beach? Or there are quiet country lanes nearby, I'm told, if you'd prefer that.'

'The beach sounds perfect,' she replied.

'Then get changed and I'll be back to pick you up in fifteen minutes.'

And with that he abruptly left her again, closing the door behind him.

She was waiting ready when he returned.

*

He kept her in stitches during their walk, telling her jokes and anecdotes about the embassy in Madrid. He also took a great many photographs, having brought a camera with him. When they met another stroller on the beach he asked the man to take a photograph of the pair of them together.

The hours fled happily and gloriously by.

They arranged to meet in the bar before dinner, and there he introduced her to the American martini, which he insisted on mixing himself.

'The secret is in the amount of vermouth you add, it has to be exactly right,' he confided, handing her her drink. He hovered expectantly, waiting for her to taste it.

'Hmmh!' she murmured in appreciation. 'Excellent, but strong.'

'Precisely the way it should be,' he said, coming round to sit on the stool beside her.

'Enjoying yourself?' he asked.

'You know very well I am.'

'And so am I.'

They had two martinis each, then went through to the dining-room, where he'd reserved a table. On one of the plates was a single long-stemmed red rose, while cooling in a nest of ice was a bottle of Krug champagne.

'You're spoiling me rotten,' she said.

'Good.'

Maggie glanced around. 'No gypsy violinists?' she teased.

'I did try, but the hotel just couldn't accommodate me in that respect,' he replied straight-faced.

She laughed, and was still laughing when the wine waiter came over to open their champagne.

'What shall we toast?' Howard asked softly when their glasses were filled, and the waiter gone.

'You choose.'

'New beginnings.'

'Perfect.'

They gazed into each other's eyes as they drank.

*

They stopped talking when they reached their floor, Howard's room being several doors along from hers. They arrived at his first.

'Maggie?' he said, his voice slightly wavering.

'Yes?'

'When I rang I said, and meant, no obligation. What happens next is entirely up to you.'

'Why don't you show me your room?' she replied.

He opened his door, and they both went in.

She lay in his arms, her head cradled against his shoulder. It had been a long time since she'd felt so mentally and physically at peace.

'I've got some news,' he said.

'Oh?'

'I'm being given four months' home leave, which means I'll be returning to the States, where I plan to stay with my parents in upstate New York.'

Her breathing ceased, then started again. He could feel she'd tensed. 'How about coming with me as my wife?'

She sat up, and stared at him.

'Well?' he queried in a whisper.

'When are you going?'

'Two months from now.'

When she didn't reply he went on hesitatingly, 'I thought you'd wind up things in Glasgow, that we'd marry in London, and have our honeymoon on the ship going over. A suite on the *Queen Mary*?'

She exhaled slowly, then nodded. 'I'll marry you, Howard. And be *proud* to do so.'

He laughed joyously, and caught her to him. They hugged and kissed, after which they fell to planning the details.

And eventually made love once more.

Howard glanced yet again at his watch. She was late and getting later. Where was she!

He was standing outside the Caxton Hall in SW1, on the borders of Petty France, where he and Maggie were due to be

508

married. With him were the Bonfiglios, Arnold and Linda, who were going to act as witnesses. Arnold was a Corps colleague, currently attached to the London embassy, and someone Howard had had dealings with in the past.

'Take it easy. You've got time,' Arnold smiled.

Howard had a terrible thought. What if she'd got cold feet and caught a train back to Scotland? Surely she wouldn't do that without letting him know? Surely she wouldn't leave him standing here? But where in God's name was she!

'You look like you're about to blow a fuse,' Linda joked.

Howard fumbled for his cigarettes, he was nervous as hell. What if . . .

At which point a taxi with Maggie inside drew up at the kerb.

Arnold paid the driver as Maggie got out.

'You're late,' Howard said.

'I thought that was a bride's prerogative?'

He smiled, and suddenly relaxed. Everything was going to be all right. 'You look stunning,' he said. This was the first time he'd seen her wedding outfit, a tailored navy-blue suit that she'd found in Bond Street.

'Thank you.'

'Well worth waiting for.'

Maggie knew he was referring to more than the past few anxious minutes.

'Here,' said Linda, and pressed a posy into Maggie's hands.

'Shall we?' smiled Arnold, indicating the double doors.

They went in, and when Howard and Maggie came out again they were man and wife.

POSTSCRIPT

It was Maggie who suggested they take a promenade round the deck before turning in on their first night at sea.

'Isn't that moon beautiful,' Maggie murmured as they walked arm-in-arm. The moon was a pale orange colour, hanging large in a profoundly black sky. All the stars were out in support, twinkling like a host of diamonds.

'Beautiful,' Howard agreed. 'And very romantic.'

She thought so too, snuggling up close to him. 'Happy?'

'Couldn't be more so.'

'Same here.'

'Do you fancy a night-cap?'

'Nope.'

'Me neither. I've got everything I fancy right here on my arm.'

She thought that sweet, and kissed him. 'I brought you out here for a reason,' she said.

'Oh?'

'I've got a surprise for you.'

He stopped, and turned to face her. 'What surprise?'

'One you'll like.'

'Well, come on then!' he urged.

'You and I are going to have a baby. I'm pregnant.'

He beamed with delight. 'A baby!'

'I conceived during our weekend at the Prestwick Airport Hotel.'

He nearly picked her up and twirled her round, then thought the better of it.

'A baby,' he repeated. 'That's a wonderful surprise.'

'I knew you'd be pleased.'

'And you?'

'Thrilled to bits.'

He drew in a deep breath. 'A baby. Wow!'

She laughed at his enthusiasm and obvious pleasure.

'Speaking of surprises, I've got one for you,' he said mysteriously.

She was instantly intrigued. 'What's that?'

'You're going to have to wait for yours, I'm afraid. But not too long, I promise you.'

'Oh come on, Howard, that's not fair!'

'You'll just have to wait. I'm sorry.'

'But I told you yours.'

'Not too long, I promise,' he repeated.

She did her damndest to find out, but he wouldn't divulge what it was. Nor would he during the remainder of that night or rest of the voyage.

Howard swung the rented Packard off the road on to the grass verge where he parked. 'I've got something to show you,' he said, and got out.

When Maggie joined him he took her by the hand and led her through a line of trees to a spot overlooking a valley.

'There!' he declared, pointing.

'You mean the house?'

'The house,' he confirmed.

The house in question was of the style known in America as Old Colonial. Newly painted, it positively gleamed white, a startling contrast to the inky blackness of the shutters flanking every window.

In front of the house was a garden bursting with flowers, a veritable riot of colour, with other gardens, trees and strips of lawn on either side of the house. At the rear was what appeared to be a garage, with an extensive vegetable patch beyond that. Round all this was a white picket fence.

There was something about the house, a warmth, a cosiness, that instantly attracted Maggie. She instinctively knew it would be a happy place to live. 'It's gorgeous,' she said.

'I'm glad you like it, because it's ours.'

She turned to stare at him. 'Ours?'

'A wedding present from my folks. They're down there now waiting to meet you.'

Maggie was dumbfounded. 'They've bought it and given it to us? But they don't even know me!'

'Oh, they know about you all right. I've told them a great deal in my letters home.'

'But a house . . . the cost!'

Howard laughed. 'My father can afford it, he's a wealthy man. But I'll explain about that to you later.'

Maggie brought her attention back to the house, and shook her head in wonder. Their house, she still couldn't believe it.

'Pleased?'

'You know I am.'

'Well, this is *my* surprise. I'm glad you like it.'

'Howard Taft, I love you,' she murmured. And couldn't have meant it more.